PLAYING

Erica knew her part
to the prince. But
around her waist and turned her face up to his
with his other hand, it seemed she had played
her part too well.

Erica opened her mouth to protest, but he
covered her lips with his own. His lips felt as
wonderful as they looked, warm and sensitive,
and she felt his hand move from her chin and
slip under her gown and chemise, to cup her
naked breast.

Erica could feel her heart pounding not in fearful
distress, but with something that seemed to
come from some warm, secret part of her she
had never been aware she possessed. The prince
smiled at her as he began to ease her gown off
her shoulders.

"Stop that at once!" she cried, struggling anew.

He chuckled. "Stop?" he asked, his voice now
husky. "But I have only just begun to melt
you, Ice Maiden. . . ."

BARBARA HAZARD won the Waldenbooks
Award for Best Selling Short Historical in 1986,
and *The Romantic Times* Award for Best Regency
Writer of the Year in 1985.

The Guarded Heart

Barbara Hazard

A SIGNET BOOK

NEW AMERICAN LIBRARY

SIGNET TRADEMARK REG. U.S. PAT. OFF. AND FOREIGN COUNTRIES
REGISTERED TRADEMARK—MARCA REGISTRADA
HECHO EN CHICAGO, U.S.A.

SIGNET, SIGNET CLASSIC, MENTOR, ONYX, PLUME, MERIDIAN
and NAL BOOKS are published by NAL PENGUIN INC.,
1633 Broadway, New York, New York 10019

First Printing, October, 1987

1 2 3 4 5 6 7 8 9

PRINTED IN THE UNITED STATES OF AMERICA

For Don
all ways—always

The author acknowledges with gratitude the information found in Susan Mary Alsop's book *The Congress Dances*, Harper & Row, Publishers, Inc., 1984, which was one of the books used in the preparation of this novel, and was its inspiration.

The brazen throat of war had ceased to roar:
All now was turned to jollity and game,
To luxury and riot, feast and dance.

—JOHN MILTON,
1608–1674

I

It was early that cool September morning when the ship docked at Le Havre, on a day that promised rain before nightfall. The wharves and buldings that made up the waterfront seemed all the same depressing gray color where they huddled together as if for protection from the restless movement of the harbor tides at their feet. Above them, heavy clouds hung low in the sky, while gulls swooped and cried as they searched the murky water for food. To the lady standing by the port railing of the ship, everything seemed to have been touched by a brush using a monotone palette, the drab scene further veiled by the tendrils of fog that clung to the small coasters and fishing dories at anchor. Even the sounds of the busy harbor seemed muted, muffled.

The lady's eyes explored the shoreline, seeking some flash of color, a bright hat, a red scarf. The only person she saw was an old fisherman. He was leaning against a piling, dressed all in faded black, from the cap that was pulled down over his white hair, to his knee-high boots. Gray smoke rose from his pipe in lazy spirals before it lost itself in the fog.

The sailors who were preparing the hawsers often stole a glance at the tall, slender figure of the woman who stared so fixedly at her first glimpse of France. She was wearing a long dark cloak that made her seem part of the leaden seascape, and her cameo profile was remote and still. As they watched her curiously, she pulled the cloak closer to her throat. Since she had never acknowledged their existence on the passage from England, they knew

she was not aware of them now, and they could look
their fill.

Her traveling companions were still below. To the first
mate of the vessel it was fitting that she stood alone.
Even though he knew she was a married woman going to
join her husband in Vienna, he could not picture her in
any situation where she would not be aloof, somehow
solitary. Even so, the mate thought her the most beautiful woman he had ever seen. She was tall, as tall as he
was, and slim and lithe. Her hair was the palest blond,
like the silver of moonlight on snow, he mused. He
wondered what it looked like when she released it from
those tight braids that were coiled at the nape of her
neck. In the flat morning light it seemed almost white,
but she would never be mistaken for an older woman.
Not with that soft, translucent skin, those startling green
eyes, and the full yet sensitive mouth that was set in a
finely boned, aristocratic face.

As the ship drew closer to the wharf, the mate was
forced to give his attention to the docking. When he
turned back later, he saw with regret that she was gone.

The lady and her belongings were not unloaded until
almost noon. Since she had, besides her baggage, five
horses and a traveling carriage, the delay was understandable. With her came two grooms, a coachman, and
an equerry. She was further attended by a middle-aged
maid, a dour woman of as few words as her mistress.
Even without all this pomp, the mate knew that anyone
would be able to tell the lady was a person of importance, merely by her demeanor.

He watched from the deck of the ship as the horses
were harnessed and the baggage tied on the roof. When
at last the lady took her seat, her maid beside her, and
the coachman snapped his whip, he could not resist waving a hand in farewell. It was a long way to Vienna, and
he was sure it would not be a pleasant journey. This was
France, after all, the France that had been England's
enemy for so many years. True, it was vanquished now,
and the Emperor Napoleon imprisoned on the island of
Elba, but it was still the France that had turned all of
Europe into a bloody battlefield. An English lady, travel-

ing alone except for servants, might well face danger as
well as discomfort. The mate wished her well, not at all
sorry that after a night ashore he himself would be returning with the ship to England.

The carriage was soon lost from sight among the buildings of the town. Inside it, Erica Stone settled a lap rug
more securely over her knees. It was beginning to rain,
and the damp crept into every crevice. If this was what
the weather was like in September, what might it be like
in January? she wondered. But then, she was sure to be
home by the new year, perhaps even in time for Christmas. She had been told the congress would last only a
few weeks. She grasped the strap beside her as the carriage lurched into a deep rut. When she looked up, she
saw her maid studying her face, her expression even
sterner than usual. Erica's green eyes lit up, and her lips
curled in a little smile.

"I can see you are wondering if it will rain all the time
we are abroad, Agnes," she remarked. "Don't worry!
Vienna is sure to be more pleasant."

Her maid sniffed, clutching the lady's dressing case
even closer as she did so. "If you say so, Miss Erica," she
said in her harsh voice. "But September means the end
of summer. Winter will be upon us before long, even in
this wondrous Vienna of yours."

Her mistress ignored her, turning her head to study the
streets they were passing through. Erica knew her maid
did not approve of this journey, that she thought it
foolish to undertake something so uncomfortable and full
of potential risk, merely to be reunited with a new husband, who, in all probability, would be coming home
soon anyway. She shrugged again. It had been her decision, hers alone. Even her father had admitted that.

"And I doubt we will get very far today," the maid
was saying now. "The captain will want to make sure we
find rooms in an inn well before dark."

When her mistress did not reply, she shrugged in turn.
Miss Erica, as she could not help calling her still, had
never been a chatterbox, and Agnes Watts was used to
her long periods of silence. She had been the lady's maid
since the girl turned eighteen four years before, and she

knew her well. Loved her, too, in her own undemonstra-
tive way, if the truth were told. She might not have
approved this mad jaunt across Europe, only because
Miss Erica was so dead set on rejoining her husband, but
she could never have been left behind.

The maid shook her graying head. It was a shame,
that's what it was. Miss Erica and Colonel Stone had
been married only a week when the summons came that
he was to make all possible speed to join Sir Charles
Stewart abroad. The colonel had been gone some three
months now, at first to Paris before he went on to Vienna, where he was helping to set up this international
congress that was to begin October 1. She didn't understand a thing about it, nor why he had had to rush off, a
new bridgegroom, too. It was too bad!

Agnes Watts studied her mistress's serene profile, and
her eyes filled with speculation. Miss Erica had always
been hard to read, and even now her maid was not sure
if she were happy in her marriage. She had not shown
any signs that she was missing her new husband in the
months since he had left, but neither had she seemed
ecstatic during the honeymoon week they had spent together. But then, the maid told herself as she put her
head back on the leather squabs of the carriage seat and
closed her eyes, that's typical of Miss Erica. And just as
well, too. I couldn't abide a lady all fancy flights and
sensibility for a minute, I couldn't!

The travelers stayed the night at a small inn some few
miles from Barentin, and were on the road early the next
day. Captain Garrity, the middle-aged equerry who accompanied them, knew the lady wished to push on with
all speed, and he approved such a course wholeheartedly.
He had hired two postilions to guide them, and the
grooms who clung to the perch behind the carriage were
former soldiers, and armed. He was prepared for trouble. He still considered France enemy territory, even though
they were nominally at peace. The captain had fought
the French for years, both in Portugal and in Spain, and
he did not trust them, not even now that Napoleon's
empire was being dissolved.

Day after day followed without incident, however.

Erica watched as the rich carpet that was France unfolded before her eyes: the farms and rolling hills, the slow-moving streams, the fields being harvested. When they passed through a small town or a remote village, she was always amazed. In contrast to the lush, fruitful land, there were so many hollow-eyed peasants, so many noisy beggars, so much crushing proverty. She had never seen anything like it in her entire life. She saw few men, although there were many women of all ages who stared at her in sullen interest. The men who were there, were elderly. And she was struck by the absence of babies. It was obvious the war had taken a hard toll of the common people, and all because a madman bent on conquest and power had used the young men and boys as cannon fodder to further his insane ambition.

The difference between her lot in life and that of these French peasants was so extreme, it was painful to contemplate. And one evening, alighting at an inn, when a little girl with big dark eyes in a drawn face had called her *"la princesse anglaise"* in a voice full of awe, she could not even smile in response.

Erica had plenty of time to think as the days went by, and sometimes she pondered her motives. If it was true that William would be back in England soon, why did she bother with this uncomfortable trip, the poor inns and bad food, the tiresome, jolting coach? She did not even have the impetus of knowing her husband had written and begged her to come, for he had not. The few letters that she had received had been brusque and matter-of-fact, with no hint of the lover. Not once had he suggested she join him. In fact, now that she looked back on it dispassionately, she had to admit he had seemed almost relieved to be leaving her. Surely that was not a groom's usual response when torn from his bride's arms! And you wanted him to go, admit it, she chastised herself, determined to be honest. Marriage had not been at all what she had expected, and the day he had waved good-bye from the bottom of the drive, she had felt like a bird released from a cage—free, and light, and alone. And then, of course, she had felt guilty that it was so.

Perhaps it was for that very reason that she was following him now. She had known something was wrong from
the beginning, and as the days after his departure passed
in much the same manner as when she had been Miss
Erica Joanna Huntington, she had begun to feel uneasy.
At last she had realized that she must go and find William, that she must try to discover what it was that was
making her unhappy and dissatisfied, no matter how
unpleasant that discovery might be.

She told herself that when they were together again
she would be able to still this little itch of disquiet she
had not been able to escape, left alone in England. She
was a fighter. All her family were fighters. She had wed
William Stone, and she would not let a mere week of
marriage determine the course that marriage would take.
Whatever the outcome of her journey, for better or
worse, she had to try.

She would have liked to see Paris. The city lay only a
few miles south of their route, but Captain Garrity dis-
suaded her. They were already behind the schedule he
had set, for many days had been rainy, the coach of
necessity slowed by the quagmire the roads became. The
captain was glad the lady was a good traveler. Not once
had she complained of weariness or boredom, and although he could see how stiff she was when she finally
left the coach each evening, she made no mention of her
discomfort. But of course the captain would expect nothing less of a Huntington—male or female.

He had agreed to escort her as a favor to her eldest
brother. They had been fellow officers in the same regiment, and Lieutenant Mark Huntington had been instrumental in saving his life at the Battle of Ciudad Rodrigo.
It was at the urging of this old comrade that the captain
had undertaken the commission, for Lieutenant Huntington was recovering from wounds and could not travel
himself. But although the captain was tireless in his determination to see her safely to Vienna, he wished to do
so with all possible speed. Erica told herself it was just as
well. When the congress was over, how much better it
would be to see Paris on William's arm, sharing the
honeymoon they had not had time for earlier.

The travelers had almost reached Metz in the Lorraine when an accident delayed them. One of the team lost a shoe, and they were forced to wait for some time by the side of the road until the grooms found a blacksmith and the shoe was replaced. The captain had paced up and down in frustration as the afternoon lengthened, refusing to join Mrs. Stone and her maid in the carriage, even though a misty rain was falling. As time passed, he had to abandon his plan to reach the hostelry in Metz where he had hoped they would spend the night. He knew from his earlier reconnoitering, however, that there was a small inn only a few miles ahead, at a minor crossroad. It was not what he would have liked for the lady, but it would have to do.

The rain was falling in heavy sheets when they got under way again, and it was almost dusk when the lights of the inn appeared through the gloom. The captain, who had ridden ahead so he could make the necessary arrangements, was nowhere to be seen when one of the grooms let down the steps and held out his hand to help Mrs. Stone alight.

Erica did not pause to look around before she hurried into the inn. It was warm inside, and there was a comforting odor of cooking. She sighed in relief as she put back her hood. Beside her, Agnes brushed the rain from her cloak.

Both women paused when they heard the captain's outraged voice coming from a room a little way down the dark corridor.

"But you must understand, sir, this cannot be tolerated!" he was saying.

Erica edged closer as a deep, bored voice drawled, "Since it must be tolerated, I suggest you begin to make the best of it. The inn is small, and there are only a few rooms, all of which I have commandeered for myself and my entourage." There was a short pause, and then that world-weary voice added, "You have heard the old maxim that possession is nine-tenths of the law, sir? Just so. I was here first, and you may be sure that not only am I in possession, I have no intention of relinquishing that possession. I see no reason why I should."

"But I cannot ask a lady to spend the night in a barn or huddled in her carriage!" Captain Garrity exclaimed. "We have been traveling all day, and she is weary and hungry. Besides, it is raining hard now."

"I have no objection to her seeking a meal here," the stranger said, sounding pleased with himself for his largess. "As to her accommodation, that is, I am delighted to say, none of my concern."

Erica had been growing steadily more angry. There was something about the man's tone of voice, his boredom with the problem, and his cynicism that set up her hackles. Now, ignoring Agnes, who was twitching at her cloak and making tuts of disapproval, she moved forward to enter the room.

"There is some problem, Captain?" she asked in an even voice as he came closer. The gentleman by the fire turned his head to inspect her idly for only a brief moment before he turned back to his contemplation of the flames. It was not at all the reaction Erica generally exacted from the male of the species, and somehow his indifference fed her anger.

"The gentleman has reserved all the rooms, ma'am," Captain Garrity said, his voice taut with outrage. "And he will not give up even one for your use."

Erica took a deep breath and motioned her equerry to be still, as she walked forward. "Good evening," she said when she was standing before the stranger. The warmth of the fire made her conscious of how chilled and tired she really was. She longed to sit down and stretch out her hands to the blaze.

It seemed a long time before the man turned his head to stare at her again. She waited, but he did not rise from his chair, nor did he speak, and she could read nothing in his harsh-featured face or the cold black eyes that studied her with such indifference.

"My name is Erica Stone. I am journeying to Vienna to join my husband, Colonel William Stone. He is one of Sir Charles Stewart's staff," she said. "I perceive you are also English, sir. Surely you will reconsider, for a countrywoman. All I will require is one room. My servants will make do with whatever space the innkeeper has for them."

The stranger sighed and propped up his chin with one well-kept hand. "I should perhaps tell you at once, madam, that I am not to be swayed by either patriotism or chivalry," he said. "Especially when I consider your journey pure folly. Vienna is to be the site of serious international discussions that will decide the fate of the civilized world. Diplomats need no women cluttering up the place, whining for balls and amusements, and distracting men from their duties. You were better off to have stayed at home."

General Sir Harold Huntington's only daughter was not used to pleading with anyone, but she made herself smile a little as she said, "I cannot believe you would be so unfeeling, sir. Whatever you may think of my traveling, you are a gentleman, are you not?"

Her adversary covered a tiny yawn, and then he sighed before he rose to his feet at last, to lean on a gold-headed cane. He was very tall, and Erica discovered she disliked looking up at him even more than she had disliked staring down at him.

"Owen Kingsley, Duke of Graves, madam," he said, not even bothering to bow. "Most definitely *not* at your service to command."

As Erica gave him a speaking glance of contempt, a small smile twisted his lips. "I do assure you that even so, I am still a gentleman. But in a foreign country, it is every man—and woman—for himself. I did not ask you to come abroad, nor to seek shelter here, and I am not responsible for your well-being." He paused, those cold black eyes intent on her face. "However, it is a pity that you yourself are a lady, madam. If you were not, I am sure some amicable agreement might have been reached, for I would have had no hesitation in asking you to share not only my room but also my bed."

Erica heard the captain's muffled oath and Agnes' sharp indrawn breath, and she raised her hand again to ensure their silence.

"I believe I would prefer to spend even a night like this under a hedge," she remarked, as if to herself, and then she turned her back on him. The duke's expression was unreadable as he took his seat again.

"Captain Garrity, find the landlord for me at once," Erica ordered, as if they were alone in the room. "There must be some attic or cubbyhole that *his grace* has overlooked."

As she swept from the room, followed by her maid, Captain Garrity bowed low before he went to do her bidding.

Owen Kingsley did not seem to be elated to be in sole possession of the parlor once again, nor did he turn his head at the torrent of French that issued from the hall. Anyone who might have observed him would have seen his eyes narrow slightly when the innkeeper offered the lady his own room, which was accepted. Not that he was surprised. It would have been a very unusual Frenchman indeed who could have turned such a beauty from his house. The duke grimaced. No doubt just picturing her in his bed would enliven his lovemaking for weeks to come.

For a while there was a great bustle in the hall as the lady's servants brought in her baggage and the low-ceilinged public taproom was made ready for the latest arrivals.

Erica did not see the Duke of Graves again that evening. She ate her dinner with her servants around her, trying to ignore the rough, hard chairs and scarred tables and the sour smell of spilled wine that had permeated the taproom over the years. When she left it at last, she saw a footman in livery standing before the parlor door, almost, she thought, as if the duke had set him to guard it from her further intrusions.

She put up her chin as she climbed the narrow stairs to the innkeeper's own room. She was glad to see that his wife had put fresh sheets on the bed, and a colorful down comforter, and that a good fire burned in the tiny hearth. She insisted Agnes sleep with her rather than on a straw pallet at the foot of the bed, and her last conscious thought before she dropped off to sleep was to hope that her male servants would not be too stiff after a night spent on similar pallets in the taproom.

When she woke early the next morning and dressed and came downstairs, she discovered that the private parlor was now hers to command. The duke had left at first light.

Intermittently that day, as she traveled on, Erica considered this Duke of Graves, wondering if he were typical of the breed. She had never met a duke before, but surely they could not all be so arrogant and insulting. But although she was still angry at his treatment of her, she had to admit that somehow she found his very indifference to her intriguing. And meeting the nobility had been one of the reasons she had come abroad in the first place. It had not been only because she wanted to see her husband and begin forging a better marriage for them both; no, indeed. She had never been anywhere in her life before this, and she had always longed to travel. When she was growing up, she had had to watch her father and her brothers go off to foreign duty. Forced to stay at home in Northumberland, she had only been able to envy them the adventure, and she did not think it was at all fair. Even when her father had retired from the army at last, she had remained in the country. The general had no interest in London or society, and seemed content to oversee his estate, correspond with other officers of his acquaintance, and relive his career by following the advancement of his three sons. Erica tried to tell herself she was content, even though she knew she was not. She was sure if her mother had lived, it would have been different, but Birgitte Huntington had died when Erica was only twelve, and outside of her father's spinster sister who lived with them and managed the household, she had known few other ladies.

As the years passed, and she had her twenty-second birthday, Erica wondered if it would ever occur to her father that she might want to wed, but the general did not seem to notice the advancing years. She remembered how pleased she had been when one of his old friends came to visit, bringing with him his eldest son. William Stone had been one of the few gentlemen she had ever met, and when, after a month's visit, he had asked for her hand, she had accepted him at once. She told herself that when she was married she would be able to travel and see something of the world. When he kissed her to seal their betrothal, it had neither stirred nor repulsed her, but she had been sure she would grow accustomed to his caresses. He was a man much like her brothers, tall and broad-shouldered and handsome. She told herself he loved her, and she would love him too, in time.

Her father was well-pleased with the match. He knew the colonel for an excellent soldier, brave and steady and born to command. To the general there were no finer attributes in a husband.

But marriage had not changed her life. There had not even been a wedding journey, for the colonel was waiting for fresh orders. They had stayed at one of his father's estates in Kent, and when William had gone to Europe, she had returned to her own father's house to await his return. Somehow, she could not like remaining with her husband's mother and father, for they were strangers still.

But no matter what the Duke of Graves had to say about the suitability of her journey, she was glad to be traveling at last. Every day was a new adventure, a new beginning. Erica wondered if she would meet the duke again in Vienna. She hoped she would not. His manner was offensive, and his drawled observation that if she had not been a lady he might have asked her to share his bed had stunned her. She knew her face had paled, and she had had to concentrate hard not to show her indignation and her naiveté.

As she stared out the windows of the coach, she realized for the first time how unsophisticated she was. Well, that would change, now that she was to enter society at last. Captain Garrity had told her that all the world was flocking to Vienna. How she looked forward to joining them!

They reached the Austrian capital late one afternoon some two weeks later. The captain had relaxed as soon as they crossed the French border, and slowed the pace somewhat. Erica was not impatient; indeed, she enjoyed the trip through Baden and Bavaria, the deep forests and fairy-tale castles that clung to crags high above the winding rivers, the cheerful peasants in their colorful dress. But now, at journey's end, she sat on the edge of her seat as they entered the city they had been traveling toward for so long.

Vienna was not large compared with Paris or London, and the palaces of the wealthy and the homes of the middle class, as well as the theaters, shops, and restaurants, seemed crowded behind the ancient ramparts that enclosed it. Erica, who had never visited a city before, thought it immense and somehow stirring. She fancied the inhabitants moved at a quicker pace, that the very air was different, more exhilarating. She was delighted to see so many green squares and parks and large horse-chestnut trees. Vienna was a bustling, happy place whose people seemed to share her delight in it, for they were all smiling as they went about their business.

The captain had to stop often to ask for directions, and Erica was glad that at least some of the Viennese spoke French. It was something she had worried about, for she had no German.

At last they turned off into a narrow, winding street not far from the Imperial Palace, which she knew was called the Hofburg. After the coach came to a halt, Erica climbed down, her heart beating fast. Before her was the tall house where William had rooms. It might be only a matter of minutes before she would see him again, she thought, and she drew a deep breath to steady herself. Suddenly she wondered if she should have written to say she was coming. She had wanted to surprise him, but now she was feeling a little uneasy at her boldness.

Captain Garrity knocked on the door, smiling down at her in relief that his mission had been accomplished as he did so. Behind her she could hear Agnes sniffing a little, and she knew the maid did not approve of the slightly run-down neighborhood, although the steps of the house had been scoured recently, and the knocker polished.

The door was opened by a short, round woman whose white hair matched the spotless apron that was tied over her black dress. When she saw Erica she dropped a curtsy and beckoned them inside.

"We are looking for Colonel Stone," the captain told her, speaking in French. "This is Mrs. Stone, his wife."

To Erica's surprise, the old woman paled and began to wring her hands. "*Armselig frau!*" she said in a distressed voice. She began a torrent of German, which Erica could

not understand. Captain Garrity translated at last. It
seemed the woman claimed Colonel Stone was not there.

"Then I will wait for him," Erica said, trying to smile
as she did so. "Please ask her to show me to his rooms,
Captain."

The woman stared at her as the captain spoke, shaking
her head as she did so. "*Nein, sehr verehrte gnädige
frau,*" she said sadly, and then she added in halting
French, "You cannot wait for the colonel, for he will
never come again. Colonel Stone is dead."

2

For a moment Erica was sure she must have misunderstood, but Captain Garrity's exclamation told her that what she had heard was all too true. She felt weak all at once, her legs quivering so, she was not sure they would hold her up. She was glad when the equerry gently helped her to sit down in a chair against the wall.

"William dead?" she whispered, looking from one to the other. "But how can that be?"

Agnes, who had come to stand beside her, and who had not understood a word up to now, stiffened.

When the elderly woman began to speak rapidly in German again, Erica held up her hands. "Please, in French, madam," she said. "I have no German."

The woman nodded, her faded eyes concerned. In a few minutes the English party had all the facts she was privy to. William Stone had been murdered three nights before as he returned to his rooms after an evening spent gambling with friends. No one had seen his assailant, and his body had not been discovered until the next morning, when a farmer delivering milk and cream had spotted it lying beside the palings of a house three doors away. The colonel had been stabbed, and his pockets emptied. The old woman assured Erica the police were investigating the murder and that everyone was very shocked. Vienna, she explained proudly, was not the kind of city that had much violent crime, and this murder, coming as it did at the beginning of the congress, was most unfortunate.

Erica took several deep breaths, and sat quietly until her pounding heart slowed its beat. Unfortunate! her mind echoed. Well, she supposed that was one way for a stranger to put it, but for her it was a catastrophe. Here she was, in a strange city far from home, and the husband she had expected to be reunited with was dead. Had been dead for three days. She put her hands to her temples and closed her eyes. If only she had come a little sooner, or not wasted so much time on the road, she might have been able to prevent it. Why, William would not have gone out gambling if she had been here.

Agnes put her hand on her mistress's shoulder and gripped hard. "Courage, Miss Erica," she said in a gruff voice. "Giving in to grief won't help. Not here, not now."

Erica swallowed the bile that threatened to disgrace her, and nodded. "What is your name, madam?" she asked the old woman.

The woman curtsied and introduced herself as Frau Heinrich, the landlady.

Erica rose then, and Captain Garrity hastened to support her. "I wish to see my husband's rooms, please, Frau Heinrich," she said. "Indeed, I suppose I must stay in them, since I have no other place to go."

"*Ja, ja.*" The landlady nodded, motioning to the stairs. As the party followed her up a steep flight, she kept up a nonstop chatter. How fortunate that she had not cleared the rooms yet, she said. But Mrs. Stone was not to be concerned. She might have them for as long as she cared to, and the rent was paid till the end of October. And she was not to worry about the police, for they had finished their inspection of them two days ago. She would be quite undisturbed.

She bustled down the corridor and unlocked a door at the end, curtsying again as she motioned Erica to enter.

For a moment Erica remained holding on to the doorjamb. She felt a great reluctance to go in, and she did not know why. Shaking her head at her timidity, she turned and asked the captain to have the grooms bring in the baggage. He saluted, and after a searching look to make sure she was all right, ran back down the stairs.

Frau Heinrich showed them the sitting room, bedroom, and dressing room, and a small room for a servant's use. There was also a small, empty kitchen. William obviously had taken his meals out. The rooms were not particularly neat, but Erica had not expected them to be. William had been an untidy man, and he had not employed a valet.

Frau Heinrich gave her the key and would have gone away, except Erica introduced her maid and asked if she might have a pot of tea sent up. The landlady nodded, coming to stand before her to peer up into her eyes. She put her gnarled, age-spotted hands on Erica's arms as she said, "There are so many widows these days, *gnädige frau*! So many!"

When the two women had left her, Erica inspected the rooms again. The furnishings were plain and inexpensive, and the carpet worn. The white curtains at the window were crisp with starch, however, and everything was spotlessly clean. One of William's uniform jackets was draped over a chair, and his dress sword was propped up in a corner. A pair of his gloves and a snuffbox rested on a small table, and papers were strewn on the desk against the wall. Erica did not want to touch anything, although she did not feel particularly sad, she just felt numb. Perhaps it was too soon for grief. Perhaps the shock of what she had discovered awaiting her in Vienna kept her from weeping for William.

As she heard the grooms coming up the stairs with her trunks, she walked into the bedroom. The big four-poster had not been made, although someone had pulled the covers up in a vain attempt to make it look neat. Erica reached down to smooth them. As she pulled the coverlet tight, she saw a lump in the middle of the mattress. Reaching between the sheets, her hand discovered something soft and silky, and she drew it out. In horror now, she stared at the scarlet chemise that was trimmed with lace and as filmy as a cobweb. A faint scent assailed her nostrils, and with some reluctance she raised the chemise to her face. She closed her eyes as the musk-laden perfume became stronger. Who owned this? Who had left it here in her husband's bed?

When she heard Captain Garrity's voice asking where she wanted her trunks to be left, she balled the chemise up in her hand and thrust it under a chair cushion.

It seemed a long time before the servants left. The

captain said he would arrange for them all to stay in one of the outlying villages, keeping the team and carriage with them, until she decided what she wanted to do. He told her he would return early the following morning, and that he was completely at her service.

Erica made herself smile at him, to ease his frowning concern. "Thank you, Captain," she said, coming to take his hand. "You have been so kind, so helpful. I do not know what I would have done without you."

After he bowed himself away, she made herself return to the bedroom. One by one she opened all the drawers of a large armoire. William's clothes were there, but that was all. As she rummaged through them, she wondered what she was searching for. More chemises? Nightgowns? Hastily she slammed the drawers shut.

When Agnes came back with a tray a few moments later, Erica was seated at the table in the sitting room, her hands clasped before her as she stared down into the street with unseeing eyes.

The maid poured her a cup of tea as she darted little glances at Miss Erica's face. She had been prepared to find her mistress in tears, but her eyes were dry. Not only that, she sat so still she appeared to be turned to stone.

"Come, Miss Erica, drink your tea," Agnes urged, patting her shoulder. "It will make you feel better, indeed, it will."

Erica sighed, and when she saw the maid's frown, she said, "I think I am still shocked. It has not begun to make any sense to me. I find William's death as hard to accept as I would a nightmare that I know will disappear when I wake." Her lips tightened. "But this nightmare will not go away, will it?"

She took a sip of the hot tea and sighed again. "How good that tastes!" she said.

"That *frau*, as you called her, sent up some biscuits too," Agnes said, indicating the plate. Erica shook her head.

A little uneasy under her maid's close scrutiny, she said, "If you are not too tired, Agnes, you might begin to unpack my things. It will be necessary to remove all the colonel's clothes first, in order to make room."

"You're never going to stay here long, Miss Erica!" Agnes exclaimed, as if she could not believe her ears.

Erica nodded. "I think I must, Agnes. At least until I have spoken to the police and the British authorities. I do not even know where his body is . . . Oh!"

She stopped, and swayed for a moment in her chair, and the maid was quick to kneel beside her and put her arms around her slender waist. "There, there, my dear," she crooned. "Try not to think of it."

Erica closed her eyes. She knew this was no time to be weak. No, she must be strong now, for there was a great deal to do, and Colonel William Stone deserved someone better than a crying, ineffective wife who "tried not to think of it." She *must* think of it, his murder, the funeral—all that, and a great deal more.

In a moment she sat up straight. "I'm all right, Agnes, truly I am. I shall finish my tea, and then I will come and help you. I suppose it is too late today to do anything, but tomorrow we must see the police and let the authorities know we are here."

Agnes nodded, reassured by her calm, even voice. "Aye, but not until you're decently dressed, Miss Erica," she said in a voice that brooked no argument. "I saw some shops close by here when we arrived. I'll be off first thing in the morning to get your blacks."

Erica would have argued, but the look in Agnes' eyes told her it would be to no avail. No recently widowed lady under her care would step a foot outdoors until she was swathed from head to toe in mourning, and heavily veiled. Erica resigned herself to it, for even though her discovery of the chemise in William's bed made her wonder what kind of man she had married, and realize how little she really knew of him, as his wife she would give him all the homage that was his due.

She was up early the next morning. To her surprise, she had fallen asleep at once, no doubt exhausted by the trauma of the day. When she first opened her eyes, it had been a moment before the painful memories came flooding back. Somehow, the scarlet chemise that was still hidden under the chair cushion came to mind at once. As it did, she threw back the covers and rose hastily from the bed William had shared with another woman, just three months after his marriage to her.

The captain arrived as she was drinking coffee, and he volunteered to take Agnes shopping so he could translate for her. Erica thanked him when he also offered to come with her later to the police station.

When the two of them had left, she busied herself trying to bring order to the room. Agnes had packed all of Colonel Stone's belongings, but she had not touched the desk. Reluctantly, Erica sat down before it to inspect the papers there. There was a great number of unpaid bills, and a few scribbled notes, mostly from fellow officers setting up appointments to dine, play cards, or attend the theater. There was even the beginning of a letter to her, a few short lines he had never completed. Erica held the letter for a moment, and then she crumpled it in her hand. It was just like all his others—comments on the weather, the congress preparations. There were no words of love, or even affection. She knew she would have to think about her marriage to William soon, and probe deeper than she ever had before, but she could not do it now.

As she tidied the desk, she caught a glimpse of something metallic in the back of the drawer. She saw it was a ring, and, curious, she took it out to study it. From its size, she knew it had to be a man's. She had never seen one like it before. It was made in the shape of two tightly entwined serpents, and somehow, although it was finely made, she thought it ugly. She had never seen William wearing anything but his signet ring, but she was sure it belonged to him. She returned it to the drawer, knowing she might never discover how he had come by it and why he had kept it.

Of much more interest to her was his account book. Erica had searched hard, but there was nothing to tell her which bank he might have used here in Vienna. As she studied the pages of the ledger, her heart sank. Apparently William had been living from hand to mouth, and he appeared to have been deeply in debt. That would explain these poor rooms, the run-down neighborhood. For a moment Erica wondered what he had done with her generous dowry. At last she closed the account book, looking thoughtful. She had some money with her, but it was not enough for her to remain here for long, nor was it enough to see her safely home in style again. She would have to write to her father and ask him for help. She was most reluctant, for to do so would be to admit that her husband had left her penniless.

She knew she could not continue to employ Captain Garrity or the male servants anymore. She must pay them their wages and let them go, for they were a drain on her slender purse. Agnes, of course, as she knew, would remain even if she were not paid.

But if she sent the others back to England, how would she get home herself? And what was she to do about the carriage and team?

She rose then to pace the room, hands to her head. What a terrible mess this all was!

Fortunately, before she should begin to brood about it, Agnes came back with her purchases. Erica could not help shivering when she saw the severe black gown, the matching gloves and reticule, and the large concealing bonnet draped in a multitude of veiling. After she had dressed, she studied herself in the bedroom mirror. She thought she looked just like a crow, albeit a mysterious one, for her features were indistinguishable under the veil. She tried not to think of how many long months she would be expected to dress this way.

When she came down the stairs, Agnes behind her, the captain was waiting to escort them. Erica was glad to take his arm, and she began to feel grateful for the veil that concealed her face, especially when they entered the police station. It seemed to her that everyone there was staring at her, staring hard.

She was received by the chief of police himself, a Baron Franz Hager. He was vocal in his condolences as he seated her in his office, although he peered at her so intently, Erica was not even tempted to put back her veil.

To her surprise, he began to question her about her husband's friends, his habits and activities. His brows rose when she told him the short time she had been married, and confessed her complete ignorance of any of Colonel Stone's private affairs.

At last, frustrated, he abandoned his questions and told her what he knew of her husband's death. He confessed they were no further along in discovering the murderer than they had been four days before. He shrugged a little as he deplored the lack of witnesses.

"It might have been anyone, *madame*," he finished at last, hands spread wide. "A common thief, perhaps, or even someone known to your husband who wanted the murder to appear a robbery."

"Where is the colonel's body, Baron?" Erica asked. She heard the rustle of Agnes' skirts as she moved closer in support, and the tiny sound helped her keep her voice steady.

"The British authorities took it away," the chief explained. "You see, no one knew you were coming, *madame*. The funeral was held two days ago."

Erica rose. "I see. I shall have to call on the British delegation next, I suppose. Thank you for seeing me, Baron. You have been most kind."

Baron Hager escorted her from the office himself, his hand under her arm as he reassured her the case would remain open until the murderer was found. She did not think he sounded very hopeful as he said it.

It was late afternoon before Erica returned to her rooms. After leaving the police station, she had gone to Lord Castlereagh's magnificent apartment in the Minoritenplatz. Since it housed his offices and staff as well as containing his private quarters, she was received with deference by one of his secretaries, even though m'lord was from home. The secretary told her all the details of the funeral, and the location of the cemetery.

As she was leaving the grand apartment, Lady Castlereagh came from her own rooms to intercept her. For the first time, Erica felt tears coming to her eyes, as the older woman, so fat and dowdy, put her arms around her to commiserate with her on her loss. Her motherly face was kind, and her manner so comforting that Erica almost lost control of herself.

The captain hired a carriage and they visited the cemetery next, stopping on the way to purchase flowers to put on the grave. Erica stared down at it, and at her sheaf of red roses lying there in brilliant contrast to the raw, dark earth of the grave. The warm October sun on her back, the rich green of the surrounding grass, and the happy sound of birdsong seemed to mock the violent death that had occurred. Erica felt numb again; she could still feel nothing but sad regret for the brutal way William Stone had died.

The next day, she remained in her rooms, but the following morning was so clear and beautiful, she could not resist going out to investigate this city she had come so far to see. Agnes insisted on accompanying her, although Erica knew she was in no danger, dressed as she was in widow's weeds. Everyone gave her a sad smile and politely made way for her.

She strolled past the Hofburg, inspecting that huge town within a town in some awe. Captain Garrity had told her it housed many of the delegations that had come for the congress, as well as the Emperor and Empress of Russia, the King and Queen of Bavaria, and the kings of Prussia, Denmark, and Württemberg, and all their entourages. Even as Erica watched from across the street, a smart carriage shiny with green varnish, the imperial arms of Austria painted in yellow on the doors, left a gateway, the matched team of blacks that drew it leaning into their collars as if on an urgent errand of state. She wondered who was inside, and on what important business. A prince? A king? Perhaps an empress?

It was a warm day for early October, and she continued her walk, investigating the streets and squares around the palace. Some of the homes she saw were large, almost palatial. As she turned a corner, she saw an officer dressed in a stunning uniform she did not recognize, helping a beautiful redhead step down from an open landau. The lady was dressed in the palest, flimsiest blue muslin, with a little blue parasol tilted over her shoulder and a saucy, frivolous hat that tipped over one eye. As Erica watched, hidden behind her veil, the lady put her hands on the officer's epaulets and stood on tiptoe to whisper in his ear. They both laughed before he bent his head to kiss her cheek. Erica felt a pang of envy. It all looked like so much fun! Not only the handsome couple she was observing, but the common people she had seen strolling or enjoying a glass of wine at one of

the numerous cafés. She had heard many different languages as she walked along, and she was caught up in the
excitement and good humor of the Viennese and their
visitors. She realized she did not want to go home, she
wanted to stay here and be part of this exhilarated throng.
She wanted to dance and play, take her place in this gay
society, share in all its festive amusements. Then she
shook her head sadly. She knew she could not do that.
She was a widow, and widows did not go out in company. Besides, Vienna was expensive, and her money
was running out.

As she climbed the steps of her rooming house at last,
she told herself she had been remiss not to contact Sir
Charles Stewart. He had been William's superior, after
all. Perhaps he might know where her husband had
banked, help her in some way.

Accordingly, she called on him the next morning. He
was occupied with appointments, but the young secretary
who spoke to her took pity on her, as busy as he was,
and asked her to come into his office. When she had
been seated there, and he asked if there were anything
he could do to assist her, Erica found herself pouring out
her troubles to him. Agnes was waiting for her in the
hall, and the man had such a kind, understanding face,
she could not help herself. Besides, his eyes bore an
uncanny resemblance to her favorite brother's.

"Oh, dear, but how very unfortunate, ma'am," Mr.
Boothby said at last. "We had no idea—that is to say, I
didn't. I knew the colonel, of course, although only
slightly." He ran his hand over his sandy head as he
added, almost apologetically, "Didn't move in the same
circles, you understand."

Erica wondered why he flushed then, and was so quick
to excuse himself when another secretary brought in some
papers. "I shall return as soon as possible, Mrs. Stone,"
he said, almost scurrying to the door. "Do make yourself
comfortable, I won't be long."

Erica rose from the chair where she had been sitting,
and began to pace the room, deep in thought.

"If I might have a moment of your time, madam?" a
deep harsh voice asked from behind her.

Erica whirled, to see a tall figure coming through a

door she had not noticed before. The sunlight streaming through the undraped windows behind him made it hard for her to identify him. Except for the bright light that silhouetted his body, he was all dark, from the top of his smooth head to his gleaming boots. He seemed menacing as he limped toward her, leaning on a cane, and she shivered.

As he came nearer, she blinked as she recognized him. "Why, it's you!" she exclaimed.

The Duke of Graves's dark face remained immobile as he turned to the mirror on the wall beside them to study his features.

"So I have always been told," he said in the cold drawl she remembered.

He turned back to her then and waved toward some chairs set near the window. "Madam?" he asked.

For some reason his courteous word seemed more an order than a request to Erica, and she hesitated. When she saw his impatient frown, however, she moved to the chairs he had indicated. She supposed it would not hurt to hear him out, unpleasant as he was.

He waited until she was seated before sitting down across from her himself. He seemed in no great hurry to speak now, she noticed, for he leaned his cane against the arm of the chair while he studied her intently. Erica was glad then for her widow's weeds, even as she began to feel a growing anger at his detailed, silent inspection.

"There was something you wanted, your grace?" she asked, stung into speech at last.

He nodded. "Put back your veil, if you would be so good, madam," he ordered. "I would see you when I speak to you."

Erica was displeased at how quickly her hands obeyed him.

"Yes, there was something I wanted, madam," he went on, staring now into her uncovered face. "I want you to seduce someone for me."

For one wild moment Erica was sure she had not heard him correctly, for he had spoken the shocking words in such a cold, matter-of-fact way. "I beg your pardon?" she asked, bewildered.

"You heard me, Mrs. Stone," he said in his abrupt

manner. "I do assure you, I always say what I mean, as
you should remember."

"But, but . . ." she began, and then the absurdity of
his request made her laugh, in spite of herself.

The duke waited until her laughter died away before
he spoke again. "I am glad that you find me so entertaining, madam," he said. "It was not, however, to amuse
you that I proposed what I did."

"No?" she asked, serious all at once. "Then perhaps I
had better remind you, sir, that I am not a promiscuous
woman. As *you* should remember."

Owen Kingsley's cold black eyes ran over her figure,
and lingered on her full, rosy mouth and green eyes. In
her black gown, and with her blond hair concealed under
the large hat, they were her only color. Dispassionately
he admitted to himself that she was altogether breathtaking, and completely unaware of it.

"You will discover seduction comes to you as easily as
it does to all other women," he told her with a grimace.
"You are perfect for the part."

"But I do not care to play the part, your grace," she
replied, keeping her voice even with a considerable effort. "And I do not have to accommodate you any more
than you felt called on to help me on the journey here."

"I am sure I heard you, not many minutes ago, telling
Sir Charles's secretary that you were in need of money,
did I not?" he asked, ignoring her challenging remarks.

"I was not aware that you were listening . . ." she
said.

The duke could tell by her constricted voice that she
was upset, but instead of flushing as other women were
apt to do in moments of stress, Mrs. Stone only became
paler, her skin even more translucent. He filed the fact
away in his head, mentally approving her control.

"I rarely announce my presence in situations like that,
Mrs. Stone," he said, "It would only have been embarrassing for you."

"Thank you. You are too good," she said, her words
so cold he could not mistake her sarcasm.

"I believe I am, but you are welcome even so, madam,"
he told her. "Now, if you are quite through compliment-
ing me, may we return to business?" He did not wait for

her response, but went on immediately, "It would be helpful to the English cause to have someone like you gathering information."

"You mean you want me to act as a spy?" she asked, her voice incredulous. He noted she seemed more upset by this role than she had by that of temptress.

"Why not?" he asked, shrugging a little. "Vienna teems with spies of every size, shape, and nationality. There are some women spies, although they are rarer, and unlike their male counterparts, they do not trip over each other in their zeal to gather the news. All you will have to do is make yourself agreeable to the certain noble gentlemen I shall point out, and get them to talk to you. At the same time, you will be able to enjoy all the balls and parties of this carnival congress we are attending. And I promise you, and that dragon of a maid you travel with, safe passage home."

"Alas, I must decline the treat, your grace," Erica said evenly, although the duke noticed her eyes resembled green chips of ice. "As fascinating—and educational—as it would be, no doubt, I do not sell my favors."

"I do not believe I stipulated that these secrets must be obtained in a horizontal position, madam," he said coldly. "Besides, it has been my experience that nothing meaningful is ever said at such a time. What you would hear during lovemaking would be of no use to me at all. Surely you must agree."

"But you did stipulate seduction, I believe?" she asked, as if confused. At his nod, she went on, "To me, seduction means intimacy."

"Your education has been neglected, Mrs. Stone," he told her. "You can easily seduce a man with only the hope of your future surrender, which, of course, you may withhold if it pleases you to do so. Women, after all, are famous for changing their minds." He sighed a little before he drawled. "And they have all the advantages."

"How generous of you to allow me discretion," she said.

"You will have to change your name and give up your mourning, of course," he went on, as if she had not spoken at all. "We will say that you are unmarried. As

such, your supposed virginal state will protect you a
little."

Erica was almost quivering with fury now. How dare
he subject her to this distasteful conversation? How dare
he ask her to spy by leading men on in order to learn
their secrets and plans? She sat up even straighter as she
said, "I think you have forgotten I am a very recent
widow, your grace. What you propose is not only insulting, it is repugnant to me."

He leaned forward suddenly, until his harsh-featured
face was only a few inches from hers. "You will learn,
Mrs. Stone, that I believe honesty is the best policy
always. Yes, you have lost your husband. A husband of
only three months, too. But since you are here in this
office, I do not think that you mourn him overmuch. If
you did, if yours was indeed that rare marriage made in
heaven, you would still be prostrate on your bed, weeping copious tears and refusing to be comforted." He
paused for only a second before he added, "And you
would have swept from the room in high dudgeon several
minutes ago, if you had not succumbed to hysterics at my
immodest request."

His cold sarcasm bit deep. How could he know she had
not really loved William? How could he know anything
about her at all?

"And what is wrong with a little flirting?" he went on,
more lightly now as he settled back in his chair. "Women
do it all the time. Do you really want to miss such a
once-in-a-lifetime chance to enjoy yourself so royally in
Vienna? You will not be Erica Stone, widow. You will
be Erica Kingsley, a cousin of mine who is staying with
me for the congress. No one will know of your indiscretion."

Erica looked at him in cold astonishment. He seemed
to read the suspicion she felt on her face, for he laughed
harshly before he said, "You may be sure your virtue is
safe with me, madam, in spite of what I said to you on
the road. What you are to do is much too important to
risk by any affair we might enjoy together. Besides, my
aunt is staying with me, and will serve as your chaperon.
Her name is Lady Eliza Ridgely. She is a widow like
yourself."

In spite of her dislike for the duke, Erica found herself

weighing the odds. The lady sounded most formidable, and she was, after all, his aunt. Since she judged the duke to be in his middle thirties, this Lady Eliza had to be an elderly, proper chaperon. And then she was annoyed that she had almost thought of capitulating and playing his game.

The duke leaned back in his chair, seemingly at ease, although she noticed his cold black eyes never left her face. She smoothed her gloves and rose.

"In spite of all these persuasive arguments, I must still refuse," she said, holding her head high. "My father is General Sir Harold Huntington. He would never permit his daughter to become a spy, no matter how worthy the cause."

The duke rose too, and she was forced to look up at him as he loomed over her. "I have two other arguments to use to convince you to do this," he said. His deep, quiet voice sent a tremor of alarm through her. "First, you might find out who murdered your husband. No one here in British headquarters believes it was a common felon, I do assure you. And second, you might discover, for your own benefit, Mrs. Stone, why a bridegroom of only a week invented the summons that took him out of your arms and brought him back to Europe."

As Erica stared at him aghast, he concluded, "You see, Colonel Stone came abroad of his own volition. Sir Charles Stewart never sent for him at all."

3

There was a discreet knock on the door then, and Mr. Boothby came in, to halt abruptly when he saw Mrs. Stone and the Duke of Graves in conversation on the far side of the room.

"I do beg your pardon, ma'am, your grace," he stammered, looking from one to the other. "I did not realize . . . I mean, I would never have intruded . . ."

The duke raised his hand and said, never taking his eyes from Erica's shocked, frozen face, "If we might have a few more minutes, Mr. Boothby?"

"Of course, as long as you wish, sir," the secretary replied before he bowed himself away. The door closed softly behind him.

Erica continued to stare at the duke, and then she sat down again in the chair she had just vacated, as if she needed its support. She was speechless with horror.

"What I told you is true, madam," Owen Kingsley said. "Sir Charles sent no orders to your husband. In fact, he was surprised to find him offering his services again."

"How do you know these things?" Erica whispered from a dry throat. "How do you know so much about me and my affairs?"

The duke took the seat across from her before he replied. "I arrived in Vienna the day Colonel Stone was murdered," he told her. "There was a great deal of talk about it, and endless speculation, as you might imagine. I questioned Sir Charles and he told me what he knew about the colonel, your sudden marriage, and his unexpected arrival. I admit I was intrigued. I remembered you from that inn in France, you see, and I wondered."

"Wondered?" she whispered.

"I wondered how any man could bear to leave you," he said, his voice emotionless. "You are a very beautiful woman. What was there about the situation that made your bridegroom so quick to resume a duty he did not owe?"

Erica swallowed and shook her head. "I don't know," she admitted.

The duke leaned forward a little. "The situation was bizarre, don't you agree? Still, I considered it nothing more than a puzzling mystery until I saw you this morning. Tell me, have you been wearing blacks ever since you heard the news?"

When she nodded, he asked another question. "And have you kept the veiling over your face when you were abroad, madam?"

Erica nodded again, barely attending. Why, why? pounded in her brain. Why had William left her when he did not have to? Was there something distasteful about her? Had she said something, done something, that had offended him? She could not imagine what it could have been, for they had never quarreled, but there had to be some reason . . .

"If I might have your attention, Mrs. Stone?" The duke's sharp voice cut into her reverie. "I find I dislike being ignored even more than most men. I am not accustomed to such cavalier treatment."

Erica forced herself to look into his arrogant face, and he nodded his satisfaction.

"The reason I ask is that it would have been ruinous to my plan if anyone had seen you as Erica Stone," he went on. "You have not been in company, madam?"

"No, I have been alone, except for my servants," Erica told him. "I did go to see the chief of police yesterday, and I called on Lord Castlereagh as well. He was not at home. I saw only a secretary, and, as I was leaving, Lady Castlereagh."

The duke frowned. "We need not concern ourselves with the Castlereaghs and their establishment, but would Baron Hager know you again?"

"I don't see how he could," Erica said. "I never lifted my veil."

Owen Kingsley leaned back in his chair, and a ghost of a smile flickered over his face. "Very good," he said, almost as if she were a small child who had just given him the correct answer. "And since no one in English society has met you, there is no impediment to my plan but your reluctance. But think, madam! Wouldn't you prefer to discover the reason for your husband's strange behavior, rather than remain in ignorance? As Erica Kingsley, you may ask any questions you like with impunity. And I can promise you will have a gay, exciting time as you do so. The city swarms with handsome officers, diplomats, and the cream of the international *beau monde*, and there are balls and entertainments every night of the week. Think of what you would be missing if you go home to Northumberland to brood." He paused for a moment, and then he added, distaste in his voice, "Winter is approaching, too. How isolated you will be there in your widow's weeds."

He stopped speaking, and Erica did not break the silence. She was thinking hard. What he said was true. She *would* brood, and all her life she would wonder, with no earthly way of finding out, why William had behaved as he had. But if she remained, she had at least some chance to solve the mystery. She knew the names of her husband's friends from the notes she had found in his desk. And as the duke had pointed out, as Erica Kingsley she could seek them out and ask about the murdered man. They would think it only idle curiosity, no more.

"I really think we must relinquish Mr. Boothby's office before dark, madam. All the secretaries have a great deal to do each and every day," the duke said with a return to his usual sarcastic manner. "If I might have your answer?"

Erica's glance at him was considering. Somehow it pleased her to keep him waiting, even though she knew he offered her the perfect opportunity to remain in Vienna, with no money worries. She would not even have to write and ask her father for assistance. And all she had to do in return was try to get a little helpful information for England from some foreign dignitaries. There was no way the duke could force her into an affair with them, or question the amount of information she brought him. That would be up to her. Even the proud Duke of Graves could not expect to eavesdrop on a seduction scene!

"Afraid?" he taunted her. "Strange, you do not look the coward."

Erica reached a decision, and she rose. Her knees were trembling under her voluminous black skirts, but she knew he could not tell. "No, I am not afraid, and there has never been a coward in my family," she said evenly. "I will do as you wish, your grace, but I will do it on my own terms, and according to my own standards."

He rose as well to lean on his cane. One black eyebrow cocked as if he were astounded by her conditions. "But of course, madam," he said. "As you see fit, naturally."

As they walked to the door, he went on, "Dismiss your servants at once. There is no need for grooms and coachman or an equerry now. And I am sure we can find you a much more fashionable dresser than your current maid. You must be turned out with impeccable style. I doubt she has the skill."

Erica stopped and faced him. "Agnes stays. I will release the others, sir, but she remains or my agreement is forfeit."

They stared as if gauging each other's mettle. At last the duke was forced to nod. "Very well, so be it," he said.

Erica wondered if she was imagining the tinge of anger she thought she had heard in his voice.

"I hope she can keep her tongue between her teeth," he continued. "Not a hint of our deception must become known, or your effectiveness in gathering information will be nil."

"She will say nothing," Erica promised him. "She is loyal to me. And since she still calls me Miss Erica, you need not fear a slip there."

The duke opened the office door and stood back so

she could precede him. "Give me your address, madam," he said. "I shall send a coach for you tomorrow at three. Kindly be packed and ready. When you enter my palace in the Johannesgasse, it must appear that you have just arrived in Vienna. Be sure to wear something light and colorful. You must not be seen in black again."

Erica gave him her direction. She noticed Agnes rising to her feet, her face full of indignation that that nasty duke had dared accost her mistress again. Erica wondered if she would have more trouble with her maid than she had thought. She knew Agnes would not approve this plan, that she would be horrified when Erica discarded her mourning and became as gay as if she had never lost a husband at all. She would have to choose her words carefully.

After waiting until they were back in the rooming house, Erica found it an even more formidable task than she had expected. Agnes was more than disapproving, she was aghast.

"You'll never!" she exclaimed, hands clutched to her heart. "What, put off your blacks like some ill-bred commoner who don't know any better? Dance and go to parties and heaven knows what-all while you live with that horrid rake? You shall not, Miss Erica! Think of your father, your name, your poor dead husband!"

Erica had not told her maid of the duke's scheme to use her as a spy. Now she repeated his suspicions that her husband had been murdered by one of the nobility. "You must see that it is the only way I can find out about it, Agnes," she said in a firm voice. "If I go home, I will never learn the truth, and I *must* know the truth. No one will suspect I am Erica Stone, for I am to pretend to be the duke's cousin. Furthermore, his aunt will be my chaperon. There will be no danger of any impropriety."

She saw the maid wanted to continue to argue, and she held up her hand. "I have decided I will remain as the duke's guest, and that is final. If you do not feel you can continue to maid me, I will understand. Captain Garrity and the others will be returning to England shortly. You can travel with them."

Agnes straightened and glared at her mistress. "Never!

If you stay, I stay, Miss Erica, and that's the end of it."

"Good," Erica said, hiding her relief. "I would miss you, Agnes, truly I would. Now, please begin packing my clothes. I must write to the captain and ask him to call tomorrow so I can release him and the others from their duty to me. I must also write some letters to the family so he can carry them with him when he goes."

The next morning, Erica was tired and heavy-eyed, for she had not slept well. There was that one unanswerable question that continued to taunt her and keep her from her rest, and it had nothing to do with the morality of spying, even in a good cause. Why had William Stone left her? *Why?*

She was almost glad when it was time to rise and dress at last, and help Agnes with the final packing. The captain came as summoned, and tried to hide his relief that he could go back to England now that the lady he had watched over planned to stay on in Vienna with friends. Erica gave him money to pay the servants, and the letters she had written to her family. She had struggled to make them as vague and ambiguous as possible so they would not worry about her.

She was standing by the window when the duke's carriage arrived, promptly at three. She stared down at the shiny rig, the four thoroughbred grays that drew it, and the footmen in gray-and-gold livery who had come to carry her trunks. She realized it was too late to reconsider now, that she was indeed committed, and for a moment she felt panicky and unsure of herself. But then she reminded herself she was a Huntington, and as such, could face whatever the future held for her with the same bravery her father and brothers had shown facing England's enemies.

As Agnes oversaw the removal of the baggage, Erica went to the desk. She had packed all of William's papers, and now she checked the drawers to make sure she was leaving nothing behind. The man's serpent ring seemed to wink up at her as it rolled forward in the drawer. She picked it up slowly. For some reason, she did not want to take it with her or ever see it again, but something made her slip it into her reticule just as Agnes came to tell her it was time to go. As she went down the stairs, Erica remembered she had felt the same reluctance when she had packed the scarlet chemise earlier.

She had told Frau Heinrich when she was leaving, and the landlady was there by the front door to curtsy and wish her well. If she was surprised to see the newly widowed Englishwoman dressed in a pale green gown with a matching bonnet, she did not say so. Erica thought she even seemed pleased she was going, but she did not wonder at it. The wife of a murdered man was only a reminder of the crime, and besides, she would be able to rent the rooms again in a minute, Vienna was becoming so crowded.

The duke's coach was luxurious to a fault. Fresh flowers in vases fastened to the side panels perfumed the air, and the dull gold velvet upholstery was soft to the touch. Erica sank back with the wild feeling that she was throwing her cap over a windmill. It was most unlike her. Beside her, Agnes sniffed.

When they arrived in the Johannesgasse and stopped before an imposing mansion, Erica had herself firmly in hand, fully prepared to meet the duke and his aunt. But the austere, elderly English butler made their apologies after he bowed and welcomed her as Miss Kingsley. As he showed her up to her room, he told her that the duke had a previous appointment, and the Lady Eliza was not at home either.

Erica tried not to look impressed by the elegance of the duke's establishment. The carpets of the stairs and her room were thick and soft, and the furnishings exquisite. Besides a large bed with cream silk canopy and side hangings, there was a marble fireplace, a chaise and chairs striped in green and gold that were grouped around a satinwood table, and a delicate gilded French dressing table whose top was covered with crystal-and-gold appointments. Beyond was a large dressing room complete with a marble tub and washstand. One entire side of the room comprised closets and drawers for her clothes.

"His grace will return at five, Miss Kingsley," the butler said as he adjusted the silk drapes so the afternoon sun would not cause any glare. "He hopes you will join him and the Lady Eliza in the drawing room at that time."

Erica agreed, smiling at him a little. He was just the kind of butler she would have expected the duke to employ, for he was as arrogant in his own way as his master.

As he left the room, she decided to have a bath in that wonderful big tub, and then rest until it was time to join her host and hostess.

At that moment, the Duke of Graves was seated in Lord Castlereagh's office, which overlooked the Minoritenplatz. His black eyes held amusement as he watched the frown deepen on m'lord's face. It was said that Robert Stewart, Viscount Castlereagh, and Alexander, the Russian czar, and Prince Clemens Metternich, the Austrian foreign minister, were the three handsomest men in Vienna. Idly the duke wondered again at Lord Castlereagh's choice of wife. The former Emily Hobart was plain and dumpy, her dress decidedly dowdy, yet by all accounts her husband never looked at another woman. Not for the first time, he wondered why.

"I am absolutely astounded by your plan! Are you sure she is capable of carrying it out, your grace?" Robert Stewart asked, interrupting his thoughts. As the duke nodded, he went on, "I cannot like it even though it will all be done quite unofficially. A young woman, newly widowed, and with no experience in subterfuge, is such a terrible risk, it makes my blood run cold!"

The duke tapped one long finger on the arm of his chair. "But as you say, sir, it will not be sanctioned by your department. The risk is only mine, and, of course, Mrs. Stone's. You must not refine on it too much. Erica Stone will do as I say. And her very naiveté will be a help. Who will believe her to be anything but what she is, a wide-eyed girl aglow with innocence and anticipation as she takes part in all the festivities of the congress? She is perfect, but you will see how my schemes answer in the end."

"She is beautiful enough to ensure that the men you

wish her to question will be attracted?" Lord Castlereagh asked in some curiosity.

"Oh, a pearl without price when I have dressed her, m'lord," the duke told him solemnly. "And in spite of my reputation for indifference to the fair sex, I am sure you must agree I am a connoisseur of beauty."

His voice was grave, and Lord Castlereagh looked at him sharply. He could read nothing, neither regret nor self-pity, on that dark, harsh face. "As you say, Owen," he agreed. "In that field you are *sans pareil*."

Suddenly he rose from behind his desk and began to pace the room. "And you foresee no difficulty introducing the woman as your cousin, sir?" he asked. "Oh, by the way, should I inform my brother Charles about her? After all, he was her husband's commanding officer."

"There is no need, sir. Sir Charles does not know her, nor does he know she is here in Vienna." The duke crossed his arms over his chest. "As for your other concern, there will be no problem whatsoever," he said, his voice firm. "You never knew my grandfather, the old duke. That is what we all called him, you know, the old duke. My father, coming into the title at last, was only called the present duke, as, I suspect, I am as well. But my grandfather! Ah, there was a holy terror for you, sir! My exploits are but poor things in comparison. He was wild to a fault, proud and unpredictable and omnipotent, and he managed to create endless turmoil in the lives of everyone around him. Two of his sons ran off as soon as they were able to do so, forfeiting their wealth and titles rather than endure his domination. Or perhaps it was to save their souls, who knows?"

He shrugged before he went on, "It will be a small matter to put it about that the fictitious Miss Erica Kingsley is my Uncle Horace's daughter, or perhaps I will use my Uncle Reginald? He went to America years ago and has not been heard from since."

Lord Castlereagh came and perched on the end of his desk. "I do not think the Lady Eliza will care for the role of chaperon, Owen," he said, speculation in his eyes.

"There is no doubt of that, but Liza will also do as I say. I have ways of ensuring her cooperation," the duke told him. Lord Castlereagh wondered at the grimness in his voice.

"There are many men who would envy your control over the women in your life, Owen," he told him with a smile.

The duke nodded his thanks as he rose and picked up his cane. "A knowledgeable hand on the reins is all that is required, and a complete indifference to either tears or entreaties," he drawled. "Women, like horses, my dear Robert, for all they are capricious and contrary, are simple creatures at heart. What they long for is to be told what to do by a strong-willed man. Surely you have noticed that it is only the ones who have cast their lot with weaklings who are unhappy?"

Lord Castlereagh laughed out loud as he rose in turn and gripped his visitor by the shoulder as he walked him to the door. "Take care my Emily never hears you say so, your imperious grace. I can assure you she does not hold your views."

He paused as they reached the door, and then he grasped the duke's arm. "How soon do you think it will be before you can set your new relative to her task, sir?" he asked, serious once more. "I admit it would be helpful to discover what the czar is thinking and planning. His intentions regarding the future of Poland are suspect. For however much he prates of their independence, I fear he means that little freedom he would grant them once he has them firmly under the Russian flag."

"I shall do my best to hurry things along," the duke told him. "I do not foresee any unusual delay. I shall rig Miss Kingsley out in style, instruct her in any etiquette she might need to know in such exalted company, and keep a close eye on her until she is easy in that company. And then, as I told you, I shall introduce her to Count Andrei Ortronsky and let, er, nature take its course."

Lord Castlereagh shook his hand. "You are a tremendous help to me, Owen. Be sure the Prince Regent shall be apprised of it in due time. I only wish it were possible to air all the ways you have been of assistance to the British cause."

The duke waved a careless hand before he made his

way down a set of back stairs and opened a little-used door that gave on an alley. He waited until a tradesman hurried by and the alley was empty. Only then did he set off on foot for his palace in the Johannesgasse.

He was seated in the drawing room sipping wine when Erica Kingsley was announced on the stroke of five. As she came toward him, he rose and smiled, holding out his arms in welcome. "But how delightful to see you at last, dear cuz," he said. "I trust you had a pleasant journey?"

As he drew Erica up from her curtsy, he put his arms around her and bent to kiss her cheek. He could feel her stiffening, and his hands tightened in warning. "We must begin as we mean to go on," he whispered in her ear.

Then he straightened, and led her to a chair near the fire, saying as he did so, "Bring Lady Liza here as soon as she returns, Rudge."

"Certainly, your grace," the butler said, closing the double doors behind him and leaving them alone.

Erica watched the duke as he took his seat again, her heart beating a little faster in her apprehension. He was not a handsome man by the standards of any time, but he had great presence. Somehow, she knew he would command everyone's eye, no matter what the competition. Tall and elegant, with a knowing look in his black eyes, he was a fascinating man even with those craggy features, that harsh, disdainful expression. She recalled his smile as she had entered the room, and thought what a shame it was that he employed it so seldom.

"It is not that I do not have the utmost faith and trust in Rudge," the duke was saying now, his cold eyes never leaving her face. "He was my father's butler; I have known him all my life. But even he might let drop a careless word. I hope you have warned your maid to be discreet as well."

Erica nodded. "Agnes understands, although she does not approve," she said.

"We do not require her approval, we require her silence and complete cooperation," the duke told her coldly. Erica bit her lip at his arrogant tones.

"I should also tell you that my aunt has no idea of your real identity," he went on. "I cannot be sure of her discretion, and so, as far as she is concerned, you are just a cousin whose existence I have only discovered. I told her you have been living secluded in the country on an estate your late father, Reginald Kingsley, purchased some time ago.

"You look very well in green," he said, changing the subject before she could ask for more details of her fictitious father. "And perhaps a deep aqua or forest green would be stunning with your eyes. Let us hope the dressmaker I sent for has some silk in those shades."

"You have hired a dressmaker for me, your grace?" Erica asked, a little bewildered.

"But of course," he replied. "Madame Rousseau is coming from Paris. I do not expect her for at least two weeks, however, so we shall have to make do with local talent. Liza will know who is best." He grimaced and fell silent.

The doors of the drawing room opened then and a tall raven-haired lady came in at a languid pace. "I must beg your pardon, Owen," she said in a slow, sultry voice. "I was delayed at the dressmaker's."

As she came closer, Erica rose, indignation growing in her breast. This lady could not possibly be the duke's aunt! Why, he was in his mid-thirties she was sure, and this voluptuous dark beauty could not be a day over twenty-five! She turned to the duke, her green eyes flashing fire.

"May I present our aunt to you, dear cousin?" he asked politely. Erica saw the amusement glowing deep in his eyes, and it fanned her anger. "Lady Eliza Ridgely, known to the family and her, er, intimates as Liza."

The lady in question studied Erica with her big dark eyes, her expression shrewd. At last she pursed her red lips and nodded. "I am so glad that you are fair," she said in her slow drawl as she sat down on a sofa nearby. "I would have hated you if you had been as dark as I am. But now I think we will make quite a stunning combination, don't you agree, Owen?"

"Breathtaking," he said, his voice devoid of emotion.

Lady Eliza waved to her new niece. "Do sit down, Erica. It is so tiring looking up at you."

"How dare you hoax me like this, your grace?" Erica

cried, speaking for the first time. "This lady is years your junior! She cannot be your aunt!"

"Many years indeed," Lady Eliza agreed quickly. "I am but in my middle twenties."

"You are soon to be twenty-nine, and you know it, Liza," the duke told her, going to lean against the mantel. As she pouted, he went on, "As for the disparity in our ages, that is easily explained, cuz. My grandfather was a very virile man. He produced his last descendant when I, my father's eldest son, was six years old. I cannot tell you how delighted the family was that Liza was his grand finale. It was getting terribly embarrassing for me, dandling my aunts and uncles on my knee."

"How many children did his grace have?" Erica asked, fascinated in spite of her anger.

"Fifteen? Sixteen?" Lady Liza asked. "I can never remember."

"Seventeen," the duke corrected her. "You forgot Felicity. You always forget Felicity."

"Your grandmother must have been a very strong woman," Erica remarked, and then she paled as both the duke and his impossible aunt laughed.

"The old duke buried four wives, Erica," the duke told her. "Liza's mother was thirty when she wed him, and he was then sixty-five."

Erica frowned, wondering about this peculiar family. As if she had read her mind, Lady Liza shrugged. "You will discover we are all more than a little mad. And even though you have been raised in ignorance of us, you are probably tarred with the same brush. I once heard Arthur Wellesley say that to him the Kingsleys appeared a trifle blurred, as if the artist who painted us had let his watercolors run."

"Hardly a diplomatic thing to say, was it? These army men!" the duke murmured. "Not that I don't agree he's probably right, mind you. However, we have the *entrée* everywhere, don't we, dear, *dear* auntie?"

Erica looked at the dark beauty and saw her flush a little. The duke's voice had held a wealth of second meaning, although what it was all about, she had no idea.

"As you say, Owen," the lady agreed, lowering her eyes and smoothing her smart silk gown.

"I have told Erica that you will know which dressmaker she should patronize," the duke went on. "You spend so much time with them, I am sure you are an expert."

As the lady nodded, he added, "Oh, by the way, did it fit, Liza?" He paused for a moment and then he said, his drawl pronounced, "Of course I was referring to your gown."

Erica was astounded when the lady addressed flushed an even deeper shade of rose. Then she tossed her head and glared at him. "I suggest you take her to Madame Lisette's. I am quite pleased with her styles, although I cannot wait for the Paris dressmaker to come," she said, ignoring his last remark.

"How glad I am that I sent for her, then," the duke said. "Perhaps she might even keep you home a few afternoons, having your, er, fittings here?"

Erica decided to intervene, the situation was becoming so fraught with tension. "Won't you take me to your dressmaker yourself, ma'am?" she asked, trying to smile. "I need expert advice. I have never lived in town, and I do not know what would be suitable."

The duke spoke before Lady Liza could answer. "That will not be necessary, dear cuz. I myself shall see to your dressing." As she opened her mouth to protest, he went on smoothly, "I do assure you I am just as capable as our dear aunt. Yes, I will look after you—in every way. I am sure you have gathered that Liza has no intention of playing more than a nominal role as your chaperon. She is hardly fit to be one, now that I come to think of it. But at least as a widow she serves propriety, as ill-prepared as she is to play the part."

Lady Liza rose abruptly, her bosom heaving in her indignation. She never glanced at Erica, for her attention was all on the duke. "Someday, Owen, you will go too far!" she cried.

"But you, Liza, will not," he told her, his voice cold. "As the head of the family, I will see that you do not. I have no intention of allowing any Kingsley to sink to the depths of a Princess Bagration or the Duchess of Sagan. I advise you to remember it, least I put a stop to these excessive . . . fittings of yours."

As she started toward him, clenched fists held high, he added, "We will excuse you now, Liza."

Erica watched, bewildered and a little frightened, as the lady stopped short and made a valiant effort to control herself.

"I know you are going to dinner and the theater with a party this evening," the duke said. "You will want to change. Erica and I dine here. We have a great deal to discuss."

Without another word, Lady Liza walked away from them to the drawing-room doors. As she put her hand out to grasp the knob, she stopped and whirled, her face contorted. "I hate you, Owen!" she cried. "Oh, how very much I hate you!"

In a flash of silk skirts, she was gone, the door slamming behind her.

4

Quickly Erica looked at the duke, but if she had thought to see him distressed by his youthful aunt's passionate declaration, she was to be disappointed. Owen Kingsley's face was as cold and contained as ever. Ignoring that cry of hatred as if it had never been made, he remarked, "You never asked her age, nor about her suitability as your chaperon, you know. If you had, I would have told you."

Erica drew a deep breath. It was obvious he was not going to discuss his relationship with the Lady Liza. She herself was committed now, and there was no way she could draw back. But she wondered for a moment what was in store for her. The duke himself was strange enough, heaven knows, but Lady Liza appeared almost unbalanced. She had not understood their conversation, or the duke's sarcastic innuendos, but it was obvious he was displeased with his aunt. And who, she wondered, were Princess Bagration and the Duchess of Sagan, that he would not allow any relative of his to become like them?

She shook her head. No doubt she would find out in time. "From what I have seen, perhaps it would be more suitable for me to act as *her* chaperon, your grace?" she asked.

The duke smiled faintly, as if to applaud her quick wit, and for some reason, Erica's heart lightened. "As you say. Unfortunately, I doubt Liza would stand for it. My aunt goes her own feckless way. I am the only person who can check her. For that reason she fears me, yes, and hates me for restraining her. But she will obey me. She knows what will happen to her if she does not."

Erica thought he sounded as grim as he looked. For a moment they sat there in silence, and then the duke rose to pour himself another glass of wine.

"Shall you join me, cuz?" he asked, holding up the cut-glass decanter.

"No. No, thank you. I seldom drink spirits, your grace," she said.

To her surprise, the duke poured her a brimming glass and came and presented it. "In that case, you must cultivate the habit," he told her. "Take it. There is a lot of drinking done in Vienna. I would have you know your capacity. And if you find you do not care for it, you can merely sip it before you put it down."

Erica took the glass he held out, and he went back to his chair. "You remind me of how very much I have to discover about you, Erica," he said. "You mentioned just now that you have never lived in town, but I do hope you are comfortable in company and can converse with wit and ease. By the way, French is the international language here. Everyone uses it, from the Russians to the Swedes. You do speak French, don't you?"

As she nodded, he ordered in that language, "Tell me about your education, your upbringing, your family."

Erica took a small sip of the golden liquid before she began. It was heavy, but not unpleasant, with a nutty aftertaste.

"That is sherry, Erica," the duke instructed her. "It is made in Spain and it contains brandy, so beware, when you are offered it again."

She nodded as she placed the glass on the table beside her. And then, in faultless French, she told him about her home, her father and brothers, and her mother's death.

"My father saw no reason why I should not have the same education as his sons, especially since Brownie was willing. Miss Brownell, my governess," she explained. She told him what she had studied, and how her father had kept her abreast of the war, and he nodded.

"Excellent. You should be able to hold your own in any political discussion," he told her, in English once more. "As soon as we find you a suitable ball gown, we will launch you in society. Perhaps even at the next ball at the Hofburg. I am sure you will enjoy that. I have been told ladies of all ages adore the Viennese waltz." His mouth twisted in a grimace as he added, "It is so romantic, is it not?"

Erica never looked away from his mocking face. "But I cannot waltz, your grace. In fact, I cannot dance at all."

"Not dance?" he asked, looking thunderstruck. "But everyone can dance, unless they are decrepit, or crippled, as I am."

"I was never taught," Erica said. "My family lived in a secluded part of the country, and there were few festivities. It was not something my father, my brothers, thought important."

The duke rose to limp about the room, his heavy frown showing his displeasure at her ineptitude. When he turned back to her, he said, "Then the only dance you *will* learn is the waltz. To attempt to add a host of others to a nonexistent repertoire would be too difficult." He paused and stared at her again, and he nodded. "Yes, it might serve us very well. It will give you distinction and make you stand out among the host of beautiful women who have come here. How interesting you will be, merely observing the grand polonaise or a stately minuet as you stand beside me. I shall have a dancing master and a pianist here tomorrow afternoon, since the morning must be spent at the dressmaker's."

"I see I had better get a good night's rest," Erica said lightly.

The duke limped back until he was standing before her. "I would advise it, my new relative," he told her, not a glimmer of a smile on his face. "No doubt you will find me a hard taskmaster, but I want you to learn your part quickly."

"What will you do with this information you seek, your grace?" Erica asked, curious. "Is there someone in the British delegation you will give it to?"

He had started back to his seat, but now he turned back to her. "Did I give the impression I was hand in glove with the diplomats, cuz?" he drawled. "It is not at all true, and I apologize if you were misled. I am here in Vienna merely to acquire some stallions and mares for my stud farm in England. I have always had a passion for equines, and the Austrians excel in breeding them. No, the information I seek is mainly for my own use, and mine alone. It amuses me to be *au courant*, to know things that others do not, to be first with the news. A failing of mine, if you like, my perpetual inquisitiveness."

Erica stared at him. "You mean I will not be helping our country at all?" she asked, appalled.

He waved a careless hand. "Oh, I might pass along a tidbit now and then, if you hear anything important. One never knows when one will be overcome with the desire to be altruistic, although I can assure you it is not a failing I succumb to very often. On the whole, I find affairs of state tiresome, and diplomats a deadly lot. They are seldom amusing, for they are so very preoccupied with the importance of their own little missions. Frankly, I try to avoid 'em as much as possible."

He paused, and his eyes narrowed when he saw the contempt on her face, the flash of her expressive green eyes. "You must curb any feelings of nobility, Erica, lest you become boring. And there is nothing more deadly, nor so quickly abandoned, as a boring woman. Not even a diplomat," he said.

At the discreet knock on the door, he turned away from her, and Erica tried to school her expression. She was disappointed by his petty motives, but now, as he went aside to talk to his butler, she realized it made her task easier. She would not have to worry about the morality of what she was doing, if it was to be used for nothing but a sop to the duke's ego. And that, of course, was why he was so inquisitive. Haughty and omnipotent, he could not bear being in the dark, even about the matters of state he ridiculed. And if she heard something important, she herself could make sure it reached the right ears.

The duke and Erica ate dinner a short time later. Throughout it, he instructed her in the society in Vienna she was about to enter. As he told her of the various heads of state, and those of their retinues she would meet, she became so interested she almost forgot to eat.

"You need not concern yourself with the King of Denmark," the duke told her. "He is a gentle, although ugly man, and he will not figure in the negotiations. He thinks to acquire Norway again, but that will never happen. Both the Russians and the British are agreed that Sweden will keep Norway. Their goodwill is needed. And you will not have to be more than passing polite to the dreadful King of Württemberg." The duke grimaced as he wiped his mouth on his napkin and gestured to his butler to remove the fish course. "Here in Vienna, he is known as the Württenberg Monster. He is so fat the empress had to have a half-moon cut out of the dining-room table to allow him to get anywhere near his plate, not that he should in his condition. Moreover, his manners, if you can call them that, are coarse and disgusting. To add to his charms, he is a homosexual."

Erica swallowed. She had never heard such things discussed openly, yet the duke spoke calmly, almost as if they were talking of the weather or of the herb sauce that had enhanced the Dover sole.

"You will like the Austrian empress, everyone does," he went on after sipping his wine. "Poor Maria Ludovica! She is Italian born, the third wife of Emperor Francis. A charming, gentle creature, blond like yourself. I have heard whispers that she is very ill with tuberculosis, a pity at twenty-seven. This invasion of her country and her palace by the world's mighty must be hard on her."

He paused to help himself to the platter of wild game a footman was presenting, and Erica asked, "What is the emperor like?"

Owen Kingsley shrugged. "A gentle man as well, some years older than his wife. He and Metternich do not often see eye to eye."

At her questioning look, he explained, "Prince Clemens Metternich, the Austrian foreign minister. A difficult man to describe, or to know, although no one doubts his allegiance to the Austrian cause." He paused, and then a sneer curled his lip as he added, "He has been beloved of many women. No doubt you yourself will find him attractive, although as a mere man I cannot tell you why he is so appealing to your sex. To me, he has always seemed pretentious and sly, a man who takes himself too seriously. I shall be interested in your opinion of him, cuz."

"And the Crown Prince of Sweden, your grace? What of him?" Erica asked eagerly.

"Ah, Bernadotte. He is an opportunist, first and last," the duke said. "He has been a French marshal, giving allegiance to Napoleon until, of course, he was elected Crown Prince in 1810. Now he is considered our ally. He is one of those men who not only know which side their bread is buttered on, but who make sure it is heaped with jam as well."

He sounded so nonchalant, Erica could not help saying, "I am surprised. Surely such behavior is deplorable, is it not?"

The duke nodded. "It is. But Bernadotte is not the only opportunist, no, indeed. The mighty Talleyrand has marched to many different drummers in his lifetime. Although of the nobility, he was president of the National Assembly after the Revolution, then Napoleon's minister of foreign affairs. And in spite of his betrayals since then, Napoleon has made him a regent in the council that has supreme authority in France during his exile on Elba. One never knows where Talleyrand will turn. Sometimes I think it depends on the direction of the most favorable wind. But he is a brilliant man, and not one to be taken lightly."

"There are so many important people here," Erica remarked, shaking her head. "I do not see how I will ever be able to keep them all straight."

The duke's face remained expressionless as he said, "And to think I have not even mentioned the more than two hundred German princes who have come to the congress! They were all deposed when the Confederation of the Rhine was formed in 1806, and now they are here to try to regain their little kingdoms. Do not regard them, they are not important."

Rudge and the footmen began to remove the plates, and Erica took a sip of the heady red wine she had just been served. "And what of the ladies, your grace?" she asked.

The duke's black brows soared. "Ah, the ladies," he said carelessly. "Yes, they are here in great abundance, needless to say. Empresses and queens, princesses and exotic dancers, singers and actresses, both wives and a plethora of mistresses of all sizes, shapes, and nationali-

ties. You will meet some of them as soon as you enter
society. You must ask me if you are confused as to their
status, so I can set you straight. Some of them fill two
roles at once, you see, being both a duchess and a courtesan, for example."

"Are you referring to the Duchess of Sagan, your
grace?" Erica asked.

His eyes narrowed. "You are quick, very quick," he
said softly, and she felt a shiver run up her bare arms.

"The duchess I had in mind is Wilhelmina Sagan, the
eldest of four sisters," he went on. "She has been married and divorced twice now, and has come to the conclusion that husbands are not only tiresome, but expensive
as well. From now on, she intends only to take lovers.
She has had many of them, Erica. She is a highly sexed
woman. What makes her of primary importance at this
particular time is that she is Metternich's mistress now."

Erica struggled to keep her expression neutral, so the
duke would not see how shocked she was. As he went
on, telling her of some of the other famous, wellborn
women present in Vienna, her head was in a whirl. It
appeared to her as if everyone here was immoral, given
over to pleasure and vice. She wondered how she would
manage, and for a moment felt a wave of doubt that she
would be able to cope with it, or even fit in. And then
she wondered if she really wanted to.

The duke signaled the servants to leave the room.
"You are having second thoughts, are you not, Erica?"
he asked as soon as they were alone, leaning back in his
chair. "No doubt it is all so different from the life you
have been accustomed to leading."

Erica looked around the ornate formal dining room
with its high walls covered with delicate murals, its gilded
woodwork and glittering chandeliers. Before her on the
polished table was a golden centerpiece of cupids and
nymphs, and the plate and crystal were unlike anything she
had ever seen before. She felt very provincial, very naive.

"Yes, I am having doubts," she told him, her eyes
searching his face. "All that you have told me is foreign
to me. I do not see how I will be able to compete in this
society, nor am I at all sure I want to. I think immorality
is deplorable."

Her eyes remained locked with his, and she saw what she was sure was a fleeting look of impatience cross his rugged features. "You will compete with ease," was all he said, however. "Remember, if you please, that you are Erica Kingsley, cousin of the Duke of Graves. As such, your position here will be assured, and you will be offered every courtesy. You do not approve of the amorous ladies I have told you about, but you will not have to associate with them. A curtsy in meeting will be all that is required. Indeed, if I were to find you contemplating entering their ranks, I would be most upset. Most upset," he repeated more softly. "I do not care to have you losing your heart, for your value to me would then disappear."

Erica paled. "There is no chance of that, your grace," she said. "As you remember, I am only recently widowed."

He rose to draw back her chair. "We will not discuss your widowhood, nor its ramifications at this time, Erica," he said. "You are excused. I suggest you go to bed. I shall expect you ready to accompany me at nine tomorrow morning."

Erica rose and curtsied, not at all reluctant to leave him. She only hoped she would be able to fall asleep, with everything he had given her to think about running around in her brain.

The next few days were as exhausting as the duke had predicted. Erica soon overcame her awkwardness in Owen Kingsley's presence, for he was always by her side. He not only chose her gowns, but all her accessories, even her sandals, ignoring her own preferences. And he was always instructing her on how she should behave.

Only twice did she protest to the point of a quarrel. The first time was when he selected a slim evening gown of deep green with a low décolleté. It was slit to the thigh, and under it she was to wear only a flimsy matching chemise. Erica refused to do so, point-blank, and the duke signaled the dressmaker and her minions to leave the room.

"This is the current fashion, Erica," he said in a weary drawl. "Surely you do not care to appear the dowd."

"Certainly not, your grace," she replied, her chin high. "Neither do I care to appear the courtesan you have warned me to avoid becoming."

As his brows rose at her daring to contradict him, she added boldly, "Since I play a virginal role, this gown cannot be appropriate."

She watched those black brows become a straight line above his cold, intent eyes, while one white hand caressed his chin, and she felt a little breathless at her daring.

At last he shrugged, as if he had seen something in her face that told him how determined she was. "Very well," he said almost mildly. "We will select something more chaste. Perhaps your very modesty, in contrast to so much wantonness, will be intriguing. Let us hope so."

It was at the hairdresser's that they next came to disagree. The fat little Belgian had been ecstatic as he loosened her tight braids and brushed her hair smooth. Erica stared into the duke's face that was reflected in the mirror as he stood behind her, and then she lowered her eyes. No one except her maid and her husband had ever seen her with her hair down since she had reached the age of eighteen. Somehow, with the duke so near, it seemed much too intimate a situation for her to feel at all comfortable.

As the duke and the hairdresser began to discuss how short her hair should be cut, and what would have to be done to turn it into a mass of ringlets, she interrupted. "I do not care to have my hair cut," she said firmly. "In fact, I absolutely refuse to consider it."

"But Mees does not understand," Monsieur Bergeau insisted in an excited tenor as he waved his hands in distress. "Everyone, but everyone, mees, wears her hair in short curls."

The duke spoke before Erica could reply. "Then perhaps that is why this lady should not," he said, much to her relief. "I think a soft chignon for daytime, *monsieur*. And in the evening, she will wear it loose like this."

He reached out then and took her hair in both his hands, his eyes remote as he admired the ripple of silver as his fingers combed the soft strands. Erica felt shivers on her neck, and she prayed he would not notice the gooseflesh on her arms.

"It is one of her assets, we will feature it," the duke went on. "And she will be in good company, for does not the czarina, Elisabeth, also wear her hair loose?"

The little Belgian pouted for a moment, and then he began to arrange the fine masses of blond hair into a large chignon. Erica could not like the little tendrils he created to frame her face, but she did not like to protest further. There was an expression on the duke's face that told her that having won yet another concession, it would be most unwise.

As they left the shop and he helped her into the carriage, he said, "Be sure your maid studies the results of Monsieur Bergeau's artistry, so she can duplicate it, Erica."

As she settled back in the carriage, Erica considered Agnes Watts. That first morning, she had appeared in the hall with her mistress, and when the duke tried to dismiss her, she had protested loudly about the impropriety of Miss Erica going abroad with him alone. The duke had glared at her until she had fallen silent, her homely face red. Before Erica could say anything at all to ease the situation, the duke took over. "Do excuse me for a moment, Erica, if you would be so good," he said, his voice so cold and forbidding Erica had started. "I have a few things to say to your maid, in private."

He had gone to the door of a nearby salon then, turning only to beckon to the maid. After he closed the door behind them, Erica had listened hard, but she could hear nothing but a soft murmur. Agnes did not speak at all. When the two reappeared at last, she did not think her maid looked at all well, and she was astounded when she curtsied and left them without another word.

She never learned what the duke had said to her maid, for Agnes would not discuss it, but she knew it must have been a powerful argument, for she never tried to attend her mistress again when she went out with the duke. And she even stopped grumbling about Lady Liza's unsuitability as a chaperon.

The dancing master and pianist arrived as promised that same afternoon, but the duke did not leave her even then. Instead, he sat in a straight chair in the ballroom and watched carefully as Monsieur deVillan explained the steps.

At first Erica felt self-conscious under the duke's cold black gaze, but she soon forgot him as she concentrated on the music. She was very tired long before the duke dismissed the two men, and, at one point, even asked if she might rest for a moment. Her tall, thin instructor looked as if he would be glad of a respite as well, for she noted a sheen of perspiration on his high brow.

"Certainly not," the duke drawled. "The waltz requires stamina as well as grace, and so you must attain that stamina." He turned to the pianist then and raised a commanding finger. "Again," he said.

Erica sighed, trying to forget her aching legs. She did not think she was a slow learner, but it was several sessions later, and many weary hours of twirling and counting to three, before the duke was satisfied. "Your services will not be required from now on," he told the instructor as he was leaving late one afternoon. "My cousin has done very well, and seems more than competent. My compliments."

"Why did you decide I was good enough now, your grace?" Erica asked, sinking down on a chair beside him to fan her hot cheeks. "I have been letter perfect in my steps for two days now. Monsieur deVillan said so himself."

The duke rose and leaned on his cane. "I dismissed him because today was the first day you did not keep peeking at your feet, as if to make sure they were going in the right direction," he said. "And for the first time as well, you appeared comfortable enough so that you might be able to converse with your partner while dancing. It is important you do so, as well as melt in his arms."

He limped away before Erica could reply, and after he had left, she sat on in the ballroom, thinking hard. She had been here in the duke's house for only a little over a week, but she felt as if it had been months. And even though they did not go out in the evening, she was always tired. And yet, for all the time she spent in his company, she knew nothing more of the Duke of Graves. He was still a cold, distant enigma. He never spoke of his interests, his home, or his family. He never relaxed in her company, so she was unable to relax either. And if the conversation was not instructional, he had nothing whatsoever to say to her. She found it not only awkward but also somehow depressing. She knew her own person-

ality was not ebullient or mercurial, but Owen Kingsley
was even cooler and more contained.

But as much as she saw of the duke, she saw very little
of his aunt. Most days, Lady Liza slept all morning,
never coming belowstairs until long after the duke and
her new cousin had left the house. Sometimes she would
appear in the late afternoon or for an occasional evening
meal, but invariably she went out later. Erica tried hard
on these few occasions to make friends with her, but
Lady Liza did not appear to welcome her overtures, and
made no effort to encourage them or respond. The duke
seemed amused.

One evening, as the lady rose to leave them before the
dessert course, he motioned to her to remain.

Erica thought she seemed about to rebel, before she
shrugged her round shoulders and leaned on the back of
her recently vacated chair.

"I shall require your company tomorrow afternoon,
dear Liza," the duke said, his courteous tone at odds
with the command in his deep voice. "I have it in mind
to take you and Erica for a drive in the Prater, now that
her new gowns are ready. She will wear amber velvet. I
am sure you will be able to find something stunning—and
complementary—to wear. Shall we say about four?"

For a moment Erica was sure the lady was going to
deny him, but after a moment she bit her lip and agreed,
her voice indifferent, as if to show how bored she was
sure to be in their company.

As the door closed behind her, the duke turned to
Erica. "I must beg you to excuse Liza's lack of enthusiasm, cuz," he said. "No doubt she planned another . . .
fitting, which now she must forgo."

As the three came out of the duke's mansion the
following afternoon, Erica in the amber velvet ensemble
and Lady Liza resplendent in deep blue silk, Erica saw a
couple about to enter the large house across the way. She
had admired the pale yellow plaster of the street front
and the lushly carved decorations above the tall windows
before, and wondered who lived there. There was something about the assured gentleman dressed in the clothes
of another era that told her he must be their neighbor.
The girl beside him was striking too.

"Who is that, your grace?" she asked, nodding in their direction.

The duke's eyes grew keen as he studied the pair. "That, my dear cuz, is none other than the great Talleyrand himself. He has taken that house for the duration of the congress. It is called the Kaunitz Palace. The lady with him is his nephew's wife and his hostess, Dorothea de Talleyrand-Périgord."

As Lady Liza stepped into the open landau, she tittered. "There has been a great deal of gossip about them and the fact that his wife was not the only distraught lady to be left behind in Paris," she said. As Erica looked a question, she added, "His mistress is the pretty Dorothea's mother, you see. How lowering to be discarded for your own daughter!"

Erica frowned a little, never taking her eyes from the pair across the way. She liked the looks of the girl, for she seemed not only kind and gentle, but amiable as well. And then her eyes were drawn to the figure of the older man beside her. Somehow he reminded her of the duke. Although they looked nothing alike, he appeared the same type of man, one who would draw all eyes with his proud posture and the arrogant tilt of his head. As she watched, he looked up, and even the width of the street between the two parties could not disguise the powerful gaze in his narrowed eyes. As the duke nodded slightly, Talleyrand swept him an elegant bow before he turned to climb the steps. Erica started when she saw how badly he limped, much more than the Duke of Graves did. She wondered if they had anything else in common.

She forgot the impressive French minister and his niece, however, as the landau entered the grand *allée* known as the Prater promenade that golden October afternoon. There were many other smart carriages there, driving slowly up and down between the rows of stately chestnut trees. She could see more people strolling across the grass, admiring the rich autumn foliage while they were entertained by wandering minstrels. It was a carefree scene, blessed by an almost summery warmth, and she drew a deep breath of pure delight when she saw the merry-go-round and the Russian swings, and heard the delighted laughter of the children.

She and Lady Liza were seated together, the duke facing them with his back to the horses. As her glowing eyes met his, his dark expression lightened. "I was sure you would enjoy the park, Erica," he said. "It is a pleasant place, is it not? How wise of the Viennese to preserve this lovely island in the Danube purely for their own delight."

"It is wonderful, just wonderful," she murmured, ignoring Lady Lisa's little pout and bored sigh.

All petulance vanished from the lady's face, however, as the duke said, "I believe that officer is trying to attract your attention, my dear aunt. Surely it is Prince Gorsky, is it not?"

Liza whirled in her seat, raising a gloved hand in salute. Erica was watching her in curiosity, so she saw the slumberous eyes begin to glow with eagerness, and the way the tip of the lady's tongue ran over her red lips.

The officer in question and several of his party rode over to the landau as the duke gave the order to halt. Soon their carriage was surrounded by thoroughbred horses on whose backs were mounted some of the most magnificent men Erica had ever seen. They wore tight white breeches that accented every muscle, above shining black boots, and their scarlet jackets, heavy with gold braid and dazzling buttons, fit like a second skin. Their plumed shakos were tilted over their eyes, the chin straps lost in their thick, full beards.

Lady Liza was soon involved in an animated, although whispered conversation with the prince, while to the duke was left the chore of introducing his cousin to the eager hussars who surrounded them.

Erica could not help but be pleased with their open admiration, but she found it somewhat overpowering after the first few minutes. There was one officer in particular, a Count Andrei Ortronsky, whose eyes devoured her face and figure in leisurely inspection. She almost felt as if this large bear of a man was disrobing her, garment by garment, and she paled.

The duke soon brought a halt to the encounter by mentioning they were blocking the *allée*, and the hussars were forced to retreat. Lady Liza pouted again as they drove away, but Erica was grateful for his intervention.

She could still feel the count's gray eyes piercing her back.

The following evening was to be her first excursion into this sophisticated society, for they were to attend the weekly ball at the Hofburg. Erica found herself looking forward to it at one moment, and dreading it the next. What could she possibly find to say in such brilliant company? What if she stumbled during the waltz? She sat before her dressing table trying to calm her fears as Agnes brushed her long hair smooth. The maid was frowning, and Erica knew she did not approve the unorthodox arrangement. Agnes had not liked the gown Miss Erica was to wear, either, but she had held her tongue. The duke had threatened to send her home if she did not, and that would never do. No, no matter how many times she had to swallow her disapproval, she would keep quiet, she told herself. Someone had to watch over Miss Erica, lest she be taken in by that terrible man. He did not fool Agnes Watts, no siree! She knew he was up to no good!

At last she lowered the pale green silk over those shining tresses and hooked it up. In her opinion, the gown was much too skimpy and tight, but she had to admit Miss Erica looked beautiful in it, her white shoulders and half-concealed breasts rising from the taut silk, and her hair flowing in a silver cascade almost to her waist. With the gown, Erica wore the Kingsley pearls the duke had lent her, and on her shining hair a bandeau of tiny white flowers.

Erica turned slowly, admiring the shimmer of the silk before she paused to study herself in the pier glass. Yes, she would do, she told herself without a trace of conceit. She had never owned such a beautiful gown, and the pearls seemed to draw attention to the whiteness of her skin. She took a deep breath as she picked up her fan and tiny beaded reticule. Beside her, Agnes arranged a stole around her shoulders.

"You see you behave yourself now, Miss Erica," she muttered.

Erica bent and kissed her cheek, touched by the fear and concern she saw in her eyes.

"Do not worry so, Agnes," she said. "Perhaps tonight

I will meet some of William's friends, and I can question them at last.''

With a last wave of her hand, she hurried down the stairs. The duke was waiting for her in the foyer. He was dressed in black, with only his dazzling linen as contrast. There was nothing outstanding about his evening clothes, no flash of jewels or decorations, but still he was a compelling figure.

As she reached the bottom step, her breathing a little shallow, he bowed to her. "Superb," he said before he bent to kiss her hand.

"Thank you, your grace," she whispered, her throat dry.

"And so you should thank me," he said in much his old way. "I have excellent taste. I knew the green silk and pearls would become you." Then he turned to his butler.

"Tell Lady Liza we are waiting for her, Rudge," he ordered. "I agree a late arrival is fashionable, but I would not care for her to miss the opening polonaise."

It seemed a very short time later that the duke's carriage entered the Hofburg. Erica could see the crowds of Viennese who milled around the arched gateway, pointing out the notables as they arrived. She wondered what they were saying about the Duke of Graves.

She managed to preserve a calm front as they entered the huge palace and climbed a wide, curving staircase in a throng of other guests. She heard many different languages being spoken around her. The duke acknowledged no one, ignoring the speculative looks his party was being given. He spoke for the first time only when he presented her to the emperor and empress. Erica sank into her deepest curtsy, her breath coming quickly in her excitement. The empress gave her a lovely smile, and Erica's heart went out to her. She looked so tired, so wan, in spite of the red spots that burned high on her cheeks. Surely it must be difficult for her to stand here greeting what seemed to be thousands of guests.

As they moved on, Lady Liza excused herself and left them to join a group of friends. And then a short, slight man in a white-and-gold uniform raised his hand and beckoned. Erica, so close beside the duke, sensed his impatience as he paused to lean on his cane. Then he shrugged. As they moved closer, she saw the officer seemed much more interested in her escort than he was in her. Indeed, when the duke presented her, Prince Boris barely spared her a brief glance, and he was soon deep in a whispered conversation with the duke. The man who was beside him, dressed in the same uniform, was not so indifferent, however. Erica caught her breath in awe as she looked up into his bright blue eyes and saw under a smooth cap of hair as blond as her own, the handsomest face she had ever seen. She lowered her eyes so he would not be able to see her confusion. She had not known that a man who sent such a strong message of masculinity could also be beautiful, but this one, now openly admiring her, certainly was.

As the duke prepared to lead her away at last, the handsome Adonis murmured to his companion, "What a beauty she is! Outstanding!"

Without thinking of what she was doing, Erica smiled and thanked him for the compliment in the same langauge he had used. He seemed astonished.

"You are Swedish too, ma'am?" he asked eagerly. "But what good fortune!"

Erica felt the duke's arm tighten in warning. "My mother was Swedish, sir. She taught me her language when I was a little girl," she said, in French now so the duke could follow.

"Yes, my uncle's heart was captured by the lady on his travels many years ago," Owen Kingslely drawled. "We have only recently made our cousin's acquaintance, for he and his wife lived secluded, and until their deaths, Erica never left Northumberland. I am delighted to introduce her to society at last."

5

"You must permit me to introduce myself," the blond officer persisted. "To meet a countrywoman of mine . . . well, almost a countrywoman, is an unexpected pleasure, so far from home."

He clicked his heels together and bowed as he said, "Prince Eric Thorson, at your service, ma'am, your grace."

Erica could feel the duke's tenseness, and see the way his eyes grew cold and watchful, and she wondered at it. And then he seemed to come to some decision, and he bowed in return.

"May I present Miss Erica Kingsley, highness," he said.

As Erica curtsied, the prince smiled down at her. "Erica . . . Eric. I wonder if such a coincidence is an omen of some kind?" he mused.

As the other Swedish prince beside him snorted, he raised her hand and kissed it. He held it for much longer than was customary, while his blue eyes blazed down into hers. Erica felt breathless, and she made herself draw her hand away, even though she did not seem able to look away from that strong jaw, sculptured mouth, and straight nose, nor the lean cheeks below those admiring eyes.

She heard a fanfare behind her, and the prince held out his arm. "May I beg that your cousin honor me with the first dance, your grace?" he asked, never taking his eyes from hers.

"Unfortunately, Miss Kingsley does not dance anything but the waltz, your highness," the duke told him, not sounding at all sorry that it was so.

The prince stared at Erica, frowning now, and she shook her head. "In that case, I shall return for the first waltz, with your permission, Miss Kingsley," he said.

Erica smiled and nodded, and the duke made their excuses and led her away to a place along the wall where they could not only observe the dancing, but be observed as well.

"You do not seem very pleased, your grace," Erica told him. "Would you prefer that I did not dance with the prince?"

"Infinitely, but you have accepted him," Owen Kingsley told her. "I give you fair warning, cuz. Be careful in his company. He may look like an angel, but he is not one, far from it. He and his cousin, Prince Boris, are two of the most vicious men in Vienna."

As if he sensed her disbelief, he added, "Surely you noticed how Prince Boris practically ignored you?"

As she nodded, he said, "That is because he is not at all interested in women, no matter how beautiful they are. No, the prince has chosen me for his lover. He has been trying to convince me to that course for some time now."

"You?" Erica whispered, her green eyes shocked. "But . . . but . . ."

The duke's little smile was grim. "There's no accounting for tastes, is there? I myself, as little interest as I have in women, have even less in men, but so far Boris refuses to take no for an answer. I know that his cousin Eric is just as much a voluptuary. He is insatiable, in fact. No woman is safe with him."

Erica's soft lips tightened. How horrible! She watched Prince Eric leading a handsome brunette into the line of dancers that was forming, and she felt a little better. At least he did not share his cousin's depravity.

As the stately dance began, the duke changed the subject, much to Erica's relief. "The room we are standing in is called the Redoutensalle, Erica. It is only the first of several vast ballrooms in the Hofburg. Two weeks ago the czar opened the ball here with the Empress Maria Ludovica. They danced the polonaise through the room, up the grand staircase, and through several other rooms before ending in the great audience chamber. A memorable evening. All the rooms were decorated in red and gold then. They are different for every occasion."

Erica looked around the huge room in awe. Tonight it was luxurious in green and silver brocade. She wondered at the expense of replacing all the tapestries and hangings for each splendid fete. Never had she imagined such wealth, such display. She felt as if she had stepped into a fairy tale, and she moved a little closer to her tall, stern escort.

The duke glanced down at her, his eyes hooded. "I shall introduce you to other men, Erica. Men more suitable for your mission than that wolfish fallen angel. But why didn't you tell me you spoke Swedish?"

"You never asked," Erica replied, intent on the dancers moving with such precise, formal steps. "I have not spoken it since my mother died. I am surprised I even remembered it."

"It is too bad you revealed your knowledge of the language," the duke complained. "We might have put it to good use at some time."

Erica tried not to think of her future spying. Somehow, tonight, she did not want to be reminded of it. She wanted to dance and enjoy herself, pretend she was truly a woman with an assured place here who came only for amusement, one innocent of any ulterior motive. Around her were the elite of the world, women in gowns so lovely with jewels so magnificent that she wanted to pinch herself to make sure she was awake. And partnering them, men dressed in faultless evening wear or colorful uniforms covered with decorations and gold braid, whose splendor rivaled the ladies they attended. Under the brilliant chandeliers they advanced and retreated in the dance, not a bit overpowered by the magnificence of the room. Erica drew a deep breath and admitted to herself that she was glad she had stayed. Vienna would be something to remember all her life.

It seemed a long time before the polonaise drew to a close to the applause of the guests. During that time, the duke had pointed out the notables nearby: Castlereagh, Prince George of Baden, the lovely Countess Julie Zichy, and Sir Charles Stewart. Erica's eyes grew keen as he did so. Sir Charles had been William's commanding officer.

She wanted so to speak to him, learn what she could of her husband's death. When she asked the duke to present her to Sir Charles, she saw his mouth twist in the familiar grimace that showed the displeasure that she was becoming accustomed to.

"I do so hope you will not become addicted to unsuitable men, Erica," he rebuked her. "One in a family is sufficient, and Liza already fills the role admirably. Sir Charles is a boor. He is not only lacking in manners, he is a drunkard, crude, and opportunistic. They say if Castlereagh were not so fond of him—they are half-brothers, you know—he would never have been included on the British staff. You would not care for him, although I am sure he would be delighted to meet you. He is another man ruled by passion instead of reason."

She tried to hide her disappointment as he held out his arm. "Shall we stroll about, cuz?" he asked. Obediently she took his arm, and he continued, "I want you to be seen by one and all, and when there is someone I want you to cultivate, be sure I shall introduce you."

As they walked away, Erica saw Lord Castlereagh and the duke exchange a fleeting glance, and she wondered if she were imagining the little nod that great man gave her tall, dark escort.

But Erica did not have the chance to meet many people then, for as the orchestra began a waltz, Prince Eric hurried to her side.

"At last," he said in Swedish as the duke relinquished her.

Taking her into his arms, he smiled down at her. "How lovely you are, Miss Kingsley," he said. Erica concentrated on presenting a cool, contained appearance, but she felt breathless. Dancing with the prince was not at all the same experience that it had been with her instructor. She prayed she would not disgrace herself.

In her determination to perform well, she barely listened to the prince's light, teasing conversation, and she never smiled. He tightened his hand on her waist as he tried harder to make her respond to him.

"Erica and Eric," he said. "Now, why do I have the feeling that our meeting was meant to be? That it is only the beginning of a wonderful, warm, fulfilling relationship?"

A little startled, Erica's eyes went to his face, now so
close to hers. He swept her in a tight turn, and her blond
hair flowed out behind her in a silver wave. "Truly you
are the stuff that dreams are made of, my dear," he
continued, made bold by the light he thought he saw
deep in her eyes. "That silver hair, your soft white skin,
those magnificent eyes. You look like an ice maiden
from one of the old Nordic tales. I do so hope that in
your case, looks are deceiving. It would be such a disappointment to discover you are not as warm and passionate as I want you to be—as I am myself."

"Your highness, please," Erica murmured. "You must
not say such things. Why, we have just met."

The prince smiled, and ignoring her reprimand, continued, "But I do not think I will be disappointed." His
eyes dropped to her half-concealed breasts. "I can see
how quick your breathing is, feel how fast your heart is
beating. No, you are not an ice maiden at all. You have
just been waiting for the right man to awaken you. Behold me, at your service, maiden."

In spite of her fears, and the duke's warning, Erica
found herself drawn to him as she stared up into that face
that was almost too handsome to be true. She wondered
what it would be like to kiss that sculptured mouth. As
her eyes studied it in wonder, he laughed. "You will
enjoy it very much, as much as I will, my dear," he said,
as if he had read her mind. Erica paled and set herself to
studying the medals that adorned his broad chest.

"I shall call on you tomorrow," he told her. "Perhaps
a drive in the Prater, if the weather is fine? Or perhaps
you would prefer to go out into the country? Vienna is so
crowded. There is hardly any place where two people can
be assured the complete privacy they crave."

"I do not know what my cousin has planned for tomorrow, highness," Erica managed to say. "As his guest, I
must pattern my days around his requests."

"We shall see," the prince told her, drawing away
reluctantly to bow as the music ended. He kissed her
hand, and as his warm tongue darted out to caress her
skin, Erica shivered. "Ah, yes, we shall see, won't we,
my soon-to-be-awakened ice maiden?" he murmured, his
blue eyes blazing. "You are . . . delicious."

Erica was more than glad to return to the duke's side and sit beside him until her breathing slowed. He made no mention of the prince, nor did he ask her what they had been talking about, and she wondered at it.

But the duke did not need to ask. Without being obvious, he had watched her while she danced, and he was well aware the handsome Swede was bending all his efforts to attach her and persuade her into an affair. He would be on his guard to prevent any such occurrence. Erica Stone had a job to do, an important job. Dalliance with an amorous prince would only hamper her usefulness.

Later that evening, the prince came back and asked her to dance again. Erica had waltzed with other gentlemen by that time, and she wondered that he was the only one who had been able to discompose her.

"They are quite breathtaking together, are they not, Owen?" Lady Liza asked as she paused beside him. The duke noted the little malicious tone in her voice. "Everyone is talking about them," the lady persisted. "I have heard such speculation, you would not believe it! Why, Comte de La Guarde-Chambonas was most fervent in his admiration for the heavenly picture they present, and Princess Lieven, ecstatic. I promised her you would bring Erica to her next affair."

The duke did not turn to his young aunt, for, as before, he had eyes only for Erica Stone. As he watched, he saw the prince bend to whisper in her ear, and he noted her confusion. Others were watching as well, some with a smile for the beautiful couple who, in their perfection, surely embodied the Almighty's original plan for how the human race should look. The prince was so masculine and handsome in his formal white-and-gold uniform, the lady so lithe and lovely in her green silk and flowing silver hair. For himself, the duke thought them too pretty together, and more than a little theatrical.

"Have a care, Owen," Lady Liza whispered, not done with malice. "I fear our new cousin is in great danger, for although the prince will not marry her, he will find some way to enjoy her."

The duke turned then, and frowned down into her sensuous, mocking face. He saw her delight for Erica's coming downfall, and he felt a spurt of anger. "I doubt that very much, Liza," he told her in a cold, harsh voice. "Everyone is not as wanton as you are. Erica will remain chaste while she is in my charge."

Lady Liza looked disbelieving, and he added, "There are some women who have a few more morals than the barnyard cat, so constantly in heat, you seem to be. Not many, I grant you, but some."

Lady Liza flushed and turned away, trying not to show her anger, the anger the duke was always able to arouse with such ease.

After the prince left her with a last whispered plea that she receive him on the morrow, Erica saw two young Englishmen in the uniform of her late husband's regiment. She made herself smile at them, and only a short time later they were bowing before her and begging the duke for an introduction. He performed it with a little amusement in his voice, and left her sitting between them, as if he knew she was perfectly safe in their company.

"I do not believe we have seen you in Vienna before, Miss Kingsley," the taller, thinner one, who had told her his name was Frederick Martin, said.

"And surely we could never forget you if we had!" Reginald Soames chimed in.

"I have only recently arrived," Erica said, smiling impartially one way and then the other. "But tell me, sirs, what regiment do you belong to? I find all these uniforms so very confusing!"

"The Queen's Own Fusiliers, ma'am," Lieutenant Soames said proudly. "A crack outfit, you may be sure, full of the best soldiers in England."

"I seem to remember meeting someone from that regiment," Erica mused, trying to keep her excitement from showing. "Now what was his name? William Sand? No, Stone, William Stone! Do you know him?"

Captain Martin's face had turned grim as she spoke. "Yes, we knew him," he said slowly. "He is dead now."

"Dead?" Erica echoed. "But when did this happen?"

"Only a short time ago, Miss Kingsley," Lieutenant Soames told her. "He was murdered right here in Vienna."

"Murdered? Good heavens!" she exclaimed. "But why? How? Who could have done it?"

Captain Martin studied her face, a little disappointed that such a beautiful young lady was also prey to the sensationalism he had noted in others of her sex.

"He was stabbed late one night," the lieutenant went on, delighted to gain her full attention, no matter how gruesome the subject. "It could have been anyone." He shrugged. "William had a wild streak, you know, he was a real peep-o'-day boy, up to every rig and row in town. And he was a heavy gambler. He had been gambling that night. Perhaps he won a great deal of money, and he was set on because of it."

"More likely he lost," the captain said, his voice gloomy. "Never knew a man to have such cursed luck, never. Why, he even had to get leg-shackled not many months ago, to escape his creditors."

"No, no, Freddie, you've got it all wrong!" Lieutenant Soames interjected. "It wasn't to pay his debts. Lord, William wasn't that simple! He just left England and avoided 'em. It was because of that woman, remember?"

The captain suddenly coughed behind his hand, his pale blue protuberant eyes flashing a message to his friend. Lieutenant Soames subsided, and after an awkward moment, changed the subject.

Erica was forced to follow his lead. She could not persist in her questions, no matter how much she longed to reveal her true identity and discover what else they knew. What woman? What was her name? she wondered, remembering the scarlet chemise she had found, even as she pretended to laugh at the sight of a very fat German princess and her equally obese partner who were dancing by, their round red faces shining with perspiration.

"Looks just like a sausage with a string around her middle, don't she, Reggie?" the captain whispered. "Why on earth some women try to wear these current styles is a mystery to me."

The duke came back a little later and excused them both. He led Erica from the ballroom so she might sample the delicacies at one of the buffets that was set up in every room, and enjoy a glass of champagne.

As he seated her at a small table for two, he asked, "Are you enjoying yourself, Erica? Is the ball everything you imagined it would be?"

Erica studied his dark, closed face, knowing suddenly that he himself was not enjoying it. She wondered if there was anything he did enjoy.

"It has been a wonderful evening, your grace," she told him with her little smile. "I would not have missed it for the world."

"And Prince Eric Thorson, what of him?" the duke persisted as he cut his salmon.

"He is very ardent," Erica admitted. "He says he intends to call on me tomorrow and take me for a drive."

"How unfortunate that you will not be home, cuz," the duke replied. "I plan to take you for a long ride tomorrow afternoon. Some fresh air and exercise will do us both good after the rarefied atmosphere we have been treated to tonight, don't you agree?"

Erica wondered why she felt a flash of resentment for his domineering ways, for she had been frightened by the prince and worried about how she was to avoid him. It was most contrary of her.

The duke sipped his champagne, his narrowed eyes studying the expressions that chased each other across her lovely face. "He will call again another day," he told her carelessly. "It is best sometimes to, er, whet a man's appetite, my dear Erica. But in the case of the prince, that is hardly necessary, and I want you to keep your distance, seeing him only in company. This evening you looked as if you would have been delighted to fall not only into his arms but also into his bed."

Erica put down her fork. "You are insulting, sir," she said, keeping her voice low. All around them, other guests were eating and talking and laughing together. She was sure none of them were enduring anything like the distasteful conversation she was being treated to.

"I am often insulting, when it is necessary," the duke agreed. "Allow me to remind you that the prince plays no part in my plans. Being only a frivolous fellow bent on pleasure, he has no information that would be of any value to me. You do remember why you are here, do you not? Why I have bought you so many lovely gowns, indoctrinated you so carefully in the little world that is the congress? How you agreed to my plans?"

He paused, and they stared at each other across the

gilt table. At last Erica lowered her eyes to her plate, wondering at the lump in her throat.

"No, I am sure you have not forgotten," the duke said, as if to himself. "But I will remind you of it again, if the need arises. Eat your supper, Erica," he added in a lighter tone. "You will need your strength. These infernal balls sometimes last until four in the morning."

Erica picked up her fork, but she had lost her appetite. How unkind he was, how cruel. All her innocent enjoyment in the evening was gone as if it had never been. She was glad for the distraction when an elderly Englishman paused by their table a moment later.

"Owen, dear boy, well met!" the man said as his sharp little eyes went from one to the other. "Now, who is this lovely young thing? Can it be that you have succumbed to Cupid's dart at last?

"No, no, do not rise, sir," he added as the duke pushed back his chair. "No need to disturb youself, lame as you are."

Erica hardly dared to look into the duke's dark face, sure he must be furious to have his disability remarked. To her surprise, he wore a faint, supercilious smile.

"Kind of you, Sir Andrew," he said mildly. "Allow me to present my cousin Erica Kingsley. Sir Andrew Braithwaite, my dear."

The elderly man bowed to her, his eyes keen. "Cousin? Cousin? Whose child?" he asked, almost quivering with his curiosity.

The duke waved a careless hand. "She is my Uncle Reginald's daughter, sir. You do remember Reginald Kingsley, Viscount Drew? After he ran away from England and my grandfather's heavy hand, he married a Swedish lady. They have been living in Northumberland with Erica for some years now, quite incognito." He threw his head back and brayed a laugh, and Erica stared at him, astonished.

"Uncle Reginald was so frightened of dear old Grandpapa, he never even came home after the old tartar died," the duke went on. "Probably thought he'd come back from the grave to haunt him for defecting from the ranks."

As Sir Andrew frowned at this levity, he added, "Erica

wrote to me, as head of the family, after their deaths. I brought her to Vienna. Well, stands to reason, don't it? Poor little girl needs some entertainment after all those years in Northumberland. Too, too dreary for her, poor poppet!"

Sir Andrew rubbed his chin, his eyes on some distant horizon. "I seem to remember the viscount, your grace, but only vaguely, you understand." He bent forward then and whispered, "I have just heard that Castlereagh and Talleyrand have been closeted in one of the ante-chambers for almost an hour now, and the czar does not appear pleased. What can it mean, do you think? A major breakthrough in the negotiations about Poland, perhaps?"

The duke hid a tiny yawn with one white hand. "Lord, who can tell? And who cares?" he drawled in a weary voice. "These diplomats, so tiresome! I do not know why they cannot hold their meetings during the day, instead of secluding themselves at a ball in an effort to make themselves interesting." He gave that empty laugh again. "As if they could, crashing bores that they are."

For a moment Erica was sure the older man was about to strike the duke, but then he straightened and said with an old-fashioned dignity, "It is a shame that you do not take more of an interest in affairs of state, your grace. Your father, your grandfather especially, would not have been so torpid and apathetic, not when England's future was at stake."

Owen Kingsley signaled a waiter to refill the champagne flutes. "Ah, but I belong to a younger generation, sir," he murmured. "And it is a well-known fact that my generation intends to go to hell in a hand basket, isn't that so? Just look at the Regent!"

Sir Andrew bowed deeply to Erica, more shallowly to the duke. "I beg to be excused, your grace, Miss Kingsley," he said, his round face very red.

The duke waved that careless hand in dismissal. As Sir Andrew moved past her chair, Erica heard him mutter, "Disgraceful! Simply disgraceful!"

"Why did you behave so, your grace?" she asked, more than a little confused. She had never seen Owen Kingsley appear so blasé, so empty-headed. Was it a part he was playing? For what reason?

"Sir Andrew Braithwaite is a prosy old bore, Erica," the duke said in his normal voice. "I did it to get rid of him, of course,"

He saw she still looked bewildered, and he changed the subject lightly. "And what did you learn from your gallant fusiliers, cuz? Any new tidbits about your husband's murder?"

Erica frowned a little as she pushed the remains of her breast of pheasant around on her plate. She did not want to tell the duke what she had learned. She did not want to admit that William had married her only for her dowry, that he had been in love with another woman all the time, that she had been a fool to accept the first presentable man who had offered for her. He was so sophisticated himself, he would probably sneer at her, enjoy a good laugh at her ignorance of the world. Besides, William's indifference was so humiliating.

"One does hope to have a reply sometime this year," the duke remarked.

"Nothing of any great import, your grace," she managed to get out, stung by his sarcasm. "They knew him only slightly."

"That is unfortunate, but you must not be discouraged," he told her. "You are sure to meet someone who can help. Perhaps I will even exert myself to aid you, since it appears to be so important to you."

Erica raised her napkin and wiped her lips to hide her distaste for his intervention. "You are too good, sir," she said. "I beg you not to trouble yourself."

The duke rose and picked up his cane. "If you are quite refreshed, shall we return to the festivities, Erica?"

She rose obediently and took his arm. As they left the room, he said, "Do force yourself to call me cousin or Owen occasionally. All this 'sirring' and 'your gracing' so constantly cannot help but be suspicious. We are family, remember."

She nodded, and he went on, "As for my assistance in the matter of your bridegroom's untimely death, I must tell you that since I so rarely exert myself and take the trouble to help others, you should applaud and encourage the nobility of my intervention, not refuse it."

They entered the Redoutensalle just as another dance

was ending, and Erica was not forced to reply, for the
duke's attention was attracted by the sight of Lady Liza.
She was still held tight in Prince Gorsky's arms, while all
around them, others were leaving the floor. The two
were staring into each other's eyes, and as she watched,
Erica saw Lady Liza's arms creep up around the prince's
neck as she raised her face to murmur something to him,
her lips only inches from his.

Beside Erica, the duke stiffened. As if aware suddenly
of the intent black eyes that stared at her so coldly, Lady
Eliza Ridgely looked around. Erica was not surprised to
see her flush and drop her arms as quickly as if Prince
Gorsky had turned into a snake.

"Ah, Miss Kingsley, how delightful to me that we are
to meet again," a deep, rough voice exclaimed, and she
turned to see the Russian hussar who had subjected her
to such an intent inspection in the park beaming at her.
He bowed to the duke and greeted him. As they stood
talking to each other, Erica could not help but compare
them. Count Andrei Ortronsky did not have anywhere
near the duke's height, but somehow he appeared tall.
She decided it must be his bulk, for he seemed almost as
wide as two men with his broad, heavily muscled torso.
His thick black hair and full beard proclaimed a strong
masculinity, and she could see more hair above his evening gloves. She was sure his entire body was covered
with that thick black hair, just like a bear's, and she was
repulsed by the thought of him naked.

He turned to her again. "I beg a dance, Miss Kingsley," he said in his broken French.

She looked quickly to the duke, hoping she might
refuse. At his nod, she made herself say, "I would be
delighted, sir."

The hussar remained beside them chatting of the ball
and Vienna until the next waltz began. Once again, the
duke had slipped into his blasé, careless pose. Erica
could see the contempt in the Russian's gray eyes for this
silly Englishman, and she was almost glad to take his
hand, allowing her own to be swallowed up by that huge
paw.

Surprisingly, the count was a graceful dancer, although
he performed the waltz with a great deal more exuber-

ance than Erica was used to, and at double time. She was glad he did not talk to her, for she was concentrating on her steps. Near the end of the dance, when she was quite breathless, she slipped a little. At once he picked her up in his arms and continued dancing, laughing hugely at her amazement.

"Put me down!" she ordered, beating that broad chest with her fists, and aware that others nearby were pointing at them, and laughing a little too.

The count obeyed her at once, a worried little frown on his face that he might have displeased her. "But I could not let you fall, little bird," he said, his voice a rumble deep in his chest. "I would not let anything bad happen to you."

"You are too kind," Erica made herself say, wondering if this whirlwind dance would be over before she was completely out of breath. She saw other Russian soldiers now, all dancing at the same breakneck speed, and it made her dizzy just to watch them.

When the music drew to a close at last, she could barely stand, and she was grateful for the count's strong arm around her waist, no matter how unsuitable it was, as he led her back to the duke. He kissed her hand in parting almost reverently, and she tried not to shiver as that thick beard brushed her skin.

"We meet again, little bird," he whispered. "It will be soon."

Erica sat down beside the duke and fanned her heated cheeks.

"I see the count has also succumbed to your charms, cuz," the duke said in an undertone. "Indeed, for a brief moment I was afraid he intended to throw you over his shoulder and carry you off as his prize, he is such a bull. But I am pleased, very pleased."

As Erica stared at him aghast, he explained, "I want you to encourage him, lead him on while you question him about the czar's plans. And I want you to do so as soon as you can manage it."

Erica stifled her wild protest for such a distasteful assignment, as an older gentleman paused beside their sofa.

"My dear sir," he said. "You must allow me to intro-

duce myself, since it appears we are to be neighbors in
the Johannesgasse."

The duke rose to his feet at once, and Erica was quick
to follow his example, for the man who stared at them so
proudly was none other than the great Talleyrand himself. He was not above medium height, but he was a
commanding figure. He was dressed in satin knee breeches
and black silk stockings, and his high-heeled shoes were
bedecked with jeweled buckles. Priceless Mechlin lace
covered his thin white hands and foamed over a satin
waistcoat and a blue-and-silver evening coat. He wore his
hair powdered. It was tied back with a silver ribbon, and
there was a faint odor of orange blossoms about him.
Although she knew he appeared an anachronism, Erica
thought him stunning, for she was sure he would have
been noticed even if he were not the only man besides
the footmen who was powdered. She noticed with some
detachment that the Duke of Graves was not at all overshadowed by his magnificence, and even felt a stab of
pride that it was so.

It was a moment before she could give her attention to
the young woman on the great man's arm. How lovely
she is, she thought in instant admiration. She was tall and
slender, and her great dark eyes were expressive.

"I am Talleyrand," the gentleman said, bowing low,
and knowing no further title was necessary. "May I also
present my niece Dorothea, Comtesse de Talleyrand-
Périgord?"

The duke introduced himself and Erica in turn, and
bows and curtsies were exchanged, and, in the case of
the two young women, small secret smiles.

Erica wondered at the instant rapport she felt as they
did so. Was it because she imagined the lady before her
to be a captive too? And then she wondered at her choice
of word. The Duke of Graves was not her captor—or
was he?

6

Erica had no time to ponder this bizarre thought, for Charles Maurice de Talleyrand-Périgord, Prince de Bénévent, Grand Dignitaire de France, and Regency Council member, began to speak. His voice was smooth and full of gentle courtesy. Erica could see why he was such a great diplomat and such an asset to his country. The three of them surrounding him listened to his every word almost fearfully, as if they might miss something important.

"You must honor us some evening, your grace, Miss Kingsley," he was saying now. "We dine at five, if that is not too early for you? It is my only meal of the day, you see."

"We should be honored, excellency," the duke said in his lazy drawl. "But only if you will allow us to return the compliment."

"Ah, but I rarely dine out," Talleyrand told him. "I must admit I find other chefs lacking, after the delights of my own superior Carême. But we should be pleased to come on another occasion, wouldn't we, *ma petite*?"

The countess smiled and nodded. "Perhaps Miss Kingsley might care to ride or drive out with me sometime," she suggested.

Not a muscle moved in her uncle's cheek, but somehow Erica knew this invitation was not as agreeable to his excellency, and she spoke up quickly, lest he find a way to circumvent it. She did not doubt for a moment that he could find that way, if he wanted to.

"I should enjoy that, Countess," she said, smiling back

at her. "I have only recently arrived in Vienna, and I have not met any ladies my own age."

Talleyrand turned to the duke and reached out to touch his cane with one of his own. "I see we have something in common, sir," he remarked. "A childhood injury?"

"No, excellency, I was born lame," the duke told him, his deep voice emotionless.

"Ah. Now I myself was dropped by a careless nursemaid when I was but an infant," Talleyrand confided. "She was frightened she would be punished, so she never told anyone, and hid the injury until it was too late to correct it." He shrugged. "It is a nuisance to be lame, don't you agree, your grace?"

"I have always found it so," the duke replied.

"But perhaps it is not the misfortune others might consider it," Talleyrand went on. "It gave me a scholarly bent, for of course I was unable to participate in games or rough play. No doubt you had much the same experience."

The duke's smile was fleeting. "Hardly, excellency," he said. "I can claim no scholarship of any kind, and had to be driven to my books. Fortunately for me, my lameness did not prevent me from becoming a horseman of note. I seem to remember spending most of my childhood on the backs of the wildest, most undependable animals in my father's stables."

"I see," Talleyrand said. "For of course there you felt whole." He gave a gentle nod of understanding. "But now, as a man grown, you must realize that physical deformities have little effect on a man's total worthiness. Lameness, even as bad as mine, is only a bagatelle."

He turned then, and bowed to his niece. "Shall we, my dear?" he asked. "It grows late, and I think we have accomplished everything we came for this evening. Your grace, Miss Kingsley. I shall look forward to our next meeting, sir. Perhaps we might discover we have . . . ah, other things in common?"

The duke bowed, but he had no comment, and Erica saw that his excellency seemed amused. She gave the countess another smile as she curtsied.

As the two strolled slowly away, the prince leaning heavily on his canes, Erica turned to the duke. His fop-

pish air had been noticeably absent while speaking to
Talleyrand, and she wondered at it, and at his penchant
for turning it on and off at will. She saw he was staring
after the French statesman and caressing his chin as if
deep in thought.

"I wonder," he murmured. "I wonder."

It was well after four before Erica was in bed at last,
an indignant Agnes bemoaning the late hour as she gathered up the green silk gown and begged her mistress to
sleep late.

Erica was tired and she dropped off at once. When she
woke at noon the following day, she did not ring at once
for her maid. Instead, she lay in the big comfortable bed
and recalled all the events of the previous evening. She
knew that even if she went to a hundred more balls in the
future, she would never forget this particular one. It
whirled in her mind in a kaleidoscope of memories. Handsome, dangerous Prince Eric, the jovial bear that was
Count Andrei, the fascinating Talleyrand and gentle Dorothea, and, woven through the tapestry in a persistent
shining thread, the Duke of Graves. He overshadowed
all the rest for her, and she pulled the satin coverlet a
little higher as she pondered why this should be so. And
then she remembered he had asked her to ride with him
this afternoon, and she sat up abruptly to ring for Agnes.

The maid brought up two nosegays with the breakfast
tray, her homely face set in lines of severe disapproval.
To think Miss Erica was attracting beaux, just as if she
had never been married or widowed at all! It was a
disgrace, that's what it was. As she took out the girl's
best habit and boots, she shook her head. She didn't
know where this was all leading, but something deep in
her bones told her there was trouble ahead.

This particular day, Erica would have laughed at her.
It was such a glorious day, so warm and sunny. How
could it be possible for anyone to be gloomy? She ate a
big breakfast and admired her posies, one from Count
Andrei, the other, with a most suggestive message in
Swedish, from Prince Eric. The duke had also written
her a short note, telling her he had ordered the horses to
be brought round at two. For some reason, she reread

those few short lines more than once, and stared at his spiky black signature as she drank her coffee.

She remembered now how he had told her he wanted her to attract the Russian hussar, and although she was reluctant to begin spying on anyone, she knew she would have to obey him. And it wasn't as if she were afraid of the Russian anymore, not after last night. She recalled how quickly he had set her on her feet when she had ordered him to do so, how he had told her he would never let anything happen to her, and the worried little frown he had worn, almost as if he were afraid he had displeased her. And how reverently he had kissed her hand in parting, such a contrast to the prince's sensual farewell. Perhaps she could keep him in check, huge exuberant man that he was, by playing the shy, inexperienced girl. She would have to see. She wondered how you went about asking an aide to the czar to reveal state secrets. Perhaps she should ask the duke.

She joined him in the foyer shortly before two, wearing a habit of dark green twill trimmed with silver buttons. On her head she wore a matching hat trimmed with white chiffon.

The duke nodded in greeting, but he did not speak until they went out, and then only to order the groom who had brought the horses from the stable to help her to the saddle. Erica's mare was a playful chestnut, and the duke's mount a large black gelding who did not look at all good-natured. He rolled his eyes and sidestepped nervously as the duke paused to have a few words with his groom. Idly, Erica wondered at their serious faces, the intent way the groom leaned forward to listen, and the grim nod he gave the duke when he mounted at last.

He was still holding his cane, and now Erica saw with astonishment that it collapsed, much like a telescope. "How very clever," she said, pointing to it with her crop.

Owen Kingsley slipped it into his pocket. "One never knows when one will have to dismount," he said, nodding a dismissal to the groom. As the two started off at a gentle trot, he added, "I have quite a large collection of canes, much as some fashionable gentlemen collect fobs or snuffboxes. Some of them are very . . . interesting."

He sounded so grim, Erica was quick to change the

subject, even though it was the first time he had volunteered any information about himself. The duke's lameness was obviously a touchy subject, one he preferred not to discuss.

The duke led the way through the streets of Vienna, always heading in a westerly direction. "I thought to show you the Schönbrunn Palace today, Erica," he told her. "It is an attractive place, and ever since Maria Theresa's reign, the grounds have been open to the public. She always said she liked her Viennese around her. Hardly regal of her, was it?"

"No, but a very kind gesture, even so," Erica replied, warming to the deceased empress. "She must have been much loved."

As they rode along, the duke told her about the lady, and pointed out any buildings or churches of interest. Erica was almost disappointed when the city fell behind them and they began to canter through the outskirts.

Schönbrunn more than made up for the temporary loss of Vienna. By its huge size and the beauty of the surrounding grounds, it was obviously a palace, but it was not overpowering with its warm yellow front and green shutters. The duke told her it had originally been intended as a summer palace, for it was situated on the River Wien. They inspected the grounds, and when she asked about the long colonnade some distance away from the palace itself, the duke suggested they dismount and investigate. Erica saw he must have made arrangements for their visit, for when he raised his hand, a groom came running to take the horses. After they dismounted, she found herself waiting once again while the duke and the Austrian groom spoke quietly together for serveral minutes. She was a little surprised at the value of the coin the duke gave him in parting. It seemed a munificent payment just to watch their horses.

As they strolled toward the colonnade, Erica matched her steps to the duke's, thinking what a good thing it was that he had that ingenious cane. There were others in the park, but it was not crowded, and she looked around eagerly, admiring the extensive flowerbeds, the velvet lawns, and the stately trees.

"The colonnade is called the Gloriette," the duke said

as they climbed the gentle rise it was built on. "It was designed by von Hohenberg in 1775."

Erica paused in delight when they reached the top. Spread out before them was a superb view of the entire park and the palace, with Vienna forming a backdrop in the distance.

"Now I know why it is called the Gloriette!" she exclaimed. "What an inspiring view!"

The duke stared down at her for a moment, and then he indicated a bench nearby. "Yes, it is outstanding," he agreed. "It is also an excellent place to talk openly, for no one can get close enough to eavesdrop without being seen."

As they sat down, he added, "In a little while we will ride on to the Vienna Woods, a favorite trysting place. I am sure you will become familiar with them in the weeks ahead. And with the ramparts around Vienna as well."

Erica frowned a little, not noticing his grimace. "May I ask you something, your gr . . . er, Owen?" she asked.

He nodded, and she raised worried green eyes to his. "I have been thinking about Count Andrei," she began. "And I have to admit I do not have the vaguest idea how to go about getting any information from him. I mean, I can't just ask him point-blank about state secrets, now, can I?"

Owen Kingsley studied her serious face, those clear green eyes, almost as if he suspected she was pretending to be an innocent. He saw nothing to indicate any deviousness, and he wondered why he felt a little uneasy that it was so.

"But it is simple, my dear cuz," he made himself say. "You merely ask him to talk about himself. There is nothing men like more than talking about themselves."

"You don't," she observed, and then she bit her lip in her chagrin at the words that had escaped her before she thought.

"But I am not an *ordinary* man," he pointed out, arrogant once more. "Take my word, the count will be delighted to oblige. And from there, you can ask him about his work, tell him how impressed you are by him, a man with the ear of the czar."

Erica was still frowning. "But suppose he won't tell me

anything, suppose he changes the subject?" she asked, leaning forward a little in her concern.

"Then you must approach from another direction," the duke instructed her. "Tell him how much you admire the czar, indeed, everything Russian. Ask him about the battles he has fought, the campaigns he has been in. He will soon be at ease with you."

She sighed, and he warned, "But do not rush him, for to do so would make him suspicious. I do not think the count is an overly clever man, but he is by no means stupid. The czar's entire staff is a formidable combination. And if you continue to hold the count at arm's length, he will be sure to try to impress you with a tidbit here, a morsel there."

He leaned toward her now, and said in a completely different voice, "My dear Miss Kingsley, it was such a morning as I have spent! Why, the czar himself requested my attendance at his meetings, and even asked my advice on the Polish problem."

Here the duke beamed and puffed out his chest, and Erica had to smile. The tall, dark forbidding duke was nothing at all like the ebullient Russian count, but he had made her see him, and hear his broken French.

"Is there a Polish problem?" she asked, remembering the content of his words.

To her surprise, Owen Kingsley frowned at her. "That is not important for you to know," he told her so coldly she cringed. "You are merely to collect information. I will decipher it."

Suddenly she was angry. The duke had spoken as if she had more hair than wit. "But you must see how much easier my task would be if I knew what you were looking for, your grace," she said quickly. "That way I could ask pertinent questions. Besides, Sir Andrew spoke of Poland at the ball last evening, and I heard several other people discussing it as well."

He stared at her, still frowning, and she added defiantly, "I am not simpleminded! Indeed, I have often been complimented on my intelligence and superior understanding."

The duke pointed to a young girl running toward them, laughing gaily over her shoulder at the boy who pursued

her, and he rose. "Shall we return to the horses now,
Erica?" he asked.

There was a decidedly militant look in her eyes as she
obeyed, and after they were safely past the laughing
couple, he said more mildly, "I am sure you are more
intelligent than most women. Lord knows it would be
easy to be! But in this instance you must accept my
assessment of the situation without question."

He fell silent then, and Erica walked beside him, her
chin tilted at a defiant angle. She was not to know the
duke only wanted her to remain in the dark for her own
protection. Even after a mere week's acquaintance he
had come to know how quick-witted she was, but he did
not know yet if she could keep a secret. There were few
women—or men—who could, as he knew well. No, much
better to have Miss Kingsley shooting random darts when
all was said and done. She would be safer that way, much
safer. And then he wondered why this seemed so rele-
vant, and so important.

The duke and Erica never regained any degree of
camaraderie that afternoon. She was still hurt at his
appraisal of her intelligence, and he seemed lost in thought.

They cantered to the Vienna Woods, which today were
crowded with other riders and carriages. It appeared as if
all Vienna were abroad, almost as if they wanted to soak
up as many of these mellow autumn afternoons as they
could before winter came.

It was almost five when the two riders arrived back at
the duke's palace in the Johannesgasse. As the groom
hurried forward, the duke's gelding reared. An afternoon's exercise had done nothing to improve his temper, Erica noted. And then the gelding lashed out at her
mare, and the chestnut whinnied in fright and tried to
bolt. Erica tightened her hands on the reins, but before
she was in any danger at all, the duke had brought the
gelding under control with one strong hand, while the
other grasped her bridle, holding both horses steady until
the groom could assist them. Erica was amazed at the
strength in those shapely white hands.

"How well you ride, sir," she complimented him as
they mounted the steps together.

One black brow rose as he glanced sideways at her.

"Naturally," he said in his old arrogant manner, and all
admiration died at once in Erica's breast. "Allow me to
reciprocate, cuz. You are an excellent horsewoman yourself," he added. Erica was not appeased.

He sounded the knocker, and just as Rudge opened
the door, something made Erica say in her sweetest
voice, "But of course. I am not an *ordinary* woman, your
grace."

In the same sweet, indifferent voice, she thanked him
for a very enjoyable afternoon, and would have swept
upstairs, her head held high, if he had not put his hand
on her arm. As she looked up at him, she thought she
saw a little amusement in his black eyes, and she stiffened.

"I have arranged to take you and Liza to Sperl's this
evening, Erica," he said. "It is one of Vienna's best
restaurants, drawing the custom of both commoners and
the nobility. The food is excellent, and the music and
dancing gay. I am sure you will enjoy watching the Viennese at play. They are such a happy people, are they
not? Not at all, er, *ordinary* either."

She glared at him and he reached out and flicked her
chin. "Run along, cuz," he told her. "The carriage is
called for at seven."

She curtsied, her green eyes flashing, and as she went
up the stairs, her back ramrod straight, he called after
her, "Wear the peach gown tonight, Erica."

She did not hesitate or acknowledge the order in any
way, and the first thing she said when Agnes came in to
prepare her bath was, "Lay out the scarlet gown, Agnes,
and the silver sandals."

The duke made no mention of this act of defiance as
the three rode to the restaurant. To her disgust, all he
did was compliment her on her appearance and remark
how wise she had been to choose the scarlet, when Liza
was so stunning in bright blue. "You look remarkably
British this evening, ladies," he said, and Liza sniffed.

She seemed to grow more cheerful when they had
been seated at a prominent table, however, and was soon
humming along with the orchestra and admiring the crowds
who swirled on the parquet floor before them. Erica's
eyes were glowing with interest. There were ordinary
burghers and their stout wives romping here, as well as

women with painted faces and low-cut gowns so blatant she knew they must be of the demimonde. There were officers from every nation, and other men who bent close in serious low-toned conversation before raising their glasses to each other with beaming smiles. It was warm in the restaurant, the air perfumed not only by the flowers on every table but also by the hearty aroma of good Viennese cooking. The music and the babble of conversation and laughter made Sperl's seem very cosmopolitan and gay.

They had finished their blue trout and were being served fillet of beef with a sour-cream sauce when Erica noticed a sudden hush. She saw that everyone near them was staring at the entrance, and she was not surprised when she saw the woman standing there between her two attentive escorts. One of them was an older man, portly and red-faced, the other a handsome officer in a Prussian uniform. But it was the woman between them who drew every eye. As she threw back her stole, Erica could see why. She was not very tall, but she radiated a power and sensuality that was obvious throughout the room. Perhaps it was the way she wore her long black hair, or the startling redness of her plump little mouth against the rich cream of her skin. Or it may have been the light in those almond-shaped dark eyes, her high pointed breasts and tiny waist. As she moved forward, the maître d'hôtel bowing low, Erica was reminded of a wave curling up on a beach, smooth and graceful and fluid.

Erica wondered who she was and why she seemed so beautiful, when, in reality, she was no such thing. Her nose was too long and her face too thin for real beauty.

"That is the dancer Isabella Sabatini," the duke told her. "She will soon be performing in a new production of *Daphne*. We shall have to attend a performance. I hear she is outstanding in her role."

Lady Liza chuckled. "But her most virtuoso performances are not given on any stage, and they are watched by only an audience of one," she remarked. "Most of the time," she added thoughtfully.

"I am sure Erica has taken the woman's measure, Liza. There is no need to state the obvious," the duke said, his voice cold. "Shall we talk about something else? A courtesan has nothing to do with a Kingsley."

Lady Liza subsided, and Erica resumed eating. And then she stiffened as the dancer removed her stole, revealing a very unusual bracelet on her upper arm. It was made of heavy gold, in the shape of two entwined serpents with large diamond eyes. Erica sat very still, wondering if her table companions could hear the heavy beating of her heart or see her shallow breathing. Surely it could not be a coincidence that Signorina Sabatini's jewelry was a perfect match for the ring she had found in William's desk. Had she given it to him? Or had he had it made to match the bracelet she wore, and paid for them both with money from his bride's dowry?

"Perhaps you should remind your dear cousin that it is rude to stare, Owen," Lady Liza said, a malicious little note in her voice. "Especially at someone the head of the house of Graves has decreed unworthy of a Kingsley's attention."

Erica made herself lower her eyes and apply herself to her excellent dinner.

"If you have quite finished, ladies?" the duke asked sometime later as he beckoned to a waiter to remove their plates. "It is time to sample one of Vienna's more delicious triumphs—her desserts."

"I really should not . . ." Lady Liza began, and he waved a careless hand.

"But you always do, Liza," he said. "Which do you think Erica would enjoy? The *sacher torte*, first created by Metternich's chef, or perhaps the *kirschen strudel* and *schlagobers*?"

Erica made herself join in the discussion, the most pleasant she had ever heard them engage in, while she tried desperately to forget the woman who might have been her husband's mistress, who sat only two tables away. She promised herself she would not look at her again, but that she would investigate her as soon as she could.

The three were lingering over their coffee when Prince Gorsky and Count Andrei Ortronsky entered the restaurant. As Lady Liza beckoned to them, the duke and Erica exchanged a fleeting glance. It begins, his black eyes told her, so be ready. Very well, her own eyes replied.

The two Russians were easily persuaded to join their party, and more chairs were brought, and another bottle of wine. The table was crowded now, and seated next to the burly hussar, Erica was constantly aware of his arm and of the muscled thigh so close to hers. She could not move away, for to do so would bring her in contact with the duke, on her other side, and he would know she was not obeying his orders. She tried to smile.

Count Andrei beamed at her. "I promised you we were to meet again, did I not, little bird?" he whispered.

"And what little bird told you I would be here this evening, Count?" she asked.

His eyes went to Lady Liza, who was leaning close to Prince Gorsky. In a moment, the two excused themselves to dance. Erica would have included the duke in the conversation, but he excused himself as well.

"I see an old friend has arrived, and I want to ask him about his new mare. Indeed, I do not know when I have been so struck! Coal black, y'know, and well set up, with such a powerful chest! Yet withal, a most intriguing grace of movement, the forward action outstanding!" he enthused as he rose. "I must see if m'lord might be willing to sell the animal, and it may take some time. But even if it does, you are in very good hands with the count," he added before he laughed. He sounded as inane as he had at the ball.

As he limped away, the count took her hand and held it in his own. "What a silly man he is," he said, pressing her fingers gently. Erica wanted to pull her hand away, but she let it remain in that huge, gentle paw.

"Shall we dance, my bird?" he asked.

"Not right now, thank you," she said with another little smile. "I have just had the most wonderful dessert, all whipped cream and chocolate. I do not think I can move."

He laughed loudly "Ah, the Viennese with their richness of food. I tell the czar we will all go home twice the size we came."

"He is such a handsome man," Erica commented. "I was almost overcome with admiration the evening of the ball when my cousin pointed him out. He is so very regal, anyone would know he is czar without even being told."

Count Andrei beamed at her. "We Russians are fortunate indeed," he agreed. "And he is not only good to look at, little bird. He has a head on his shoulders and a brain in that head. Yes, Alexander will make sure that all goes well for Russia here."

Erica remembered that the duke had warned her not to rush the count, or be too obvious about her purpose, and she changed the subject, asking him to tell her about his home and his family.

The count beamed at her as he replied. As he waxed eloquent about his mother and brothers, his little sister, and the family estate near St. Petersburg, Erica tried to tell herself that what she was doing was not wrong. Whatever information she gleaned from the garrulous Russian hussar would go no further than the Duke of Graves. She still did not understand why he wanted the knowledge so badly that he had invited her to stay with him in Vienna and expended so much money on her clothes and dancing lessons. The little fear that she had once had that it might be only a trick to get her to agree to an affair had been discarded days ago. The duke was a cold man, not interested in her, or in any other woman that she could see. She wondered if she would ever understand him or his motives. And then she was recalled to the crowded, noisy restaurant when the count begged her to attend a military review as his guest.

"The czar wishes to show Vienna—and the other nations—the superiority of his army," he told her with a twinkle. "There will be the review itself first, then an exhibition of riding and Russian dances. Do say you will honor me, little bird!"

"It sounds very exciting," Erica made herself say. "Of course, I must ask my cousin for permission. He . . . he is my guardian while I am in Vienna, you see."

The count rolled his eyes. "That one?" he asked a little scornfully. "I would wish you had another, more sensible man to watch over you, my bird, one who did not think horseflesh the most important thing in the world."

He saw Erica's smile fade, and he patted her hand. "No, no, not to distress yourself! I will ask the duke to come with you, and send my carriage for you both."

He winked at her and nodded toward the dance floor, where Lady Liza and Prince Gorsky were dancing even more closely than some of the painted demimondaines and their eager escorts. "I am sure the Lady Liza will come too," he said. "Sergei Gorsky is one of our best dancers."

The duke came back a short time later, full of the gossip he had heard in his absence, and Erica gave a little sigh of relief that her first venture into spying was over. She had to admit she had not learned anything, but she had made sure of the count's interest in her, and arranged another meeting.

The duke was pleased to accept the count's invitation to the review to be held the following week, and Lady Liza was quick to agree to make one of the party as well, when she and the prince finally rejoined them.

She was all complacent smiles until the duke rose a short time later. "We must toddle along now, highness, Count, positively we must," he said, motioning to the ladies. "We have another engagement this evening. Beg you to excuse us."

Good-byes were said all around, and once again Erica found her hand being kissed after an almost reverent bow from the count.

Lady Liza pouted all the way back to the palace. "I don't see why we had to leave so early, Owen," she complained. "We had no other engagement, and you know it."

"No, we do not," he agreed. "But a good night's sleep will do you good, Liza. You must keep up your . . . strength, you know."

As she tossed her head, he added, "I am surprised that you have yet to learn that too much familiarity breeds, er, contempt."

Lady Liza drew a deep breath, and Erica was sure there was a major storm brewing. But to her surprise, the lady only glared at her nephew. She must have seen something in his dark eyes that told her that any invective would be most unwise, for she settled back in her seat and turned to stare out the window of the carriage. She did not say another word, not even to thank him for the delicious dinner, and she left them abruptly and went to her room as soon as they reached the house.

The duke did not seem to notice her rudeness. He took Erica into one of the smaller salons to question her about the count's conversation. Erica was glad when he nodded a dismissal at last, seemingly not at all disappointed by the scarcity of information she had gleaned. His only comment was that it had not been at all necessary to include him in the invitation to the military review, for he did not intend to be constantly in her company when she was with the count. Erica did not dare tell him that she longed for his protection.

As she curtsied and left him, she wondered at his crisp, matter-of-fact air, so different from his often silly, careless behavior in public. She realized the duke was acting a part, although for what reason, she had no idea.

Erica found it hard to get to sleep that night, but it had nothing to do with her new role as a spy. No, instead she found she could not stop thinking about the implication of what she had learned, now that she had seen Signorina Sabatini and her unusual jewelry.

As soon as Agnes had finished brushing her hair and left her for the night, she went to her jewelry case to inspect the serpent ring again. She saw it was indeed identical to the dancer's bracelet, and she could not restrain a shiver. She dropped the ring back into the case and closed the lid in haste, almost as if the act of putting it out of sight would dispel her ugly thoughts.

But the ugly thoughts could not be banished that easily, as she found out when she climbed into bed. At last she stopped trying to get to sleep, and began to think. She knew she had to accept not only William's philandering but also the fact that he had married her just for her money, exactly as the two officers in his regiment had claimed. That would explain why he had left her so abruptly, when there had been no need to do so. It was more than humbling, it was a plummeting tumble into reality, but if she were to be honest with herself, she had to accept it. But oh, how demeaning it was to discover that Erica Joanna Huntington, who had been so pampered and admired all her life, had been only a means to an end for him; to learn that he had never cared for her at all.

She stared up at the canopy, her eyes narrowed. How could she ever have thought she might come to love such a man someday, have his children, share a lifetime with him? How could she have been taken in so, been such a bad judge of character? Granted, she was a neophyte in matters of love, the ways of a man and a maid, but she was not a fool!

And then she rolled over and pounded her pillow in angry frustration. Stupid, stupid! she whispered. Of course you were a fool!

7

Life for Erica settled into a pattern from then on, a gay whirlwind of activity and amusement on the one hand, interspersed with periods of reflection and brooding over her late husband and his treachery. The duke was quick to notice how distant she could become in a moment, how quiet and introspective, and he wondered what was troubling her. He had to admit that Erica Stone was a complicated woman, as deep as she was beautiful. It was a combination he had never come across before.

The Parisian dressmaker and her assistant arrived at last, and were installed in a large room on the third floor. Madame Rousseau was delighted with both the ladies she had come to dress, and she set to work with a will, devising new ball gowns and walking ensembles that would not only be all the crack but also place the Kingsley ladies in a class apart. Agnes Watts and Lady Liza's maid were pressed into service as well.

Erica wondered in the days that followed what had happened to Prince Eric. He had sent her a passionate note and more flowers, but she had not seen him. She did not know that the duke had given his butler orders to deny Miss Erica if the prince should call, so she had no idea how many times he had come and been turned away.

It was only by accident that she ran into him again one afternoon as she was returning from a shopping trip with Lady Liza. The prince, who was coming down the steps of the duke's palace, gave the two ladies a deep bow, although his bright blue eyes never left Erica's face.

"At last we meet again, dear lady," he said, taking her hand in his. "Can I not persuade you to go for a stroll with me? It is such a pleasant afternoon!"

There was amusement in his voice, for the day was cloudy and threatened rain. Lady Liza smiled as she waved her hand.

"Do run along, Erica," she urged. "I will take these parcels to Madame Rousseau. There is no need for you to come in."

"But I do not have my maid with me . . ." Erica began, and both the prince and Lady Liza laughed at her.

"This is Vienna, goose, not stodgy London town," Lady Liza told her. "Away with you! Enjoy yourself!"

Erica gave her a troubled glance. It seemed to her that Lady Liza was being deliberately provoking. She knew the duke did not want her to associate with the Swedish prince, yet here she was, as good as promoting the scheme.

The prince tucked her hand in his arm. "I will not take no for an answer," he told her. "And my thanks, kind lady, to you," he added with a twinkle for the unexpected conspirator he had gained.

Noting how he waved his carriage away, Erica told herself she was being silly to worry so. There were many others abroad that afternoon, so it was not as if she were in any danger of being alone with him on the crowded streets.

"I am angry with you, you know," he told her in Swedish as they began their walk. "Very angry. I have even considered punishing you, but perhaps I will not."

"Angry, your highness?" Erica asked, wishing he would not hold her quite so close to his side.

"Yes, angry. I have been calling on you ever since the ball, but you will never see me. Now, why is that? Can it be that you find me . . . distasteful?" he asked, his voice disbelieving.

Erica cast a sideways glance up at his face. She saw that he was furious, for his mouth was set in a hard line, and those blue eyes burned with a dangerous light.

"I did not know," she found herself saying. "It must be that my cousin, the duke, gave such orders. He is my guardian, you know."

Prince Eric's face brightened a little. He was used to disapproving papas and male relatives, and had circumvented many a one of them before this to gain his ends. "But how gothic of him, don't you agree?" he asked, smiling down at her now. "I am positive he is jealous. But it is most unfair to you, my pretty one, and to me. Why should we suffer because the duke is crippled and ugly, and so unattractive, in fact, he can make no woman love him?"

Erica found herself wanting to deny that Owen Kingsley was any such thing, but she held her tongue.

"You are more beautiful than I remembered," the prince murmured next. "But I wish you were wearing your hair loose. I cannot like to see it bundled into that oh-so-proper chignon. It makes you seem even more the ice maiden, and, as I am sure you remember, I have plans to melt that lady shortly."

"Highness, you go too fast," Erica scolded him. "I hardly know you, or you me."

"How I am looking forward to getting to know you, Erica," he said. "Intimately."

She paled a little and changed the subject. She noticed that they had come quite a distance from the duke's palace, and she wondered when the prince would suggest they return. Perhaps if she said she was tired?

"I shall take you to the Silbernen Kaffeehaus, my pet," he said next. "It is a popular spot, and we can enjoy some refreshment while we begin to make each other's better acquaintance."

Erica agreed calmly, but she had to shiver as he leaned closer and whispered, "You see how good I am being? How noble and forebearing? At least for a little while," he added.

He turned away then to hail a cab, and as much as Erica disliked his conversation and the calm assumption that it was only a matter of time before she became his mistress, she had to admit he was just as handsome as she remembered. They had not passed a single woman or girl in the street who had not stared at him, almost in awe. Today he was wearing a dark blue uniform that fit him like a second skin, and its gold epaulets and brass buttons only seemed to call attention to the purer gold of

his hair. And she had to admit as well, in spite of knowing what a dangerous man he was, she herself was not
immune to his masculine magnetism. His obvious admiration and desire for her even soothed the still-raw agony
of her husband's rejection.

She was grateful that when they were seated in the
hansom, he chatted of other things, parties he had attended, and people he had met here. And she was grateful as well that the coffeehouse was crowded when they
reached it, the tables set too close for any dalliance.

The prince ordered coffee, but when he would have
selected a pastry for her, she denied him. "They look
delicious, but I must not," she told him with a little
smile. "If I continue to eat all this food, I will have to
order new gowns."

His eyes dropped from her face to caress her throat
and breasts. She was glad she was wearing a modest
walking gown, although she wished it did not fit her quite
so well. Suddenly she felt his thigh pressing against hers
and moving slowly up and down under the long damask
tablecloth, and she moved away quickly.

"No treats now?" he asked with an innocent smile.
"But I do agree it would be a shame if you put on any
more flesh. Alas, I cannot help but wonder if this self-
control you show is not a bad sign, however. I do so hope
that control does not extend to other appetites of yours."

Erica looked around in dismay. There were two elderly couples at a table only a foot away, and she was
sure they had overheard.

The prince took up her hand and kissed it slowly,
finger by finger. "Do not worry, Erica," he said calmly.
"They cannot speak Swedish. Why, we can say whatever
outrageous things we want, and no one will know. How
exciting it will be, how different."

Erica removed her hand from his grasp. "But I do not
want to say anything outrageous, your highness, and I
beg you not to do so either," she said in French.

He sighed in mock disappointment as the waiter served
their coffee, but he behaved himself from then on. Erica
wished she could relax, but she found it impossible to do
so while she was waiting for the next *double entendre*, an
improper suggestion, or even an outright proposition.

As she finished her coffee, she said, "I really must go now. It grows late, and the duke is taking me to the opera this evening."

He beckoned to the waiter. "I shall see you home, my lovely one. And on the way, we can make plans for future meetings."

Erica preceded him to the door. As he opened it for her and she stepped outside, she came face-to-face with Signorina Sabatini, and it was all she could do not to gasp. Up close, the dancer was even more exotic than she had appeared at Sperl's, for she radiated a much stronger aura of eroticism. Erica could even smell the heavy musk perfume she was wearing, and it removed any lingering doubt. This was indeed the owner of the scarlet chemise.

She saw the dancer look beyond her after only a brief, cursory glance, her slumberous almound-shaped eyes brightening as she did so.

"Highness," she said slowly in a deep, husky voice. "How delightful to see you again so unexpectedly."

"*Signorina*," the prince replied, his voice noncommittal.

The dancer's dark eyes flashed as she looked back at Erica again. Her plump red mouth curved in a smile as she inspected her from head to toe. "Ah, I see," she said. "But of course."

Still smiling, she picked up her skirt and stepped past them without another word. Erica looked a question at the prince, but he had turned away to summon a cab. She had no way of knowing that he had spent all last night with Isabella Sabatini and another dancer from her company, in a passionate *partie de trois*.

On the drive back to the Johannesgasse, Erica had no chance to ask the prince about the encounter, for he steered the conversation to her coming engagements, and when they might meet again.

When he learned that she was to attend the Peace Ball to be given by Prince Clemens Metternich and his wife at their villa in the Renweg the following evening, he assured her he would be there as well. "And perhaps we might even find a moment to be alone?" he pleaded. "There is sure to be a huge throng; Metternich has been planning the ball for months, and it appears all Vienna has been invited. The duke will not notice your disappearance; I will be discreet."

Erica was delighted to discover just then that they had reached the duke's home, so she was not forced either to agree or to disagree with his plan. And if the ball were to be as crowded as he claimed, perhaps he would not even be able to find her, she told herself.

The prince escorted her up the steps to sound the knocker for her, and his kiss on her gloved hand was a mere courtesy. Erica was not fooled. She could tell by the secret look he gave her that he was reminding her of the evening they had first met, when he had kissed her hand and caressed her skin, and how he longed to do it again.

Erica tried hard to hide her feelings of depression at dinner that evening. The prince would have been annoyed at how quickly she forgot him, for all her thoughts were about the Italian dancer who had been William's mistress.

She had stared hard at herself as she was being dressed. What was there about her that was inferior to that exotic foreigner? She knew she was not bad-looking, and her figure was good, she thought as Agnes helped her into a new gown of soft aqua silk. Of course, her bosom was nowhere near as prominent as the *signorina*'s, nor her waist as tiny, but her legs were longer, and she had a neater ankle. And then, as she stared into the mirror, she realized that it had nothing to do with her looks, for the *signorina* was nowhere near as comely. No, it must be because Isabella Sabatini was a more exciting woman, she thought in dismay, more vivacious and enticing. But I didn't even know how to make love—why, William was the first man I ever kissed! she cried inwardly as Agnes fastened on a pearl necklace. Could her very inexperience in bed have disgusted her new husband, after the practiced, supple expertise of the Italian dancer?

The duke noticed how quiet she was, and he made a special effort to conduct most of the conversation with Lady Liza, who was dining with them before going on to a private party. That lady did not appear to notice Erica's distraction, and he wondered why she seemed so excited. Owen Kingsley made a note to himself to set an investigation in train tomorrow. He did not trust Liza; he was sure she was up to no good.

Erica began to enjoy the evening only after they arrived at the opera. She had never been to the theater; it was all so new and exciting. They were to see a performance of Mozart's *The Magic Flute* that was being given at the Theater an der Wien, and the duke had reserved a box. When the lights dimmed and the music began to float up to her, Erica not only stopped brooding, she was filled with delight. It was such a glorious, tuneful spectacle, the singers in their fantastic costumes—an Egyptian prince, high priests, slaves, and genii, even a bird girl. The duke watched the way her eyes shone and a little smile played over her face, and he was pleased.

He was not so pleased at intermission when he saw the Swedish prince waving from another box across the way. He frowned so blackly that Prince Eric did not even try to come and make his bow.

Erica was quick to refuse another visit to Sperl's after the performance, claiming she was tired. In reality, she was afraid she might see William's mistress again, an encounter she would prefer to avoid.

The duke did not press her, for he had seen the little droop of her mouth when he suggested it, and he thought she must be weary indeed. When they reached home, Erica gave him her hand as she thanked him again for a wonderful evening. He watched her climb the stairs, humming a snatch from one of the arias they had heard. As the butler coughed, he turned away with a frown.

It rained late that night, but when Erica woke early, she saw it promised to be a fine, warm day. She sent a message to the stables, determined to have an early ride. The duke had given her permission to ride alone, provided she had a groom in attendance. As she mounted the chestnut, she saw Countess de Talleyrand-Périgord coming down the steps of the Kaunitz Palace across the way, and a groom holding two horses ready. Dorothea was pulling on a pair of riding gloves, her crop tucked under her arm. Erica waved to her and rode over.

"Good morning, Countess," she said, bowing a little over her saddle. "I see you are going riding too. Will you join me?"

Dorothea de Talleyrand-Périgord hesitated for only a
moment. Her uncle had warned her about the inadvis-
ability of becoming intimate with an Englishwoman, but
she had thought him too cautious. What had she and the
lovely Erica Kingsley to do with treaties and diplomacy?
she thought. Besides, she liked the girl's looks, those
clear green eyes so full of intelligence and sensitivity, and
she wanted her for a friend. Dorothea knew she was a
shrewd judge of character, and politically astute, for her
uncle had complimented her on those qualities many
times before. Now she knew she could keep the conversation innocuous. And she needed a friend badly. In
spite of the fact that her three beautiful older sisters were
also in Vienna for the congress, she saw far less of them
than she had expected. They had their own friends, their
own sets. Her serving as hostess to the elderly Talleyrand
had removed her somewhat from their sphere.

"I should be delighted, Miss Kingsley," she said with
her warm smile. "I am glad to see that you, like I, do not
waste the best part of the day. Henri?"

She beckoned to her groom to help her mount, and a
minute later the two young women were riding off side
by side, followed at a discreet distance by their grooms.
These two men eyed each other with mistrust and an
instant dislike. The duke had brought his entire staff
from England, rather than risk any Austrian spies in his
employ, and Henri had been brought for the same reason. Neither groom could speak the other's language, so
they preserved a cold, watchful silence.

Their mistresses suffered under no such handicap, and
were soon deep in a conversation about Vienna and the
Viennese people, and the immense victory parade of the
Austrian Army that was to be held later that morning in
the Prater.

Erica was content and happy when they returned to
their respective palaces an hour later. She felt as if she
had found a real companion, someone who shared her
interests and concerns, no matter how different their
upbringing. They made arrangements to drive out together early the following week, and shook hands, smiling, as they said good-bye.

Erica wondered at the immediate rapport she felt for

the French countess. She had been brought up to hate everything French, even threatened as a child by her nanny, who told her that wicked Boney would come and get her if she didn't eat up her vegetables. And when all was said and done, after all, the countess had married a man of the same nationality as the soldiers Erica's father and brothers had fought in Spain and Portugal. One of her adoped countrymen had wounded Erica's beloved oldest brother, Mark. Why, with Dorothea, was it so easy to forget all that now?

She frowned a little as she dismounted and slowly climbed the steps, turning when she reached the door to look back at the Kaunitz Palace. As she did so, an empty hansom cab clip-clopped by, its driver singing an aria from the opera she had heard last night. When he saw her looking at him, he smiled and doffed his hat. Erica smiled in return, taking a deep breath of the clear morning air. It must be bewitching Vienna that had changed her outlook, she thought. It was such a happy, trusting city, so full of innocent gaiety and goodwill. It seemed to demand that the old enmities be put aside, for in Vienna they were out of place. Now was the time to heal the wounds of war, restore peace to the world. Perhaps it was not too fanciful to imagine that a beginning had taken place only this morning between two young women who a little while ago had been on opposite sides and who now were able to clasp hands and smile.

All the ladies who had been invited to attend the Metternichs' ball that evening had been asked to wear olive wreaths in their hair, their gowns either silver or blue to honor the occasion. The Peace Ball, as it had been named, was being held to commemorate the first anniversary of the Battle of Leipzig, and it would conclude a memorable day. Erica had attended the parade with Lady Liza and the duke after her ride with the countess, and she had been moved by the crush of people, the clamor of martial music, and the cheering Austrians. As their soldiers marched by them in what seemed an endless stream, the brass buttons of their uniforms and their shining sabers and lances glinted in the brilliant sunlight. They had all the assured vigor of youth, and their pride was contagious. Erica had been almost reluctant to return to the palace at last, to rest for the coming evening, even though the duke warned her that the Peace Ball would not be over until dawn.

Madame Rousseau had made the design of the gowns Liza and Erica would wear this evening her first priority. Liza had chosen a rich deep blue silk, cut so low over the shoulders and bosom that Erica did not see how she was to dance in it without suddenly finding herself naked to the waist. Her own gown, with a more modest neckline, was made of cloth of silver that fell in soft, shining folds to her ankles and was caught up under the bosom with a narrow silver satin sash.

Erica was pleased with her ensemble, the diamond pendant and earrings the duke had lent her giving it that perfect final touch. She thought the gown with its unadorned simplicity made her look elegant and sophisticated. When she came downstairs, the duke complimented her, and she smiled at him.

"Tonight you look very much the ice maiden all Vienna is calling you, cuz," he told her. "Why, even your hair is more silvery."

Lady Liza, who was coming down the stairs behind them, laughed. "A veritable icicle, in fact," she mocked. "That gown practically cries out, 'Touch me not, for I am pure and virgin!' "

Erica tried not to show how upset she was by the sarcasm. She had no idea why Lady Liza took such great delight in taunting her, hurting her feelings.

All the way to the Metternichs' villa in the Renweg, she wondered why Liza Ridgely was so difficult. She had tried many times to be friendly, but the lady was no more approachable now than she had been at first meeting. The Duke could have told her that Liza envied her the very qualities she mocked, that she was jealous of Erica's startling beauty as well.

Erica forgot the unsatisfactory Lady Liza when they reached the prince's villa, dressed, as it was, *en fête*. She had thought the ball in the Hofburg could never be surpassed, but it appeared she had been wrong. There were some eighteen hundred guests attending the Peace Ball and dancing in the classical pavilion with its tall columns that had been built especially for the event. She had a chance to observe the brilliant throng as they performed the courtly polonaise and the Russian dances in honor of the czar.

Alexander was in fine form tonight, flirting impartially with any pretty woman near him. He wore uniform, striving as always to be as one with his gallant soldiers. He was resplendent in tight white kidskin breeches and gleaming high boots, and his form-fitting tunic with its high stiff collar was covered with jeweled decorations. Erica thought him a handsome man with his fair hair, but she had heard enough whispers about him to wonder at his morals. It was said he treated his wife, the lovely and much-loved Elisabeth, shamefully, and that he flaunted his mistresses, even going so far as to insist that his empress accompany him to their parties. And this was the man she was to investigate for the duke! She hoped her playacting as an unmarried girl would keep him away from her. She had heard enough stories about Alexander to know that no woman he fancied was safe with him, from highborn titled ladies to the lowliest prostitutes.

The Lady Liza had left the duke and Erica as soon as they quit the receiving line. Owen Kingsley took her to watch a ballet and a *tableau vivant* that was given to amuse the guests who did not care to dance, and when she did dance, he was always there when she came off the floor. Count Andrei had beamed at her as he begged that she honor him with the first waltz. She had agreed, hoping the feverish pace with which he performed it would not cause her to lose her step this evening. The duke even allowed her to go into the gardens alone with him later, when the balloons were sent up. With most of the other guests, they watched the fireworks that were released from the balloons, fireworks made especially to display the arms of the sovereigns at the congress. Erica had never seen anything so spectacular, and she clapped her hands in delight as they exploded overhead, lighting up the dark sky in myriad arcs of brilliant falling color. Count Andrei appeared as affected by the display as she was, and he had to wipe his eyes when the Russian flag was honored.

Prince Eric appeared shortly thereafter. The duke was

nowhere in sight, and the count had hurried away in response to an urgent summons from one of his compatriots, reassured that she would be well-taken-care-of when he saw Lady Liza in a group of guests nearby. As Erica moved toward them, the Swedish prince bowed and took her arm, turning away from the crowd to lead her deeper into the gardens.

"If you please, your highness, where are we going?" Erica asked, wondering why she was so breathless every time she was near this handsome, dangerous man. "I do not think I should leave Lady Liza and the other guests. I am sure my cousin, the duke, would not approve."

Prince Eric laughed down at her worried little frown. "But we are not alone, for there are many others here, Ice Maiden," he told her. "I know you will want to see the miniature temples to Apollo and Minerva that the prince has had built. And we can listen to one of the orchestras that are hidden throughout the gardens for the guests' enjoyment."

Erica looked around and saw some other couples ahead of them, and she relaxed, determined that nothing would spoil this fabulous, fairy-tale occasion. "Isn't this the most enchanting evening?" she enthused. "The fireworks were splendid, were they not? And to have a ballet . . . all these wonderful displays!"

Prince Eric turned down a narrow side path. "It is wonderful indeed, but in my opinion it has reached perfect enchantment only now," he told her.

He indicated a bench nearby. "Shall we sit and listen to the music, Erica?" he asked.

Erica did not see how she could refuse without appearing ungracious. She noticed it was darker here, and there was no one nearby, and her heart fluttered uneasily as she seated herself. Some little distance away, an orchestra was playing a waltz softly, and she was reassured by their presence, for it meant she was not really alone with him at all. The prince sat down close to her, sliding his arm around her waist as he turned her face up to his with his other hand.

As Erica opened her mouth to protest such intimacy, he bent swiftly and covered her lips with his own. His lips felt as wonderful as they looked, warm and sensitive, and for a moment Erica surrendered to pure sensation. But then his tongue invaded her mouth and began to explore it in slow, sweeping thrusts, and she felt his hand move from her chin and slip under her gown and chemise, to cup her naked breast. It was all accomplished with practiced expertise in the twinkling of an eye. Erica tried to get away, but he was holding her so closely, his arms imprisoning hers against her sides like iron bars, that she could neither free herself nor force him away. As she struggled harder, his hand tightened on her breast and she exhaled sharply into his mouth. To her horror, she felt her nipple begin to harden under those strong, exploring fingers. His tongue moved more quickly now, darting in and out of her mouth and curling around her own as if urging it to respond.

When he released her, Erica could feel her heart pounding not only in fearful distress but also with something else that seemed to come from some warm, secret part of her she had never been aware she possessed. The prince smiled at her as he began to ease her gown off her shoulders.

"Stop that at once!" she cried, struggling anew.

He chuckled. "Stop?" he asked, his voice husky. "But I have only just begun to melt you, Ice Maiden." One of his hands captured both of hers behind her, forcing her to arch her back to avoid pain.

"Let me go! I am not melting!" Erica said, fierce in her denial of any such thing.

"No?" he asked, looking down. Erica's eyes followed his. To her dismay, her breasts were completely exposed and trust forward in the bold pose he had forced her into. Only the tight sash under them kept the silver gown from falling to her hips. She could feel how taut the fabric of the gown was as the sleeves bit into her arms, and she prayed it would not rip.

"You may say you are still cold, but your body speaks a different language, my girl," he told her before he bent to kiss one nipple, after a moment taking it into his mouth to caress it with his tongue.

Erica closed her eyes in despair as warm sensation coursed through her body. "No, no, you must not," she moaned.

The prince looked up into her face, admiring the shining silver of her hair as she tossed her head in wild desperation. As he moved to kiss her other breast, he whispered, "Ah, but I must. You are so delicious. If only I were able to sample all your delights . . . now . . . here . . . at once."

Erica could feel the cool night air on her legs as he lifted her gown and ran his hand slowly up her leg. When he reached the quivering skin above her stocking, she thought she would faint. She felt a writhing mass of contradictions. One part of her wanted to run away, but that other part that she had never imagined, deep inside her, was begging him not to stop. She knew she would be lost in a moment, and with her last bit of self-control she said as firmly and evenly as she could, "If you do not let me go at once, I shall call for help."

Just then she heard voices coming nearer, and the prince released her. As his eyes caressed her nakedness, she struggled to adjust her clothes.

"But can it be that you are indeed a virgin, Erica Kingsley?" he asked in disbelief. "I did not think there was a single one left in Vienna over the age of twelve."

Erica rose unsteadily to her feet. "Whatever you think, I am not to be had in a dark garden like any little housemaid," she said coldly. "I would remind your highness that I am the Duke of Graves's cousin. You insult him as well as me with this forced intimacy."

The prince rose leisurely and put his hands on his hips, staring down at the front of his uniform. Erica tried not to gasp when she saw the way his tight breeches were stretched by the mound between his legs.

"Just see what you are missing," he invited, and then he reached out as quick as a cat and pulled her to him to kiss her again. As he ground his hips against her soft belly, Erica could feel his lust growing, and she was afraid that her haughty words would have no effect on him after all.

The voices were louder now, as their owners paused and discussed the side path, and he let her go. Erica was quick to step back out of reach.

"I do so hope you can find your own way back to the festivities, my dear," he said, those blue eyes bright with desire. "As you can see, I am in . . . no shape to escort you."

As Erica turned to flee, his confident voice stopped her. "You may be sure we will conclude this episode to my complete satisfaction in the very near future, Ice Maiden. And, I promise you, to yours as well," he whispered. "I do not fear your kinsman, oh no. The duke is a fool, ineffective and worthless. He does not keep the Lady Liza in line, so why would he object when I become your lover? And I will, believe me, I will, one way or the other."

He chuckled, and Erica began to run. The guests she had heard had moved on, so she did not pause until she was some distance away, lest he change his mind. When she was sure he was not following her, she stopped and straightened her gown before she dipped her hand into a nearby fountain to bathe her hot cheeks. She lingered in the gardens as long as she dared, to make sure her breathing had returned to normal.

The duke was waiting for her as she came up the red-carpeted steps to the brilliantly lighted pavilion, and her heart sank. She gave him what she hoped was a casual little smile.

"The prince allowed you to return unescorted after your tryst, Erica?" he asked, his voice as cold as any winter wind from the north. "But how very ungentlemanly of him, when you have just granted him your complete surrender."

8

Erica wondered how the duke knew she had been with the prince. Was he omnipotent? Did he know everything? In some despair, she turned away to enter the pavilion. He stopped her by taking hold of her arm and leading her aside.

"Just a moment," he said as he reached out to straighten the wreath of olive leaves she wore on her hair. "I see you are as wanton as Liza, no ice maiden at all, in fact," he told her more coldly, and she quailed. How could she have forgotten that wreath, even as upset as she was? She felt a deep agony at his words, and she had to swallow hard to contain her tears.

"I have told you before that you must not fall under Prince Eric's spell, yet what do you do but run to him like any other easy jade, the first chance you get?" the duke continued, remorseless now in his disgust. "Count Andrei has been looking for you. I shall take you to him, and I trust you will remember why you are here for the remainder of the evening. I do assure you it is not for any quick physical gratification."

"It is not what you think," Erica said quickly, stung by his sarcasm. "I can explain it, indeed, I—"

"But I do not care to hear your explanation, Erica," he interrupted her harshly. "I am sure it would be like many I have heard before. He is so handsome and virile . . . you could not help yourself . . . he forced you . . . it will never happen again!" His words scalded her and she fell silent as he went on, "I must insist you temper your ardor for the pretty prince and follow my instructions. We have a pact, and I intend to see that you honor it."

Erica stared up into that dark, forbidding face. She saw he would not listen to her, and that even if he did, he would not believe her. Somehow, his mistrust made her sadder than she had ever been in her life. She forced herself to put up her chin. "I have not forgotten, your grace," she said evenly. "I am a Huntington. My family always keeps its word. There is no need for you to be concerned."

She turned and left him then, running too swiftly for him, leaning on his cane, to follow her. When he reached the pavilion she was nowhere in sight, and he began to search for her. He found her at last in one of the supper rooms, sipping champagne with the count, and he turned away, wondering as he did so why he was not more pleased to see her obeying his commands.

He admitted he had been angry with her, and disgusted by her behavior. Somehow, it seemed so much worse than Liza's, for Liza looked the part she played—seductive and hot. But Erica Stone was a cool, quiet woman who appeared the epitome of modesty and control. When he had seen her coming up the steps from the dark garden, looking self-conscious and with that wreath set tipsily on her shining hair, he had been enraged. For one impossible moment he had wanted to take her back there and make love to her himself—coldly and brutally. He had seen how upset she became at his words to her, and he had steeled his heart against the pleading in her green eyes that he believe her lying explanation. Women! he thought as he took a glass of champagne from a footman's tray. But why am I surprised at Erica? She is just like all the rest.

Erica had seen the duke enter the supper room and look around, and she concentrated on the burly Russian beside her, trying to forget the pain she still felt. She saw the count was wearing a little frown, and he seemed absentminded and very different from his earlier, happy self.

"There is something troubling you, sir?" she asked softly. As he looked up, she added, "You do not seem to be enjoying yourself anymore."

The count sighed. "In truth, little bird, I am not. The czar spoke to Prince Metternich a little while ago, almost insulting him. Of course, it was because he blames him for this impasse the congress has reached over the question of Poland."

He paused to rub his hand over his eyes, And Erica held her breath. She did not dare to speak, although she knew she should be prodding, questioning him. But her silence served her well, for after a moment to swallow the rest of his wine, the count went on, "Of course, the czar is determined that Russia will have Poland when all these negotiations are over. He feels Metternich is trying to circumvent that, perhaps currying favor with England and Prussia by agreeing to their plans for that poor, torn country. But the czar is more than a match for a mere Austrian! You must not worry, little bird," he added, reaching out to gently touch her hand where it lay on the table between them. "No, no! Alexander plans to approach the German princelings. They are angry that Metternich has agreed that their territories will go to Prussia to form a new Germany."

Erica's eyes widened and her breathing grew shallow. She had heard enough people talking about the Polish impasse since she entered Viennese society to know this was exactly the kind of information the duke wanted her to discover. She would never have thought Count Andrei would be so open with her. It must be his worries about his czar, and the possible repercussions from his words to his host, that had loosened his tongue.

As if he agreed with her, the count patted her hand and smiled. "But you are not interested in these dull affairs of state, are you, my beautiful little bird?" he asked, his deep voice teasing. "How bad I am! I should be telling you of your beauty, admiring you, wooing you."

He leaned closer and his gray eyes adored her face and shoulders. "Ah, yes, wooing you," he said more slowly.

Erica moved her hand a little, and he let her go at once.

"Not to fear, my bird," he whispered. "I will not hurt you. I will never hurt you. But tell me, do you feel anything for me? I cannot tell from your eyes."

Erica lowered her lashes. How horrible this was, she thought, knowing somehow that he was in earnest, and an honorable man, different from the randy prince. She realized the count was waiting for her answer, and she made herself say, "It is too soon, Count. I like you, but . . . but I cannot tell . . ."

Count Andrei laughed deep in his chest as he rose to help her from her chair. "I shall not to rush you, little one," he said, forgetting some of his French in his eagerness to reassure her. "Ah, no. I want you, but I know how to be patient. You will see."

It was very late before the duke came to find her and tell her the carriage had been called. He was all cold politeness as he wrapped her cloak around her shoulders against the dewy chill of early morning. Erica had avoided him ever since he had accused her of being a wanton, but now that she was with him again, his words came rushing back, and she was miserable.

Lady Liza appeared beside them, barely bothering to hide her yawns. Erica thought she looked as if she had had a rousing evening, and far too much champagne. Her hair was tousled, and her gown slipping from her shoulders. She giggled when the duke ordered her adjust it, but she obeyed him. Erica remembered then how Owen Kingsley had told her she was just like Lady Liza, and she cringed when she saw what a blowsy, abandoned-looking woman she was in the early-morning hours. Even the other guests nearby were not the glittering fashion plates she had seen earlier. There was a large stain on a pair of white breeches, a uniform tunic missing a button, a bedraggled muslin flounce. Even the duke sported the beginning of a dark beard on his harsh-featured face and firm jaw, which made him look even fiercer and more saturnine. It was almost as if they had all stayed too long at the ball.

The three of them joined the other guests who were standing on the steps of the pavilion waiting for their carriages. It was a perfect crush, and somehow unearthly, in spite of the pitch torches whose light flickered brightly over the assembled company. People near them spoke in whispers, as if they did not care to distrub the dawn.

Erica suddenly remembered what the count had told her. When Lady Liza turned aside to speak to one of the other guests in line, she leaned closer to the duke and whispered, "I must speak to you alone as soon as we reach home, your grace."

She made herself look into his face and she saw that he meant to deny her. "It is not about that," she added quickly. "It is important!"

Owen Kingsley shrugged, his hooded eyes inspecting her face as if he were trying to catch her in some duplicity. "Very well," he said.

He looked away from her then, showing her as clearly as if he had spoken that he had no desire to converse with her further, and Erica felt the same pain he had caused her once before this evening. She wondered that such a marvelous occasion had turned so sour. It had been so beautiful, so festive, so full of promise! Yet now she felt a tiredness that she knew had nothing to do with the strenuous waltzes she had engaged in or the lateness of the hour. She turned to look at the eastern horizon, determined to overcome her depression. She knew now that life was hard in many ways, and there were bound to be disappointments along the way, and hard blows to accept and overcome. The happy ending she had sought when she had married William had eluded her; she wondered if she would ever find one. Certainly not here among strangers so different from her, she told herself.

She watched as the narrow gray line at the horizon broadened and slowly turned to gold and the first rays of the sun lit the remnants of Prince Metternich's Peace Ball. Instead of making her feel better, it made her feel infinitely worse. In the clear morning light, everything that last night had seemed so magical and enchanting now appeared tattered and tawdry.

Beside her, the duke watched her serene profile, that feminine yet determined chin, the soft, composed lips, and those brooding green eyes, and he wondered what she was thinking. It was impossible to tell. He had the feeling she had retreated behind a wall as thick as that of any fortress.

It was full daylight before the carriage drew up at last before his palace in the Johannesgasse. Lady Liza did not bother to speak as she started up the stairs, holding tightly to the handrail in her weariness. The duke gave Rudge their cloaks and beckoned Erica into the small salon they had used before. He shut the door behind them and waited until she was seated before he said, "There is something important you have to tell me, madam? Before you begin, let me say again that I have no intention of discussing your disgraceful behavior at the ball. If there is indeed something else, I beg you to be brief. It grows late."

Erica looked down at her clasped hands, and then straight into his black eyes. "I have heard something of great import from Count Andrei," she said, following his instructions. "He told me the czar as much as insulted Prince Metternich tonight because he is very angry at him. Somehow he found out that the prince has aligned his country with England and Prussia, that he has agreed to their plans for Poland. The czar intends to woo the German princelings, and when he has them on his side, win through that way."

She paused and waited, holding her breath for his reaction. To her surprise, he looked almost bored, and he covered a yawn before he spoke. "Indeed?" he asked, leaning his arms on the back of a large wing chair. "Is that all?"

"Yes, that is all I learned," Erica said, wondering that he could be so blasé. Surely this was important news for England! "Will you tell someone in authority about it, your grace?" she could not help asking.

The duke looked astonished at her daring to question his intent, but she did not look away. "Perhaps," he said carelessly. "Then again, perhaps not. It is only a little piece of news. And where else can Alexander go for support but to those disgruntled little Teutonic highnesses? I am sure Castlereagh is well aware of his dilemma. But it grows late. Go to bed, Erica. You are excused."

He yawned again, and waved a careless hand in dismissal, and she rose, perturbed at his nonchalance and more than a little distraught. This was not just idle gossip! She knew it was urgent news the British must have as soon as possible. She wondered if he would even bother to tell anyone, and she was about to dare to insist he do so, when he held out his hand.

"Before you go, give me the diamond set, madam," he said. "I will put it in the safe."

A little discomposed at the abrupt change of subject, she reached up and swept her long hair to one side, so she might unfasten the necklace. As she handed it to him, she saw his intent, considering glance, and she paled. He never took his eyes from her as she began to unfasten the earrings, and she was reminded of that day at the hairdresser's when she had thought they were participating in a scene better suited to husband and wife. It was the same way now, and much too intimate for comfort. Her hands trembled. It was almost as if she were undressing before him, and after he had locked the jewels away, he would undress too, and get into bed beside her.

He nodded carelessly as she gave him the earrings, before he limped to the door and opened it for her. There was not the trace of a smile on his face or in his eyes.

Reminded again of his accusations, she paused, her head held high. "Whether you want to hear it or not, your grace, I must tell you, on my honor, that you are mistaken in me. What you assumed happened did not, although not from any forbearance on the part of the prince. He is everything you said he was. But I am none of the things you called me. Good night."

She marched past him through the hall and up the stairs, her tired body ramrod straight. Somehow she had the feeling he was watching her, but when she looked back at the top of the flight, the door to the salon was closed.

Erica slept most of the day. She did not hear the traffic passing beneath her window, nor the cheerful birdsong in the garden below. When she woke at last, it was midafternoon, and she still felt weary and depressed. She stretched and yawned, wishing she had been able to sleep longer, and then she sat up in bed quickly as she remembered what the count had told her. She knew that no matter how casually the duke might treat her revelations, she would not rest until she made sure this important information was in the right hands.

She propped her elbows on her upraised knees while she considered how this might be accomplished. Certainly it was too dangerous to commit to writing. The duke had told her how the spies of Baron Hager steamed letters open, even confiscated the contents of wastebaskets and pieced together torn pieces of paper in their zeal to make sure nothing would escape them.

Erica frowned, and then her eyes widened. Of course! She could go to British headquarters herself! She rang the bell for Agnes and spent the time waiting for her planning how she would do it.

She knew, even posing as the duke's cousin as she did, she could not just walk in and demand to see Lord Castlereagh, but she was loath to give the information to anyone else. Then she remembered his wife, and how kind she had been to Erica Stone, widow, putting her arms around her in her blacks and soothing her in such a motherly way.

She would call on the lady, and when they were alone, she would ask her to summon her husband. It did not matter that she had never been introduced to Lady Emily, for she could send in a note with her card that would explain the intrusion. She jumped out of bed and ran to the desk, not even bothering to put on her robe and slippers.

Agnes began to scold her for her carelessness when she came in, but Erica raised her hand. "Lay out the dark green walking dress and hat, Agnes, and hurry! And as soon as I am dressed, I will need you to go with me, so fetch your shawl and bonnet. Never mind that tray—move!"

Agnes put down on a table the tray containing the hot coffee and poppy-seed rolls she had been carrying, and went to do as she was bidden, her homely face serious. She knew that tone. Miss Erica did not use it often, but when she did, it was best to obey without asking a single question.

It was only a short time later when Erica swept down the stairs, Agnes at her heels. As she pulled on her gloves, she suddenly realized she was being most unfair to the duke. Perhaps he was closeted with Lord Castlereagh right this minute. What a fool she would look if she also appeared, and how angry he would be at her intrusion!

"Has the duke left the house, Rudge?" she asked,

smoothing a glove and holding up her hand so Agnes
could button it.

The old butler looked shocked. "Certainly not, Miss
Erica," he said. "After such a late night, he is still
abed."

Erica's soft lips tightened. So he did not intend to use
the information she had brought him for anything more
than his own peculiar satisfaction. Well, we will see about
that, she told herself as she asked Rudge to fetch her a
cab.

Agnes would have questioned her after she gave the
cabbie the address of British headquarters in the Minoritenplatz, but Erica told her to hold her tongue. She spent
the journey frowning down at her gloved hands, deep in
thought.

The young secretary who took her card and note said
he was not at all sure Lady Castlereagh was receiving
visitors. Erica gave him her warmest smile, and he flushed
before he said he would go and inquire. He hurried away
as if he wished there was something of greater import he
could do for this lovely young lady.

Erica had made her note as intriguing as possible,
hinting at the need for urgency, so she was not surprised
when the secretary came back and told her Lady Castlereagh would see her at once. Telling Agnes to wait for
her in the hall, she followed him to the Castlereaghs'
private suite of rooms.

She found Robert Stewart's wife somewhat untidy. It
was obvious she had only recently got up and dressed,
for her hair was still arranged in last night's coiffure,
parts of which straggled around her face, giving her a
slightly demented air, which her untidy *toilette* did nothing to dispel.

"Miss Kingsley?" she asked doubtfully, rising with Erica's
note in her hand. Then she smiled and clapped her
hands. "How very pretty you are, my dear!"

Erica made herself smile. "Thank you, m'lady, and
thank you for seeing me. As I mentioned, it is urgent. I
wonder if you would be so good as to ask your husband
to join us? I have something to say to him, and it cannot
wait."

Lady Castlereagh peered at her, a slight tinge of doubt

on her pudding features before she shook her head at her own foolish thoughts. Robert had never been unfaithful to her, and she knew that no matter how beautiful this Miss Kingsley was, he was still true to his vows. She smiled a little as she rang the bell. When would he even have had time? He had worked like a slave ever since they had arrived in Vienna.

The two ladies sat somewhat uncomfortably in each other's company until m'lord arrived. It did not seem appropriate to chat of home, or even of the Peace Ball or other festivities. They were both glad when Robert Stewart came in and shut the door behind him.

Erica had seen the British foreign secretary only at a distance, for the duke had never introduced her. She liked his looks. He was as handsome as his wife was plain, and yet there was something in the glance they exchanged that told her how close they were, what a good marriage they had.

"How may I serve you, Miss Kingsley?" the great man asked, coming to take her hand.

Erica looked at his wife. "If I might see you alone, sir?" she asked, hesitating a little over this strange, bold request.

"But of course," Lady Castlereagh said with a twinkle in her eye. "I must confer with the chef in any case. Delightful to have met you, Miss Kingsley."

As she rustled to the door, trailing a ripped flounce, and with her untidy hair flying, her husband smiled, but he did not speak until she had closed the door softly behind her.

It did not take Erica long to tell Lord Castlereagh exactly what Count Andrei had revealed the evening before. She did not mention the duke, thinking it might get him in trouble if it were known he was spying on the congress. At the very least, it would lower him in everyone's estimation, and somehow she was reluctant to expose him to any more ridicule. His reputation was not good, as it was. She had heard enough derisive comments to know that he was considered a foolish man, intent only on amusing himself in Vienna while he searched for the perfect stallion—a man of no importance at all.

Lord Castlereagh listened to her, his face serious, and

then he thanked her for coming and told her the information she brought would be put to good use.

As she rose to leave, he asked, "Does the Duke of Graves know you are here, Miss Kingsley?"

Erica frowned a little, a fact he noted at once. "No, he knows nothing about it," she said, wishing she did not have to lie. "I . . . I thought it better to bring it directly to your attention."

"I do not consider it wise for you to make a habit of calling here, Miss Kingsley," he said next. Erica stared at him. "You may be sure we have our own sources, and I would not like to think you were in any danger. Headquarters is under constant surveillance, and your visit has been noted. I am sure you realize that the count would be very angry with you if he found out you were repeating his confidences, that you were the one who told us the czar's intent."

Erica nodded and bit her lip. She did not even want to contemplate what the Russians would do if they found out she was a spy.

Lord Castlereagh bowed as he bade her good-bye, and she left without saying another word. She was already worrying about how she would get word to him if she heard anything else important that the duke would not bother to report.

As soon as the door closed behind her, a broad grin crossed Lord Castlereagh's handsome face as he went to the desk to pen a short note to Owen Kingsley.

When Emily Stewart came back a few minutes later, he was still smiling.

"Yes, she was very pretty, dear Rob, but do take that fatuous look from your face lest I become angry," she said, shaking her finger at him. "The very idea, allowing yourself to be closeted in here alone with her! How I am put upon!"

Her husband rose and took her in his arms to kiss her soundly. "But, my dear, I have not been so entertained in a sennight," he told her.

"What did she want?" Lady Castlereagh asked, curious now.

Her husband smiled down at her. "She came to give me the same information his grace did at nine this morning," he said. "You remember I was just about to go to bed for a few hours' rest after the ball when he arrived? You may imagine how difficult it was for me to keep a straight face, especially when Miss Kingsley assured me the duke knew nothing about the affair. Odd, that. Can she be protecting him, do you think? And from what?"

Lady Castlereagh appeared lost in thought, and then she smiled too. "It is possible," she said. "His performance as a superficial man is very convincing. And perhaps she is fond of him. Oh, how wonderful it would be if they fell in love! I have always thought it such a shame that the duke refuses to consider matrimony, that he is so cold to my sex."

Her husband hugged her again and went back to the desk. "He is afraid of rejection, m'dear," he said. "He cannot believe any woman would want a cripple, unless it was for his title and his wealth, and that he will never accept. Owen Kingsley is an idealist, a hopeless romantic under that crusty arrogance he sports. He will not settle for anything but perfection and true love."

"Just like we share, Rob?" Emily Stewart asked over her shoulder as she tripped away. England's foreign secretary blew her a kiss before he picked up his quill to finish his note.

Erica did not see the Duke of Graves for the rest of the day. When she came down to dinner, she discovered that he had gone out, and she was not pleased that she and Lady Liza would be dining alone together. However, that lady seemed a little abstracted, and she put her hand to her head more than once, and only toyed with her food, causing Erica to believe she was still recovering from the excess of champagne she had enjoyed at the ball. Lady Liza excused herself as soon as dinner was over, and Erica settled down in the library to read.

She was still there, completely absorbed, when the duke came home. As he closed the library doors behind him with a snap, she jumped, hands to her heart. Her book slipped unnoticed to the floor.

"Did I startle you, Erica?" he asked. "But I *do* live here."

Erica stared at him in some suspicion. He seemed different somehow, and she did not trust the change. As she watched, he limped over to the chair across from her and sat down.

"There is something we have to discuss, ma'am, and it might as well be now," he told her, never taking his eyes from her face. "It has come to my attention that you called on Lord Castlereagh this afternoon. May I ask why you did such a thing?"

Emily felt her heart sinking. How had he found out? Was he angry? What would he do to her for her defiance? she wondered.

"I am waiting for your answer, my girl," he said. "I do not intend to grow old in the process."

She put up her chin in that now-familiar gesture. "Yes, I called on him," she said, knowing only the truth would do. "I asked for Lady Castlereagh first, in case anyone noticed I was there. Surely it is correct for one lady to call on another?"

"You have not told me why you went," he reminded her.

"I had to tell the foreign secretary about the czar's plans," she said, wishing he did not look so stern and forbidding. "I knew that you would do nothing about it, and I knew it was too important to disregard."

The duke rose and came to draw her to her feet. He gripped her shoulders hard, and Erica tried not to wince. "You will never do such a thing again, do you hear me?" he said quickly, his voice showing the anger he had been hiding. Erica shivered as he shook her a little. "Little fool!" he went on. "Every spy in Vienna knows that you went there by now, and even if they cannot know the purpose of your visit, they will be suspicious of you from now on. You have put yourself in jeopardy, and all because you took matters into your own hands, bypassing my authority and against my express orders."

Erica twisted free of his bruising hands and backed away from him. She was unable to take her eyes from his furious face. "But it was essential to the negotiations!" she cried. "I had to do it! The Huntingtons never shrink from the duty they owe their country!"

The duke limped back to his chair. "Ah, what patriotism," he said with a sneer, and then he pointed to the chair where she had been sitting. "Sit down!" he thundered.

As she hesitated, he began to get up again and she slipped back to the chair at once. She knew he would not hesitate to use force, and she was a little frightened of him.

"It might interest you to know, dear noble and officious patriot, that Robert Stewart already had that information," he said next.

Erica's eyes widened. "He did? But how did he get it?" she asked. "He certainly never said anything to me about it."

"No doubt he hesitated to puncture your self-righteous piety," the duke told her coldly, and she cringed. "I told him myself," he went on. "Right after you went to bed this morning."

He saw Erica's mouth drop open a little, and the way she frowned.

"Perhaps that might teach you to be less busy in the future, madam," he went on, snapping out his words crisply. "I gave you an order, and you deliberately disobeyed me. I will not tolerate such behavior. If there is even one more instance of your willfulness, I will see that you are sent home. Do I make myself clear?"

Erica nodded, biting her lower lip. "But why did you change your mind?" she asked, as if perplexed, and ignoring his scalding lecture as if it had never been made. "You told me it wasn't of any significance, that you had no intention of putting yourself to the bother of passing it on. I . . . I don't understand."

The duke rose and poured himself a snifter of brandy. As he twirled the amber liquid in the glass, he said, "I told you once before that it is not necessary for you to understand anything. Do as you are told, no more, no less."

"But that's not fair!" she cried, stung at last. "It is to treat me as if I were a child or an idiot! And I am not, as I have told *you* once before."

The duke had raised his snifter to inhale the heady aroma, but at her impassioned words he lowered it to stare at her. He saw that she was very pale, and she was clenching her hands at her sides. He could tell how upset she was, and he wished he might reassure her, but that was not possible. If she continued to take matters into her own hands, she would be in danger. And ever since he had read the note from Robert Stewart that had been delivered to the back door in a basket of fruit, he had realized that any danger that involved Erica Stone was something he did not care to contemplate. He was surprised to find how strongly he felt about this, and he wondered why it was so important that nothing happen to her while she was under his care. Nothing at all, neither the attentions of a lascivious Swedish prince nor the angry revenge of a burly Russian hussar. He remembered now how inordinately pleased he had been to find out that she had told Lord Castlereagh that he himself knew nothing at all about the news she brought, almost as if she hoped the foreign secretary would think that if he had, naturally he would have come himself, and at once. He could still remember Robert's postscript, word for word. "Miss K. appeared determined to shield you from my sneers, old boy," he had written. "Now, why is that, do you suppose?"

Recalled to the angry Miss Kingsley, the duke made his frown even darker. "I drink to your superior intelligence, madam, but still I must insist that you tell no one but myself the things you learn," he said. "And I will have your promise that you will obey me in this."

He glared at her until she nodded a reluctant agreement. But when he settled down with his brandy and one of the London journals he had arranged to have sent on to him, and suggested she resume her reading, she was quick to excuse herself and leave the library.

Somehow, the news from home was not very intriguing to the duke that evening.

9

The military review that Count Andrei had invited them to was to take place the following morning. Erica was already in the hall when the duke came downstairs shortly before ten, the hour the count had arranged for his carriage to collect them. He himself was involved with his regiment, and would not be able to join them until the review was over.

Erica was wearing a form-fitting scarlet gown cut along pseudo-military lines, with loops of braid over one shoulder, and brass buttons marching in a double row to the waist. On her head she wore a dashing little black hat that tilted over one eye and had sweeping plumes that reached her shoulder.

The duke's cold black eyes inspected her attire. Erica was annoyed to find she was holding her breath. At last he nodded.

"Very apropos, cuz," he said in a bored drawl. "I see Count Andrei is a doomed man. Who could resist you in that gown? Let us pray he does not lose his head, toss you over his saddle bow, and gallop away in an easterly direction."

Erica put up her chin. She had no idea how to respond to the duke's sarcastic flattery, for she was feeling distinctly awkward in his company after their scene in the library the night before. Even this morning she could still hear his cold voice demanding her obedience, and feel his hands bruising her shoulders as he called her a little fool. Now, as Lady Liza rustled down to join them, she turned away from him to compliment her on her attire. This morning she was all in white, but the smoldering, expectant look in her dark eyes belied its modesty.

Erica was glad Lady Liza had so much to chat about when they were being driven to the review. She told them exactly what they were to see, and in which order, and when the duke questioned her as to the source of her information, she tossed her head and flushed a little as she said Prince Gorsky had told her all about it at the ball.

"One wonders that he had time," the duke murmured. "However, it is encouraging to know that he manages to stop and, er, speak, every once in a while."

It was obvious that Owen Kingsley was in a very bad mood this morning, and Erica changed the subject before Lady Liza could reply. Not for the first time she wondered at the relationship between the duke and his younger aunt, and she wondered as well if she would ever understand them.

The count had arranged for a friend of his to escort them to the reviewing stand. Erica looked around with her usual interest. Several heads of state were present, as well as common people who milled about on either side of the stand, pointing out the various nobles. On this lovely sunny morning there was an air of festivity and goodwill, and a great deal of laughter and animated conversation, which abated only when the czar took his seat to the applause of the guests.

He was dressed as an officer of the guards, with the blue order of Saint Andrew across his chest. Heavy gold epaulets adorned his shoulders, which seemed very broad above the tightly cinched black belt he wore at his waist. His face, under his plumed two-cornered hat, was solemn and dignified, and he held himself as if he were well aware he was the cynosure of every eye.

Erica was fascinated by the review itself. Regiment after regiment cantered up, halting as one man and wheeling their horses to salute their czar. She was especially taken with a band of cossacks on their sturdy, shaggy ponies. They wore belted shirts over wide white trousers that were tucked into high boots, and tall fur hats, and their lances shone as they raised them in unison and with one voice roared their reverence and obedience to the czar. Erica felt as if she had stepped into another world that was strange and foreign. During the riding exhibition that followed, she was awed by the feats of horsemanship they performed on their rough ponies, the daring with which they rode full tilt at each other, screaming challenges over their lowered lances. At one point she had to close her eyes, she was so sure a deadly collision was about to occur. She opened them only when the other guests applauded, to discover both riders bowing safely over their painted saddles. In her mind's eye, Erica could see bands of these cossacks tearing across the frozen steppes and tundras of Russia, intent on mayhem and plunder, and she shivered.

"Are they not magnificent?" Lady Liza demanded, leaning forward, her red mouth slighty ajar in her admiration.

The duke turned to stare at her. "Indeed," he drawled. "If only they were not quite so . . . so *Russian! Too* fatiguing!"

He had spoken quietly, and in English, but Erica saw the annoyed glances that were directed his way, the contempt in a curled lip, a cold eye, and she wanted to beg him to put off this foppish air he maintained in public. It continued to puzzle her, for when they were alone the duke was a sensible, straightforward man. In company he almost seemed the fool. It was most incomprehensible.

But she forgot him as the next part of the entertainment began. Burly Russian soldiers performed their native dances with passionate fervor. She had never seen men dance together, but as she watched them, she realized these were completely masculine affairs in which any woman would have been out of place. Erica did not see how the dancers could remain balanced when they sank to their haunches and, with arms folded across their chests, heads held high, threw out one leg and then the other in violent rhythm. Lady Liza applauded wildly, and threw a kiss to one of them. Erica saw the kiss returned as the dance ended, and she knew Prince Gorsky had been one of the company. She wondered where Count Andrei was, for she had not been able to distinguish him from the others. There were so many broad, muscular soldiers, so many thick black beards.

He appeared at last when they left the reviewing stand. He was perspiring under his heavy bearskin shako, and his cheeks were flushed with his efforts. "Did you enjoy it, little bird?" he asked eagerly, taking her hand in greeting.

"It was splendid, just splendid," Erica told him. She could feel the duke stirring beside her, and she hurried to ask the count about his regiment, lest Owen Kingsley disgrace himself yet again.

The duke excused himself shortly before refreshments were to be served. "I do believe I shall toddle along with Lord Hazelbeck," he said. "Oh, by the by, the horses were magnificent! I must think about possibly cross-breeding one of the cossack ponies with an English mare. It might produce an interesting strain . . . hmm?"

He seemed lost in thought as he began to leave, and then he turned back and waved a limp hand. "Beg you to take care of my cousin for me and see her safely home, there's a good fellow."

The count tucked Erica's hand in his arm and bowed slightly. "She will be safe with me, your grace," he assured the duke, not even bothering to hide his disdain.

Owen Kingsley did not seem to notice. As he limped away, the count snorted and said, "Fool! And a cripple, to boot!"

On his face Erica could see the healthy, physically strong man's revulsion for deformity, and she had to bite her tongue to keep from defending the duke. It was not his fault that he was lame, and she found she agreed with Talleyrand. Being crippled was only an annoyance; it could not affect the quality of the man himself. And in spite of Owen Kingsley's propensity for playing the fool, somehow after last night she knew he was a formidable man—in every way.

Erica allowed the count to lead her to the colorful tent that had been erected a little distance away. They were soon joined by a number of his friends as refreshments were served. Lady Liza and Prince Gorsky were seated close together at the table, whispering to each other.

Erica knew Liza had not even noticed she was there, nor anyone else, and she felt uneasy.

After they had eaten, the count took her up to the czar and introduced her, his voice reverent as he did so. Erica sank into her deepest curtsy and lowered her eyes.

"So you have captured an English lady, have you, Andrei?" the czar asked, smiling at his burly aide. "One must commend you on your good taste, although perhaps it was a regrettable move on your part."

He paused as Count Andrei frowned, and then he added, "I only mean that if I had seen the lady first, you would not have had a chance with her. Such lovely hair, such perfect features wasted on a mere count? Why, she is fit for royalty!"

At once Count Andrei put his hand to his heart and gestured to Erica as he bowed, and the czar laughed, well-pleased. "I am teasing you, my friend!" he said. "I would never ask you to make such a sacrifice."

Erica felt a spurt of anger, not only at being discussed as if she were not even there but also at the count's willingness to give her up if his czar wanted her. She managed to keep smiling, but inside she was seething. She was not Count Andrei's possession to be bestowed where he willed, and she never would be. She decided she did not like Russians very much, after all.

She was cool from then on, but when they were both seated in the count's carriage, she remembered her mission. "Thank you for introducing me to the czar, sir," she began. "What an impressive man! I do not wonder at the devotion you—all of his people—shower on him."

The count beamed at her and took her hand to press it gently between both of his big ones.

"His highness seemed in a very good humor this morning," she said hastily. "I am so glad he has recovered from his anger of the other night."

The count's smile faded. "As you say, my bird. There is nothing Alexander likes more than to be with his soldiers. But he has not forgotten the treachery of Metternich. Even now, his plans to thwart him are under way. The prince will soon discover how very unwise he was to anger our czar." He paused, and then he added,

"You did not notice that Count Nesselrode, our foreign minister, was not in attendance this morning? Nor Baron Stein, who is in charge of German affairs? It was for a very good reason. They are calling on the Germans, persuading them to our side."

Erica murmured her admiration, even as she filed the information away. The count changed the subject then, as the carriage entered a gate in the ramparts and began to clatter over the cobbles.

"I am taking you to Princess Bagration's, my bird. She has invited a select few of her Russian compatriots to a reception in her apartments in the Palm Court."

By this time Erica had heard a great deal of Princess Bagration, the lady all Vienna called the naked angel. Pretty and blond, she was addicted to extremely low necklines and gowns that were so gauzy, and with so many strategic slits, they revealed all her charms. She was also insatiable, often taking several lovers at a time, who visited her one after the other for what the Austrian spies who haunted the court called "an intimate audience." Erica wondered if she should object to going there, and she looked a little nervously at her escort.

He was smiling down at her, a tender light in his gray eyes. "It is not to worry, little bird," he said. "I watch over you. You need never fear. I know you are a good woman—how do you say it?—pure, innocent."

Erica thanked him as he leaned closer and kissed her hand, although she could not help remembering how quickly he had been prepared to make her a gift to his czar.

Princess Bagration was in fine form that day. Her greeting to Erica was languid, but the stream of Russian she directed to the count had him red-faced, while all around them, other officers roared with laughter and clapped him on the shoulder. Erica was delighted when he led her away to a sofa and a quiet *tête-à-tête*.

She noticed Lady Liza clinging to Prince Gorsky's arm, and she also saw her look around before the two left the room in an almost furtive manner.

It was some time later that there was a violent disturbance. An elderly Austrian burst into the room dragging a young girl with him. She was in a state of dishabille, and crying hysterically. In harsh tones the Austrian admonished the princess for allowing one of her beastly countrymen to lure his daughter to a private room where he locked the door before he attempted her seduction. The large reception room hushed as he spoke, but when he finally left, his weeping daughter covering her eyes in shame, the company burst into animated conversation. Erica heard a lady nearby say it was the Austrian's own fault. "Imagine bringing a young virgin to *this* house!" she told the group she was in. "Madness, pure madness!"

"Ah, madam, but we are all of us so impetuous," a Russian officer insisted. "When we see something we want, we take it. It is only Russian nature to do so."

Erica paled, and Count Andrei leaned closer to whisper in her ear, "Yes, Nikita is right. We are like that. But I beg you to remember, my little bird, that it is not because I do not want you that I have restrained myself. No, no. It is because I know you are so fine."

It seemed a very long time before the count took her home. Erica had seen nothing more of Lady Liza, and when she asked if they should not look for her, or at least wait until she was ready to leave, the count looked uncomfortable.

"The prince will take her home when he is ready to do so," he told her, his voice stiff.

Erica nodded, suddenly aware that somewhere in the princess's enormous suite, Prince Gorsky and Lady Liza were making love. She wondered at their daring. Surely it was most unwise with such a throng of people present. She hoped the duke would never learn of it.

When she arrived home, she discovered the duke had gone out to the Spanish Riding School, and she went into the library to wait for him. She spent the time pacing and thinking hard. This afternoon she had seen a world very unlike hers, and it troubled her. How could people of the nobility be so amoral, so completely intent only on satisfying their lust? That Russian officer must have known the young Austrian girl was frightened and unwilling, but he had not stopped his seduction. He wanted her; therefore it followed that he must have her. Prince Eric was

just such another. Thank heaven Count Andrei had a
few scruples! she thought with a shiver, not that she
would ever trust him completely. And the women here
were no better than the men. It was true that Lady Liza
slipping away with the prince had been shocking, but
Erica had listened to enough gossip this afternoon to
know that what she had done was common practice. She
had overheard a conversation about the Duchess of Sagan
and her torrid affair with Clemens Metternich. Erica
remembered the prince strolling through the pavilion at
his Peace Ball, his wife on his arm, and both of them
smiling as they greeted their guests. And they had children, too. How painful it must be for Laure Metternich
to ignore the whispering, and his unexplained absences,
while still presenting a calm, assured front to the world.
Erica did not think she would ever be able to do that
herself. And as for the famous Princess Bagration—well!
She might be related to the czar, but her behavior was a
disgrace. Erica had even heard two ladies tittering over
the fact that they were visiting what all Vienna called a
bordello! When she remembered the gown she had told
the duke she would never wear because it was so immodest, Erica almost laughed. The princess had appeared to
be attired for bed rather than dressed for a formal reception, and several other women, for she could not call
them ladies, had been similarly gowned. Erica frowned.
She had never thought of herself as a prude, but she
wondered if she were the only woman in Vienna who
thought it was important to care deeply before she gave
herself. But even if she were, she would not, could not
compromise. This time she would make sure she loved,
and was loved in return.

The duke came in then, and she was able to forget her
distressing thoughts as she told him what she had learned
from the count. Owen Kingsley heard her out without comment, only frowning a little. At last he told her it would
be helpful if she could find out not only whether the
Russian go-betweens had been successful but also any
further schemes of the czar. She noticed his frivolous air
was completely missing; rather he seemed stern, almost
abstracted. He did not even remonstrate with Lady Liza

that evening, although Erica knew he was aware of how late she had come home, almost two hours after her own return.

Erica did not see the count again for several days. He sent her flowers and a note explaining he was busy executing a special commission for the czar.

Thus released, however momentarily from her spying, Erica found she was able to enjoy herself again. To her relief, Prince Eric kept his distance, although she saw him staring at her one evening at the theater, and again, a few days later, deep in conversation with Lady Liza at Princess Fürstenberg's *soirée.* She wondered what they found to talk about, for Liza Ridgely was still involved with Prince Gorsky, and was seldom home.

The afternoon Erica was to drive out with Countess de Talleyrand-Périgord, she was in an excellent mood. Although it was November now, the warm weather still lingered, and the countess gave her coachman orders to drive to the Vienna Woods.

"It is such a glorious day, isn't it, Miss Kingsley?" she asked.

Erica begged her to call her by her first name, and the countess smiled as she agreed, stipulating that Erica must call her Dorothea as well.

"There is so much formality at this congress," she said. "I tell my uncle I weary of emperors and princesses, kings and countesses, there are so many of them. Of course, as his hostess, I must be always smiling and pleasant. No doubt you have had much the same experience?"

Erica admitted she had not, wondering as she did so why the duke seemed to have so few friends and did so little entertaining.

"You are lucky," the countess told her as the carriage bowled along the road leading to the famous woods. "But please tell me something about yourself, where you grew up, your family and friends."

Although she knew how important it was for her to maintain her masquerade, Erica wished she did not have to invent a story. She would have liked to tell Dorothea the truth.

The two were soon chatting as if they had known each other for years. Erica was stunned when the countess began to speak of her own life. She was so poised and sophisticated, Erica had thought her older than the twenty-one she said she was, and she had not known she was a married woman with children.

She saw how her new friend's face clouded over when she discussed her marriage. "I was wed to Edmond—Comte de Talleyrand-Périgord—five years ago," she said quietly. "It was the czar's wish, and as the duke of Courland's youngest daughter, I had little to say about it." She sighed and confided, "I was very much in love with another gentleman, but . . . but the match was not encouraged."

Erica reached out impulsively and squeezed her hand. Dorothea smiled at her before she went on, "We lived in Paris, and my mother came to stay with us. How mama-duchess adored the city, and Napoleon! Well, at least she was happy."

She made a face. "I myself never liked the man, or his court. It was not easy for me there. My husband and I have little in common besides our three children. My youngest son is only a baby. It was very hard for me to leave him and his brother to come here, even though I knew how much my uncle needed me."

"But I thought you said you had three children?" Erica asked, a little confused.

"Yes, but my beloved little daughter, Charlotte-Dorothea, died of the measles a few months ago. She was only two," the countess told her, taking her hand-kerchief from her reticule to wipe the sudden tears from her eyes. Erica's heart went out to her. "I was dis-traught," she went on after a moment. "I ceased to want to live myself, by my uncle saved me from despair. He is such a wonderful, kind man! Indeed, it was because of his support in that difficult time that I agreed to come to Vienna."

Fortunately, for Erica did not know what to say in reply, the carriage halted then in one of the small villages that were scattered through the woods, and the two of them repaired to the local inn for refreshments.

Dorothea soon lost her pensive air after they had ordered tea. "Have you heard about the Carrousel that is to be held November 23, Erica?" she asked, her dark eyes sparkling now. "It will be the most exciting event, and I have been asked to help with the preparations!"

Erica did know, for all Vienna was discussing it, but she had not heard any details. Now she listened with great interest as the countess told her about the coming festival. "It is to be a reenactment of a medieval tournament," she said. "And it will be held in Fisher von Erlach's Imperial Riding Hall, with twenty-four of the best horsemen in Vienna impersonating knights. I am to be one of the ladies of the tournament."

"How grand," Erica enthused. "I do hope I can see you there."

"Oh, you are sure to be invited," Dorothea told her. "The Duke of Graves has the *entrée* everywhere. My uncle tells me he is a man of impeccable bloodlines, and descended from royalty, besides being one of the wealthiest men in England."

The two lingered over their cakes and tea while Dorothea asked Erica's advice about her gown for the Carrousel. "We are to wear costume, of course," she said. "I have a marvelous idea for one that is truly medieval. Just imagine a long black tunic with slashed sleeves worn over a satin underskirt. If only I could decide on the color of the skirt. What do you think of scarlet?"

Erica considered for a moment before she suggested white. "Surely black and white would be stunning," she said.

Later, on the journey back to Vienna, Dorothea asked Erica if she knew Count Karl Clam-Martinitz. Erica thought she seemed a little self-conscious as she did so. She herself had met the Austrian major at a ball, and had thought him a handsome, clever man with great wit. Now she told Dorothea so.

The countess blushed. "Yes, he is handsome, is he not? I have fallen in love with him, Erica, and he with me. I never thought to care for anyone that way again, after losing my first love, but Karl, oh, he is so wonderful!"

Erica stared at the countess, noting her little smile and

dreamy eyes. "But how sad, for what can you do about it?" she asked. "After all, you are a married woman."

Dorothea turned to look at her new friend in some amazement. "Yes, but it was an arranged marriage, and it has never brought me happiness. Now I have the chance for some joy at last, and I have no intention of letting that chance go. Karl and I are lovers, of course." She peeked at Erica, and something she saw in her face made her laugh. "I can see you think I am disgraceful, my dear, but please do not hate me. It is the way of the world, as you will find out someday soon. However, for your sake, I hope you can marry where you love, although I warn you it is a very rare thing indeed. No, most of us of the nobility have to marry to suit our families, for a title or an alliance or wealth. Is it not so in England? Besides, I have done my duty and given my husband two sons for his noble line. What I do henceforth is my own business. I doubt we will ever live together again."

Erica was shocked by this frank speaking, but she was not required to think of a response, for the countess continued without pause. She told Erica all about the Austrian count, how they had met, and when they had fallen in love.

When Erica said good-bye sometime later, she was still confused. Here was another woman taking a lover as casually as she would take another cup of tea, and right after the death of her daughter, too. But no, she was not being fair to Dorothea. Erica knew instinctively that she was good at heart. She was not at all like her three sisters: Wilhelmina, the Duchess of Sagan; Pauline, who was Princess Hohenzollern-Hechingen; and Jeanne, who had married an Italian duke. Their exploits in Vienna were legend, and it was a rare conversation that did not include some gossip about them, for with their numerous affairs they scandalized even the tolerant world that was Vienna. Only their birth saved them from ostracism.

As Erica went up to her room, she wished she could talk to someone. She was so confused! And still so naive and unsophisticated—a true country mouse! she told herself. She sank down into the chair beside her window to stare with unseeing eyes into the street below as she

recalled what Dorothea had told her about her life. But
did she really envy the countess, when all was said and
done? Dorothea had had a loveless childhood, moved
from one dismal, uncomfortable castle to another. She
had not been close to her older sisters, and her mother
had been too busy with her own love affairs to pay her
much attention. She had had only her governess and
tutor to amuse her. And then to be forced to give up the
man she had been devoted to throughout her teens, and
forced into a marriage of convenience with a stranger!
Perhaps she was right, and life did owe her some happiness. Perhaps a strict moral path was not always the right
way, not when your life had been predetermined, and
you had no choice.

Erica sighed, missing her mother badly, as she still
sometimes did. If she had been alive, she could have
spoken to her about Dorothea, Vienna, the congress.
But her mother had been gone for years. If only I could
speak to Lady Castlereagh, she thought. She is a good
woman, and I am sure she could advise me. Or perhaps
the Duke of Graves? Her lips curled in a little smile as
she pictured herself asking that cold eccentric about love.

Count Andrei Ortronsky called on her the following
morning, roses in hand. As she came into the salon
where Rudge had put him to wait for her, he rose eagerly
from his chair and came toward her in a rush. Erica
made herself smile and curtsy, although her initial reaction had been to step back in alarm.

"At last to see you again, my bird!" the count exclaimed, taking her hand in his and pumping it hard.
"How beautiful you are—more beautiful that I remembered. Here, these are for you."

He thrust the roses into her arms and beamed at her.

Erica thanked him, and asked him to be seated. When
she had asked Rudge to put her bouquet in water and
bring the count a glass of wine, she took a seat opposite
him.

"I am so glad you are here. It must mean you have
finished your commission, Count?" she asked. Smile,
Erica, smile! she told herself.

"Finally, yes, it is done," he told her. "These are

terrible times, my bird. I myself do not understand why
England and Austria—even France—remain so stubborn.
Surely the czar's desire to keep what he has conquered
should not be questioned. Let others make concessions,
that is not the Russian way."

"But doesn't everyone at the congress have to make
some compromises if there is to be peace?" Erica prod-
ded, to keep him talking.

"Everyone *else*, my bird, everyone else. Why, I have
heard the czar say that if he is forced to it, we will go to
war again."

"Oh, I do so hope that will not be necessary!" Erica
said. She felt it was the first honest thing she had said
since entering the room. "We have been at war for such
a long time, indeed, almost all of my life," she continued. "Is it not possible for us to live in peace, at long
last?"

The count shrugged and threw out his hands. "Peace
would be nice, of course, but a peace without honor is
impossible for any true Russian to endure," he told her.

Erica thought he looked stern and cold, and she changed
the subject. She could hardly ask point-blank about his
commission for the czar, or Alexander's future plans,
without arousing his suspicions. Something she had seen
on his face a moment ago, some hint of the barbaric
cruelty he was capable of, made her leery. The count was
falling in love with her, and so he smiled at her and
treated her as someone precious. But Erica knew that if
his czar gave the order to kill her, he would do it without
a moment's hesitation. She shivered.

The duke's arrival signaled the end of the visit. The
count asked Erica to drive out with him that afternoon,
and under the duke's eye she was forced to agree, with
every indication of delight.

When he had bowed himself away, Erica remained standing where he had left her, a worried little frown on her
face.

"You are disturbed about something, cuz?" the duke
asked, his black eyes keen.

Erica told him what the count had said, pacing up and
down now in her agitation. "More war!" she ended,

loathing in her voice. "Will it never end? One of my brothers has been so badly wounded he will never fight again, but Geoffrey and Peter will be in the front lines once more."

"Perhaps it will not come to war, in spite of the count's assessment of the situation," the duke told her. He watched as she turned and stared at him, and he found himself saying, "There is much to do yet in the way of negotiation, and willing statesmen to do it. I am sure all is not lost, not yet."

Erica nodded her agreement before she asked to be excused. The duke's calm words did not reassure her. He was not interested in politics or peacemaking. How many times had she heard him say he thought them boring? And since that was the case, how could she take any comfort from his view of the situation?

She spent the rest of the day writing letters home and helping Agnes with some sewing, until it was time for her drive with the count. Dressed in a smart afternoon gown and hat, she went down to join him at three. As he escorted her to the carriage, she noticed that the skies had darkened with heavy clouds as the afternoon wore on.

The count sat very close to her, and she tried to hide her uneasiness. Again he talked of his home and family, and told her how she would love Russia. Erica tried to change the conversation to a discussion of the congress, but this afternoon he did not follow her lead.

The carriage had left the city, and as it tore along a winding country road, Count Andrei took her hand and pressed it to his heart. "Yes, my bird, I have a beautiful estate. I hope with all my heart to show it to you someday," he said, and then he raised her hand and kissed it.

Erica shrank back on the squabs of the carriage seat. "Please, Count," she said. "You go too fast. We . . . we are strangers still."

For a moment she thought he would argue, and she held her breath. Then he smiled at her and put her hand back in her lap. "As you will, my bird," he whispered, never taking those intent gray eyes from her face. "I will be patient. You see how you have enslaved me? I obey you without question. But someday *you* will obey *me*. How I live for that day!"

Erica thought they would never return home, for the drive seemed endless. At last the count gave the order to return to the city. It was almost five when he set her down again in the Johannesgasse. As he said good-bye, he reminded her he would be expecting the first waltz with her at the Hofburg ball that evening. Erica, relieved to be released from the intimacy of a closed carriage and his overpowering presence, smiled and agreed.

As she entered the hall, she saw that a letter had arrived for her from home, and she picked it up eagerly. As she slit the seal, Lady Liza came out of the drawing room.

"So, you are here at last, Erica," she said, leaning against the doorjamb and smiling her malicious little smile. "I am afraid you must go out again. I saw the Countess de Talleyrand-Périgord this afternoon, and she asked me to tell you that she would like you to come to the Kaunitz when you return from your drive. She said she has something to tell you, something important, and it will take only a moment."

Erica put her letter back on the table. "Thank you, Liza," she said. "I will go at once. I wonder what it can be?"

Lady Liza laughed as she moved languidly to the stairs. "Some girlish bit of gossip, no doubt, that will not keep. Do run along."

Erica stared at her for a moment, wondering at the suppressed excitement she thought she heard in her voice, before she opened the door and ran down the steps.

The afternoon had grown increasingly dreary, and now, at five o'clock, an early dusk was falling. Erica waited until a hackney cab clattered by, and then she crossed the street. As she stepped up on the opposite curb, she barely registered a carriage coming up behind her, for she was thinking about Dorothea's unusual summons.

Just before she reached the steps of the palace, she became aware of running footsteps, and she turned, not alarmed, but curious. Her eyes widened as two men in dark clothing reached her and stopped. Before she could even ask what they wanted, or think of calling for help, one of them grabbed her by the arms, while the other put a large hand over her mouth. Erica began to struggle, her heart pounding in sudden fright, but it was no use. The two men were strong and determined. It was only the matter of a moment for them to bustle her into the carriage next to them. Even in all her terror, Erica noticed the imperial arms on the door, the shiny green varnish of the familiar Austrian equipage. Once she was pushed down on the seat, the man who was gagging her removed his hand, and Erica started to scream. But her valiant effort to save herself came to nothing as a foul-smelling cloth was pressed over her nose and mouth. She was unconscious before the carriage even began to move.

10

It was a long moment before Erica remembered what had happened to her when she recovered consciousness. She felt disoriented, and a little sick to her stomach, and for some reason, her mouth was very dry. She put her hand to her head, keeping her eyes closed as memory returned and her breathing grew shallow with fear again. She had been kidnapped and drugged by those two strange men—but for what purpose, she had no idea. She was stretched out full length on something soft, and there was no movement, so obviously she was no longer in the coach. With her eyes still closed, she pondered that coach, the same as those she had seen when she first came to Vienna. But who in the Imperial Palace would want to kidnap her? Was it possible that Count Andrei or the czar had discovered she was spying on them? she wondered, her heart leaping with dread.

She was not required to ponder the mystery for long.

"Are you awake, Ice Maiden?" a soft voice asked, and her eyes flew open in astonished horror.

"I rather thought you were," Prince Eric told her, coming from the chair he had been leaning against to sit on the sofa by her side.

Erica looked around. She had never seen this large elaborate sitting room before, but she knew she must be in the Swedish prince's quarters in the Hofburg. She wondered if it would do any good to call for help.

As if the prince divined her thoughts, he said, "Do not scream, my beautiful one. It would do no good, for there is no one to save you. Prince Boris is the only one who has rooms nearby, and he knows my purpose. He will not help you." He chuckled richly. "My, no, quite the contrary. He is, er, involved himself this afternoon with a strapping German prince. Boris found his dueling scar irresistible."

Erica stared at that handsome face that was now wreathed in a smile of complete satisfaction. She found it was twice as horrible that a man so steeped in evil could look like an angel rather than the devil he really was.

"I am sorry you had to be drugged, my dear," the prince was saying. "But I did tell you the situation would be resolved shortly, to my complete satisfaction, did I not? And since I have been denied access to you, I had no other choice but to spirit you away. I have never been refused by any woman, but after my initial anger wore off, I found that your reluctance added zest to the affair. Yes, Ice Maiden. Our coupling will be a wonderful, passionate thing that will have you begging for more. My word on it."

He saw the revulsion on her face, and he added, "Would you care to wager on it?" Then he chuckled. "But no, I am a gentleman. It would not be fair to let you lose your money on such a sure thing."

Erica was positive she had never heard anyone so conceited, so confident of his prowess as a lover. He reached out then and calmly began to loosen the ties of the heavy dark cloak she had at some time been wrapped in.

"Where . . . where did this cloak come from?" she asked, her lips so dry it was hard to force the question past them.

"It was necessary for the subterfuge," Prince Eric told her. She was delighted when he stopped removing the cloak as he explained, "Even in the Hofburg, kidnapping ladies for the purpose of seduction is frowned on. My men were given orders to say that you were Princess von Sigmartin and that the reason they were carrying you was that you had been taken ill. The princess will not mind us using her name. We have spent some very enjoyable hours together, and she is a complete madcap. Perhaps I shall tell her about it someday. She is sure to find it amusing."

He laughed as he reached for the ties again, and Erica made herself say, "Might I have a glass of water, highness? My mouth is so dry."

He rose at once. "But of course. Anything that is in my power to give you, Erica."

He went to a drinks table set against the wall and poured her a glass from a tall silver pitcher. Frantically Erica began to think of how she could escape him. She believed him when he said only Prince Boris would hear her if she cried out, but surely there must be some way? She wished she did not feel so muddled, so helpless. She knew she would need all her wits about her if she were to get away.

The prince clicked his heels as he handed her the glass, and as she sat up to take it, she noticed he was wearing a serpent ring identical to the one she had found in William's desk.

"What a very unusual ring," she managed to say, although her heart was pounding so in her breast, she had trouble breathing.

The prince looked down at his hand, as if he had forgotten he was wearing the ring, and he frowned a little.

"The mating serpents," he said, his tone musing. He stared at it for a moment, and then he removed it and placed it on the table beside the sofa. "It is not appropriate at this time," he said.

Erica saw that he was prepared to forget it, and she made herself say, "I believe I have seen jewelry like it before, although I cannot remember where."

As Prince Eric took his seat again, he smiled. "It would be unusual if you had not. The dancer Isabella Sabatini gives them to her favorite lovers. If this congress lasts much longer, every man in Vienna will be sporting one." He chuckled, and Erica took a swallow of water to steady herself.

"When did she give you the ring?" she asked.

"You are very interested in my *affaires,* are you not, Ice Maiden?" he asked. "But you need not worry about her. The lady and I have an understanding. Although we still meet, we are free to take others as well. It adds spice. But to answer your question, she gave it to me as a reward a few weeks ago. I amused her by disposing of a rival of mine for her favors."

"Disposing of him?" Erica whispered.

"Yes, I believe that is the correct term," the prince said. "I had him set on and killed. He was in my way with his gifts of money and jewelry. He was so mad for Bella he would not permit her to entertain other men, and I wanted her. You do see why it was necessary for me to, er, get him out of the way?'

Erica stared at him, horrified. He was the one who had had William killed, and only because he wanted the same woman for a few weeks before he tired of her. What a monster he was! And she was here in his rooms, his captive. Suddenly she felt faint, and she had to put the glass down on the table and grasp the sides of her head for a moment as the room whirled around her.

"Still dizzy, my dear?" he said courteously. "Well, as impatient as I am to begin, I can wait. You may very well be dizzy when I make love to you, but I want it to be the result of my touch. And we have the entire evening ahead of us, perhaps even the night as well, for I have no other engagements. We shall see. It all depends on whether you please me or not. No, no, do not concern yourself! I am sure you will, once I have taught you the essentials."

Erica forced herself to look into his hot, lustful eyes without shuddering. With another man she might have tried pleading, trying to appeal to his better side. With Prince Eric that was not even a remote possibility. She knew now he had no better side.

"But the duke—surely he will search for me," she said as she reached for the glass again to take a big swallow of the cool water.

"How will he know where to look?" the prince asked, his tone that of a reasonable man. "No one saw you being kidnapped, and no one knows where you are. The Duke of Graves may well suspect that I have you, but I do assure you, my dear Erica, he would never dare invade the Hofburg and insist on searching my rooms. To do so would precipitate an international incident of dire proportions. The duke is not man enough to risk that. No, you are my prisoner for as long as I want to keep you here. But what a fascinating thought!" he added, as if to himself. "I wonder if it is possible . . . ?"

"Aren't you afraid of what the duke will do to you when you finally let me go, and I tell him?" Erica asked, swallowing hard at the thought of days spent here, being used for this monster's pleasure.

The prince crossed his booted, tightly breeched legs. He was not wearing his uniform jacket, but rather a soft brocaded dressing coat with a silk ascot at his throat, and he was very much at his ease.

Now he chuckled in genuine amusement. "But when I am done with you, Ice Maiden, you will not want to tell him. No, instead you will make up some tale to satisfy him, for you will want me so badly you will do anything to keep me safe for further passionate trysts." He grimaced a little before he added, "Not that it would matter if you did tell him. The duke is a fool, a weakling as well as a cripple. He would never dare to challenge *me!*"

Erica bit her lip to keep from crying out that she would never want him, that she had never hated anyone more. But when she remembered how her body had betrayed her at the Peace Ball, she was not so sure. Was it possible to loathe someone and still desire him? She shook her head. Surely not now, after what she had learned. She knew that deep inside she would always detest the prince, not only for this but also for what he had done to her husband. But to escape him, she had to get away soon . . . somehow . . . some way!

The prince rose again and her green eyes grew wary as he came to take her glass and sit down beside her on the sofa. His arm slid around her waist and pulled her close. He was not rough with her; indeed, she found the situation even more macabre because he treated her so gently.

"You look like a terrified fawn," he told her as he finished undoing the ties of the cloak and opened it. As his hands removed the pins securing her chignon, he added seriously, "You must not be frightened of me, Erica. You will see. I will be as gentle as I can, for I know you are a virgin. But once that little initial pain is over, you will discover how proficient a lover I am, and you will be transported to a wonderful plane of pure sensation. There is nothing like it in the world. It cannot be described."

His hands combed through the silvery strands of her hair as it tumbled down her back, and he picked up a tress to kiss it before he added, "You are a very fortunate woman, Erica Kingsley. There are many of your sex who would envy you that you are my choice. You see, even I, with my strong appetite, can satisfy only so many."

His hands went to the neck of her gown, and he began to unbutton it. Erica made no protest. Her mind was working so quickly, it was as if her body were frozen, unfeeling. The prince stopped after a moment, to slip one hand inside her gown to caress her soft skin while the other hand went to her back to press her close to him as he bent his head and kissed her. Erica closed her eyes in dismay. She knew that the prince was determined to make love to her, that nothing she could say or do would stop him, that it was only a matter of time before he had her naked in his arms. As his lips pressed hers and his tongue invaded her mouth again, she suddenly thought of a plan.

When he raised his head, she made herself sigh and put her arms around his neck so her hands could play with his golden hair.

"Ah, so you have come to see the wisdom of cooperation, have you, Ice Maiden?" he whispered, trailing kisses down to the hollow of her throat. "Do you admit you want me too? Tell me!" he demanded.

"Yes, oh, yes," she made herself say with another sigh.

His hands became more urgent on the buttons of her gown now, and Erica forced herself to draw his head up so he would kiss her again. She tried to put more feeling into her response, and tentatively her tongue caressed his. Both his hands stilled for a moment before they fastened over her breasts to play with the nipples through the fabric.

When the kiss was over, they were both breathing hard.

"My dear Eric," she whispered, "I . . . I must retire for a moment."

He stared at her doubtfully, and she squirmed a little and lowered her lashes. At that, he smiled. "But of course, love. All that water you drank. I understand."

Erica's answering smile was brilliant as he helped her to her feet and led her to the adjacent room. He could not know it was a smile of heartfelt relief that her ploy had worked so well.

He left her at the door of his bedroom. "The dressing room is through there, Erica," he told her. "You will find whatever you need, and I will contain my impatience until you call me back to you."

Erica held her breath as he hesitated before he added, "Do not undress. I reserve that pleasure for myself."

Erica made herself nod as she lowered her eyes in what she hoped he would think was girlish confusion, but she did not dare take a breath until the bedroom door shut behind him. Thank heaven he was so conceited he could not even imagine she might try to escape him!

Quickly now she ran to the dressing room, a fervent prayer on her lips. To her great relief, she saw the other door that led from it, and she opened it cautiously. As she had hoped, it gave onto a wide corridor that fortunately was empty of people. She did not hesitate as she clutched the cloak around her and began to run. The corridor seemed endless, and at any second she expected to hear him cry out behind her, his booted feet thudding as he pursued her and brought her back to his rooms. She did not think he would be gentle with her then.

She turned into the first cross corridor she came to, but she did not stop running. When she reached two flights of stairs, one going up and the other down, she took the one that went up to the next story. He would not expect her to do that, and if she could confuse him, it would help her escape. At the top of the stairs she began to run in the opposite direction. A valet, with a freshly ironed shirt and a pile of cravats over his arm, stared at her in astonishment, but to her relief, he only bowed as she hurried by. She did not slow her steps until she was several floors and acres of corridors away from the Swedish prince's rooms. There were more servants in this part of the palace, and she held her head high and tried to act assured as she passed them. More than once she heard snickers and whispers behind her. The servants obviously thought she was some grand lady returning to her own rooms after an afternoon of dalliance. No doubt such sights were commonplace during the congress.

At last she came to a small alcove where two chairs were placed, and she sank into one of them while she considered what she was to do next. She knew she had to leave the palace as quickly and as secretively as she could, but she had no idea how she was to accomplish that. She clutched the cloak closer around her as she realized that even now Prince Eric was probably searching for her. And in spite of all her twisting and turning to make it difficult for him to follow, she might bump into him right around the next corner.

Just then a little maid came out of a room across the hall. She squealed in fright as she caught sight of Erica in the big dark cloak. Erica made herself smile. The girl had a round, kindly face and honest blue eyes, and she decided she had to take the chance and trust her.

"I am sorry I startled you," she said in French. To her relief, the maid curtsied. "I wonder if you would be so kind as to help me?" Erica asked. The maid looked doubtful, and she added quickly, "I was drugged and brought here by an evil man, and I have just escaped from his rooms. But I have no idea how I am to leave the palace, indeed, even where I am in it. Can you tell me where I should go?"

The maid's hands had crept up to her face as Erica spoke, but now she nodded decisively as she came forward and led the way toward another flight of stairs going down. "This way, *madame*," she said. "Poor lady! Not that I wonder at what happened to you."

As the two of them went down the stairs, she added, "The goings-on among some of these foreigners, you wouldn't believe. I have had some close calls myself since this congress of theirs opened, and me promised to my Johann, too. It's shameful, shameful! I can tell you I'll be glad when they're gone at last."

She led Erica through a pair of baize-covered doors and down a series of shabbier corridors. "Best you leave the back way, *madame*," she said. "There's a gate we servants use when we want to go in and out unnoticed."

Erica saw her blush a little, and knew she slipped out to meet her Johann that way.

The maid pointed to a door ahead of them. "There," she said. "That leads to a courtyard, and set in the outer wall is a small wooden gate. It's half-hidden in the ivy, but you'll find it."

She smiled and the two looked at each other, both pleased they had outwitted another lusty male.

"Thank you. You have been so very kind," Erica said, wishing she had her reticule with her so she could give the girl some money.

The maid did not seem to expect anything, for she only smiled again before she bobbed a curtsy and ran back the way they had come. Erica moved just as fast, and it was not long before she was taking a deep breath of the cool night air and thanking providence for her escape.

It took her a moment to find the door the maid had mentioned, and it was hard to open, and so stiff it creaked. Erica peered up and down the street before she stepped out to close the gate behind her. Then she wrapped herself more securely in the cloak, pulling the hood well forward to hide her face before she walked quickly away.

She felt a few drops of rain as she reached a brightly lit intersection, but she knew where she was now. It would take her only a few minutes to reach the duke's palace and safety.

She hurried through the streets, head down so no one would recognize her. There were many others abroad, mostly men at this hour, and she knew that the rain, which was falling more heavily now, saved her from their attention. Everyone appeared to be in a hurry to reach his destination before getting soaked through.

Erica turned into the Johannesgasse at last, and she almost ran in her eagerness to reach home. She hesitated only a little when she was a few houses away, for she would not have put it past the prince to send his men after her again. To her relief, no imperial carriage was anywhere in sight.

It seemed to take an age before Rudge answered her knock. As he held the door wide, she stepped inside, trying to smile at him. She put back the hood of her cloak, ignoring the look of astonishment that passed over his generally imperturbable face. Erica had no idea how disheveled she looked, the wet, overlarge cloak dripping puddles of water on the gleaming parquet floor, and with her hair flowing down her back in complete disarray.

And then her smile faded as she realized she had never taken the time to rebutton her gown. She could not give Rudge the cloak he was so clearly waiting to receive.

The door to the drawing room opened then, and the Duke of Graves stood on the threshold. Erica stared at him, her heart sinking as she saw how his harsh face darkened with anger.

"Ah, cuz, there you are at last!" was all he said, however. "Do me the favor of attending me for a moment, if you please. I would hear if your errand of mercy went well."

He beckoned, and Erica forced herself to walk across the hall and pass him to enter the room. Behind her, she heard him say, "That will be all, Rudge. See that we are not disturbed."

Erica stopped in the middle of the room and turned. The duke had closed the door and was limping toward her. Her hands, which were holding the edges of the cloak together, trembled.

"Let me take that for you," Owen Kingsley said.

Erica backed away from him. "No, you must not!" she said, and his brows shot up.

"But you are dripping wet. You will make yourself ill if you do not remove it," he said. Calmly he reached out and loosened her grasp, to sweep the cloak from her shoulders.

Erica's hands flew to her bodice, trying desperately to button it. The duke stood perfectly still, staring at that expanse of smooth, satiny skin. Erica saw how his hands crushed the damp cloak between them, and she tried not to shiver.

"I am sure there is some perfectly plausible explanation for your appearance, Erica," he said at last in his usual sarcastic drawl. "Although it is most unusual to find you coming in half-clothed and with your hair in such tangled disorder."

Erica forgot the buttons as she reached up to smooth her hair. Then she shrugged as she realized it was no use. She would have to tell the duke what had happened. "Yes, there is an explanation," she said slowly. "Might I sit down, your grace? I am so very tired. I feel as if I have been running for miles."

He motioned toward a chair and she sank into it, trying to ignore her damp stockings and sodden sandals. "I have just escaped from Prince Eric's rooms in the Hofburg," she told him baldly. "He had me brought there by two of his men."

"Indeed?" the duke asked as he laid the cloak over a chair. He made no move to sit down. "And when did this happen?" he asked.

"Shortly after five," Erica told him.

"Are you sure you did not go to him of your own accord?" he asked coldy. "Perhaps after your session in the garden at Metternich's, you wanted more of his love-making? Do not lie to me, Erica. I will have the truth."

Erica shook her head, feeling bone weary. "You must believe me!" she said, her voice desperate. "I have avoided the prince ever since that night, which is why he had me kidnapped."

The duke stared into her pale face, noting the steady green eyes that never left his. Oddly enough, he found he did believe her. "How did he accomplish this, Erica?" he asked. "I assume the men did not march up to the door and demand you, or Rudge would surely have told me of it."

Erica shook her head. "No, I was in the street. Lady Liza told me Dorothea wanted me to call for a moment when I returned from my drive with the count, for she had something important to tell me."

"I do not understand how you could have been so rash," the duke said in the coldest voice she had ever heard him employ. "After all my warnings and your own experiences with him, you knew very well how dangerous a man he is. And yet, what must you do but run out of the house without even your maid in attendance. What folly!"

"But I was just going across the street to the Kaunitz!" Erica protested.

"What happened next?" he asked, ignoring her passionate words as he folded his arms and leaned against the table behind him.

"I heard a carriage, and then the rush of footsteps,"

she said, trying not to shiver as the awful fear she had
felt during those moments came back to her. "When I
tried to call out, a man put his hand over my mouth and
another forced me into the waiting carriage. I would
have screamed, fought them, but they drugged me."

The duke's eyes grew even bleaker. "And when you
came to yourself?" he asked.

"I was lying on a sofa in the prince's rooms in the
palace," she said. She closed her eyes for a moment,
more to shut out the duke's harsh, angry face than her
memories.

"Your reputation will be ruined, for it will be all over
Vienna tomorrow," the duke told her. "The Hofburg
swarms with Austrian spies, all reporting to Baron Hager.
No one enters or leaves unnoticed. Why, it was even
known when the opera singer Josephine Wolters donned
boy's clothes in order to visit Prince Volkonsky there."

"Maybe no one saw my face," Erica offered. "The
prince told me the men said I was a princess who had
been taken ill. And I was wrapped in that big cloak."

The duke snorted at such naiveté, such a fragile little
hope of social salvation. "And of course the guards at
the palace are so used to thugs carrying in unconscious
women, they never inquired further?" he snarled. Erica
stared at him hopelessly.

Suddenly he looked at the clock on the mantel. "It is
just six-thirty now, I see," he said. "He didn't waste a
second, did he?"

Erica's face was white with shock, her eyes huge. "What
do you mean?" she whispered.

"Why, only that the prince must have done the thing
in record time," he said coldly. "But how distressing for
you, my dear. Making love is so much more enjoyable
when it is savored rather than rushed, as I am sure you
know."

Erica ran to him and grasped his arms. "You do not
understand!" she cried. "Nothing happened, nothing at
all!"

"Ah, I see. *Nothing* again." He nodded wisely. "The
prince merely wished you to share a glass of wine with
him, discuss last night's party, give your opinion of one

of his new coats, is that it?" he asked, his lip curling in disdain.

Erica tried to shake him, but he was like a rock, firm, immovable. "Of course not!" she said, panting in distress. "He . . . he did kiss me, caress me. He even began to undress me." She made herself keep looking at the deepening anger in his black eyes. "I saw I had no way to escape him by protesting, for he would just have . . . have raped me. So I pretended to agree to make love."

She stopped and lowered her head at last, and the duke took her chin in his hand. "Look at me, Erica," he said, and at the first gentle tones she had ever heard in his voice, she did so in astonishment.

"Was he fooled?" he asked. At her nod, he went on, "But surely not for long?"

"No, but very soon I told him I had to be alone for a few minutes," Erica whispered. As the duke looked amazed, she said in a rush, "It was the only thing I could think of!

"He showed me the dressing room and left me there," she went on tightly. "And when I looked around, I saw, as I had suspected I would, another door to the hall. I had prayed it would be so, as it is in most establishments, so a servant can enter and leave without disturbing his master."

"Very ingenious, very ingenious indeed," the duke complimented her. "But he must have come after you. How did you escape? Not only from him, but from the hordes of other people in the palace? It was a busy time of the afternoon, too. All those servants bringing hot water, freshly ironed gowns, linen . . . I do not see how you managed it, looking as you did."

"It wasn't easy," Erica admitted. "I ran as fast as I could at first, turning this way and that through what seemed a score of huge hallways, and up and down a dozen flights of stairs. I was soon quite lost, but far enough away from his rooms so I did not think he could find me. And then I asked a maid to direct me to the nearest door."

"And she didn't report you?" the duke asked in disbelief.

Erica shook her head. "No, for I told her what had

happened to me—oh, using no names, of course! I took
the chance because she looked kind and good. And she
was, she did help me. She even told me of a little-used
gate only the servants knew of, so I could slip away
unobserved."

She saw the lingering doubt in his eyes, and she went
on quickly, "I swear no one saw me leave, your grace! It
was almost full dark and there was no one nearby. And it
began to rain."

"We will have to wait and see what is being said
tomorrow," the duke mused. "If you were unseen, we
can do nothing about this. Not that the prince will escape
my wrath and retaliation eventually, Erica, you may be
sure of that."

He sounded deadly in earnest, and Erica wondered
what his reaction would be if she told him she had
discovered the prince was William Stone's murderer. But
she could not do that. It would all come out if she did:
the fact that her husband had never loved her at all, his
unfaithfulness, and the way he had spent her dowry on
another woman. She could not bear that the duke should
learn the extent of her shame. Suddenly she was surprised to find herself weeping. She was mortified, but all
the events of this afternoon, and the duke's mistrust of
her, had sorely tested her. She had felt alone and helpless in the palace, praying she could be here, safe beside
him once again, but now she realized that she was alone
still.

As Owen Kingsley saw her hands come up to cover her
face, and the way her slim shoulders shook with her sobs,
he moved toward her involuntarily to take her in his
arms. She was crying hard, but he saw how straight she
stood, how she did not make a sound, and he wondered
at the lump in his throat. He knew very well that most
women would have been in hysterics by now, screaming
or fainting in their distress. And how many of them
would have the wits or the courage to effect an escape as
cleverly as Erica had? Truly she was a remarkable woman.

He let her cry until all her tears were shed, holding her
close to him and smoothing her hair with a gentle hand.
At last he felt her grow calmer, and he took out his
handkerchief and tilted her chin up so he could wipe the

tears from her face. Those beautiful green eyes were
hidden now under her lowered lids, but her soft mouth
trembled. As he stared at it, he saw it was still swollen
from the prince's hot kisses, and he could not resist
bending down to cover it with his own. He kissed her as
softly as if she were a child, waiting for some sign of
protest. To his delight, she grew very still, her lips parting under his as naturally as if this was their hundredth
kiss, not their first.

At her unexpected surrender, he kissed her more deeply,
his hands burying themselves in the silver cascade of her
soft hair. He caressed the back of her neck before he
moved his hands slowly to her waist. She was warm and
pliant in his arms, and the sweet scent she wore, com-
bined with the cool dampness of autumnal rain that clung
to her, stirred his senses. He could feel the fists she had
made of her hands open as they lay on his chest, and he
willed her to put her arms around him. As if she had
read his thoughts, she reached up shyly.

Lost in the wonder of her, it was a long time before he
raised his head a little. His dark eyes were hungry as he
inspected her beautiful face. She was breathing faster
now, her eyes still closed, and as he watched, one last
tear escaped her wet, darkened lashes, to run down her
cheek. Gently he kissed it away.

She opened her eyes as his lips touched her skin, to
stare up at him in awe and wonderment. He smiled.

And then, when he saw the light that began to shine in
her eyes, he remembered who he was, who she was, and
the important tasks they had to perform, and he cursed
himself silently for the loss of that iron control he had
maintained for so long.

"Owen?" she whispered, her voice so tender and so
bemused that it stabbed his heart. Her hands moved to
his dark hair. At their soft, tentative touch, the duke had
to concentrate on standing very stiff and very still. There
was nothing he wanted more in all the world at that
moment than to kiss her again, kiss her until they were
both lost.

He put her away from him firmly as he pondered what
he could conceivably say or do to defuse this impossible,

dangerous situation. As she grasped the tabletop beside her to steady herself, he found wisdom.

"I only kissed you because I wanted you to remember what a real embrace between a man and a woman is. A kiss that is given and received with affection," he told her, making himself speak coldly and evenly. "Consider it a valuable lesson, Erica, and use it to forget the prince's lust and what he tried to do to you. That kiss we shared will make it easier for you to do so."

He saw the dismay that came over her face, how she shook her head and reached out to him with a trembling hand, and he turned away from her before he was completely lost. As he limped to the drinks tray, he said over his shoulder, "Let me get you some brandy, Erica. It will warm you, make you feel better after this afternoon's ordeal."

He concentrated on pouring the amber liquid into two snifters and twirling them slowly, for he needed the brandy as much as she did. As he did so, he wondered what he was to do now. He could hardly just change the subject. Perhaps he might suggest she remain home this evening and rest. Certainly she could not return to the Hofburg to attend the weekly ball there now, only a few hours after her escape from it. Someone might see her and wonder at it. His mouth twisted, and he took a deep breath.

But when he turned around, the snifters in his hands, he saw that he was alone in the drawing room. Erica was gone.

11

When Agnes Watts came in answer to her mistress's summons, she was more than indignant, she was angry.

Erica stood in the center of her sitting room, her feet wet and the hem of her gown sodden. Her long hair hung in tangles down her back, and she had not bothered to do more than fasten a few token buttons of her bodice as she was leaving the drawing room. But it was the hurt, lost look in her eyes that fired her maid's wrath the most. Agnes was sure that nasty duke had taken advantage of her mistress, and as she hustled the girl out of her wet clothes and wrapped her in a warm robe, she mumbled imprecations and threats.

She was soon worried, as well as angry. Miss Erica did not speak more than a few words, and even though she had never been a chatterbox, this was unusual. Agnes had to bite her tongue to keep from questioning her as she ordered hot water for a bath and a pot of tea brought up. That would make Miss Erica feel better, she was sure. Her mother had always told her there was nothing like hot tea with lots of sugar for shock. And after she was in bed, warm and comfortable again, surely she would tell her longtime maid what had happened to her.

As Agnes poured the hot water into the big tub from the copper cans the kitchen maids had brought up, she began to plan their journey home. She would begin packing at once. Surely Miss Erica would not stay here, not with *him*, not now.

But Erica refused to listen to her when she proposed

166

leaving Vienna. She told Agnes about the prince's kidnapping, for she knew she had to give her some explanation, but she did not tell her that he had murdered William, nor how the duke had kissed her only a little while ago.

At last she asked Agnes to snuff most of the candles so she might sleep for a while, before the maid was to go and make her excuses to the duke and Lady Liza. She was to say that Miss Erica was not feeling well and would neither join them for dinner nor attend the ball.

"Aye, I'll do that. You just rest, Miss Erica. I'll bring you a nice tray later," Agnes said as she tidied up, darting worried little glances at her mistress as she did so. Miss Erica lay quietly in the big bed, her eyes closed. As Agnes shut the door of the bedroom softly behind her, she wished they could leave Vienna. It was a terrible place if some foreign prince could have a girl drugged and brought to him, and no one did anything to stop him. As she clumped down the stairs to seek out the duke, she wondered what his grace would do to punish the man. After all, Miss Erica was his guest. He could not let this insult pass without retaliation.

She found him in the drawing room sipping brandy and brooding before the fire, and she gave him Miss Erica's message. The duke nodded and waved a careless hand in dismissal, but Agnes stood her ground.

He did not appear to notice that she had remained, and finally she gave a gruff little cough. Owen Kingsley turned and inspected her with his cold black eyes, not a muscle moving in his harsh face.

"There was something more?" he asked in his usual drawl.

Agnes took a deep breath. "Indeed there is, your grace," she said, her eyes snapping. "What do you plan to do to pay that there Swedish prince back for what he done to Miss Erica, that's what I'd like to know."

The duke looked astonished at her daring to question him. "What I shall do is none of your affair," he said. "You may leave me."

"No, I won't," Agnes said stoutly. "He should be punished, and you're the only one who can do it."

The duke half-rose from his chair, but she held her

ground. She saw what she hoped was a small glimmer of
admiration pass over his dark face. "He shall be punished eventually," he said. "Unfortunately, it is not possible to call him out now."

"Why not?" Agnes asked, hands on hips.

"Think, woman!" the duke said. "To do so would be
to give all Vienna a spicy *on dit.* Erica's name would be
on every tongue, and she would be ruined in spite of the
fact that she escaped him. Is that what you want for
her?"

Agnes shook her head, and then she curtsied, her face
thoughtful. As she turned to leave, the duke murmured
behind her, "Thank heaven I have satisfied you at last,
Miss Watts. I was afraid you were going to take root
here."

Agnes did not pause as she marched to the door. She
didn't like the duke one little bit, but she could see the
wisdom of his words. And it was bad enough that Miss
Erica had discarded her blacks and was pretending to be
someone else in Vienna, without adding gossip to her
plate.

When she brought up a tray two hours later, she found
her mistress staring up at the silk canopy over her bed.
She helped her to sit up, and as she arranged the lace-
edged pillows behind her, begged her to make a good
meal.

But the tray she removed later had barely been touched.
Agnes shook her head at the little Miss Erica had eaten.

Erica was glad when Agnes finally left her at last. She
had slept earlier, worn out from her experiences that
afternoon, but now she knew she had to think, and think
hard.

She sat up in bed and pulled the spare blanket over her
shoulders. The fire Agnes had banked was still glowing,
and she stared into it, wondering if she would ever, ever
understand. She wasted no time thinking of Prince Eric
and what he had done. He was a terrible man, but she
would make sure he never had a chance to come near her
again, even if she had to take not only Agnes but also a
sturdy footman every time she stepped outdoors.

No, it was the Duke of Graves and the kiss they had
shared that troubled her. Erica clutched the blanket tighter

as a little shiver ran over her body. She wondered why he had kissed her at all. He had never appeared to care for her or think of her as anything but the spy he was using here at the congress. He had always treated her to a cold indifference, never bothering to be pleasant or friendly. Perhaps he had been sorry to see her crying, she thought. But she knew instinctively that Owen Kingsley was not the kind of man who would be moved by a woman's tears. And he had been so angry with her when she first came in looking the perfect wanton he had called her once before, with her hair loose and her gown undone.

But he *had* kissed her. Not with anger or rough passion, or even the eager lust the prince had shown her. Her eyes widened and began to glow as she remembered that kiss. He had begun so gently, that even though she had been startled, she had not been afraid, not while held in those strong, safe arms. She had been unable to resist returning that kiss and putting her own arms around his neck. His lips had seemed made to fit hers; she could still feel their firm contours when his kiss had deepened and grown more intense. Yet she had not been terrified of him, as she had been of the prince. Somehow their embrace had seemed so irrevocable, so right.

And then she shook her head. And what do you know about it, my girl? she asked herself. The duke was only the third man you have ever kissed! First, there had been William. His kisses had been hearty and brief, and she had felt nothing in response, not even when he made love to her. She remembered lying in bed staring up into the darkness as he snored beside her, and wondering if this quick, fumbling release he sought was all there was to love and marriage.

The prince was the next man who had kissed her, of course. It was true his practiced expertise had drawn a response from her, but it was not a comfortable feeling, but rather one that evoked fear and, somehow, shame. Could it be because she did not love him that his kisses had been so alarming? But if that were true, did the way she had felt in Owen Kingsley's arms mean she was in love with him? Erica shook her head. That could not be.

She would admit she found him a fascinating man, although one who was difficult to fathom. But how could she love someone so shallow, so prone to play the fool? She thought of her father and her brothers, brave men all, and steady and serious. She had always revered them, and when she had thought of her future lover sometimes, as all girls did, she had imagined him in their image.

And how was it possible to care for someone who treated you like an idiot, a tool, and who spoke to you only to give you orders and instructions? she wondered. Owen Kingsley was a man who kept himself locked away behind high private walls, revealing nothing of his past, his dreams for the future, or his deepest yearnings.

The candle beside her bed sputtered, and she saw it was almost gone. Suddenly she was very tired. She yawned, and discarding the blanket she had wrapped around her shoulders, snuggled down under the covers again. Tomorrow, she thought drowsily. I'll think about it again tomorrow.

Downstairs, in the library, Owen Kingsley was also staring into a fire, but this one burned brightly, since Rudge had just added more wood when he came in to replenish the brandy decanter.

The duke had eaten dinner with Lady Liza. He had explained that Erica would not be joining them because she had been caught in the rain and taken a chill. He was abstracted as he added that he himself would not be attending the ball that evening, and so he did not notice the secret little smile Lady Liza wore as she drank her soup.

She had gone to the ball some hours ago, and he had spent the evening alone. For once he did not think of Liza and what she might be up to with her Russian lover. He knew the affair with Prince Gorsky was coming to a head, for the agent he had hired to watch her had reported her every move. The prince must either marry her or relinquish her. The Lady Eliza Ridgely must not become just another mistress, but Owen Kingsley told himself he would deal with that when the time came.

Tonight he had to think about Erica and what had passed between them.

He still did not know why he had taken her in his arms and kissed her. It was most unlike him. His only experiences in the past had been brief encounters with prosti-

tutes, for which he mocked himself later. But he knew
he had kissed Erica Stone as a man would kiss a woman
with whom he was deeply in love.

Owen Kingsley remembered how furious he had been
when he had seen her coming in looking as she had. Was
his reaction jealousy? He felt a black rage still that the
prince had dared to abduct her, touch her, while he knew
he could do nothing about it—not yet. He grimaced and
sipped his brandy. Was he feeling proprietary toward the
girl, he wondered, because she was, after all, a woman
he had hired to spy for him? Wouldn't he be just as
angry if a servant of his had been treated that way?

He laughed harshly, knowing that not only he would
not, he was evading the real problem of his attraction for
her. Erica Stone was a beautiful woman. It would be
hard for any man not to want her. But she was more than
a lovely face and body. He admitted she had impressed
him, not only with her pleasant personality and good
manners, but with her courage and intelligence as well.
And what a quick wit she had! To think she had gone to
the mighty yet unknown Castlereagh in spite of him, she
was so determined to help her country. He smiled a little
as he thought of that. Then he remembered how she had
spoken up to him more than once, and become angry
when he had treated her like the foolish woman she was
not. Suddenly he could hear her saying in an airy little
voice that she was not an *ordinary* woman. How true a
statement that was!

He rose and went to lean on the mantel, his crippled
leg braced on the fender as he brooded down into the
fire. He knew he could never have any woman, never
mind Erica Stone, on the terms he wanted. He accepted
that, for he had always known it. But then, why did you
kiss her? his conscience asked. You are not some tender
young man to be swayed either by a woman's beauty or
by her grief.

I think I went to her because she cried without making
a sound, he admitted to himself. How like her that was,
to be so valiant. And although she had never said so, he
knew how much she hated the role she was forced to play
here, although she performed her part with a calm good
sense he could only applaud. He knew Erica would love

deeply someday, but he also knew she would love that
way only once. Not for her the casual love affairs all
Vienna was so intent on. The man who won her love
would be rich beyond belief. How sad it was that he
would not be that man—that he never *could* be that man.

He sat down again, and as he stretched out his lame
leg to ease the familiar ache in it, he stared down at it
with loathing. It was several moments later before he
shook his head. So, he told himself, you must pretend
that you kissed her because you admired her, for there
can be nothing more. But this prosaic acceptance of the
facts did not ease his mind. He could still feel her soft
lips opening under his, feel her pliant curves pressed
against him, breast and hip and thigh. He could still feel
her hands in his hair, hear her voice whispering his
name, see the light that began to glow in those beautiful
green eyes.

He cursed, and tossed down the remaining brandy in
his snifter with a complete disregard for its distinguished
age.

He knew he had no choice but to keep his distance. He
would be cold and correct, treat their embrace as if it had
been merely the lesson he told her it was, something that
would ease her over her memories of the ruttish prince.
He wondered if she believed what he had told her. To his
own ears it had sounded a rather lame explanation.

The duke rose and staggered a little from the amount
of brandy he had consumed. He cursed silently and at
length as he limped to the door, calling himself every
kind of fool, and in more ways than one. His work here
at the congress was going well, and nothing—nothing!
—must jeopardize it, most certainly not a slim girl with
speaking eyes and hair so glorious he never saw it without wanting to bury his face in it. His work was all-
important, not only to him but also to his country. He
would be on his guard to remember that, he promised
himself.

As he climbed the stairs slowly, he reviewed the net-
work of spies he had set up so carefully here in Vienna.
There was his groom, Albert Pray, such a gray little man.
He was not really a groom at all, but he had been
brought from England because of his fluent French and

German and his ability to blend so easily into the background. Then there were the Austrian and German grooms employed at the Hofburg. It had taken a great deal of gold to win their allegiance, but the news they delivered was more than worth it. People of the nobility were prone to speak openly in front of servants, almost as if they believed the lower orders were all deaf. And no one would ever think anything of his conversing so often with grooms, not when he had so painstakingly set up the charade of his intense interest in horses and blood stock, and his complete unconcern in the work of the congress.

There was also the French prostitute Mimi Lebrun. The duke grimaced again. No one would suspect that his visits to her were only to collect all the pillow talk she had gleaned from her customers. She had the added advantage of living close to Lord Castlereagh's headquarters in the Minoritenplatz. Indeed, the back of the house where she had rooms shared the alley that led to m'lord's back door.

As the duke reached his rooms, he paused and stared at another door further down the hall. There was also Erica Stone, he reminded himself. The information she could glean would be more valuable than all the rest put together. He must remember that, and still these infantile, fruitless longings he had.

Erica woke at her usual hour the next morning, but she did not feel much refreshed by the long sleep she had had. Agnes begged her to stay in bed and rest, and Erica found she was not hard to persuade. Every time she thought of dressing to go down and meet the duke's cold black eyes, she flinched.

It was early afternoon before the maid came up with a note from Owen Kingsley. Erica was seated at the desk in her sitting room, trying to write a letter describing the congress to her brother Mark. When she saw the duke's spiky black handwriting, her pen dropped from nerveless fingers.

His note began abruptly. He told her the count had called and had been very upset to find her still indisposed. He said he had made an appointment for her to go for a drive in the Vienna Woods with him at two, since there was no reason he could see for her to continue to hide upstairs, not when there was a job to be done. "I do assure you, Erica, Prince Eric will not dare accost you, not with Count Andrei standing guard," he wrote. He then said he had spent the morning making calls, and since no one had mentioned her name in connection with the Swedish prince, it was obvious she had had a lucky escape. Below his name he had added a postscript. "I have arranged for Percy, the youngest and strongest footman, to attend you whenever you leave the house. Agnes Watts may frighten me, but I am not sure she would intimidate an ardent, angered Adonis."

Erica reread the note, her eyes thoughtful. It sounded just like the duke. There wasn't a hint of the man who had held her in his arms and kissed her so tenderly. She sighed as she rose to dress. He was right. It was cowardly of her to hide, she thought. Her father would be ashamed of her.

Still, she was relieved when she came downstairs shortly before two, to discover the duke had gone to inspect the horses at a famous stud farm outside Vienna.

The weather had turned colder all at once, and the count himself spread a fur rug over her knees. "I cannot to have you getting cold, my bird," he said as he took his seat beside her. "No, no! Nothing must happen to you, lest you become ill again. I was so sad when you did not come to the ball last evening, and there is nothing in the world to equal a sad Russian, you know."

He laughed uproariously and patted her knee. Erica tried to smile as he added, "But today I am happy again, for I have captured you, and we are alone."

"All is going well for you and the czar?" Erica asked, wishing his intent gray eyes were not so fervent.

"Better and better," he told her. "Alexander has chastised both the Austrian and Prussian ministers for their foolish plans for Poland." He laughed again. "Your Castlereagh is left standing alone, or as good as. You remember, my bird, I told you the czar is a wise man. We have even heard that some of Castlereagh's staff are having second thoughts about his ability to handle the negotiations."

"Indeed?" Erica made herself say. "But how did you

find out? I have been told the British are very secretive, that the secretaries stay up long into the night burning papers, and that all correspondence is carried in diplomatic bags by special couriers."

Count Andrei grinned as he put one finger next to his nose. "I cannot tell you *how,* but I *can* tell you that we have our sources, oh, yes! Baron Hager is not the only man with spies, and there is very little that cannot be obtained if enough money is offered."

Erica tried to preserve a faint interest in her expression, but inwardly she was horrified. Could it be true that there was a leak at British headquarters? Was there someone there who would betray his country for money?

The count took both her hands in his. "But enough of this dull talk, my bird," he said. "I have made arrangements for us to take tea in a little inn deep in the woods. We will arrive soon, and I can hardly contain my impatience. There is something important I must ask you, little bird, but I will wait until then."

Erica's heart sank. His gaze was so tender, his words so full of second meaning, she knew she must prepare herself for a difficult time. He raised one of her gloved hands and pressed it to his heart, and she made herself smile before she withdrew it.

When they reached the inn, she saw that it was charming. They were ushered to a private parlor where a large stove set with colorful tiles gave off a welcome heat. The table, covered with a linen cloth, had been placed before a window that overlooked a tiny dormant garden. The pleasant gray-haired landlady, who was dressed in black with a white apron tied around her waist that was so stiff with starch it crackled, took her to another room to freshen up.

When she rejoined the count, tea had been brought, along with a plate of sandwiches and one of pastries. While they ate and drank, the count chatted lightly and she was able to relax, but when the servants removed the dishes at last, he came and knelt beside her. Erica's eyes widened as he grasped her hands and once again held them pressed tightly to his heart.

"You can guess what I am about to say, can you not, my lovely one?" he asked, his gray eyes devouring her

face. "Surely it is plain to see that I have come to care
for you, to revere you for your goodness and your beauty.
I thought when first we met to enjoy only a few pleasant
weeks of flirtation, for I must tell you I never thought to
marry an Englishwoman."

Erica stifled a gasp as he went on eagerly, "But it was
not to be a light affair. I came to see my life would never
be full and happy without you beside me. I love you, my
bird, and want to marry you and carry you back to St.
Petersburg with me!"

Erica wished she could look away from those eager
gray eyes, his beaming face. As she stared down at him,
wondering what she was to say in reply, he lifted first one
of her hands and then the other, to cover them with
kisses.

As he raised his head, she made herself say, "You
honor me, Count, but . . ."

He waved a playful finger at her. "Not *Count* anymore, my Erica. Now I am Andrei!" he said. "But what
is your answer? You look so . . . so cool, I never know
what you are thinking."

Erica lowered her eyes to their clasped hands. "I do
not know what to say," she began slowly. "I like you
very much, but I had no thought of marriage."

The count laughed. "But for one such as you, my
Erica, only marriage is possible. Surely you know that."

Erica could feel her face paling, and she drew her
hands from his. "Of course," she agreed, wondering why
her lips were so dry. "But to live in Russia, so far from
my country, my home . . ."

"Russia will be your country, and you will have a fine
new home," the count assured her, still kneeling at her
feet. She wished he would get up. He looked so incon-
gruous, such a big, burly, black-haired man to be playing
the humble petitioner. "Know that I do love you truly,
Erica Kingsley," he said softly.

His use of her fictitious name gave her courage. "I
thank you, Co . . . Andrei," she said. "But it is not for
me to accept an offer of marriage before consulting my
guardian, the duke."

The count's hands formed into fists. "That man!" he

exclaimed. "Such a fool as he, to have any say about your future! I get angry every time I think of him!"

His face above the full black beard was growing red, and Erica said quickly, "Whatever you feel about Owen Kingsley, he is my cousin and the head of the family. You should have gone to him before you even approached me."

She stopped speaking as she wondered what the duke would have said if the count had asked him for her hand. To her relief, her burly suitor went to stare out the window, his hands clasped tightly behind his back.

She was startled when he whirled suddenly and bowed to her. "You are right!" he exclaimed. "In my eagerness to win you, I forgot what a lady of your station deserves. I promise we shall say no more about this, but I promise as well that I shall call on the duke as soon as I can. We will be together, my shining princess, and how happy we will be! And you are not to worry that the duke might refuse me. No, indeed. I am related to Russian royalty, and wealthy as well. There can be no reason to deny our marriage."

He moved toward her, arms outstretched and a beaming smile on his face, and Erica rose to gather up her gloves and muff. "I think it would be better if you took me home now, Andrei," she said, going to fetch her cloak. He hurried to her side and took it from her to wrap it tenderly around her shoulders.

"It shall be as you wish, my bird. I live only to obey you," his husky voice breathed in her ear. Then she felt his lips and warm breath on her hair.

For a moment Erica felt as if she might begin to cry. How dreadful this was, to deceive this good, decent man! She was ashamed of herself. As he led her out to the coach, she drew a deep breath of the cold November air to steady herself, and noted the heavy snow clouds massing overhead. The lingering warm autumn was over, and tardy winter had arrived at last. Somehow the weather seemed most appropriate.

On the drive back to Vienna, the count questioned her about her home. Erica knew she would never be able to invent a fictitious estate with any conviction, so instead she described her real home in Northumberland.

"It sounds a lonely place," the count remarked at last.

"Yes, it is not very populated," Erica agreed.

"And it is in the *north* of England too," he mused, and then his eyes twinkled. "It will not be so much a difference for you, Russia, my bird."

Erica turned away to glance out the coach window, and he chuckled. "But I forget my promise already," he mourned. "How fortunate that we have arrived back in the Johannesgasse! Tell me, my Erica, is the duke at home now?"

Erica shook her head. "He has gone out of the city this afternoon," she said, relieved that it was so. She knew she must have a chance to speak to Owen Kingsley before he received the count.

Count Andrei bowed deeply after he helped her from the coach, and his lips lingered on her hand in farewell. "I shall count the minutes until we meet again, my bird," he whispered.

Erica made herself smile a little before she climbed the steps. At the door, she turned to see him blowing her a kiss. Her eyes widened as she saw another carriage across the roadway beyond him, the cold handsome face of Prince Eric framed in its window.

She had forgotten the prince, and that would never do. She knew he must be furious with her for tricking him and pretending to agree to his lovemaking, before making good her escape. As Rudge finally opened the door after what seemed an age, she also knew that the prince would be sure to seek revenge. More than most men, he would take her deception and refusal hard. She must never forget that. She must always be on her guard.

Before she went up to her room to remove her outdoor things, she asked Rudge to let her know as soon as the duke arrived home.

Agnes was nowhere in sight, but Erica did not ring for her. After she had hung up her cloak, she went to the window, standing to one side so she would not be seen. She noted the prince's carriage had left, and she sighed in relief. Then her eyes were drawn to the Kaunitz Palace as a footman hurried up the steps to knock on the door.

She had completely forgotten Dorothea, and after the

countess had sent for her yesterday, too! A fine friend she was, she thought as she hurried to her desk. She would send a note of apology, making up some explanation for not calling on her as Dorothea had requested.

She rang for a footman to deliver her note, and watched as he ran across to the palace. But Dorothea and all her harrowing adventures with the prince vanished from her mind when she saw Owen Kingsley and his groom cantering toward the mansion.

No sooner had the duke dismounted than she was hurrying to the mirror to smooth her hair and straighten her gown. She made herself leave the room before she could begin to wonder how she would manage to behave at her first sight of him since their kiss.

She reached the bottom of the flight just as he turned from handing Rudge his gloves and beaver. She thought his voice seemed cold and indifferent as he said, "So you have returned too, cuz. Shall we have tea?"

Erica shook her head. "I have just had tea with Count Andrei, your grace, but if I might have a moment of your time . . . ?" she managed to get out.

He bowed slightly and limped to the salon door. A footman hastened to open it for him as the duke said, "But of course, cuz, as many moments as you like," he murmured as she passed him, head averted.

She did not speak until the duke had limped up to join her near the fireplace. She wondered that she could feel so cold next to such a cheerful blaze. Before the duke could speak, she took a deep breath and began. "I have heard from Count Andrei that the Russians have a spy at British headquarters," she said, all in a rush.

The duke's black brows drew together in a frown. "A spy? Are you sure?" he asked, his voice tense. "Tell me exactly what he said."

Erica repeated as many of the count's words as she could remember.

"Are you sure he said they had their own sources, that there was little that money could not buy?" Owen Kingsley asked when her voice died away.

Erica nodded. "He would not tell me any more, and I could not press him," she explained. "But he seemed very sure of himself. I do not think he was only boasting

when he told me that some of Castlereagh's staff begin to
doubt his prowess in the negotiations."

The duke limped to the sofa, waving his hand at a
facing chair. "Please sit down, Erica," he said as he took
a seat. "This afternoon's ride has wearied me."

Erica did as she was bidden, her eyes never leaving
that dark, rugged face. Hardly daring to breathe, she
watched as his eyes grew distant in contemplation, while
one hand absently massaged his crippled leg. Only the
sound of the fire and the ticking of the clock broke the
heavy silence.

Finally the duke looked at her again. "It will be necessary for you to find out more from the count, Erica," he
ordered. "If the Russians do have a spy, we must discover his name and dispose of him as soon as possible."

Erica wondered at his crisp, authoritative tones. This
was the man who pretended to be a fop, a fool? The man
who claimed complete disinterest in affairs of state? But
then the import of his words registered in her brain, and
she started and leaned forward.

"I cannot do that," she said, as crisply as he had
spoken. The duke glared at her, amazed, as she continued, "Count Andrei asked me to marry him this afternoon. I told him I could make no decision until he had
spoken to you, as head of the family."

She thought she saw the duke sneer, and she added
defensively, "It was all I could think of to say at the
moment!"

"You could just have refused him," Owen Kingsley
said mildly. "Surely you know the form, cuz. 'You pay
me a great distinction, Count, but I am unable to accept
your hand for I do not return your regard,' et cetera, et
cetera."

"I couldn't do that!" Erica cried. "He is a good, honorable man, and he loves me. I could not hurt him by
turning him away so coldly!"

"So you left me the distasteful chore, eh?" the duke
asked. Before she could reply, he went on, "It is, however, fortunate that you did not refuse him outright. Now
it will be a simple matter for you to continue to question
him."

"What?" Erica asked, rising to her feet in her distress.

"You want me to agree to marriage just so I can continue to spy?"

The duke's expression was enigmatic. "It will not be necessary to agree to anything," he said. "You may say you must have time to think about it, for it is such a big step. Prattle on about leaving your home, your family; mention your fear of the unknown, the wolves, the barren steppes, the strange language. I do assure you he will wait for you for as long as you choose, Erica."

As he grimaced, Erica lost her temper. "I have told you that Count Andrei is an honorable man. I cannot, in good faith, do such a vile thing to him. To lead him on, letting him think he has a chance, and making his pain worse when the moment comes that *you* agree I can release him, is too horrible an action for me to contemplate. I tell you I refuse, and my refusal is final!"

Her impassioned words rang in the room, and as the duke got to his feet, his dark eyes never left her face. Erica could read nothing there, neither anger at her defiance nor admiration for her standards. "It is unfortunate that you have such nice scruples, Erica," he said, his voice as expressionless as his face. "However, since you are so adamant, I must find another way. What that might be, I have no idea."

"I would be most happy to help you discover the British spy in any other way, your grace," Erica volunteered.

The duke studied her and then he turned away. "Perhaps there will be something you can do. At this time, I cannot tell," he said as he limped to the door.

Erica frowned at his back until he turned, his hand on the knob. "I take it I may expect the count early tomorrow morning, cuz?" he asked.

She nodded, feeling unhappy, and he added, "I shall be as kind as I can, so do not look so blue-deviled. It will be a simple matter to salvage his pride by implying your own wishes were disregarded by me, for I have an English nobleman in mind as your future bridegroom. One of higher rank than the count, and with more wealth. That will soothe his wounded feelings, I am sure."

Erica curtsied as he left the room, and then she sank back down into the chair nearby. She was still sitting there staring into the fire and remembering all his words, his expressions, when the footman she had sent to the Kaunitz Palace knocked and came in to present a note to her on a silver salver.

She opened it with listless fingers, but as she read the countess's words, her eyes widened. Dorothea disclaimed any knowledge of the summons to visit her. "Not, my dear Erica, that I am not glad to see you at any time," she wrote. "But I did not ask you to call yesterday. Surely there has been some mistake?"

She concluded her note by suggesting a meeting on the morrow for a shopping expedition, and Erica crumpled the note in her hand.

How could this be? she wondered. Surely Lady Liza had been most definite that it was Dorothea who had asked to see her; she could not have been mistaken in her words! Her face grew still as she considered the sultry brunette who was the Duke of Graves's young aunt. Was it possible? Could even someone as unpleasant as Liza Ridgely be so base as to help Prince Eric stage his seduction scene?

12

When Owen Kingsley left the salon, he did not go upstairs to his rooms to change from riding clothes, as had been his original intent. Instead, after telling Rudge he was not to be disturbed, he went into the library to settle down in a comfortable chair before the fire to think. His crippled leg was aching abominably, for he and Albert Pray had had to walk quite a distance through one of the poorer sections of Vienna for their meeting with the Austrian groom. As he propped his leg up on a footstool, the duke grimaced. The meeting had been unproductive, for the groom had been unable to discover anything of importance during the past week. The duke had taken note of the man's nervousness, the way his eyes darted constantly from right to left, as if he were in mortal terror of being discovered conversing with two Englishmen. Owen Kingsley shrugged. He did not fear betrayal. He had told the groom at the beginning of their arrangement that he would not hesitate to denounce him to the Austrian authorities if he tried to cross him.

He put the unsatisfactory Austrian from his mind as he recalled what Erica had told him. He knew it was imperative to get the news to Robert Stewart with all speed, but he was uncertain how this might best be done. If there had not been a suspected spy at headquarters, he would have gone to the Minoritenplatz at once, aching leg or no. But now he did not dare. He had been there too many times already; surely his visits must have been noticed and reported, as well as his furtive way of entering and leaving the building.

His eyes grew cold as he considered this. As far as he knew, his cover was unbroken, and that, in the face of the news he had just received, was unusual. Could it be that the count had only been boasting to Erica after all?

The duke shrugged. False rumor or not, he must tell Castlereagh, and tell him quickly. And as little as he dared making an appearance at headquarters now, so too did he shrink from committing anything to writing and having it delivered there.

He rose suddenly to go to his desk and glance over the invitations he had received. Tonight there was a ball being given by Countess Julie Zichy. Would Castlereagh attend? The duke had no way of knowing, but he knew he must put in an appearance himself, just in case, no matter how much he longed for his own fireside this evening. He sat down at the desk and took a thin sheet of paper from one of the drawers and pulled the inkwell closer. He could not write much, but he could trust Robert to read between the lines and arrange some kind of meeting shortly.

After he was done and had folded the paper into a small square, he summoned his butler. Rudge appeared almost at once, and his expression did not change when his master requested that Albert Pray be summoned.

But as Rudge bowed and went to do the duke's bidding, he tried to stifle his resentment. To his mind, the duke spent far too much time in the company of a humble groom, a groom, moreover, who had only recently been employed. But then, Rudge decided in resignation, the present duke was a strange man. There were times when he was everything the most exacting butler could desire: arrogant, pretentious, cold, formal, *ducal*. But then there were all those other times. Rudge sighed as he straightened the cards on the foyer table. He had been only a very young footman when the present duke's grandfather had been master, and at the time he had been terrified of him. Now that he was grown old, he could understand and value the man they had all called "the old duke." He had been a noble it must have been an honor for any butler to serve.

It was not long before Albert Pray appeared in the library. He shut the door carefully before he bowed and came to stand in front of the duke's large mahogany desk.

"Something's amiss, Albert," Owen Kingsley said abruptly. "I have had word that there's a spy in British headquarters."

Pray looked shocked. "Surely not, sir," he said in his soft, expressionless voice.

"Unfortunately, I have the intelligence from an impeccable source," the duke told him. "I have written to Castlereagh, and I hope to be able to give my note to him this evening. If he does not attend the ball, however, I shall require you to make sure he gets it somehow, and without anyone seeing you do it. Don't ask me for suggestions, Albert, for I've nary a one to offer you!"

Mr. Pray allowed himself a small, satisfied smirk. "No need to trouble yourself, your grace. I'll see to it, all right."

"Yes, I am sure you will," the duke said. "Make sure you are on duty this evening. It will be an easy matter for me to hand you the note as we leave the ball, if Castlereagh does not come."

The groom saluted, and the duke waved his hand in dismissal. He did not even notice when the library door closed, for in his mind he was reviewing the British secretaries. They all had access to the information the Russians wanted, and he tried to think which one of them might be tempted by enough gold to betray his country. For the life of him, he could not come up with a single candidate. Of course, it could be one of the servants. He himself employed grooms to spy for him. Then he shook his head. Robert had chosen all the attendants carefully; besides, they would not have the chance to hear anything important. Everyone at headquarters was well aware of the need for the tightest security. It was one of the things that was making the Austrian police chief's life miserable these days.

The duke rose and stretched. It grew late and he had to change for the evening. Suddenly he thought of Erica again. He must remember to have his valet find out which gown she was wearing so he could select the appropriate jewels from the safe. He rather hoped she would wear green, for of all the jewels, he most admired the emerald set that was such a foil for her eyes.

*   *   *

Erica's first thought after reading Dorothea's note had been to confront Lady Liza at once, while anger still burned hot in her breast. When she learned from Rudge that the lady had not returned from a riding expedition, Erica made herself go to her room. The Zichy ball was this evening and she wanted to bathe before she dressed.

When she sank into the big marble tub at last and closed her eyes as Agnes bustled around warming towels and laying out her ball gown, Erica realized that it was better that she have a chance to compose herself before she saw the duke's aunt. She would have to have it out with her sometime soon, but not until she had herself under firm control.

Erica came downstairs just as Rudge was sounding the dinner gong. She was wearing one of her more dramatic ball gowns. It was a deep forest green in color, and the low bodice and tiny sleeves were embroidered all over in a delicate design of silver threads and bugle beads. At her throat and on her wrists she wore the Kingsley emerald set. Matching combs held back her silvery blond hair, which, as usual for evening, was flowing down her back.

Lady Liza was resplendent in scarlet satin. As Erica entered the room, she looked up from a collection of fashion plates she had been leafing through, to give her a knowing little smile. Erica stared at her as she made her curtsy. She could tell from the lady's expression that she had been the prince's accomplice indeed, and that she was delighted to think that he had succeeded with his seduction. Erica's lips tightened with scorn.

Dinner was a quiet meal. The duke was preoccupied this evening, and barely touched his food, and he wore a little frown. Lady Liza chatted gaily for a while, her words full of second meaning whenever she addressed Erica directly, but in the face of barely monosyllabic replies, she soon fell silent as well.

When they reached the ball at last, Erica could feel her heart pounding in her breast, although no one could have known it from her self-contained expression and calm clear eyes. She saw Prince Eric at once. He was dashing in another skintight uniform, but of Count Andrei there was not a sign. Indeed, although the czar and the Empress Elisabeth were there, few other Russians were in attendance. Erica had heard how disgusted the Austrians were becoming with these eastern guests. Enough talk had flowed out of the Hofburg about their arrogance and bad manners to make the Viennese begin to scorn them.

Erica could feel Prince Eric's cold eyes on her, and she stayed as close to the duke as she dared. As was her custom, Lady Liza had deserted them at once for a group of friends, but not before she had nodded to the prince and winked at Erica with a saucy smile that made Erica long to slap her.

Even in her own preoccupation, Erica noted how keenly Owen Kingsley searched the ballroom, although his hooded eyes did not linger on anyone in particular.

The duke felt a stab of relief when he saw Robert Stewart leading his wife forward for the first dance. Sometime later in the evening, when it would not be obvious, he would find a way to slip Castlereagh the note that was concealed inside his left evening glove.

He led Erica to a sofa against the wall and set himself to amusing her in his old foolish manner with stories about the other guests as they twirled by them in the dance. The ballroom of the Zichys was crowded, and in spite of the cold air outside and the snow flurries they had encountered on the drive here, it was warm and airless. When Erica picked up her fan, the duke took it from her and began to ply it for her himself.

Several guests paused to speak to them, including the French minister, Talleyrand, and his niece. Erica thought Dorothea looked especially lovely this evening in a soft peach gown, with roses in her cheeks and her dark eyes glowing. Erica was not surprised. She had seen Dorothea waltzing with her handsome Austrian lover, and for a brief moment she had envied them their happiness, and wondered if she would ever know its equal.

The duke excused himself sometime later. Erica tried to smile, but he saw the fright that came into her eyes for a brief second.

"It will be all right, Erica," he told her, speaking softly so no one else could hear. "I shall take you to the Countess de Talleyrand-Périgord. I can assure you Prince Eric will not dare try anything here." As they strolled

over to where Dorothea was holding court, he added, "If
he should ask you to waltz, refuse him. You have my
permission to be as cold and cutting as you care to."

Erica tried to enjoy the banter and laughter of the
circle she had joined, but she was always aware of the
Swedish prince's angry face, those cold blue eyes that
never seemed to leave her. Even Dorothea noticed it, for
she raised her handkerchief and whispered behind it,
"Whatever is Prince Eric looking so black about, my
dear? Can it be that you have had a falling-out? I long to
hear all about it!"

Erica promised she would tell her sometime soon, then
quickly changed the subject. A fellow officer of Count
Karl Clam-Martinitz's took her in to supper and seated
her at a large table near Dorothea and her lover. Although she smiled and laughed, Erica thought the evening would never end, and she was more than ready to
make an early departure when the duke suggested it
later. She thought he looked tired, and he was limping
badly, but he did appear easier than he had on their
arrival. Lady Liza pouted when she was told the carriage
had been called. Prince Gorsky had not been at the ball,
but Erica had seen her laughing and dancing with a
handsome German officer, so obviously she was not missing her lover overmuch.

No one spoke on the drive home. The duke stared out
at the cold dark streets that were filled with swirling
flurries that could be seen only when the carriage passed
a glowing lamppost. Lady Liza had closed her eyes and
leaned back against the squabs, her full red mouth set in
a petulant line because her pleasure had been interrupted. Erica found herself free to study the duke's rugged profile unobserved. She wondered at the ache in her
throat as she did so, the little feeling of depression she
had.

The duke handed both ladies down from the carriage
and ordered a groom to help them up the steps that were
fast becoming slippery with snow. Erica saw him pause to
speak to his favorite groom, and it was some minutes
later before he joined her in the salon. She had already
removed the emerald set, and now she held the jewels
out to him without a word.

The duke took them from her hands without comment. "Not a very enjoyable evening for you, cuz," he remarked as he went to the safe to put them away.

"Nor for you," she found herself replying. As he turned to frown at her, she paled. "Please excuse me, your grace," she said. "I find myself uncommon tired, and I would go to bed."

He nodded, his dark eyes never leaving her face as she curtsied and made to leave him. As she reached the door he said, "I suggest you remain abovestairs tomorrow, Erica, at least until I have received the count and denied his pursuit of your hand."

Erica nodded before she slipped through the door. She felt dull and heavy, and somehow, very sad. She could not help remembering Owen's kiss every time she looked at him, but from his cold, formal manner it was obvious he had forgotten it completely.

Before Agnes left her for the night, Erica asked the maid to let her know when Lady Liza called for her breakfast tray, for there was something she wished to discuss with her without delay.

It was almost noon before Agnes came to tell her that Lady Liza was awake at last. Erica felt she had been up and dressed for hours, hours that she had tried to fill with writing letters and trying not to think about what was taking place in the drawing room below her. She was sure the duke was refusing Count Andrei's suit in his usual sarcastic manner. She was sorry for it, but she knew that that refusal now was the kindest, indeed, the only thing that she could do that would be at all honorable.

Erica waited several minutes before she went along the corridor and knocked on Lady Liza's door. Her maid opened it and curtsied, holding it wide. Through the open bedroom door beyond, Erica could see that Lady Liza was still in bed, propped up on a number of lace-edged pillows as she ate her breakfast.

Erica asked the maid to leave them, and she shut the door firmly behind her. She had never been in Lady Liza's suite before; she wished she did not have to be here now. There was a musty odor of old scent that was heavy and cloying, and the rooms were very untidy. The scarlet gown Liza had worn last evening had been thrown carelessly over a chair, and her chemise and sandals dropped on the floor. The dressing table was littered with cosmetics and jewelry, and it was dusty with spilled powder.

"What a horrible time to come calling, when I am barely awake," Lady Liza drawled, her dark eyes mocking. "It must be something of *great* importance, dear, *dear* Erica."

Erica saw she was wearing a nightgown so tight and flimsy that her ripe breasts were clearly visible, their large dark nipples thrusting against the fabric. She determined to ignore the lady's nakedness even as she wondered why Liza did not have the decency to cover herself. "It is very important, that is true, ma'am," she said, coming to stand at the foot of the bed. One of Liza's dark brows rose, although she continued to smile over the rim of her coffee cup.

"I am sorry to disturb you, but I had to find out why you told me Dorothea wanted to see me the other afternoon," Erica went on. "Your message was false, as I discovered when I wrote to apologize for not coming."

Lady Liza widened her dark eyes. "But you do not appear at all pleased, and here I thought you had come to *thank* me!" she said innocently. "After all, even though you could not bring yourself to abandon your virginal state willingly, I was sure that once you were forced to lose it, you would be both relieved and delighted."

"So you did help the prince," Erica said, trying hard to keep her voice cool and even, although her hands had formed fists in the folds of her skirt.

Lady Liza nodded, a smile of satisfaction coming over her face. "He was so mad for you, my dear, I was gratified to be able to do it. You see, I could not bear to have you miss such an exciting experience with one of the handsomest men I have ever seen. He might have tired of your girlish reluctance and left you for another. Men can be so . . . so impatient! But now you have been fortunate that he was your first."

She put her cup down on the tray and sat up a little straighter. Leaning forward, her eyes avid, she asked, "How was he, Erica? Gentle? Accomplished? Did he take the time to give you pleasure as well as take it himself? Sometimes an Adonis can be so inconsiderate, although something tells me the prince is a lover without equal." She sighed and added, "I even found myself envying you for quite an hour after you left the house. Do tell me all about it!"

Erica grasped the bedpost to steady herself. "How could you do such a terrible thing?" she asked, her green eyes flashing. "Had you no thought for the terror I felt, my shame and helplessness?"

Lady Liza looked amazed. "You mean you *didn't* enjoy it?" she asked in some astonishment. "But, Erica, that is ridiculous! I tell you that preserving your innocence any longer would have been silly. You have been missing so much! And there is no need to worry about how your future husband will react on your wedding night. You can simply tell him you had a riding accident when you were young." She leaned back on her pillows, stretching her arms wide as she yawned. Her large breasts were thrown into even more prominence in the pose, and to Erica she looked the complete wanton.

"That is what I told my husband, and he never doubted me," Lady Liza went on. "Or if he did, he wanted me too much to complain. *I* made sure of that. He never knew how many lovers I had before him, nor how many I entertained during our short married life together. Men like to think they are the only ones with an appetite for lovemaking, and the only ones free to indulge in it, but they would be surprised if they knew how many young things there are who are just as voracious as they themselves. It is nothing to be ashamed of, Erica. Let your prince take rooms somewhere in town, and meet him there as often as you can. You will soon thank me for my good advice."

Erica stared down at her, speechless, as she chuckled and added, "But come, my dear, do tell me everything that happened between you. It is the least you can do to repay me after all my help!"

Erica looked down at that sensuous figure, the eager face framed in clouds of black hair. "I am sorry to disappoint you, m'lady," she said coldly. "Unfortunately, there is nothing to tell that would satisfy your voyeurism. I managed to escape from the prince before he succeeded in raping me."

"I don't believe you!" Lady Liza exclaimed, and then her eyes narrowed. "So that was why the prince looked so angry last night, so cold," she said slowly. "I wondered why he did not even dance with you. But, oh, what a little fool you were to run away!"

Erica stared at her as if she were some new kind of species she had never seen before. "I came to see you because I want to know *why* you did it," she said, forcing herself to speak calmly. "I refuse to believe your actions were a result of altruism, as you claim. You have made it so very clear ever since I arrived that you do not like me or care to be friendly."

Lady Liza shrugged before she threw back the covers and swung her legs over the side of the bed to stand up. "Hand me my robe, there's a good girl," she ordered.

When Erica did not move, she shrugged again and reached for it herself, cursing when she discovered one of the sleeves was inside out. Erica tried not to look at that lush body, the thick triangle of black curls between her legs that was so obvious in the transparent gown.

As Lady Liza pulled her robe on and tied the ribbons at the neck, she said carelessly, "I really don't know why. I suppose I did it for the fun of it."

"For the *fun* of it?" Erica asked, her voice incredulous. "What kind of woman are you to think the rape of another amusing?"

Lady Liza went to her dressing table and sat down to brush her hair. In the mirror, her dark eyes met Erica's indignant ones, but her expression did not change. "A woman like any other, as you will discover you are someday," she said. "At least you will if you are not in truth the ice maiden they name you. Perhaps I am only more honest than most. I know I have more appetite than others of my sex, for I have been told so, time out of mind, by some very satisfied lovers."

She smiled and leaned forward to rub some carmine-colored cream over her red lips before she added, "Since you do not want him, perhaps I shall arrange a tryst with Prince Eric. It would be such a nice change from my dark Sergei, and I do so hate to think the prince might be . . . *suffering* in any way."

She waved a careless hand and added, "Do go away

now, Erica! And you may take your precious virginity with you . . . it sickens me!"

Erica let go of the bedpost, but she did not move. She did not dare, for she was so angry, she was afraid she might do Lady Liza some harm. "I shall be delighted to leave you, ma'am," she said formally. "But before I go, I must warn you not to try anything like this again, or I will be quick to tell the duke. Somehow, I am sure he would not be pleased with your behavior."

Lady Liza spun around on her stool, her eyes wide and frightened, and it gave Erica the courage to go on, her head held high, "However you may choose to live your life is, of course, your own business, m'lady. But how I choose to live mine is not. Do not interfere with me again."

She walked steadily from the room, but as she closed the bedroom door behind her, she heard Lady Liza's taunting laughter begin, and her lips tightened.

Once in the hall, she had to lean against the wall for a moment to steady herself, and it was here that the duke found her. He thought she looked ill, and he could not help asking quickly, "Erica! Are you all right?"

Erica forced herself to stand up straight and return his gaze. For a moment she toyed with the idea of telling him of his aunt's perfidy, but somehow she could not bring herself to do it. She felt it would make her Lady Liza's equal to be telling tales now, although she knew she would not hesitate to do so if she tried anything like it again.

"I am fine, your grace," she made herself say instead. "I turned too quickly, and it made me dizzy."

He did not believe her. He could see plainly the sick disgust in her eyes, and for a moment he looked in speculation at Liza's door. But when he saw Erica curtsying, he hurried to say, "I have seen the count. He is more than disappointed—indeed, at one point I thought he intended to try to murder me."

As Erica's eyes widened he shrugged. "You are not to be concerned, cuz. The count knows that you will never be his, and he has accepted it. I made the matter very clear. And although I do not think he will, if he should tax you with it, just say you are sorry, that you had no idea your bridegroom had already been chosen for you, but that, of course, you are honor-bound to accept my choice."

Erica nodded, and then she remembered the prince. "I do not think Prince Eric will be disposed of so easily, sir," she said. "I could see last evening that he is waiting for revenge."

The duke considered her from his great height. "Yes, you are right. Always remember it, and never leave the house without taking Percy with you."

Erica would have left him then, but he reached out and touched her arm. "A moment more, Erica," he ordered. "We have been invited to dine this evening at the Kaunitz. I want you to look especially beautiful. It will help your acceptance in Talleyrand's circle. And the Comte de La Besnadière might well be there, and the Marquis de la Jullier. They are two gentlemen whose views of the congress I would very much like to have."

Erica stared up at him, wishing she might refuse this new commission. The duke's face was stern and unyielding, and she was forced to nod before she left him without another word. As she went back to her own rooms, she wondered where this would all end, and when. The congress seemed to go on and on, with no sign of agreement between the nations, only this endless maneuvering and subterfuge. She was so very tired of it all!

She could hardly wait to be alone. She still felt a little sick and depressed from her scene with Lady Liza. She had not known there were women who were so evil, and she wished she still thought well of her sex. But what she had learned of Liza Ridgely, and of Isabella Sabatini before her, had destroyed all her innocence.

The duke watched Erica until she entered her room and closed the door behind her. He wondered what Liza had been saying to her to make her look so distraught, what had left her green eyes so full of lingering distaste. He almost went after her to demand an explanation, until he remembered his appointment with Castlereagh. After going apart and reading the duke's note last evening at the ball, the minister had made it a point to murmur his instructions. They were to meet in half an hour in the Stephansdom, Vienna's impressive cathedral.

The duke, attended by Albert Pray, took a cab there. The groom was instructed to stand guard some distance away and cough twice if he saw anyone who seemed interested in two English gentlemen admiring the rich baroque interior of the cathedral.

As he limped up the side aisle, the duke noted Robert Stewart had brought Lady Emily with him. The lady's smile was fleeting as she moved away from her husband to inspect the tomb of Frederick III, leaving the two men to converse in whispers as they slowly advanced up the aisle toward the main altar.

"I have given your communication a great deal of thought, Owen," Castlereagh began. "If it is true, it is a serious blow."

The duke thought Robert Stewart did not look at all well. His handsome face was set in serious lines, and he was so pale it appeared he had not had much sleep since hearing the news. "Erica said the count was very sure of his facts. I think we must assume he was telling the truth, sir," he told him.

Castlereagh nodded. "Can Miss Kingsley find out anything more?" he asked. "I admit I do not have the vaguest idea how I myself can ferret out the spy, not without tipping my hand by setting everyone to watching each other. And what an atmosphere of distrust that would create, and at such a time, too! You know negotiations have reached an impasse now that the alliance between Prussia and Austria is no more. We are much closer to world war again than we have been at any time since the congress began, Owen."

The duke nodded. As they passed a young woman dressed all in black who was on her knees in one of the pews telling her beads, he pointed to the arches overhead, as if in admiration.

Safely past the praying woman, he said, "I realize that, sir. But Erica Stone's influence on the count is a thing of the past. He has asked her to marry him, and she has refused to play coy and lead him on while continuing her spying. She told me she could not do that to an honorable man, so I was forced to deny his suit only this morning."

Robert Stewart cast a sideways glance at his tall companion. He could not tell how Owen Kingsley felt about this new development, for his voice had been as expressionless as his rugged face. "Then what are we to do?" he asked, at a loss.

"I shall have to think about it in more detail, sir," Owen replied. "Perhaps it is not one of the secretaries after all. If it were, I am sure my own role here would have been discovered by now, for they all know how often we have been closeted together, and how I come and go via the alley, which is hardly appropriate for the Duke of Graves! But I could swear no one suspects me."

Robert Stewart looked a little brighter, for he had hated to think that one of his own chosen men was betraying him. "We must arrange to meet again in the near future, Owen," he said. "Send your man to my stables if you have news. Tell him to give your message only to the groom, George Baskins. I can be sure of him. He has been with me all my life."

The duke nodded and turned away to limp back down the aisle, leaving Lord Castlereagh to rejoin his wife. He noted the widow in her blacks was still deep in prayer. He could see her lips moving, and as he passed her, one black-gloved finger came up to wipe away a tear. She looked so sad, so defeated, with her slim shoulders bowed in misery. He wondered whom she was mourning—a gallant husband or lover fallen on the battlefield? How fortunate the man had been, to have inspired a devotion that existed so strongly even now.

Owen paused, his dark eyes full of pain. And then his mouth twisted in a grimace when he realized that he had been envying a dead man simply because a woman had loved him enough to mourn him.

13

Erica was delighted when she discovered that Lady Liza was not to join them for dinner at the Kaunitz that evening. Although she knew it was impossible, she wished she never had to see the duke's youthful aunt again. Still, for this evening at least, she was able to look forward to a pleasant time. As she and the duke strolled across the street, Erica matched her steps to his without even being conscious of her action.

As usual, Owen Kingsley was dressed in quiet but precisely tailored evening dress. Erica, as ordered, had taken great pains with her own *toilette,* and the duke complimented her on her sophisticated gown of violet silk. "I am sure his excellency will recognize the fine hand of one of his countrywomen at once," he told her as they waited for the butler to answer his knock.

The duke and Erica followed the butler up a beautiful limestone staircase to the second floor, where he announced them at the door of a formal drawing room. It was paneled in gold and white, and on this cold November evening the elegant room was heated by a large porcelain stove built into one of its corners.

Talleyrand came to greet them and bid them welcome, his niece on his arm. The duke saw that there were some twenty guests, among them the two French envoys he had mentioned to Erica. He watched her graceful curtsy to their host, and the smile she gave him when he complimented her on her gown.

"Ah, but these young ladies we both have attending us

197

are an inspiration, are they not, your grace?" Talleyrand
asked the duke, a twinkle in his eye.

"Indeed they are, excellency," Owen agreed. "Erica
brightens my palace with the same warm glow a lighted
candle brings to a dark room. I know the Comtesse
de Talleyrand-Périgord does the same for your establishment."

Erica was astonished, and she did not dare look at the
duke. Never had she heard him speak in such a complimentary way, and so warmly! Instead, she made herself
laugh a little before she said, "Gentlemen, gentlemen!
You must take care lest you turn both our heads, is that
not so, Dorothea?"

Her friend smiled. "Indeed. However, one cannot but
wonder what they are about to request us to do. Surely
such encomiums can only mean a most unpleasant chore
ahead for us."

Talleyrand rapped her on the hand in mock reproof,
his haughty expression softening as he admired her. As
usual he was wearing powder and old-fashioned dress,
and he held every eye. "Naughty child," he scolded.
"Have a care, or I shall send you back to entertain
Princess Galintin again."

Dorothea drew back in pretended horror as the others
chuckled. The princess was elderly and very deaf, and
her idea of a pleasant conversation was to speak out on
any subject she chose, no matter how unsuitable, in a
piercing, carrying voice. This evening she had already
subjected Dorothea to an interrogation about her Austrian lover that had had the countess unable to control
her blushes.

When their host and hostess left them to receive some
new arrivals, the duke led Erica around the room, making sure to introduce her to the two men who were such
important members of the French staff. He saw their
admiration, and he wondered why he was not more pleased
when the Marquis de la Jullier made such a lingering
show of kissing Eriea's hand.

Carême, Talleyrand's famous chef, had outdone himself once again, and the dinner that was served the guests
was excellent. Carême was known for his inventive soups,

and the rich onion one that began the meal was made even more delicious with the grated cheese that adorned its steaming top. Talleyrand was not at all reluctant to admit that the addition of cheese had been his suggestion.

Erica was seated next to the French *marquis*, and, obedient to the duke's instructions, she made a special effort to interest him. She did not think it would be too difficult to do so, for he bent toward her at every opportunity to whisper in her ear. Erica could see he was much more interested in the low-cut bodice of her gown than her conversation, but she did nothing to discourage him even as she felt distaste once again at the role she was forced to play. She knew the *marquis* was a married man, but his wife had remained in Paris, a fact he was quick to mention, along with his loneliness. Erica tried to look intrigued by the revelation.

At last she asked him his views on the congress, but he neatly changed the subject as the footmen served them some white asparagus, and salmon in dill sauce. She realized it would be much more difficult to get this man to confide in her than it had been the boastful Russian count. The *marquis* was older and much more worldly than Count Andrei Ortronsky.

As his eyes caressed the swelling curves of her bosom again, Erica hid a sigh. She did not like the *marquis*, not one little bit. Middle-aged, he was no taller than she was herself, and he had a thin, aristocratic face that she could see he painted discreetly. He was all haughty superiority, holding himself as if he were a man as important as Talleyrand. Erica thought him not only conceited but also unattractive.

During the game course of quails, which were perfectly roasted and garnished with dark red brandied cherries, she tried again. "Delightful as such evenings as this are, I find I am growing homesick, sir," she told him, sighing a little. "Sometimes it seems to me that we have all been in Vienna for years rather than months. I wonder when it will end."

The *marquis* bent closer, his hooded eyes never leaving the cleavage her gown displayed as he said, "But now that I have met you, *ma demoiselle d'argent*, I find I do not care how long we must remain!"

Erica made herself smile at his compliment before she acknowledged defeat, for this evening at least, and turned her attention to her other dinner partner.

Erica was standing with Dorothea and some others, chatting after dinner, when she heard a lady near her say to her companion, "Has the latest escapade of Sir Charles Stewart come your way, m'lord?" She turned a little to listen, even though she pretended she was still involved with her own group. She saw the gentleman shake his head before the lady said eagerly, "It is too bad! I have heard he had the audacity to commandeer a hackney yesterday to drive it slowly past the Hofburg, singing a bawdy song at the top of his lungs!"

The lady tittered and added, "Of course, Sir Charles was drunk, and at three in the afternoon, too. And the poor horse! He had been decked out in flowers and hardly knew how to go on, the man's driving was so erratic."

"I wonder the English brought him here at all," her companion remarked. "Surely he does nothing for their cause with his drunken sprees and endless love affairs. Have you heard of his latest mistress?"

Erica saw the lady lean forward to whisper in his ear, rolling her eyes as she did so.

The gentleman laughed. "Yes, my dear, it is none other than our own lovely Madame Theresa Beauvelle. I must say I was surprised to find her here in Vienna at all. Everyone in Paris knows how badly off her husband left her at his death last year, with all those heavy debts, that run-down château. One would have thought her hard pressed to find the money for such an excursion."

The lady whispered in his ear again, and he laughed again as he led her away.

Erica had wondered as well why Sir Charles was part of the British mission. She knew he was Lord Castlereagh's half-brother, and, it was said, a brilliant man in his own right when he was sober. But he was also impetuous and quick to anger, and, more often than not, in his cups. But then Dorothea asked what she planned to wear to the Carrousel in two days' time, and Erica put from her mind the incomprehensible man who had been her late husband's commanding officer.

It was only a little after nine when the duke came to tell her all the guests were about to take their leave. "The countess told me her uncle is weary," he explained as they made their way down the lovely staircase. "Well, he is a man of sixty, and the pace of his days here, to say nothing of his worries and the manipulations he is forced to, would be enough to tire a much younger man."

He waved a maid away and helped Erica put on her cloak himself. His big hands were impersonal as they drew the hood up over her shining hair. The little snow that had fallen the night before had melted, and it was cold and clear. As they walked back across the street, the duke leaning on his cane, Erica looked up at the brilliant stars overhead. It was a beautiful night, one that made your heart lift as the cold touched your skin, and the exhalation of your breath became a white cloud before your face. She had always loved the crisp, exhilarating air of winter, but when the wind caught the edge of her velvet cloak and blew it open, pressing her thin silk gown against her legs, she could not help but shiver.

Once back home and divested of their cloaks, the duke escorted her to the small salon they used so often. Erica went to stand before the fire, pretending to warm her hands and wishing she might excuse herself. She still felt awkward when she was alone with Owen after the kiss they had shared. She wondered if she would ever regain her former detachment, as he so clearly had.

The duke sat down in his usual wing chair and motioned her to the seat across from it before he began to question her about the *marquis*. Erica admitted her inability to get him to discuss anything but the possibility of an affair between them.

Owen noted her distaste, the way her soft lips curled in a scornful smile, and before he thought, he said quietly, "I wish you would not lose that wonderful innocence of yours, Erica."

As Erica's startled gaze met his, he added, "It pains me to see how different you are now from when we first met. You have become cynical and sophisticated here in Vienna."

Erica continued to stare at him. "But if you had wanted

me to remain the same, your grace, you should not have set me the tasks you did," she said, having trouble with her breathing. "However, it is too late for me to change now. I am not simple little country-bred Erica Stone anymore. I have seen too much, heard too much, . . . learned too much."

Her voice had grown sadder as she spoke, and now it died away. In the sudden silence the duke remarked, "I suppose growing up was inevitable, no matter where you might have been. However, I beg you to remember that Vienna and the nobility here are not the entire world. And even here, things are not always what they seem. Keep an open mind, Erica, and your good heart."

He saw that her green eyes were still intent on his, and, afraid he had said too much, he changed the subject. They sat together for almost an hour, chatting idly of this and that: the delicious dinner and assorted guests, Talleyrand's outmoded dress, and Dorothea's preoccupation with the Carrousel. Once again Erica was reminded of a married couple reliving an evening they had just enjoyed together, and telling each other everything they had heard. The duke even sounded like a husband when he asked her what she planned to wear to the Carrousel, that event that according to the Viennese was to be the most impressive fete to be held that winter.

"The pale green ball gown, your grace," she said, looking down at her clasped hands so she would not have to meet his dark eyes. She was afraid he would be able to divine her thoughts.

"Ah, yes, that green. An excellent choice," the duke remarked. "Be so kind as to pour us both a glass of wine, Erica," he continued. "My throat grows dry."

As Erica rose to do his bidding, the duke was free to stare at her graceful figure and rounded arms, her pale blond hair as she stood at the table containing the wine and glasses Rudge had brought in earlier. Idly he wondered if she would ever relax her formality and call him Owen again.

He took the glass she brought him, careful not to touch her hand. As she sat down again, he said, "I have been meaning to ask you if you have any further recollection of anything Count Andrei said to you about the British spy."

Erica shook her head. "I told you everything he said, your grace," she replied. "He spoke of it so briefly. In fact, I had the suspicion he felt he was at fault even to mention the spy's existence to me."

The duke sipped his wine, and then he frowned. "I have gone over and over what I know of the people at headquarters," he said absently. "I would swear they are all trustworthy; why, I am personally acquainted with most of them, and at least know the families of the rest. But who else can it be?"

"Perhaps a servant?" Erica volunteered, wondering why he was discussing this so openly with her. It was most unlike him.

The duke shook his head. "Servants cannot be a possibility, for although they were all carefully selected, Castlereagh has instructed the secretaries to talk freely only when they are alone. Complete security is always observed."

For some reason, Erica suddenly remembered the French couple and their discussion of Sir Charles Stewart and his new mistress. She also remembered that Sir Charles was often drunk. Might he not, in that condition, grow careless, especially in bed with a lovely woman, satiated and content after their lovemaking?

"Now what are you thinking?" the duke asked, his deep voice a little amused. "Your face was a study in contradictions," he told her. "There were all kinds of emotions chasing each other across it, one right after the other. Can it be you have thought of something that would help solve this mystery?"

"You will think me ridiculous—" Erica began.

"I shall be quick to inform you if you become ridiculous, Erica," the duke interrupted in quite his old manner. "Now, tell me what you were thinking about."

Erica put her wineglass down, a little frown between her brows. "It is probably nothing at all," she said slowly, "but tonight I heard two of the guests talking about Sir Charles Stewart and his new mistress. She is a French widow, a Madame Theresa Beauvelle."

"But what does Sir Charles or his new mistress have to do with spying?" the duke asked. "Surely you cannot think *he* would go to the Russians?"

Erica heard his impatience, and she hurried to say, "No, no, of course not! It was only that I remembered Andrei saying how easy it was to get information if you offered enough money for it. And tonight I heard how poor Madame Beauvelle is. It seems her husband left her with a mountain of debts and an impoverished estate. The gentleman talking about her was surprised she even had the means to travel and stay here. It occurred to me that she herself might be the spy. Perhaps she scraped together enough money to come here in search of a rich husband or a generous lover, and found out when she arrived how very lucrative spying could be. She might well be wheedling the information out of Sir Charles when he is in his cups or in her bed."

She stopped and put her hands over her mouth. She had been thinking out loud, and she was horrified at what she had just said to the Duke of Graves.

He did not appear to notice, for he was frowning himself now. "But Sir Charles knows the delicacy of the negotiations," he argued in rebuttal. "He would not jeopardize the peace, England's interests . . ."

Suddenly he stopped speaking, and emboldened, Erica asked, "But does he think of England when he has been drinking heavily, sir?"

The two of them stared at each other, and then Owen nodded. "Perhaps not. This must be investigated," he said, tossing off the rest of his wine before he rose and picked up his cane.

Before he could excuse himself, Erica asked him quickly why he so often played the fool. He stared at her as she went on, "I know you are not a fool, and yet you seem content to let other, less worthy men mock you. Why is that, when you are the least foolish man I have ever known?"

She waited, a little breathless at her daring, and he shrugged. "I have a reason, Erica," he said. "A reason it is better you do not know. I do, however, thank you for the compliment."

As he bowed, he added, "In this matter you must trust

me and believe that I know what I am about. And now, I must ask you to excuse me. I need to think about what we have discussed, and make some plans."

Erica rose in turn. "Of course, your grace. But I do hope you will allow me to help you if that is possible."

She found she was holding her breath as she watched him limp to the door of the salon. He paused there and said, "We shall see. Since a woman is involved, you might very well be able to do something. I bid you good night."

Erica stayed in the salon for some time, deep in thought. It was very strange. Sometime during their discussion, she had reached a decision about the Duke of Graves and his reasons for being here in Vienna. She had wondered on other occasions at his posing in public as a silly dilettante, interested only in horses and amusing himself, for she knew he was not silly. Nor could she believe any longer that he had set her to spying merely to satisfy some whim of his to be first with the news, as he had told her originally. He was playing a part, even as she was, although for what reason, she could not tell. She did not know why he would not explain it to her. Was it because he did not trust her? She shook her head. It was true they had not known each other for very long, after all. But then she remembered that Owen never spoke of himself, neither his past nor his dreams and ambitions for the future. Yet tonight she had become sure that he had a very good reason for everything he did here, that he had come with a definite purpose in mind. She hoped she would discover what it was before she had to go home.

She did not see the duke all the following day, and she wondered what he had been doing. Just before the dinner gong, Lady Liza came into the drawing room, dressed for the theater. Erica was amazed at how casually the lady behaved, almost as if they had never had a confrontation at all. To make conversation, Erica asked if Liza had any idea of the duke's whereabouts.

"He will be down presently," his aunt said carelessly as she admired a gold bracelet she wore. "He has been out inspecting horses again today, and when I passed him in the hall, he said he has had dinner delayed because of his late arrival home."

She shrugged as she went to a mirror to inspect her coiffure. "How any man can be interested in horseflesh to the exclusion of all else, I have no idea," she said carelessly. "Sometimes I think our dear Owen a veritable monk. Someone should tell him there is another kind of flesh, and very nice it is, too."

She laughed at her own wit, and Erica picked up a journal to read. She had no intention of discussing the duke's lack of amorous affairs with his impossible aunt, even though she herself had wondered at his abstinence. It was so very unusual, here in Vienna.

After dinner, Erica spent the evening alone. All gay laughter, Lady Liza had gone out to her theater party, but Erica did not miss her company. No, it was the duke she found herself missing. He had been preoccupied during dinner, and excused himself afterward, saying he had a previous engagement. Erica wandered into the library, wondering why she felt so bereft now that he had gone. The house was very quiet, and she made herself read a book until Rudge brought in the tea tray and it was time for bed.

The next morning she woke to discover an indignant Agnes twitching back the draperies from the windows as if they were her mortal enemies, and muttering to herself as she did so. "What on earth is wrong, Agnes?" she asked, yawning and stretching.

The maid brought her her breakfast tray, setting it down in her lap so hard the soft rolls bounced on their china plate and the marmalade quivered in its cut-glass dish. "I'll tell you what's wrong, Miss Erica," she said, putting her hands on her hips. "And it *is* wrong! To think of you accepting such a gift from the likes of . . . of *him!* Never!"

Erica stared at her before she poured out a cup of coffee. "What gift? From whom?" she asked, her voice reasonable.

"It was delivered this morning before you rang for me, Miss Erica, so I brought it up with me and opened it," Agnes explained. "I thought it was a new gown you had ordered, and I didn't want it to get wrinkled, crushed in the box."

Suddenly she turned and went into the dressing room. Erica sipped her coffee, wondering what it could possibly be to get her maid in such a state. That it was from the duke, she did not doubt, for Agnes always called Owen Kingsley "him" in that same scornful tone.

Erica's eyes widened as Agnes came back holding a full-length hooded cloak of white ermine before her as if it were contaminated with plague germs. *"This* is what came, *this!"* she exclaimed, shaking it a little.

Erica wanted to beg her to be careful. The cloak was the most beautiful thing she had ever seen. Pure white, and thick and glossy, it was lined with darkest green satin. She put her cup down on the tray with a shaking hand. "Was there a message with it, Agnes?" she asked.

Her maid nodded as she laid the cloak carefully over a chair. Erica saw that she could not resist smoothing the fur as she did so.

"It's from *him,* and this came with it," Agnes announced, holding out a sealed note. "I recognized his handwriting. But, Miss Erica, you'll never, never take it! Why, such a thing would be *terrible!* You are not the duke's relative, you are a widowed lady. If you accept that there fur, he'll think bad things of you. Not that I suspect he doesn't already," she muttered to herself as she reluctantly handed Erica the duke's note.

"It will be all right, Agnes," Erica said calmly. "I shall discuss this with the duke as soon as I am dressed. Please leave me now. I shall ring when I want you."

For a moment Agnes thought to continue to argue, but the look in Erica's eyes, and her tone of voice, warned her it would be most unwise. Mumbling to herself and shaking her head, she stomped from the room.

Erica waited until the door closed behind her before she slit the seal of the note. It was quickly read, for it was as short and impersonal as all his previous notes to her had been.

"I noticed how chilled you were the other evening, returning from the Kaunitz," it began. "Since it appears we must remain in Vienna for some time yet, you must have a warmer cloak, one more suitable for winter. Sick, you would be no good to me at all."

He had signed it abruptly, and Erica had to smile.

How like him it was to be so sarcastic, so cold! She ate her breakfast in a hurry, her eyes often straying to that opulent spill of warm pure white draped over the chair nearby. She knew Agnes was right. This was a gift she could not, *must* not accept. It was too expensive, too distinguished an attention.

Still, when she pushed her tray aside and rose at last, she could not resist going over to the cloak to pick it up and wrap it around her shoulders. She could see in the pier glass how very stunning it was. With only her green eyes and rosy lips as color, she had never looked more the ice maiden that Prince Eric had named her. As she turned slowly, the fur edges of the cloak caressed her skin wherever it touched it, sending little shivers racing up and down her spine. She could even feel the rich satin of the lining through her thin nightgown.

It was some time before she could bring herself to remove the cloak and place it back on the chair.

She did not listen when Agnes helped her to dress and did up her hair in the now-familiar chignon, scolding and advising all the while. After the maid's first few sentences, she knew the rest would be mere repetition. Nevertheless, she hugged her before she left the room to seek out the duke.

She found him in the breakfast salon, deep in reading his morning post. As she hestitated at the door, he looked up, his rugged face immobile.

"If I might see you, your grace?" she asked.

He nodded, and she made herself take the seat beside him that Rudge was holding out for her.

"Pour Miss Kingsley some coffee, Rudge," the duke instructed. Then, turning to Erica he added, "You have had breakfast, cuz?"

"Thank you, yes," Erica replied, smiling at the old butler as he filled her cup.

"That will be all, Rudge," the duke ordered. "I'll ring if we need anything more."

Erica stirred her coffee. When she knew the butler had gone, she raised her eyes to Owen's, but she was not allowed to speak.

" 'I thank your grace for the lovely furs,' " he began, his voice cold and his face still expressionless. " 'However, I find I cannot accept a gift of such munificence. It would not be at all . . . fitting for a lady in my position, one, moreover, who is not a relative.' "

Erica stared at him. He had taken the words right out of her mouth! Why, he had even sounded the prim young thing, all sensibility and correctness.

"Do I have it right, Erica?" he asked, passing her the cream and sugar.

Erica put up her chin. She had come in determined to reject the gift of the cloak, and his mockery had only reinforced her decision.

But before she could begin her refusal, the duke continued, "Yes, yes, I am sure you have a great deal to say! But in order to save time, allow me to refute all your arguments at once. A, it is true you are not a relative of mine, but here in Vienna you play my beloved cousin. And B, it is also true the cloak was expensive. However, since it is well known throughout the *ton* that I have wealth beyond imagining, not even white ermine will be remarked. It is just the sumptuous fur the Duke of Graves might give his lovely cousin, if, indeed, her father, Reginald Kingsley, had not already done so, since it is the only fur that could begin to do her justice. And C, no, your velvet cloak will not do very well at all. What possible help do you think you will be, sick in bed with pleurisy, coughing and wheezing and miserable? Do be sensible, Erica!"

Erica waited for a moment, a look of polite interest on her face. "Are you quite through, your grace?" she asked, her voice courteous. At the duke's nod, she went on, "Although I hesitated to interrupt you, I must—"

"Most wise of you," Owen remarked as he poured himself another cup of coffee. "I am likely to become irritated when I am interrupted."

"So am I!" Erica said quickly, her green eyes flashing now.

The duke's brows rose, but he made a courtly gesture. "Do go on, cuz. I promise you may speak for as long as you care to," he said almost meekly.

Erica wondered if she were imagining the amused gleam in his dark eyes, and she felt herself paling. "You have some powerful weapons in your arsenal, your grace, but even so, I cannot accept the cloak. As Agnes said, it would not be at all suitable."

"Ah, I wondered when we would reach the ever-faithful, ever-watchful Miss Watts," the duke said. "I am sure she had a great deal to say, both about me and about the cloak, this morning. No wonder you are looking a trifle pulled. I do wish you would let me send Miss Watts home. The woman is an abomination."

"Because she sees how improper such a gift is?" Erica asked. "Especially for a stranger who happens to be newly widowed as well?"

The duke put his coffee cup down. "You know, I had forgotten that part of your history," he mused. "Strange that you have not mentioned it lately, or seemed at all intent on discovering your husband's murderer anymore. Now, why is that, do you suppose?"

"You will kindly not attempt to change the subject, sir!" Erica ordered, suddenly angered. "I am not a fool and I do not find the way you are treating me at all amusing!"

"No?" the duke asked. "But people are very seldom amusing at breakfast, haven't you always found it so?" As Erica half-rose, he held up his hand. "Cry truce, Erica! I will not tease you anymore, but neither will I permit you to refuse the cloak. You are here in my house, and you, like everyone else here, will do as I say. When you leave Vienna you may leave it here or throw it in the dustbin, but while you are my fictitious cousin you will wear it on each and every appropriate occasion. I trust I have made myself sufficiently clear?"

His voice had grown cold again, cold and stern, and Erica saw that any further argument would be useless. Here, the Duke of Graves was omnipotent. She nodded, and rose to curtsy without protesting further. As she walked to the door of the salon, Owen spoke again. "By the way, Erica, was it the right length? I told the furrier that the top of your head came just to my shoulder, and he made the cloak to that measurement."

Without thinking, Erica nodded again, and the duke smiled. "I knew you could not resist trying it on," he said smugly.

Erica longed to tell him exactly what she thought of

him, but she took a deep breath, turned on her heel, and left the room. As she closed the door behind her, she could hear his deep chuckle, and it did nothing to improve her mood.

When they met again in the hall later that morning, she was still angry and upset after the stormy scene she had had with her maid. When the duke asked her to drive out with him, she refused, her voice as cold as his had ever been.

Still, she was glad they had a few moments alone that evening before dinner. She was dressed for the Carrousel in the pale green ball gown, but that gown, even as magnificent as it was, paled beside the jewels the duke had sent to her room for her to wear. She had been stunned to discover not only the emerald set but also the diamonds. She felt overdressed, almost weighed down with the fortune that hung around her neck and glittered on her wrists, fingers, and ears. There was even a delicate diamond tiara she had never seen before. She wished she might refuse at least half the jewels, but the duke's valet had been most insistent that his grace expected her to wear them all.

As she entered the drawing room and curtsied to Owen, he raised his quizzing glass in inspection. "Excellent," he said, without the trace of a smile. "I know you think my choice this evening excessive, cuz, but I do assure you every woman there tonight will be decked out as you are. I have heard some of them are even borrowing jewels from relatives. You and I might consider all this a vulgar display, but you will be right in fashion. The gown is stunning, by the way."

"I wonder you can even notice it, your grace," Erica said as she sank into a chair and arranged her shimmering skirts.

When he did not reply, she looked up in some surprise. He was staring at her, his rugged face serious above the stark white of the linen that set off his dark evening dress. Tonight he was wearing a waistcoat of pearl gray embroidered with silver threads. Erica thought he looked much more elegant than she did.

As he continued to stare at her, she had the odd

thought that he was about to say something important, but instead he only turned away to get them both some sherry.

"I am glad we have a few moments alone, sir," she said as she accepted the wine. "I have been wondering since our conversation the other evening if you have discovered anything more of the spy."

The duke looked at the drawing-room door as if to remind her of Lady Liza's imminent arrival, and Erica said softly, "It is all right. As I was coming down, I heard your aunt berating her maid for doing her hair badly. She will be some time yet."

Reassured, the duke took the seat beside her. "There is no news as yet," he told her. "I have set a plan in motion, however, and we should know soon if your suspicions bear fruit. Madame Beauvelle will be at the Carrousel this evening. I will point her out to you. Perhaps you might watch her, unobtrusively, of course. I doubt she will give herself away at a fete, but one can never be sure."

Lady Liza appeared before Erica could question him further, and they adjourned to the dining salon. Tonight the duke's aunt was dressed in primrose, and she wore as many jewels as Erica did.

When it was time to leave for the Imperial Riding Hall, Agnes brought down Erica's new ermine cloak. Her lips were set in a disapproving line and her eyes snapped with indignation. Erica saw her hesitate as the duke took the fur from her hands, but she did not speak before she gave him a shallow curtsy and stomped back up the stairs. The sniff she gave as she did so, and her rigid back, made her disapproval plain.

"How gorgeous! But where did this come from?" Lady Liza asked as the duke put the cloak over Erica's shoulders. Hastily Erica herself raised the hood to cover her hair.

"Our cousin needed a warmer garment for this cold winter," the duke explained. "I told her to consider it an early Christmas gift."

Liza's eyes narrowed, and she looked from one to the other in speculation. "Indeed?" she drawled.

Erica stiffened, and she had to make herself return the

lady's mocking gaze. She had not considered how the Lady Liza, indeed the world, would take this gift.

As they went down the steps to the waiting carriage, Liza whispered to her, "But how very clever, my dear! Now I understand why you refused Prince Eric and why it has been so important to preserve your maidenly modesty. After all, a minor member of the Swedish nobility is not to be compared with a wealthy English duke, even if he is crippled and unpleasant. Sly puss!"

14

The duke had arranged for them to be seated very near the box in which the ladies of the tournament were arrayed like so many colorful exotic flowers in their medieval gowns and flashing jewels. Erica recognized Dorothea at once in her black-and-white ensemble, even though, like the twenty-three others, she was heavily veiled. As the two exchanged waves, Erica wished she felt more festive. There was an expectant air in the massive hall with its many gleaming wall sconces that set off the delicate carvings on the white-and-gold wood-work, paneling, and graceful columns. Every seat in the hall was filled, and she saw Owen had been right. Never, in all the weeks she had been in Vienna, had she seen so many beautiful jewels, such rich gowns. Yet in spite of the excitement and anticipation, the constant hum of conversation and gay laughter around her, her heart was heavy.

Once again Lady Eliza Ridgely had managed to ruin the evening for her with her mocking insinuations. Erica knew all Vienna would be quick to agree with the lady's assessment of the state of affairs between the Duke of Graves and his young blond cousin. She wondered if Owen were aware of this, and how he would respond when he did hear the whispering that was sure to begin.

She made herself talk to the people seated near her, but she was glad when a trumpet fanfare announced the beginning of the tournament. Twenty-four of Vienna's best riders entered the hall single file, each one mounted on a coal-black horse. They trotted at first, then cantered, and at last circled the vast arena at a gallop that seemed to threaten the very foundations of the building itself.

As the knights reined in abruptly before the box that held their favorites, the guests rose as one to applaud and exclaim. The ladies the knights were honoring removed their veils and leaned forward to greet their champions. Erica saw Dorothea hand Karl Clam-Martinitz a white silk scarf which he fastened around his right arm so he might display his lady's favor in the joust.

The exhibition of horsemanship that ensued was magnificent, even by Vienna's high standards. The knights charged each other, brandishing lances that were adorned with colorful pennants. The display was so realistic that once again Erica had to hold her breath and close her eyes, sure that serious injury could not be avoided. And unlike the Russian military review, this evening there was a mishap. One of the knights, unhorsed by his opponent, had to be carried from the hall. Erica was glad it was not Dorothea's lover. Beside her she could hear the Duke of Graves discussing the merits of the horses with another gentleman close by, in his old careless manner. He seemed so untouched by the young knight's fate, that even though she knew it was only an act she wanted to beg him to stop pretending to be so careless and silly.

The ball that followed the tournament, and the feast that was spread before the guests, was almost an anticlimax. With the others, Erica watched the knights and their ladies open the ball with a quadrille. They were heartily applauded and cheered, and Erica was not surprised at the happiness on Dorothea's face. She had worked so hard to make this a memorable occasion, and she had succeeded beyond her wildest hopes.

Erica forgot the countess in a moment, however, when the duke pointed out Madame Beauvelle in a whispered aside. She was standing quite close to them, and Erica had the opportunity to study her closely. She was of less than medium height, but she had a voluptuous, graceful figure, and her dark red hair was arranged in a mass of ringlets above a somewhat sharp-featured face. As she opened her fan, Erica saw the magnificent diamond bracelet she wore that was quite a half-inch wide, and she was discouraged. Surely a lady on the brink of ruin would have to sell her jewels; perhaps the Frenchman had been mistaken in the lady's misfortunes?

As the orchestra began a waltz, Erica was dismayed to discover the supercilious Marquis de la Jullier bowing before her. She tried to smile as he led her forward, all airs and graces. Throughout the dance, Erica made herself talk lightly of the tournament and the display, no matter how the *marquis* tried to get her to agree to an affair. He was much more direct this evening, and Erica was delighted when he returned her to the duke's side. She could tell the *marquis* was becoming impatient with her artless refusal to understand his intent, and she decided she must talk to the duke about him and beg him to release her from this onerous chore. She did not think she would ever be able to get any information from the man, for he seemed to have no interest in the congress beyond the opportunity it gave him for a love affair.

She saw Madame Beauvelle and another lady leave the room together, and she begged the duke to excuse her. He waved a careless hand, still deep in a discussion of blood stock with Lord Hazelbeck.

Erica followed the two women to the ladies' withdrawing room.

They were so busy conversing, they did not appear to notice her as she waved away one of the maids who had come to assist her and pretended to inspect the hem of her gown.

"My dear Theresa," she heard the other woman say, "I have been longing to ask you about your bracelet. Surely it is new, is it not?"

Madame glanced down at her wrist and smiled. "Indeed, my dear Monette. Do you like it?"

She held out her arm so the thick glittering band could be admired.

"I would sell my eyes for it!" her friend exclaimed, envy plain in her voice.

Madame Beauvelle chuckled as she sat down at a dressing table to pat her dark red curls.

"But where did you get it, Theresa?" her friend persisted. "Can it be that your new lover is so generous? How fortunate you are!"

Madame gave a very French shrug. "He is not *that* generous! But there are other ways a woman can get jewels here in Vienna, if she knows how to go about it," she confided as she applied powder to her nose.

Erica turned slowly before a pier glass, frowning a little as she inspected her gown. The movement seemed to catch Madame Beauvelle's eye, for she put her finger to her lips and shook her head at her friend. "But no more of that now, *chérie*. Come, we must return to our party. The gentlemen will be wondering what has become of us."

The two left the withdrawing room, and Erica was not long in following them. She wondered if what she had just heard confirmed her suspicions. Had the lady bought the bracelet for herself with money the Russians gave her for the information she brought them? She had made it very clear that Sir Charles had not given it to her, after all.

When Erica rejoined the duke, she found him with a group that was discussing the czar's absence.

"Such a shame he has been taken ill and could not attend," an English gentleman was saying. "He would have enjoyed the tournament so."

"There are so few Russians here tonight, had you noticed?" an overdressed lady of considerable girth remarked. "And I have heard that Count Ortronsky has returned to St. Petersburg."

She gave Erica an arch glance and added, "It is said that he has succumbed to an illness, too. One brought on by unrequited love."

She tittered, and Erica was not sorry when the duke excused them both. As they entered the anteroom, he said softly, "Yes, Count Andrei has gone. I heard of his departure earlier today. It seems he begged the czar to release him, for he had no heart to remain. You will not be troubled by him again, Erica."

Erica would have told him of the conversation she had heard between Madame Beauvelle and her friend, except Prince Eric paused before them just then and bowed.

"Your grace, Miss Kingsley," he said formally, although his icy blue eyes never left Erica's face. She could not restrain a shiver, being so close to him again.

"Highness," the duke said just as formally. "But surely it has been a long time since we have seen you, isn't that so, Erica?"

To Erica's ears, Owen's voice was insolent, telling the prince plainly that his absence had been neither noticed nor regretted. She could feel the muscles of the duke's arm tighten under her hand, and she made herself say, "Indeed," as coldly as he had spoken.

"May I beg that Miss Kingsley honor me with a waltz, your grace?" Prince Eric asked, ignoring the undercurrents that flowed among the three of them.

The duke stared at him until he was forced to stop glaring at Erica and return that cold, indifferent gaze. Owen waited until he had his full attention before he drawled, "My cousin is engaged for all the waltzes this evening, highness. And I think it would be safe to say that she will always be engaged in the future as well."

Erica could see the flush that began above the gold-braided high white collar of the prince's evening uniform, and she pressed the duke's arm in warning.

"Beg you to excuse us, highness. Come, my dear," Owen murmured before he strolled away with her. Behind them, they left a furious Swedish prince.

"I wish you would not anger him further, your grace," Erica whispered when they were out of earshot. "To do so can only lead to trouble!"

"I doubt that," the duke said, bowing a little to Talleyrand and his circle as they passed him. "Ah, Princess Lieven! How delightful to see you! Don't you agree with me that there has never been a more festive evening?"

Princess Lieven not only agreed, she waxed poetic about the wonders they had been treated to. Erica smiled and pretended to listen, but she could not put Prince Eric's hot anger from her mind. She had seen him many times since her escape from his rooms, sometimes on the street or when she was driving or riding, and she was glad the duke had insisted she take the footman Percy to watch over her wherever she went. She knew the prince had not given up his pursuit of her, although she knew that if he ever did get her alone, there would be no kindness or concern, no love in what transpired between them.

It was very late when they left the ball, and even after they arrived home, Erica was unable to tell the duke what she had learned in the ladies' withdrawing room. This evening, Lady Liza did not leave them alone and seek her bed. Instead, she watched them both closely, her dark, slumberous eyes shrewd. Erica could see she was convinced they were having a discreet affair, and her remaining in their company, discussing the Carrousel, was only a means to thwart them, make them wait for the magical moment they could be in each other's arms. Erica smiled grimly as she bade them both good night. How little the lady knew, after all.

She sought the duke out again in the breakfast salon the following morning. Owen dismissed Rudge to listen carefully to her account.

"It does appear that you were right, Erica," he said when she had finished. "How wondrous a thing is woman's intuition!"

"What will you do now, your grace?" Erica asked, ignoring his sarcastic compliment in her impatience to have the spy unmasked, and British headquarters safe once more.

"I?" the duke asked, his voice deprecatory. For a long moment he looked into Erica's clear green eyes. He had been about to fob her off with some light story as he had before, but he remembered her questioning him about his acting the careless fool in public, and he knew any more subterfuge was not possible, not when he was alone with her and her honest eyes regarded him so steadily.

"I must wait awhile longer before I do anything," he told her, amazed at the power she had over him. He saw her make a quick, impatient gesture, and he added, "We must be sure, very sure, before we act. But I expect proof positive in a day or so. Be assured you will know of it as soon as I have it."

With this, Erica had to be content. She longed to ask him how he intended to get that proof, but his stern expression told her the subject was closed.

After Erica left him to prepare for a luncheon with the Countess de Talleyrand-Périgord, the duke sat on in the breakfast salon. He had set Albert Pray to watching the pretty Madame Beauvelle as soon as Erica told him of her existence. So far, his groom had nothing to report, but surely it could not be much longer before either the woman contacted the Russians or they approached her. And when that meeting occurred, he would have all the proof he needed.

He stared out at the light snow that was beginning to fall. He was not sure how he would handle the situation from then on. He dreaded having to tell Robert Stewart that his own dearly beloved half-brother was responsible, however inadvertently. Castlereagh had so much on his mind right now, so many worries about a possible outbreak of war again, and Britain's inevitable part in it. And Owen knew Robert had overstepped his bounds here at the congress. He had been sent mainly to seek an agreement and ban on worldwide slavery, but he had interpreted his orders much more broadly than that. The Whig opposition had already attacked Lord Liverpool and the Tories about Castlereagh's role here; what might they not do if he plunged the country back into war again? No, Owen could not tell Robert about Sir Charles, not with that on his mind, for he knew how his friend brooded, how subject he was to moods of deep depression.

The duke canceled several appointments he had for that day. For some reason, he felt he must remain at home, in case Albert came to make his report. He spent the day catching up on his correspondence. There were several matters back in England awaiting his decision that he had put aside for much too long. Since he had left his secretary in London, he was forced to pen his instructions himself. By late afternoon his hand ached as much as his leg ever had.

His vigil was rewarded. Shortly before teatime, Albert Pray entered the library to tell him that two Russians had visited Madame Beauvelle only an hour ago. "They weren't in uniform, your grace, but I recognized them," the groom told him with grim satsifaction.

When the duke congratulated him, he smiled his gray little smile. "It was not too difficult, sir," he said. "You see, they were speaking Russian as they passed me on their way into the house. Sir Charles had been there earlier. He spent two hours in the lady's apartments and seemed well on the way to being cup-shot when he left."

The duke thanked him and dismissed him. He sat on in the gathering dusk without bothering to call for candles for almost half an hour before he rose and limped from the room.

For a while there was a great bustle in the hall. A footman was sent running upstairs to fetch the duke's hat and coat, another to order the carriage brought round, and Rudge was told to inform the ladies that they were to dine without him if he had not returned at the usual time.

Owen found Sir Charles Stewart in his rooms, about to dress for dinner, and he was received at once. Sir Charles was some years younger than his half-brother, and hot-tempered and erratic. The duke had little sympathy or liking for him, in spite of his brilliant mind. He was often rude and overbearing, and he was addicted to women and drink. And in this particular instance, one of his casual affairs had almost led to disaster for his country.

Sir Charles was all smiles at first, offering the duke a glass of wine that was refused, and settling down for a comfortable chat. It was not long, however, before the duke's revelations had him on his feet blustering and shouting.

"How dare you, sir?" he bellowed. "My affair has nothing to do with any leakage of information from headquarters! Why, I have never . . . Besides, I am sure Theresa would not . . ."

The duke eyed his florid, agitated face with distaste. Sir Charles was so angry, the veins in his neck looked like knotted cords. "This Theresa is a French widow in extremely straitened circumstances," he reminded him. "She has been seen sporting some new and expensive jewelry. Of course, if you yourself bought her that jewelry, there is nothing more to say, and I'll apologize and take my leave." Owen's voice seemed even cooler and more controlled after Sir Charles's ranting.

Sir Charles peered at him, a little doubt coming into his eyes. Then he laughed and went to pour himself another glass of wine. "You're a cold fish, your grace," he remarked as he took his seat again. Suddenly he was very much the man of the world, striving hard for control and nonchalance. "But even you must know how things are when a man takes a mistress," he went on. "No, I have not bought Theresa any jewelry yet. I had her moved to a better apartment, and I give her an allowance." He paused and winked at the duke. "It is too soon yet to see whether she is exciting and accommodating enough to warrant further gifts. But you know the form."

"I have no idea how such arrangements are reached," Owen told him. "I have never kept a mistress."

Sir Charles appeared stunned. "Never?" he asked in some awe, and then he chuckled again. "Ah, well, there's no accounting for tastes, now, is there? I do assure you, your grace, I'm a broadminded man, although it's strange, that. I would not have thought it of you."

"Allow me to correct any misconceptions you have about my sexual preferences, sir," Owen said even more coldly. "When necessary I frequent brothels. I only meant I have never met a woman I wanted to tie myself to for even a short duration, merely for the sake of convenience."

When Sir Charles had no comment, he went on, "But we stray from the point. It is not only *madame*'s jewelry. She was visited this afternoon by two Russians a short time after your departure. Unless she is . . . involved with others, as well as yourself, I consider that proof positive. Cast your mind back. What did you talk about this afternoon? Did she ask you any questions? How much do you drink when you are with her, and do you remember what you have said when you are in your cups? You see, someone is telling the Russians our plans, and this in spite of the tightest security. It has to be your mistress, sir—there is no one else."

As the duke concluded, there was silence in the room. Charles Stewart sat staring into space for a long while, and then he buried his face in his hands. "Dear God, what have I done?" he whispered.

The duke sat quietly. He knew no response was required, or at all necessary.

At last Sir Charles raised bloodshot eyes to his face. His mouth was twisted with emotion. "Have you told Robert?" he asked in a dead, helpless voice.

The duke shook his head. "No, my lord, I have not. I rather thought you would prefer to do that yourself."

Sir Charles nodded, his expression bleak. "Thank you for that, your grace. It was good of you to be so forbearing. I shall go at once and tell him, and beg his forgiveness. There will be no repetition of this, and you may be sure I will deal with Madame Beauvelle as she deserves."

The duke rose and picked up his cane. As he did so, Sir Charles came to take hold of his arm. "Does anyone else know of this, your grace?" he asked, his florid face contorted.

In his mind's eye Owen could see Erica's lovely face, her clear green eyes. "No one who will ever say a thing about it, sir," he reassured Sir Charles, knowing somehow that he spoke nothing but the truth.

"Thank you," Sir Charles got out before he turned away abruptly, as if he could not keep control of his features for a moment longer.

The duke left his rooms as quietly as he had arrived. When he entered his carriage again, he gave the order to return to the Johannesgasse. He had toyed with the idea of warning Madame Beauvelle that her secret was known, but he found he had no desire to see the woman. Sir Charles would take care of her, he was sure.

Owen told Erica the whole story later, when they were seated together in the library after dinner. For once he was glad Lady Liza was going to a ball with her Russian lover. Erica sat quietly throughout the telling, and he thought how unusual a woman she was, not to interrupt him even once. She had some questions at the end of his tale, however, and when she learned he had not seen Madame Beauvelle, she took exception to this omission.

"But you should have seen her, or at least written to her, your grace," she said, looking distressed. "That way you could have given her time to escape Sir Charles's wrath. Who knows what he will do? Why, he might be so angry he will harm her, perhaps even kill her. Do you want that on your head?"

The duke admired her flashing eyes. "She is our enemy, Erica," he said. "For someone as despicable as she is, no consideration is possible. If she were English, she would have been hanged for her treachery, perhaps even drawn and quartered."

He saw she was about to protest further, and he raised

his hand. "Leave her, Erica!" he ordered, his deep voice harsh. "I will not warn her, nor shall you. Madame Beauvelle deserves whatever she gets."

Erica sank back in her chair, her eyes remote. She knew the duke was right, but still she regretted letting another woman face whatever fate awaited her, without preparing her for it.

And then another thought occurred to her, and her eyes widened. "Your grace?" she whispered, and he leaned forward at the distress he saw in her eyes.

"But in what way am I different from Madame Beauvelle?" she asked somewhat desperately. "I am a spy too, am I not? And therefore as despicable as she is?"

The duke made himself sit quietly, although he longed to go to her and take her in his arms, she looked and sounded so distraught. "There can be no comparison, Erica," he made himself say calmly. "You are not thinking clearly and with your usual good sense. You are English, and whatever information you have discovered has been used only for my own satisfaction, or to help your country. *Madame* spied for personal gain, for money; she had no higher motives. Do not let me hear you say anything so ridiculous again!"

"But I *have* spied for personal gain," Erica mused in a sad little voice. "I agreed to your offer so I could stay in Vienna and find out who murdered William. And I have accepted all those beautiful clothes, the ermine cloak—why, I am as guilty as *madame!*"

Owen Kingsley rose and came to lean over her. He grasped the arms of her chair tightly, lest he lose his head and sweep her up to embrace her. As he stared at her, he saw how hard she was trying to control herself.

"I tell you again, you are nothing like her, nor are you guilty of anything more than the sin of helping your country! You are good, fine, and I will not have you denigrating yourself!" he said harshly. "Furthermore, your reason for staying after your husband's murder is most understandable. As for the gowns, even the ermine cloak, they are only the necessary costumes you don, as an actress would, to play a part on the stage that is Vienna."

She turned her head away, and he reached out to grasp her chin so she was forced to look at him. "We will not discuss this again," he said. "But I beg you to remember that what you have done, especially in discovering the person who was giving British secrets to the Russians, could only be applauded if it were to become known. Why, Castlereagh himself would have the Prince Regent decorate you with the highest medal in the realm if it were possible."

Owen wondered if he had said enough to convince her. He did not straighten up or let go of her chin until he saw a little amusement come over her face at the thought of the Regent pinning a medal to the front of her gown. At that, he made himself limp back to his chair and pick up the book he had been reading earlier.

As he opened it, Erica said, "I will accept your assessment of the situation, sir. Indeed, it is more comfortable than my previous thought." She paused for a moment, and then she said quickly, in an unsteady voice, "How I wish it were all over, this congress! I have hated what I had to do every moment I have been here. If only I could have done with spying and subterfuge!"

For one wild moment the duke wished he could release her from her promise. She had sounded almost desperate in her dislike for the course he had set her. But he knew that was not possible. No, until the congress concluded, Erica Stone must remain here and continue to help him. England came first. He made himself ignore the pleading in her eyes, and his own feelings, as he said, "Again I beg you to remember that what you do is invaluable. And negotiations are coming to a head, one way or the other, or so I have been told. You will soon be able to go home again."

Erica had no comment to make about such optimism. They sat quietly together without speaking for a while, Erica gazing into the fire lost in her thoughts, while the duke, his book forgotten, admired her cameo profile. He was thinking how wonderful it would be if he could spend all the evenings he had left to him on earth just like this, when she turned toward him.

Erica was startled when she saw his intent, serious gaze. Had he been watching her all this time? She had been sure he was reading his book, but there was a light in his dark eyes that she had never seen there. Before she could even wonder what it meant, it was gone.

"Your grace, may I ask you something?" she made herself say.

At his nod, she went on, "I wish you could at least release me from the chore of trying to attach the Marquis de la Jullier. He is not a man to be satisfied with a coy courtship or some light flirting, for he has made it very clear what he wants from me. And I . . . I do not like him." She shuddered in distaste. "His eyes are like maggots crawling over my skin, and when he touches me, his hands are so hot and dry. Besides, he will not talk about the congress or any French plans. All he wants to discuss is *amour . . . amour . . . amour!*"

She made a wry face, and Owen tried not to think of the *marquis*'s lecherous eyes devouring her, or his hands on her soft skin. He was not successful.

"Very well, you may abandon him," he said, giving up the battle without much of a fight. Erica's sudden smile faded as he added, "I shall find someone else for you in a few days."

She sighed to herself as she reached down to pick up her own book. Although she held it in front of her from then on, and remembered to turn the page every so often, she did not see a single word. In her mind, she was going over everything they had talked about tonight, and trying to put it in its proper perspective.

A log crackled in the fireplace, and she started a little. Suddenly she remembered the scene at dinner, and how uncomfortable she had been. Lady Liza had been quite blatant in her hints at the table that the duke and Erica shared more than a cousinly relationship. Of course it was the ermine cloak that had aroused her suspicions. Erica squirmed a little. Only yesterday afternoon Dorothea had also remarked the cloak, and the generosity of the duke. Erica had changed the subject quickly when she saw the questions forming on her friend's lips, the little roguish look in her eyes. But if both Dorothea and Liza thought she was having an affair with Owen Kingsley, might not society come to the same conclusion? Perhaps she should tell the duke what Lady Liza was thinking, what all Vienna was sure to be buzzing about in a few days. She wondered he had not thought of that possiblity when he bought her the fur. And although she felt beautiful and pampered, and somehow wrapped in more than warmth and luxury every time she wore the cloak, still she wished he had never given it to her. It could only lead to trouble.

The trouble arrived the next evening. For once, Lady Liza had no engagement, nor did the duke and Erica. Liza managed to restrain herself before the servants, but when the three of them gathered in the drawing room after dinner, she was even more obvious than she had been before.

The duke was seated before the fire, sipping port, when she said, "I must apologize for not going out, my dears! I am sure you are longing to be alone, and here I sit playing gooseberry! Alas, that I have become a most unwelcome chaperon, after all!"

Owen put his glass of port down on the table beside him. "That will be quite enough, Liza," he said in his coldest manner. He never took his dark eyes from her smiling, triumphant face as he added, "There is no need to belabor the point. Both Erica and I are well aware of your belief that we are lovers. However, I think we will dispense with your innuendos and little barbs now. I do not find them particularly amusing, nor, am I sure, does Erica. Incidentally, you are far from the mark. We do understand, however, that you must ever judge others by your own wanton behavior."

Lady Liza tossed her dark head. Erica could see the storm signals flying in her cheeks, and the way her eyes narrowed, and she put her hand to her throat in some distress.

Suddenly Liza laughed. "Poor, poor Owen," she crooned. "How sad it is that you have never understood the power of love, that you deny yourself its satisfaction and release. There is nothing wrong with passion or surrender, you know." She laughed again, a high, somewhat bitter laugh. "Not that either one of you will ever know anything about it," she added, sneering.

Owen rose then and limped up to his youthful aunt. Lady Liza stood her ground, a mocking little smile on her sultry face and her chin lifted defiantly.

"I do believe you are mistaken there, Liza," he told her. "It is true that neither you nor I will ever know love:

I because the capacity for it has been left out of my makeup, and you because you will always confuse passion with that finer emotion. But somehow I am sure Erica will know it someday. I think it is that about her that makes you dislike her so much, because she will have richness that you will never know.

"But I told you that will be enough, Liza," he continued, grasping her arms so hard she gasped. "I find it boring to have to repeat myself. You will say no more on this subject, not to us, and most certainly not to others. Whatever Vienna cares to believe, at least they will not hear any gossip from you. I believe I do not have to tell you how unpleasant it would become for you if I find you are not following my orders?" He waited until she lowered her eyes and nodded a little. "In that case, I think we will excuse you for the remainder of the evening. Perhaps a good night's sleep might improve your disposition and make you less waspish."

Erica watched as Lady Liza wrenched loose from his grasp and walked hurriedly to the door of the drawing room. Before she reached the door, the duke's cold voice stopped her. "By the way, dear, *dear* Liza, may I point out that any further assistance that you might be prepared to give a certain Swedish prince would also be most unwise? *Most* unwise."

His voice had grown colder and more deadly as he spoke, and Erica felt a chill run up her spine. So the duke had known all along that Liza had helped Prince Eric, she thought, wondering why he had not mentioned it before.

Liza turned, and Erica could see she was very pale. "Of course, Owen," she said in a constrained, quiet voice. "Your wish must naturally be my command. It is sad that *my* wish never became *your* command."

Erica looked from one to the other as they stared at each other without speaking. It was very quiet in the drawing room, and she wondered what had happened between them at one time to make them such antagonists. And if, as it surely appeared was the case, they disliked each other so much, why did they live together? Not for the first time she wondered if she would ever understand the Kingsleys. They were a family unlike any she had ever known.

As Lady Liza left the room and the duke returned to his seat by the fire, she also wondered why he had said what he had about being sure she would find true love someday. And, more important, why he had claimed he would never know it himself because he was incapable of ever loving anyone. She found herself hoping, for his sake, that he was wrong.

To her surprise, he spoke openly about Lady Liza's insinuations, telling her she was not to concern herself with them. Encouraged by his frankness, Erica almost asked him about his relationship with his young aunt, but something warned her this was not a subject he was prepared to discuss. "How did you know she helped Prince Eric, your grace?" she asked instead.

Owen shrugged. "It was a stab in the dark, although I did remember your saying it was Liza who told you the countess asked you to call that afternoon. She will do nothing more, now she knows I am aware of her perfidy."

Erica did not look at him as she said, "But even if Lady Liza does not spread any gossip, don't you think it is entirely possible that society might draw its own conclusions about us? The ermine cloak is such a distinguished attention!"

She looked up, startled, as he laughed. "And why would such conclusions concern either one of us?" he asked, his voice rich with scorn. "It might bother an ordinary man, but as I have told you before, I am not ordinary. Neither are you. What Vienna thinks, or says, is unimportant. People will always talk, especially about their betters. Ignore them, Erica, as I do."

Erica hid a sigh. It was easy enough to say, but she was sure it was going to be difficult from now on to ignore the whispering and the rumors. She wished Owen had never bought her that cloak!

15

At the end of November the duke invited Talley-rand and the countess to join his party and attend a concert to be conducted by the great Beethoven himself. The concert was to be given in one of the halls in the Hofburg, lent to the maestro by the Austrian government, and it was an event all Vienna had been awaiting eagerly. Beethoven was an adopted son, and although he was completely deaf now, and becoming even more eccentric and irascible, he was universally admired. He was also a great favorite of the English. In March 1813 he had composed a piece to commemorate the defeat of Joseph Bonaparte's troops at Vitoria in Spain. He called it "Wellington's Victory," and although many serious students of music pointed out it was nothing more than a piece of pompous trash and unworthy of its composer, it was hailed in Vienna as a triumph. It seemed that Ludwig von Beethoven could do no wrong.

Talleyrand could not be persuaded to dine before the concert, but he graciously consented to being taken up in the duke's carriage afterward. Erica was disappointed that Dorothea, out of respect for her uncle, also declined the dinner invitation.

Since it became obvious that Lady Liza had no interest in the concert or in any domestic matters, Erica herself was happy to oversee the menu and all the arrangements. The duke had not mentioned any further spying to her, and she intended to enjoy the respite while she could.

To her relief, dinner was excellent, and everything went well. Erica realized she had Rudge and the chef to thank for that. Lady Liza served as hostess, of course, taking her place opposite the duke and accepting all the compliments on the dinner and the occasion. Erica did not mind in the least. She was delighted at any opportunity to disappear into the background, for the whispering, the little insinuations she had predicted, had begun, and she longed to be less conspicuous.

After dinner, she was forced to put on her ermines for the drive to the Hofburg. As Lady Hazelbeck and Princess Zichy openly admired them, Erica wondered how anyone could be inconspicuous, draped in such opulence. Why, the rich white cloak was just like waving a red flag at an angry bull! But she knew she had to wear it. Only a few evenings ago, before a visit to the theater, she had come down in her velvet cloak, and Owen had sent a footman upstairs for the ermine one before he would let her leave the house.

Seated in the carriage waiting for Dorothea and her uncle to join them, Erica was glad of the fur. It was bitter cold, and there was a nasty wind blowing. Sometimes she thought the golden autumn just past had been a dream. Now it seemed as if Vienna had always been caught in winter's grip.

The hall at the Hofburg was crowded with some sixteen hundred guests. Erica had never heard a full orchestra before, nor seen the great Beethoven himself, and she stared at him eagerly when he entered the hall and mounted the rostrum to tumultuous applause. Around her people were standing and cheering as they would for an idol, and she wondered at it. Beethoven seemed only an ordinary man, after all. Short and stocky, he had a leonine head of bushy hair. But even from a distance, Erica could feel the power of his piercing black eyes and see his mighty frown. The duke had told her the maestro was completely deaf; she wondered what it must be like to see this madly adoring crowd, yet be unable to hear a single "bravo."

The Eighth Symphony, the music that was played that evening, was unlike anything she had ever dreamed possible. At first she had watched Beethoven, stunned by his passionate gestures and wild abandon. But she soon forgot him as the rich fullness of the music filled the hall, shocking her with its melodic power. Once again, and in spite of everything, she was glad she had stayed in Vienna. To think she might have missed this once-in-a-lifetime performance, that she might never have known the beauty such music had! She knew she would never forget tonight.

At the conclusion of the last movement, she sat stunned, while all around her the audience clapped and cheered. In the confusion, she saw the Duke of Graves looking at her, his eyes considering, and she made herself smile. He nodded, an answering smile lighting his dark eyes, as if he understood the emotions she was feeling, and concurred with them completely.

The balls and dinner parties, the receptions and teas that she went to in the days that followed the concert seemed very ordinary to Erica. As December passed, she heard some rumors of the congress, but nothing seemed to have changed, nor had any progress been made. The czar was still ill, and would see no one but his own staff, and diplomatic negotiations appeared to have ground to a halt. It was almost as if everyone was waiting for Alexander to recover before the business of the congress could be resumed.

Erica went riding one clear, crisp morning with Dorothea, and the two talked about the congress. The countess was completely at ease with Erica now, and she spoke more openly about her uncle and what he was doing for the French cause.

"I fear those black war clouds that hang over us all," she told Erica. "My uncle is so serious, so preoccupied!"

"Perhaps it will not come to war. We must hope so, indeed, pray that it might be avoided at all costs," Erica replied, thinking of her beloved brothers.

"But Talleyrand has asked Louis XVIII for a partial mobilization of the French Army," Dorothea persisted. "Surely, if he considered such a move necessary, he thinks we are close to another conflict."

Erica tried to keep her expression neutral. This was important news, and yet she wished with all her heart that Dorothea had not told it to her. On the ride home, she agonized over what she should do. She knew, deep inside, that she should tell the duke, and at once, but she could not bring herself to betray her friend. But would it be a betrayal? she wondered, her brothers' handsome faces and strong bodies coming to her mind. Could she keep silent when Geoffrey and Peter, and thousands of young men like them, might be forced to fight again, to face the possibility of terrible wounds, perhaps even death?

She went up to her room to think, glad the duke had been nowhere in sight when she entered the house. She was afraid he would be able to tell she had heard something momentous, just from the look on her face. She passed Lady Liza on the stairs, and they exchanged nods. Liza had been very quiet and circumspect since her confrontation with the duke, a state of affairs that Erica was grateful for, and hoped would continue.

Several blocks away, the duke was closeted with Lord Castlereagh in his private apartment at British headquarters. He had entered through the back alley, via the house where Mimi Lebrun had rooms, and he was sure he had not been observed. Now he leaned back in his chair and told Robert Stewart everything he had learned since their last meeting.

"My Austrian groom tells me the French are up to something, m'lord," he concluded at last. "What it might be, he has no idea as yet, but it has been remarked in the Hofburg that communications between Talleyrand and Paris have increased tenfold."

Robert Stewart stopped pacing and rubbed his chin, his eyes worried. "I am aware of it, Owen," he said. "I have even been considering a rather bold new move. It is clear that my original plan has no hope of succeeding, but perhaps if we can get the French on our side, forming a new coalition that will include the Austrians, we might win through that way. I must think it over carefully, however. Tell your spies to remain alert. Whatever they can pick up might be valuable."

Owen nodded, and Castlereagh came and took the chair beside him. "How fares Miss Kingsley these days, Owen?" he asked in some curiosity. Lady Castlereagh had heard the rumors that were circulating about the lovely blond and the Duke of Graves, and had been quick to apprise her husband of them.

"Erica is well, sir," the duke told him. "She is upset at

the gossip that is being spread about us, even though I told her to ignore it. But women, as you know, are so sensitive."

"Has she heard anything of interest lately?" Castlereagh asked.

Owen shook his head. "She asked me to release her from entangling the Marquis de la Jullier, and I agreed. The man's too shrewd to tell her anything, and he was becoming most persistent in his desire for an affair. I had thought to set her to the task of interrogating the Countess de Talleyrand-Périgord instead, but somehow even *I* do not dare risk that. The two are close now. Can you imagine her reaction if I asked her to spy on her friend?"

He smiled a little, and Robert Stewart studied him closely. He wondered if Owen had any idea how his expression lightened and his rugged features relaxed when he was discussing Miss Kingsley.

"No, you cannot ask that of her," he agreed. "She has been so helpful to us, I would wish it possible not to have to set her any more tasks. Why, her discovering it was my brother's mistress who was spying on us was of invaluable assistance."

He grimaced, looking saddened, and Owen said, "I heard Madame Beauvelle left Vienna rather abruptly. That was Sir Charles's doing?"

Castlereagh nodded. "Yes. He told her that if she did not go back to Paris within two days' time, he could not guarantee her safety. At least that is what he told me he said. Somehow I am sure he put it more strongly than that." He sighed, and put his hand to his forehead, effectively hiding his eyes. "I can never thank you enough for the delicacy with which you handled that situation, Owen," he said, his voice constricted.

The duke waved a careless hand. "Do not refine on it too much, my dear fellow. I beg you will not let it color your relationship with your brother, for I know how much he means to you. Besides, it might have happened to anyone." He rose then and picked up his cane, hat, and gloves.

Robert Stewart got up to walk him to the door. "Not just anyone, Owen," he said wryly. "I cannot imagine you, for example, succumbing to such an indiscretion."

The duke stared down at him, his expression unreadable. "Of course not," he said. "But then, I am not as other men, as you are well aware, sir."

After he had left the room, Robert Stewart stared after him, rubbing his chin in thought again. "No, my poor friend, you are not like other men," he whispered. "I wish for your sake that you were, that you would let yourself fall in love as others do, that you did not consider yourself only an object of pity."

Erica could not bring herself to tell Owen what Dorothea had let slip. For days afterward she was preoccupied, and the duke wondered about it. But from experience, he knew she would keep her own counsel until that time when she resolved whatever was bedeviling her. He wondered if it were still only the gossip, or if perhaps she grew homesick as Christmas approached. She had never been away from home at such a time before; surely she must be missing her father, her brothers, and all the preparations that such a festive season entailed.

Accordingly, although he had no heart for it himself, he ordered Rudge to have the palace decorated and a Yule log brought in. He even bought gifts for all the servants and a diamond pendant for Liza. For Erica he purchased a huge ermine muff to match her cloak, and he invited a few compatriots to a festive dinner and carol-sing on Christmas Day.

Erica paled when she opened the box that contained the muff, although she only thanked the duke in her usual quiet voice. Lady Liza was so vociferous in her enthusiasm for the glittering pendant that Erica's lack of animation was not remarked

Owen was surprised to discover that Erica had bought him a gift, as well as some scent for his aunt. He opened the large box she gave him almost eagerly

Inside, carefully wrapped, was a framed etching of the Schönbrunn Palace that showed the Gloriette in the distance. He stared down at it, remembering their ride there so many weeks ago, the things they had said to each other, and the orders he had given her

"Thank you, Erica," he said at last. "How pleasant it

will be to have this hung in my library at home. It will always remind me of Vienna.''

Erica had bought other gifts as well: a warm new shawl for Agnes, and a pretty porcelain box shaped like a bluebird for Dorothea, but she had agonized over her gift to Owen the most. She did not want it to be too personal, and yet she wanted something that would commemorate their time together. She wondered why he looked a little strained as he thanked her.

She had not seen him as much in the past few weeks as she had formerly. Frequently the only time they met during the day was at dinner. But whenever she heard a rumor at any of the parties she attended, she was quick to tell the duke about it, although she never mentioned Dorothea's disclosure that the French Army was being mobilized. She had come to accept the fact that for her, at least, friendship with Dorothea was more important than spying.

Everyone in Vienna had even greater cause to celebrate Christmas and the coming of the new year of 1815. Castlereagh, after considering all the ramifications of his new plan, had moved swiftly, drawing up a secret treaty in his own handwriting which he presented to Metternich and Talleyrand. Both off them accepted it at once. The three powers signed the agreement on January 3. It effectively aligned their nations in time of war, and they were aware there would be war if Prussia did not retreat over the issue of Saxony.

To everyone's great relief, the Prussians relinquished their demands, and even the Russians accepted the *fait accompli* with a good grace. As Castlereagh had foreseen, the Emperor Alexander did not dare stand against three such great powers, firm in their new alliance. His gamble had paid off.

Erica felt more relieved than anyone else in Vienna. Now she would not have to worry about betraying her friend or seeing her brothers go off to war again. She felt as if a huge weight had been lifted from her shoulders when she heard the good news.

She began to wonder, however, that the duke did not suggest she leave for England. Surely there was no need to keep her here, not now. But when she mentioned this to him as they were driving home from the theater one evening, he refused to consider it.

"There is a great deal more to do here at the congress, Erica," he told her. "Besides, you would not care to miss the festive day that is planned at Schönbrunn, now, would you? Or the house party early in February at Burg Kobenzl? Count Kobenzl, I have been told, is determined his guests will have a wonderful time. There will be hunts and shooting parties, balls and masquerades, even sleigh rides and skating. No, no, you must not go home before that."

Erica subsided on her side of the carriage, wondering why she was so relieved. For as much as she missed her father and brothers, something that was stronger than any attraction her home might have for her made her want to stay here. She did not understand it; she only knew that it was so.

When they arrived home, Rudge handed the duke a sealed note, bowing as he did so. Owen took it into the small salon after motioning Erica to precede him. She was glad to do so because it was fairly early, since they had not gone on to a restaurant after the performance. She took a seat and waited while the duke read his note.

She was startled when she heard his muffled oath. Turning toward him, she saw that he was pale, his rugged features grim. As she watched, he limped to the fire and threw the crumpled note on the blazing logs.

"There is something wrong, your grace?" she asked anxiously.

"Indeed," he said through gritted teeth. "The note was from my dear aunt. The Lady Liza left Vienna this evening."

"Left?" Erica echoed. "But where has she gone so suddenly?"

"To Russia, she says, although I am sure she has not progressed very far as yet. It seems Prince Gorsky has been recalled home, and they could not bear to be parted." His voice was rich with sarcasm as he added, "Liza claims he means to marry her, something I very much doubt."

He looked disgusted as he sat down across from Erica and stretched his crippled leg before him. "I have been

remiss, as regards Lady Liza," he said almost as if he
were thinking aloud. "I saw that things were coming to a
head, but I thought there was time yet, that the prince
would remain in Vienna until the congress was dissolved.
Now I shall be put to the trouble of going after her and
bringing her back."

Erica could think of nothing more delightful than to be
rid of the lady, and knowing that the duke also appeared
to dislike his aunt, she wondered why he was so determined to keep her in Vienna.

"But if they love each other, your grace, perhaps it
would be kinder to let her go with him?" she asked a
little diffidently.

The duke snorted. "Love? Liza does not know the
meaning of the word. She is in heat, and that is all. Oh, I
do beg your pardon for my bluntness, Erica, but there is
no other way to describe my dear, *dear* aunt. It was ever
thus."

He looked at her almost as if he were considering her
for the first time, and she made herself meet those dark,
intent eyes with composure.

"I have never told you anything about Liza, have I,
Erica?" he asked. As she shook her head, he added,
"Perhaps it will make it easier for you to understand her,
if I do, although I know I can rely on you to keep what I
am about to tell you to yourself, not only now, but for all
time."

"You can be sure of my discretion, sir," Erica told
him.

"I know I can," the duke said simply, and then he sat
quietly, as if gathering his thoughts. Erica watched him
without speaking.

"Liza was a strange child," he began at last. "We grew
up together, of course, for my grandfather kept the whole
family close, living together at Graveshead, the ducal
seat. For some reason, Liza attached herself to me as
soon as she was out of leading reins, and I became her
big brother. It was not a role that pleased me as a boy,
but there was no denying her. She always had the most
monumental temper tantrums if she were crossed in anything. My grandfather laughed at her, saying she was a
more worthy descendant of his than some others of his

children and grandchildren." He laughed bitterly then, and shook his head. "The old duke was wrong. He was so very wrong.

"When Liza reached her teens, she discovered she was not interested in a brother anymore. She wanted something else." He paused, as if wondering how to put it, or as if he were afraid Erica would be horrified at the telling. "There is no way to put it nicely," he said. "You see, Liza wanted me to be her lover."

Erica stared at him. "But that's . . . that's incest!" she whispered.

Owen nodded. "It is, indeed. I told her I would never agree, but she would not take no for an answer. She had always been so much indulged by a doting, elderly father, she couldn't begin to imagine not getting her own way in everything. Sometimes I would find her in my bed when I went to my room for the night, so I had to forcibly eject her. It was then I began locking my door to keep her out. And sometimes she would try to tempt me by removing her clothes when we were alone. You must understand I was not much more than a boy myself. It was very difficult for me. When she threatened to tell her father I had attacked her if I did not agree to her plans, I went to my own father. He could not tell the tale to the old duke. He knew he would not be believed. He did, however, arrange for me to live in London, and travel. For a while, Liza wrote me passionate letters, but eventually she discovered all the other young men in the world—grooms and farmers and neighboring squires' sons. Her escapades were legend."

He sighed, staring into the fire with unseeing eyes, and Erica took a cautious breath, afraid to disturb him in his painful memories.

"At last she ran away with a Gypsy, and her father, the old duke, could not ignore her promiscuity any longer. He had her brought back and the family closed ranks to protect her. An early marriage was arranged for her when she was only sixteen. Unfortunately, her husband did not survive for many years. By the time of his death, both my grandfather and my father were dead, and I had come into the title. Liza became my responsibility, as she is today. The only way I can control her is to keep her

with me always, and give her no money of her own. She
is my dependent, you see. She ran through two inheri-
tances from her father and her husband. I admit I have
even threatened her with poverty if she will not obey me,
and this has kept her in line, at least until now."

His voice died away, and Erica stared at him horrified.
What a terrible burden he had carried, and she had never
suspected it.

"But you cannot want her to remain with you, your
grace," she found herself saying. "Surely if the prince
marries her, you will be free of her forever. And Lady
Liza is shrewd. She would make sure of his promise
before she went with him, would she not?"

"There is that," the duke admitted. "In her note she
said she had given up any hope of my capitulation, and
since that was the case, Sergei was as good as any other.
And it would be a relief to be rid of her at last."

"Then why not let them go?" Erica asked, a little
puzzled."

The duke's dark eyes inspected her face before he
shook his head and laughed. "But, my dear Erica, you
are not thinking," he said, his voice mocking. "We cannot remain here together without Liza, for to do so
would be ruinous to your reputation. The little speculation about the ermine cloak would be a pale thing beside
the blaze of gossip that would ensue. And how the old
tittle-tattles would relish the tale!"

Erica looked away from him in confusion as he added,
"I shall go after Liza tomorrow and bring her back.
Perhaps I can persuade the prince to wait for her, after I
explain our situation to him, one gentleman to another."

He paused, lost in thought, and Erica sat quietly, wondering again why he simply did not make arrangements
for her to leave Vienna. If he did so, he could be free of
Lady Liza forever. But perhaps he had something important for her to do, she thought.

Owen was recalled to his surroundings a few minutes
later. He stared at Erica's profile, thinking what a restful
woman she was, how companionable even when silent.

"You must be very careful while I am gone, Erica," he
said, suddenly remembering the Swedish prince. "I have

no idea how many days this will take, although I shall make all haste."

Erica nodded. She knew whom he was warning her against, and there was no way that she would put herself in any danger.

When she came down the next morning, she discovered the duke had left at first light, with his groom, Albert Pray, in attendance. They had gone on horseback, since it was faster than traveling by carriage. Erica was a little disappointed that the duke had not left her a note saying good-bye, but then she scoffed at herself as she went into the breakfast salon and allowed Rudge to serve her. The duke had bid her a civil if restrained farewell the evening before. There was no necessity for anything more.

As she ate her breakfast, she pondered again the story he had told her. She had never liked Lady Liza, but she had never imagined her to be such a horrible woman. Yet now a great many things that had puzzled her in the past had been made clear. She knew now why the duke kept her so close to him, why he was so cold and stern in his dealings with her. She tried to picture how difficult it must have been for him, a young man being pursued by a close relative he knew was unbalanced. Her heart went out to the boy that he had been. But he had solved the problem, and honorably, too. She realized that Owen Kingsley was quite a man, one even more impressive than she had come to believe he was.

It was four days later before a dirty traveling carriage with the imperial arms of Russia emblazoned on the door pulled up before the duke's palace in the Johannesgasse in the early winter dusk. It was accompanied by two familiar outriders. Erica was at the window of her room when it arrived, and her hand went out in an unconscious gesture as the duke dismounted and stumbled a little in his weariness. She did not hesitate. Picking up her skirts, she ran down stairs to tell Rudge his master had arrived, and to order wine brought and dinner put back, before she went to the door to greet the travelers.

Lady Liza swept into the house first, her dark eyes stormy. She pulled off her gloves and furs and tossed them to a footman, completely ignoring Erica in her petulance at being separated from her lover.

Erica looked beyond her to see the duke coming slowly up the steps. "Welcome home, your grace," she said as she curtsied. Behind her, Lady Liza made a derisive sound as she went to the stairs.

Erica ignored her as she took Owen's arm. "Come into the salon, sir," she invited. "There is a good fire, and I have ordered some refreshment. You look tired."

"But how very wifely you sound, dear Erica," Lady Liza called down from the landing. The duke glared at her, and she colored and tossed her head as she turned away.

"I will have a tea tray sent up to you, m'lady," Erica told her retreating back, and then she forgot her as she followed a limping Owen into the room they had used so often.

For a while there was only general conversation between them, but at last the footman who had come to attend the fire bowed himself away, and Rudge closed the door behind him after bringing the sherry. Erica brought the duke a glass, searching his face as she did so.

He looked very tired, and she saw how he winced as he tried to find a comfortable position for his leg. One lock of dark hair fell over his rugged forehead, and she had to clench her fists to keep from smoothing it back or bringing him a footstool. She was a little surprised to discover how much she had missed him.

"All is well, your grace?" she asked as she took a seat a little distance away from him.

Owen nodded. "Yes, all is well. I found Liza and the prince only two days' journey from here. They had been delayed by an accident to one of the carriages. The prince was most agreeable to my bringing my aunt back, after I explained our dilemma. He told me he had not wanted to elope with Liza, for he knew it was not the honorable thing to do, but that Liza had insisted on it. He says he will wait for her in St. Petersburg until I can send her on to him."

He shook his head, looking puzzled. "It is strange, that," he mused. "He appears to love her deeply, and yet he saw how she reacted to my appearance on the scene. It was a classic tantrum, complete with screamed invectives and a storm of tears because she was being thwarted. I am sure it would have frightened any other man away. But Prince Gorsky only put his hand over her mouth and ordered her to be quiet. And, Erica, she obeyed him!"

Erica almost laughed out loud at his look of stunned disbelief. "Ah, well, sir," she said with a little smile, "perhaps the lady has met her match at last."

The duke's sudden grin lightened his stern features. "As you say, cuz," he drawled. "Now, if I can only keep her discreet until their reunion. The prince may be prepared to wait; whether Liza can remain celibate is another matter."

The outing to Schönbrunn had been postponed several times during January. The plan was to have everyone travel by sleigh, and the weather had been capricious throughout the month. At last there was a heavy snowfall, and the twenty-second was named as the day for the party. Erica was glad of her new fur cloak that bitter morning, and for the huge fur muff that kept her hands so warm. Lady Liza was also resplendent in new sables, a gift from her fiancé.

The duke's carriage conveyed them to the Josephplatz, where thirty sleighs were waiting to transport the guests. Erica looked around eagerly. The Austrian emperor and his empress were to lead the parade, followed by a bevy of pages and a squadron of the Imperial Guard. Erica saw that the empress was also wearing white ermine, and a hat of bright green that was adorned with plumes and diamonds.

There was some confusion at first, but at last the procession started off, traveling at a walk so the Viennese could admire the festive sleighs and their noble cargoes, and the decorated horses covered with the tigerskins that drew them. At the end of the parade there was a huge sleigh containing an orchestra valiantly playing military marches for the guests on their journey.

Erica had never seen anything quite like it, and in spite of the intense cold, she felt a surge of anticipation. Owen sat across from her, noting the excitement in her green

eyes and admiring the delicate rose the cold air brought
to her cheeks.

At Schönbrunn the guests were served an elegant ban-
quet. It was followed by a display of skating by a young
Englishman from Castlereagh's staff. He performed all
manner of intricate figures, even drawing the initials of
the highborn ladies present on the ice with the blades of
his skates. He was warmly applauded.

Following this display, the guests returned to the palace to watch the opera *Cinderella,* which was followed by
a new ballet that had been commissioned especially for
the occasion.

Erica and the duke were joined by the Countess de
Talleyrand-Périgord as they strolled about admiring the
high-ceilinged, gracious rooms of the palace. Everything
was white and gold, with rich rococo decorations all
displayed in the soft glow of massive gold chandeliers
and candle sconces. Dorothea was much taken with the
Chinese room and the Grand Gallery, and said she had
never seen anything so impressive.

"Yes, but it is strange," Erica mused as they entered
yet another elegant room. "The palace is so rich and
beautiful, and yet to me it appears homelike. I do not
understand how this can be."

"You are right, Erica," the duke remarked. "I never
come here but that I seem to hear echoes of some of
those sixteen children Maria Theresa had, as they ran
laughing through the halls. Sometimes I am almost positive that just as I enter a room, a little girl in a pinafore is
disappearing through the opposite door."

"Ghosts, your grace?" the countess asked with a smile.

He shook his head. "I do not know. However, I am
sure if there are any ghosts here, they are happy ones. It
is such a happy place."

It was with reluctance that the guests finally went out
to the sleighs again. It was very late, and bitterly cold,
and they were not looking forward to the torchlight procession back to Vienna. Snuggled into her fur cloak with
her hood pulled close and a hot brick at her feet, Erica
wished the day had gone on and on. Even Lady Liza
brooding beside her could not diminish the enjoyment
she still felt. She looked up to see the duke regarding

her, and she smiled at him. Her smile faded when she
saw he did not return it. In the flickering torchlight, his
face was very dark and serious. She wondered what he
was thinking as the sleighs raced over the frozen roadway, their runners squeaking on the dry, crusty snow.

Would she ever understand Owen Kingsley? Was he
always to remain an enigma?

16

A week later, the duke received a communication from Lord Castlereagh that begged him to call at head-quarters as soon as he could. Albert Pray brought him the note. He had formed a friendship with George Baskins, Castlereagh's groom. They met often, supposedly to share reminiscences about the county where they had both been born, although Berkshire was discussed only when they were in earshot of others.

Owen Kingsley waited impatiently the next day until it was late enough so a visit to Mimi Lebrun would not be remarked. He passed Lord Hazelbeck on the stairs, and handled their encounter in the brothel with more aplomb than that embarrassed young peer did, suddenly reminded of his long-suffering wife.

Owen Kingsley sat in Mimi's room listening to her quick prattle and sharing a glass of wine until he was sure Lord Hazelbeck had left the premises. This was no hard-ship, for he had grown fond of the little Frenchwoman. Short and shapely, with a head of crisp black curls, she accepted her profession with a shrug. One must eat, no? she had asked the duke, before her eyes began to dance as she disclaimed any interest in being a scullery maid instead.

And Mimi had proved to be of inestimable assistance. Once she had told him of a plan that was afoot to assassinate Castlereagh, and he had been quick to foil it and make sure the conspirators knew their plotting had been discovered. And many times she had repeated men's boasting, revealing remarks about their missions in Vienna and their countries' objectives. The duke had wondered what there was about the sex act that made some men so careless with strangers, even as he was grateful that it was so.

Today Mimi had nothing of interest to report, but he gave her the usual payment anyway. She had told him she was saving her earnings to provide for her in her old age, grinning at him she did so. Even though she was barely eighteen, the duke was not tempted to join in her laughter. Prostitutes faded quickly. He knew Mimi might have need of the money much sooner than she thought.

After he had safely negotiated the alley and slipped in the back door of headquarters, he made his way to Robert Stewart's rooms.

"Thank you for coming, Owen," Castlereagh said as he indicated a seat. "I have important news from England. The Duke of Wellington is on his way to Vienna even now, to take my place here. I have been recalled."

Owen leaned forward, a little surprised at this unusual turn of events. Neither he nor Robert had ever envisioned such a thing happening. "May I ask why, sir?" he drawled. "Surely all your efforts here can only be applauded! But wait! Perhaps that is why you have been called home, to accept the plaudits of a grateful nation?"

Castlereagh laughed. "Nothing would be more unlikely! I go only so I can explain to an angry House of Commons why I exceeded my authority and took the steps I did here."

The duke looked disgusted. "They should greet you with a royal procession and medals, sir," he said.

Castlereagh waved a deprecatory hand. "There is another reason I must leave Vienna, Owen," he said. "It was necessary to get the Duke of Wellington safely out of France. You are well aware that in November he was the target of an assassin's bullet in Paris that fortunately missed its mark. But how to remove him from danger without offending the French or losing face? *Voyons!* A statesman of such importance must naturally be welcomed here at the congress, but his arrival is logical only if I leave so he can take my place."

He sighed and added, "There has been much unrest in France. No one, not even those nobles who clamored for

the return of the old royalty, can find anything inspiring
in the leadership of King Louis. Affairs are in disarray,
for as Wellington told me in a letter, the French may
have ministers, but they have no ministry. Besides, there
are all those disgruntled soldiers from Napoleon's Grande
Armée. They have been sent back to their villages to
starve on half-pay, and they are angry. Never doubt that
it is Napoleon who has their loyalty, not the Bourbon
king. Thank God the man is on Elba! If he were in
France, the army would flock to his standard at once,
and then, God help us all!"

He sat down behind his desk, making a steeple of his
fingers to regard Owen Kingsley over them. "The duke is
due to arrive any day now. I shall remain here a week or
so to brief him, and then Emily and I are for home." He
smiled a little. "She has already begun to pack, with a
great deal of glee, I might add. My wife has not liked
living in Vienna, or the congress. She thinks it too frivolous a city, and much too full of immorality."

"I shall miss you, sir," Owen Kingsley said. "Will you
tell the duke of the arrangement we have had?"

Castlereagh nodded. "With your permission, of course,
Owen. I had to find out how you feel about Arthur, and
if you would care to work with him. I would never
suggest such a thing if it did not have your complete
approval."

He waited a little anxiously until the duke said, "I
have no reluctance to do so. I know the duke to be
intelligent and clearheaded. I am sure he will make an
excellent ambassador. Tell him he may rely on me, as
you have done."

"You relieve my mind," Castlereagh told him. "And
now, may I ask another favor, my friend? I wish you
would write to me often and let me know how things go
on here. Of course I will have the official reports, but I
need to have you add flesh to those bare bones with
your own astute observations in order to get the complete picture."

The duke agreed, and the two continued to chat for
almost an hour. As Owen got up to leave at last, he said,
"I shall be out of town for two weeks or so, so we must
say good-bye now. All the Kingsleys have been included

in Count Kobenzl's invitation to his castle on the Danube. Erica is looking forward to it, I know, and as for myself, I will be delighted to remove Liza from Vienna. She has already begun to flirt with other men and forget her betrothed. With Liza, out of sight is truly out of mind. But in the country it will be easier to keep an eye on her. Women, Robert, can sometimes be an abomination, don't you agree? I think God put them here on earth not only to propagate the race but also to bedevil us, punish us for our sins, and keep us humble."

He bowed, and Castlereagh was quick to come to his side and grasp his hand. The duke stared down at him, his black eyes amused. "No, Robert, I shall not permit you to utter a single graceful compliment or voice a word of thanks," he warned him. "I have enjoyed myself too much for that, you know I have."

Castlereagh laughed as the two shook hands.

"Give my regards to Lady Castlereagh, and tell her I wish you both a safe journey home," the duke told him, clapping his old friend on the shoulder. "I will come and see you as soon as I reach England myself, when the congress is over."

While the duke had been closeted with Castlereagh, Erica had been taking tea with the Countess de Talleyrand-Périgord in the Kaunitz. She knew she would miss her friend in the next two weeks, for Dorothea was not attending the house party at Burg Kobenzl.

At last Erica rose to go home. As she picked up her ermines, Dorothea sighed. "Such a gorgeous cloak!" she enthused, coming to stroke the soft white fur.

"And so much trouble as it has brought me," Erica told her a little bitterly.

As Dorothea looked a question, she explained, "You know what the gossips are saying, I am sure. I told the duke it was much too blatant a gift, but he would not listen." She sighed. "But oh, how I hate it when women smirk at me so archly and whisper behind their hands!"

"Human nature, my dear Erica," Dorothea told her. "But, and you must forgive me for prying, I myself have wondered about your relationship with the duke. I could not help but notice the way he looked at you that day at

the Schönbrunn, and how easy you were together, sharing
the same thoughts and opinions. I do not think you are
having an affair with him, but tell me, do you love him?
There is something in your own eyes when you look at
him that makes me wonder."

Erica paused, holding the fur cloak close to her. She
was more than a little stunned. Whatever could Dorothea
mean? She was not in love with the duke, nor he with
her. She wondered what the countess would say if she
confessed that all they shared was a business arrangement and nothing more.

"No, I am not in love with the Duke of Graves," she
made herself say. "I feel affection for him, of course. He
is my . . . my cousin, and he has been very good to me,
letting me stay with him during the congress. But love?
No, no!"

"But *could* you love him, Erica?" Dorothea persisted.
"It isn't that you think him too old for you, is it?"

Erica sank back down on the sofa she had so recently
vacated. "No," she said slowly. "He is only in his middle
thirties, and that is not too old for someone soon to be
twenty-three."

She frowned a little at her thoughts, and Dorothea
said, "It is strange with older men. I have felt so much
closer to my uncle lately. He seems to need me more and
more. Karl is angry with me, for I have had to stop
seeing him so often so I can spend more time with
Charles. It is not that I do not still love Karl, but . . . but
I feel such a strong bond with my uncle."

She colored up a little as she added, "Sometimes I
catch him looking at me the same way the duke looks at
you, Erica."

"How is that?" Erica could not refrain from asking.

"As if he were hungry for me," Dorothea confessed.
"The duke stares at you the same way when he thinks no
one is watching. And in their eyes there is sorrow as well
as hunger."

She turned toward the window and added, "It is as if
they both know they can never have either one of us."

She sighed then, before she turned back to her friend.
"But perhaps I am only being fanciful! Forgive me, my dear.

"Now," she said more briskly, throwing off her pensive air, "be sure you remember everything that happens in the country, for I will be anxious to hear all your adventures when you return."

Erica kissed her good-bye and promised she would not forget a single thing, before she went down the broad stairway, deep in thought. Talleyrand was making his laborious way up it, leaning on his canes, and she paused on the landing to curtsy.

"My dear Miss Kingsley," he said, bowing in return. "You have left Dorothea in her rooms?" At her nod he added, "Good! There is something I wish to discuss with her. Thank you."

For a moment Erica saw a light in his eyes as he looked up the flight to where his niece waited, and she knew what Dorothea had meant. Whether or not Owen looked at her that way, which she could not believe, it was obvious that the elderly Talleyrand was in love with Dorothea.

As she continued down the flight, Erica felt uneasy. What good could come of such a passion? Surely Dorothea would never consider an affair with her uncle, even if she were not in love with Karl Clam-Martinitz. Besides the family relationship, Talleyrand was sixty, and crippled.

As she beckoned to Percy where he waited for her against the wall, she frowned. But Owen was crippled too, and that didn't make any difference in the way she felt about him, now, did it?

Erica walked carefully across the snow-covered street, wondering if what Dorothea had implied this afternoon could possible be true. And how would she feel if it were? she wondered. Then she shook her head. Dorothea had a more vivid imagination than she had thought. True, her uncle appeared to be falling in love with his young and beautiful niece, but Erica knew the Duke of Graves was in no such danger where she was concerned.

The Kingsleys left Vienna two days later, part of a group of carriages all traveling together to Count Kobenzl's country estate some thirty miles from Vienna. Behind their carriage came another with their baggage, both ladies' maids, and the duke's valet. Erica saw that Albert Pray was trailing the duke's favorite riding horse and that two other grooms led horses for Lady Liza's and her use.

By the time they reached the castle, late in the afternoon, Erica was heartily sick of Lady Liza's company. Liza had sat on her side of the carriage, seldom bothering to contribute to the conversation, and yet, by her very presence, managing to disrupt what should have been a pleasant drive.

Erica forgot her as the castle came into view. High up a steep, winding road above a picturesque village, it looked as if a giant baby had flung down some toy blocks complete with towers and battlements, high stone walls, and gilded domes, and then laughed in delight as it clung to its precarious perch. It reminded Erica of one of the fairy tales she had heard in her childhood.

"Yes, it is very medieval, it is not?" the duke asked. "But it has been modernized to a great extent. The count married heiresses—twice—so you must not fear cold dank walls and the winter wind keening through the corridors. I would not have come if that were the case."

"But how disappointing!" Erica mourned as the carriage slowed and the team leaned into their collars in the steep ascent. "Then surely there cannot be a ghostly lady moaning and clanking her chains, either. And I was so looking forward to her!"

"I wonder who else will be here?" Lady Liza remarked, ignoring this levity as unworthy of her attention. "Have you heard of the other guests, Owen?"

The duke admitted he had not. "But of course it will be the same people we have been seeing in Vienna, Liza. I'm afraid there will be no *new* conquests for you," he said.

Lady Liza looked away from his dark, mocking eyes, and she did not say another word, even when their carriage rumbled over the drawbridge and drew up before the fifteen-foot-high oaken doors. A number of footmen were waiting to assist them, and the count himself stood there to greet them.

Erica had a warm smile for her host. She had always liked Count Kobenzl. A short, stout man in his late fifties, he had a merry air about him, as if he enjoyed life to the fullest, and was ever ready to laugh at his own vagaries. He was known in Vienna as one well-versed in the art of amusing himself as well as others. Childless,

and a widower for the second time now, he spent his
time planning and carrying out elaborate parties like the
one they had been bidden to today.

A footman escorted both ladies and their maids up the
broad, winding stairs, while the duke enjoyed a glass of
wine with his host and the other male guests who had
just arrived. Lady Liza had been placed in a room facing
the courtyard, while Erica found herself several corridors
away in a large, luxurious room that overlooked the
Danube. As she inspected the view, the river seemed like
a shining, twisting silver ribbon very far below her.

Agnes took her fur cloak and muff. After the trunks
had been brought up, she unpacked them, chatting all
the while. Later she went to get hot water so Erica could
wash before dinner.

"Your room is comfortable?" Erica asked as her maid
brushed her hair smooth for evening.

"Aye, comfortable enough," Agnes said. "I share with
Lady Liza's maid, and at least the room is heated, something I doubted, Miss Erica, when I saw this old place
looming up ahead of us on the road. But all these stone
stairs and long corridors! I wouldn't care to live here for
long!"

Erica smiled as she rose so Agnes could lower the gold
silk evening gown over her head and hook it up the back.
Her own room was full of modern amenities, but enough
of the castle's past remained in the thick, curved walls,
the narrow windows, and the heavy arched doors with
their iron fittings so that no guest could ever forget that
this castle had been built originally for defense.

After she had been dressed, Erica found she was a little
early for dinner, and she dismissed her maid. "Go and
have your supper, Agnes," she said. "I will wait here
until I hear the dinner gong."

Agnes curtsied and left her, and Erica amused herself
by inspecting her room more closely and making up
stories about the knights and ladies of old who might
have slept here. She saw a door in the far wall she had
not noticed before, and she went to it in some curiosity.
She knew it was not the dressing room, but she wondered if it led to a sitting room or some other antecham-
ber. A smile curved her lips as she had the fancy that it

might open to reveal a twisting narrow flight of stone stairs leading down to . . . perhaps the dungeon? Feeling a little daring, she softly turned the iron handle and opened the door to peer inside.

She gasped as she found herself confronting the Duke of Graves. He was standing before a long mirror, adjusting his cravat while his valet stood nearby holding his evening coat. Her startled eyes met his in the glass.

"I beg you pardon, your grace!" Erica exclaimed. "Why, I had no idea my room adjoined yours!"

The duke turned to her, his expression unreadable. "Nor I," he said coldly, waving his valet away.

As soon as the servant had left the room and closed the door behind him, Erica asked, "But why did the count put us together like this?"

"I imagine because he has heard the gossip about us in Vienna, cuz," the duke said in that same even voice. "No doubt he thought to make our stay even more . . . pleasurable. Stefan is a man who tries very hard to indulge his guests."

Erica's grasp tightened on the heavy door. "I see," she managed to say. "Excuse me, your grace. I will not trouble you again."

The duke hesitated for a moment before he nodded in dismissal. Erica backed through the door and closed it softly before she leaned against it and put her hands flat on the wood behind her.

Owen had treated the matter of their adjoining rooms casually, but she was very embarrassed. In fact, now that she thought it over, the whole situation was dreadful! How could she go down that long flight of stairs and face the count, indeed, all the guests? She wondered how many of them knew of the arrangement. The dinner gong sounded then, and she took a deep breath and put up her chin. She could not help the gossip, nor what people believed of her, but she would not dignify it by worrying about it. Let them think what they chose!

The duke was leaving his room as she came down the hall, and he extended his arm. Erica had no choice but to take it. She was glad when he began to discuss the statues placed in niches along the wall, and the count's paintings that brightened the stairwell as they made their way to dinner.

The company had assembled in what was now called the drawing room, although its title of centuries ago, "the great hall" was still appropriate. Erica recognized all the guests, but her heart missed a beat when she saw that Prince Eric had been invited, as well as his awful cousin, Prince Boris. Now she would have to be on her guard throughout their stay, but she felt a little better when she saw there were some forty guests assembled. In such a large house party, she might even be able to avoid the prince completely. She felt the muscles in the duke's arm tighten as he too saw the handsome blond Swede, and she was very glad he was beside her.

Dinner was a gay affair. Erica had been placed between a charming French count and a German princeling, both of whom flirted with her in spite of the fact that neither one of them would ever see fifty again. Across from her Erica saw that Lady Liza's attention had been captured by the Russian officer beside her. They seemed to be having a very serious discussion, and once Erica saw him pat her hand.

The count had arranged for a trio to play during dinner, and when the guests adjourned to the drawing room later, they discovered the carpets taken up and an orchestra installed to play waltzes for an impromptu ball.

Erica danced with both her dinner partners before she went to join the duke. He was standing before the massive fireplace leaning on his cane while he conversed with their host.

"Ah, my dear Miss Kingsley!" Count Kobenzl welcomed her with a warm smile. "What a delight it is to have you here! I trust you found your room satisfactory?"

Erica could not read any innuendo in his merry voice, and she made herself smile in reply. "Thank you, Count," she said. "It is lovely, as is the rest of the castle, which I long to explore."

The duke held out his arm. "Then shall we begin now, cuz?" he asked. "I am sure you will find the library especially fine."

Obediently Erica curtsied to the count, who was beaming impartially at them both. "Go along, *mes enfants*," he said, making shooing motions. "By my decree, guests do exactly as they please at Burg Kobenzl, even if all

they wish is to be alone together. Then I know they will
be happy. And when my guests are happy, so am I!"

The duke led Erica from the drawing room and down a
long corridor. Neither of them spoke, and the only sound
was that of their footsteps as they echoed on the stone
floor, the measure of the duke's stride interrupted by his
limp.

The library was very large, with a vaulted ceiling of
plaster decorated with rich rococo designs. The many tall
bookcases were topped by heavily carved Gothic arches,
and there were tables and chairs and two enormous globes
set in brass stands for serious scholars. A massive fireplace was built into one wall, with some sofas beside it.
As the duke indicated the sofas, Erica had the feeling
they were both in some luxurious cave.

To her surprise, the duke did not mention their host or
his insinuations. Instead, he said as she took her seat, "I
am sorry the prince is here, Erica. I had not realized he
was to be one of the party."

"But I might be able to avoid him, there are so many
people here, your grace," Erica made herself say. "And
perhaps he will leave me alone now."

The duke frowned as he took the seat opposite her. "I
don't believe there is so much hope of that," he said.
"He is still angry. And although he was careful not to
stare at you, I noticed that he managed to keep you
under observation during dinner."

"As Prince Boris did you," Erica found herself saying.
"But how put upon we are by eager Swedish royalty, is it
not so, your grace?"

She was glad to see Owen smile a little at her attempt
at a jest. "I don't know which one of us is more to be
pitied," he remarked, his tone lighter. "However, I do
believe it might be better for you to stay very close to me
while we are here. No matter what interpretation the
count and the others choose to place on it." he added.

Erica nodded. "I would be easier," she admitted. "But
surely neither one of us will have a shred of reputation
left by the time we leave."

The duke smiled again. "How fortunate it is that Erica
Kingsley will disappear as soon as the congress is over,"
he said. "Now, *my* reputation can only be enhanced if

people think you chose me for your lover, but as Miss Kingsley, *yours* will not. No doubt you will find it a relief to resume your widow's weeds and your own name again."

Erica found herself wanting badly to deny any such thing, and she bit her lip. She told herself it was not only because she did not want to think that her time here with the duke was coming to an end but also because she would so much rather not have to become Erica Stone again, a woman who had been married for her money by a philandering husband who had never cared for her.

She looked up from her clasped hands to see the duke regarding her, and suddenly she felt she must tell him what she had discovered about William. They were alone now, and not likely to be interrupted, and she had carried the burden of what she had learned too long alone. Besides, in order to protect himself, the duke must know the prince was capable of murder if anyone got in his way.

"May I tell you something, your grace?" she asked, leaning forward so she could speak in a softer voice.

"Of course. Anything at all, Erica," he said, his black eyes never leaving her face.

"Your speaking of my becomings Erica Stone again reminded me," she began. "You see, I found out who killed my husband several weeks ago, but I could not bring myself to tell you. I was so ashamed! But now, somehow, I find that what was once so painful has become less so with the passing of time."

She paused, but the duke did not interrupt her. After a moment, she began to speak, telling him all about the serpent ring she had found in William's drawer and the matching bracelet on Isabella Sabatini's arm at Sperl's, as well as the perfume she wore that matched the scent on the scarlet chemise that had been in her husband's bed.

The duke watched her, noticing when she swallowed a little in her distress. He tried to make his expression calm and sympathetic, for he knew what telling this must be costing her. And to think he had never guessed she knew! Somewhat cynically he had imagined that she had forgotten her dead husband in the excitement that was Vienna.

He was recalled to her story as Erica went on, "When

I was in Prince Eric's rooms, I saw he was wearing an identical ring, and I asked him about it. He told me quite openly that the *signorina* had given it to him, that she gave one to all her favorite lovers. And he admitted that he had had a rival disposed of because the man kept her his exclusive property with his lavish gifts of money and jewelry, and he—the prince—wanted her too.

"You see, William never loved me at all, your grace," she finished, looking away from him for the first time. "He only married me for my dowry, and he left me as soon as he could. You must understand why I felt I could not tell you—anyone!—such a degrading thing."

"But why do you tell me now?" Owen Kingsley asked, his deep voice a little unsteady.

Erica looked back into his eyes. "For two reasons," she said. "First, I think I wanted to be as honest with you as you were with me when you told me about Lady Liza. I have not liked keeping the truth from you. It seemed so devious. And I had to tell you now because Prince Eric is here at Burg Kobenzl. I wanted you to know exactly how vile a man he is, one who will not even hesitate at murder to get what he wants. Now you will be on your guard."

She paused and sighed a little. "How unfortunate it is that the prince can never be brought to justice!"

The duke nodded. "You are right, for if the truth came out, your part in the story must also become known. You would not only be exposed as a woman pretending to be someone she is not, you would be held up to ridicule. But, Erica, the prince has a great deal to answer for, even more than I thought. You may be sure he *will* answer for it someday."

She bent her head, and he got up to pour them both a glass of wine. As he stared down at the bowed head with its rippling spill of silver hair turned gold in the firelight, he felt an anger he had never known he was capable of, to think she had been hurt so.

As he handed her the glass, he said, "Forget your husband, Erica. The man was a weak fool. To think he scorned you and your love for a wanton Jezebel! Believe me, you are well rid of him."

Erica sipped her wine. She felt a sense of great relief

that she had told Owen the story at last. It was as if in sharing it with him, its power to hurt her had been banished forever.

"Well, I suppose it is wicked of me to be glad William is dead, but I cannot regret it," Erica admitted. "I might have had to spend a lifetime with him."

"You will forget him," the duke reassured her. "No matter how much you thought you loved him when you married him, he will soon become only a faint memory."

Erica did not look away from the duke's dark eyes. "But I never loved him, your grace," she explained, wondering why she felt it was so important that he know this. "He was the only eligible man I had ever met. And my father approved the match; my brothers liked him. I told myself I would come to love him in time, for my aunt assured me that would be the case."

"Your aunt?" the duke inquired, suddenly feeling a great deal happier.

"My father's sister, Anne Huntington," Erica told him. "She has lived with us ever since my mother died."

The duke did not point out how unlikely it was that an aging spinster could know anything at all about love between a man and a woman, and had been very far from the mark as well.

Before they could continue what he had found a fascinating conversation, a footman came to tell them that tea was being served, and they rose to rejoin the other guests.

Erica slept very well that night, a deep, dreamless sleep. In the room adjoining hers, the duke sat up for a long time. In his mind he was going over everything she had told him, and searching for the perfect way he might repay the Swedish prince for what he had done.

When he went to bed at last, he smiled grimly as he realized that the revenge he intended to take—and had always intended to take—had little or nothing to do with the murder of a fellow Englishman.

17

The count had spared no effort or expense to make sure his party at Burg Kobenzl was a success, and in the days that followed, almost everyone had a wonderful time. There were sleigh rides through the surrounding countryside and deep forests, and an informal feast given in a huge hall that was followed by gaily dressed peasants performing their native dances, and singing for the assembled guests. One evening they were treated to a puppet show that had been written especially for the occasion, and in which the puppets slyly poked fun at those in the audience watching. Even the count was mocked, and he roared with laughter. The haughty Princess de Vincenzi was therefore forced to seem amused when one of the female puppets imitated her breathless manner of speaking and proud demeanor. Erica and the Duke of Graves did not escape either, but it was all done in such a spirit of fun that Erica could only laugh and send the duke a helpless smile.

Sometimes there were shooting contests in the cold, crisp air, and here, taught by her father and brothers, Erica more than held her own with the gentlemen. She noticed that Owen was by far the best shot of all, however.

And of course many of the guests often put on their skates to enjoy the frozen village pond before adjourning to the local inn for hot chocolate and pastries.

Many times Erica was forced to speak to Prince Eric, and even dance with him, and she was relieved and a little puzzled when he treated her to a frosty politeness. She mentioned this to the duke, but Owen did not relax his vigilance. He was sure the prince was planning something, although he had no idea what it might be.

There were two other guests besides Prince Eric who did not appear to be having a very good time. Prince Boris was sulking because the duke's obvious preference for his lovely blond cousin made it very plain he had no interest in any kind of an arrangement with him; and Lady Liza, who found herself constantly in the company of the Russian officer. Ivan Torkashev was a close friend of Prince Gorsky's, and he had taken it as his personal mission to watch over his friend's fiancée and keep her amused. With such a serious watchdog always in attendance, Owen was able to give up his surveillance of his aunt. He made it a point, however, to be very attentive where Erica was concerned.

They had been at the castle for a week now, and one evening the count arranged a gala ball. Erica wore her dark green silk, the one covered with silver embroidery, and the Kingsley emeralds. The duke thought she looked very beautiful as he watched her dancing from his position along the wall. He saw Prince Eric staring at her as she laughed up at her partner. Then the prince's lips tightened in a grim smile as he turned away.

It was very late when they all retired. Erica dismissed Agnes just as soon as she had been undressed. She knew she should be in bed, but for some reason she was not at all tired tonight. She put on her robe and wandered over to the window. There was a little moonlight, and she could see the Danube sparkling like molten silver far below her. The room was almost dark, for Agnes had extinguished the candles before she left, and there was only the glow from the dying fire to light it.

As Erica leaned against the velvet drapery, idly thinking of the Duke of Graves and what they had talked about this evening, she heard a faint noise. She turned, wondering what it could be.

The scratching came again, and tracing the sound, she stared at the door to the hall. It was so dark she could barely see the latch, and she moved forward as quietly as she could. It sounded very much like someone was trying to gain entry to her room. For a moment she thought of calling to the duke, but then she shook her head. It was

late, and he was probably asleep. Besides, the door was
locked. No one could get in.

To her horror, the latch lifted then and the door opened.
Two masked men dressed all in black stood there, and
then the taller of the pair dropped the key he held and
came toward her in a rush. Released from a stunned
paralysis, Erica started to scream for help. Her cry was
cut off before it even began, as a hard hand clamped
over her mouth. Frantically she tried to twist and turn
and kick, to escape her captor. She knew it had to be
Prince Eric, but who was the other man? His horrible
cousin Boris?

The prince was forcing her ever closer to the bed. As
he pushed her against it and the other man giggled,
Erica's foot lashed out to the nightstand beside it, to
topple it. The crash of the heavy table and all the orna-
ments that had been placed on it sounded very loud in
her ears. She prayed the duke would wake up at the
noise of it, even through that solid wooden door that
separated them. If he did not, there was no hope for her.

Erica began to feel faint, her heart was pounding so in
her fright. Suddenly the door to the adjoining room was
thrown open and she saw the Duke of Graves standing on
the threshold. The light from his room spilled into her
own, and Erica could see that he was still fully dressed
except for his jacket and cravat. Swearing, he twisted the
top of the cane he held to draw out a sword.

As he limped forward, the second man cried out, " 'Ware
the duke—behind you!"

Any doubt of her assailants' identity disappeared as
Erica heard the Swedish her mother had taught her so
long ago.

Prince Eric thrust her into the arms of his cousin
before he darted to the fireplace to grasp the poker. Erica
could have wept. Without his cane, Owen was not quick
enough to prevent him from reaching it. She struggled to
get away from Prince Boris so she might help the duke as
he prepared to engage his unlikely opponent.

The thin sword flashed in the light from the fire, but
she could see it was going to be a very unequal match.
What could Owen, even as tall and strong as he was, do
against a sound man armed with a heavy iron bar? Of

what possible use would a thin, fragile sword be against such odds?

To her surprise, the duke did not hesitate even for a moment. It was as if he himself knew he had little chance, and so he attacked at once. His first thrust was aimed directly at Prince Eric's heart. The move took his opponent by surprise, but he made a quick enough recovery to parry it slightly with the poker. Instead of killing him, the sword sank deep into the flesh of his upper arm. Stunned, he cried out then, a harsh sound of pain as he dropped the poker and retreated to clutch his wound. Prince Boris threw Erica to the floor to attack the duke behind. As he picked up a heavy pewter vase the table nearby, Erica screamed. In desperation, and on her hands and knees, she scrambled toward the discarded poker.

The duke had dodged at her cry, so the vase, which had been aimed at his head, only brushed it before it landed on his shoulder. The blow unbalanced him, and he fell.

Erica screamed again and again as she struggled to her feet, waving the poker. The two masked princes turned and ran from the room.

When they were gone, she slammed the door behind them and locked it with trembling fingers. As she turned back, she saw the duke still stretched out on the floor, and she hurried to kneel beside him, her breath coming in little pants. Carefully she lifted his head and laid it on her breast, putting her arms around him in support.

"Owen! Owen, my dear!" she cried softly. "Are you all right?"

The duke had not lost consciousness, but his head was reeling, and his shoulder felt as if it were on fire from the blow he had received. But at her soft cry the pain became unimportant. She had called him "Owen" and "my dear"! He kept his eyes closed, breathing in the sweet scent of her and reveling in the feel of her pliant breast beneath the thin nightgown she wore, where his cheek rested.

He felt the soft cloud of her hair brush his face as she bent her head to kiss his forehead and cheek.

"Owen, love, speak to me!" she begged, her voice breaking.

Almost reluctantly he opened his eyes. She was very

close to him, and her green eyes widened and began to shine when she saw he was all right.

"Oh, thank heaven," she murmured, holding him even closer. "I was so afraid you had been badly hurt!"

Owen realized that if he did not do something soon, he would be unable to prevent himself from kissing her. Kissing her, and a great deal more besides. He struggled a little, and she released him and sank back on her heels.

As he sat up and put one hand to his head, he said, striving for normalcy, "Is there some water, Erica? I feel a trifle dizzy still."

He watched as she rose in one fluid motion to run to the dressing room, noting her slim ankles and slender bare feet. It seemed no time at all before she was kneeling beside him again, glass in hand.

The duke sipped gratefully. "Thank you," he said as he handed back the empty glass.

"You should not thank me, Owen," Erica told him. "It is for me to thank you for saving me from the prince and his cousin."

"How did they get in?" he asked. "I told you to keep your door locked."

Erica pointed to the key over by the door. "They must have found an extra one," she said.

The duke grimaced as he rubbed his shoulder to bring back the circulation. "No doubt they bribed a servant," he said as he grasped the bedpost to pull himself to his feet. Erica rose with him, one arm around his waist. Clasped to her side, he could feel her all along the length of his body, and in spite of his iron control, his arm slipped around her waist in turn.

"Are you sure you should stand up?" she asked anxiously. The duke stared down into her lovely, worried face and at the soft skin of her throat and breasts that was exposed by her open robe. He shook his head at his thoughts, and the dizziness returned. As he staggered a little, Erica pushed him gently back down onto the bed.

"You must rest, my dear," she told him as she sat beside him. "You will only hurt yourself if you try to move too quickly."

The duke groaned. It was agony to be so close to her when he wanted her so badly.

Erica watched him, wondering if he needed more attention than just time to rest. But something in his eyes told her it was not the blow that he had received that was making him feel so weak. He looked as he had the afternoon he had kissed her in the drawing room. Remembering that kiss, she swayed toward him.

He caught her in his arms then, and she raised her face to his. Groaning again at his weakness, he bent and kissed her.

It was just as wonderful as it had been before, and she put her arms around his neck with a little prayer of thanks. She could feel the muscles in his big shoulders tense as she touched them, and his mouth become even more insistent and hungry on hers. At last, with the greatest reluctance, he drew back.

When Erica felt him trying to remove her hands and put her away from him, she opened her eyes. She saw the distant, bleak look was back in his own dark eyes, and that dear mouth that had kissed her with such love and longing was set in a thin line of denial.

"Owen," she whispered. "No, I won't let you leave me."

He put her hands aside and rose, grasping the bedpost again. For a moment Erica felt a stab of doubt. But as he turned away a little, as if he could not bear to look at her, the firelight showed his long hard length in profile and she saw how much he wanted her.

"You don't know what you're saying, Erica," he told her, his deep voice harsh and cold.

Erica did not hesitate. Lying back on her pillows, she held out her arms to him. "Yes, I do," she said. "I do. I want you to stay with me."

Her voice was not the least bit unsteady or shy. She knew now that she loved Owen Kingsley, had loved him for a long time. When she had seen him engaging the prince with only that thin sword, she had been terrified. Not for herself anymore, but for him. She had known then that she could not bear it if he were to be hurt. And when she had seen him lying on the floor, the wave of feeling that had swept over her had been like nothing she had ever experienced before. The only time she had felt remotely like it was when she had seen her brother Mark

come home from the Peninsular War, his handsome face
scarred and his empty left sleeve pinned to the shoulder
of his uniform. But the loving pity she had felt for her
brother was nothing like the love she had for this man.

Dorothea had been right after all. How strange that
her friend had been able to comprehend the love that she
herself had been so busy denying.

Now she waited, watching Owen in the flickering firelight as he did battle with himself. She did not know why
he pretended he did not love her, want her; why he had
kept her at arm's length with a wall of cold formality all
this time. Perhaps she would never know. It was strangely
unimportant to her, as was the world's opinion of their
lovemaking. What was important was that she and Owen
were here, together, that she loved him, and he needed
her.

She studied him, admiring the broad shoulders that
stretched the linen of his evening shirt, the powerful
column of his neck, that rugged, hawklike profile. He
was frowning as he turned back to her, and there was
such agony in his eyes that she cried out a little.

"Do not look that way, my dear," she said, sitting up
to reach for his hands. "It is right. I have never felt so
strongly about anything. Come!"

The duke gave up the struggle that he knew he did not
want to win as he sat down beside her and took her in his
arms again. He stared down at her and saw the way her
eyes glowed with love, and he shook his head, bemused.
Perhaps he was dreaming, perhaps tomorrow he would
wake and discover it had been only his own desperate
yearning that had created this vivid scene.

But as his fingers touched her soft skin, and she reached
up to smooth back his disheveled hair, he knew it was no
dream.

Erica had never felt so loved, so cared for, as when
Owen kissed and caressed her. His hands trembled a
little, and she pressed closer to him in reassurance. He
was so careful of her as he undressed her, telling her in a
reverent whisper how beautiful she was, how precious.

At last he rose to remove his own clothes, and Erica
lay back on the pillows and watched him through half-
closed eyes. She had to swallow when he took off his

shirt and she saw those muscled arms, the broad power-ful chest that narrowed to slim hips and sturdy thighs. And then he limped to the door between their rooms and closed it.

She wanted to cry out and beg him not to, for it was very dark now, with only the little glow from the fire. But before he came back to her, he bent to throw an-other log on, and as it caught and the flames sprang up, the room became lighter.

He sat on the edge of the bed and removed the rest of his clothes before he stretched out beside her, and the hands she had missed even for that short time were caressing her and holding her close again.

Erica tried to lie still, as she had been taught, although she found it very difficult. Everywhere his fingers touched her seemed to begin to glow and melt.

"Erica?" he asked, as one hand caressed her breast and the other pressed her hips closer.

She opened her eyes and saw him smiling down at her. Then he nodded. "Thank heaven, love," he drawled. "I thought you had fainted, you were so still."

Erica shivered as his fingers trailed down her belly and he bent his head to kiss her breasts.

"But I must not move," she whispered somewhat breathlessly.

He raised his head to stare at her. "Not move?" he asked in disbelief. "Why ever not?"

Erica could feel a blush beginning right under his gently probing hand. "My aunt told me not to," she said. "She said a good woman was expected to lie still and let the man do everything, that it was only prostitutes who made a show of enjoying love."

The duke threw back his head and laughed. "How fortunate for some lucky man that Miss Huntington never married," he said between chuckles. "My darling, inno-cent Erica, she was wrong."

"But William didn't seem to think—" Erica began.

The duke's hand stopped its fondling to cover her mouth. "What your late and unlamented husband thought is not at issue here, my dear, and there is no need to whisper," he told her sternly. "You have my permission to do whatever seems appropriate to you at the moment.

I do not want your aunt's idea of tight-lipped resignation, I want the warm, vibrant woman you are. And if you do not touch me soon, I shall think you were lying when you said you wanted me."

Shyly Erica put her hands on his broad chest. She could feel his rapid heartbeat, the way that chest was rising and falling with his quickened breathing.

"Truly, Owen?" she asked.

"Truly, Erica," he said solemnly. "Cross my heart."

Now it was her turn to laugh as she threw her arms around him and squirmed even closer. Her laugh was cut off abruptly as his mouth found hers again.

Erica had no way of knowing how gentle the duke was as he made love to her, how careful he was not to rush her or frighten her. She only knew it was all so different from William's quick, fumbled mating. It seemed an age before Owen joined his body with hers, a wonderful, sensation-filled age that had her breathless with passion and surrender, and longing for what must come next.

Suddenly she felt a flood of warmth course through her, and she cried out. Only then did the duke abandon his careful, patient waiting and allow himself the luxury of release. A moment later Erica felt him shudder as he gave an exultant cry.

They lay panting in each other's arms, still one, and Erica closed her eyes. She felt like crying with joy, for from the top of her head to the tip of her toes, her body was singing.

"How wonderful you are," the duke murmured, his deep voice ragged with emotion. "How beautiful and dear."

"And you, Owen," she whispered back. "How glad I am that we have found each other. I love you so much."

The duke did not answer. Indeed, he could not speak at the moment, and so, instead, he kissed the hollow in her throat as he felt his eyes grow damp.

Erica dropped off to sleep in his arms. He could tell when her breathing slowed that she was asleep, but he made no move to leave her. Before he drew the coverlet up so she would not catch a chill, he admired her once again. He knew she was all soft, yielding flesh, but still she reminded him of the inside edge of a delicate seashell, creamy and pink and gold. Reluctantly he covered them both, and lay back beside her on the pillows.

The duke did not get much rest that night. He did not want to sleep, he wanted to remember all that had happened, and the things she had said to him, imprinting them in his mind so he would never forget them. He knew that no other night of his life would be as wonderful, and that he would never be so happy again. Making love to Erica had been unlike anything he had ever known or even dreamed of. She was as different from a prostitute's practiced caresses as a masterpiece is from a child's rough drawing.

He smiled a little when he remembered how innocent she had been, lying beside him like a marble statue until he told her she would not be a wicked woman if she showed her delight. And then, released from that frozen propriety, how overwhelming her response had been, how freely and generously she had given of herself. The sweet scent of her still teased his senses, and he buried his face in her long hair to breathe deeply, being careful not to disturb her rest.

But after dozing for a while, he found himself awake again, and as the sky began to lighten and the room turn from black to gray in the approaching dawn, sanity returned. He had been weak when he should have been strong. But wasn't that permissible just once? he asked the gods in silent agony.

He knew he would have to pay for the joy he had had, but he knew it was worth all the loneliness and the pain the future held. At least he had loved her once, known the ecstasy of holding her in his arms; making them one.

He realized he could not have Erica, for he had always known it. And what she felt for him was only gratitude that he had saved her from the prince. Oh, she might think she loved him, but he knew how impossible, even laughable, that was. She was too fine and beautiful for a cripple with a twisted, ugly leg. When she was thinking more clearly, she would wonder at her actions and be repulsed by what she had done.

The duke grimaced. He would have to leave Burg Kobenzl, make some excuse that he had been called back to town. That way she would not have to be embarrassed and reminded of her fall from grace. And he would not have to watch her revulsion in the clear light of day, or listen to her trying to be kind as she told him she had made a terrible mistake.

But what of Prince Eric? He could not leave Erica here with him, for wounded or not, the man was still dangerous. Like a snake, he would not hesitate to strike again. His fellow conspirator, Boris, was of little concern to the duke. He would not try anything more, not now when he knew his name was known. The duke was sure he had only abetted Prince Eric as a way to repay Erica for attracting the man *he* wanted.

Owen nodded then. As soon as it was light, he would go back to his own room and write two letters, one to the prince that would ensure his quick departure, and the other to Erica. That one would be the most difficult letter he had ever penned, but he knew it must be written. And in it he would thank her for the gift she had given him, and make light of the situation, so she could be easy again. He would tell her he was going back to town to allow her to recover, and he would beg her not to take seriously what had been only a pleasant interlude. And he would promise her it would never happen again.

Then, when she came back to Vienna with the others, he would be just as he had been before, cold and sarcastic and formal. She was a guest in his home, and he should be shot for the way he had abused her trust. Thank heaven there was his work with Wellington to keep him busy, and all those loose threads that must be sewn together before the congress adjourned.

And for her sake and her future happiness, he would manage to be just strong enough.

He could not resist kissing her and holding her again before he left her, and, half-asleep, Erica murmured and caressed him with gentle hands. The feel of that perfect body pressing close to him was too much for him, and silently, tenderly, he took her again.

When he rose at last, he saw she was smiling in her sleep, and his lips twisted as he limped back to his own room to dress and order coffee before he began to write those letters.

It was very late when Erica woke and stretched. She felt wonderful. There was a tiny singing along all her nerve ends still, and she felt warm and womanly and adored.

She blew a kiss to the duke's door before she went to the dressing room to wash and don her discarded nightgown again. As she rang for Agnes, she wondered how long it would be before she would see Owen again, and she blushed a little as she imagined what it would be like to exchange glances in a roomful of people. She wished they were here alone, that she never had to dress again, that he would come through that door right now and take her in his arms.

Agnes did not appear to notice how different she was, and Erica wondered at it, for she was sure her happiness must be written plain on her face. But the maid only brought her the breakfast tray, and, as Erica sat up and arranged the pillows, went to open the draperies.

"It's another frigid morning, Miss Erica," she said. "There's supposed to be snow later, but to my mind, it's much too cold for that! I hope you weren't planning a ride or some such today. Better to stay cozy by a nice warm fire with a good book!"

As Erica opened her napkin, her lips curled in a secret smile. How she would adore to stay cozy beside a warm fire—but not with a good book.

She was pouring a cup of steaming coffee when Agnes bustled up to the bed again. "I almost forgot!" she exclaimed, reaching into her apron pocket. "There's a letter for you—from *him*."

Erica reached for it eagerly, before she dismissed her maid. "I'll ring later, Agnes," she said, trying not to stare at his black handwriting. "I feel lazy this morning, and will take my time getting up."

As soon as the maid had closed the door behind her, Erica was opening her letter, her breakfast forgotten.

But as she read it, her delighted smile faded, and she began to shake her head. "No, no," she murmured. "Oh, Owen, *no*!"

The duke had written as he had planned, and the letter was cold and formal. He told her he would be forever grateful for what had passed between them, but that he understood it was only an enjoyable interlude, and he would not presume on it. No, everything would be as it had been before. She had his word for it.

And he wrote that he was going back to Vienna, so she need feel no embarrassment, and would have the opportunity to recover her *sang-froid*. He assured her she had no need to fear Prince Eric anymore, for the prince and his cousin had left the castle very early that morning. And he had signed the note with his title—and not a single word of love.

Erica read it twice, and then she pushed her tray aside and ran to the door that connected their rooms. Throwing it wide, she surprised a little housemaid who was stripping the bed. Erica could see that all Owen's things were missing, and tears welled up in her throat. Without a word to the maid, she turned away and closed the door. He was gone; it was not just some horrible dream.

She read his letter again, and her soft lips tightened. It had not been just "an enjoyable interlude," most certainly not for her, and not for him either. She knew this as certainly as she knew her own name. And for whatever impossible reason he had written that letter and gone away, she would not accept it.

For a moment she thought of ordering the carriage and going after him, but she knew she must not do that. There would be enough talk about his sudden departure, as well as that of the Swedish princes. No, she must not expose both Owen and herself to conjecture and ridicule. She would wait, no matter how hard it was, until she could return to Vienna as originally planned. But then Owen Kingsley would see. Oh, yes, he would see!

It was a very long six days later before Erica, in company with a disgruntled Lady Liza, arrived in the Johannesgasse again. The Russian officer had insisted on accompanying their carriage to make sure of their safe return.

At Burg Kobenzl, as Erica had suspected, there had been a great deal of talk about the duke's defection and the way the two Swedes had left the same day at dawn.

"There is some trouble in paradise, I think," the count had said, twinkling at Erica. She denied it at once, proud of her cool composure. It was easy enough for her to make up a story about a stallion the duke had despaired of acquiring suddenly becoming available.

Erica made herself become the perfect guest. Whatever the count and the others planned, she agreed to with every semblance of delight. She danced and skated and rode, she played at whist and billiards, and she smiled and laughed as if she didn't have a care in the world.

But every night after she was in bed alone, she would remember Owen here beside her, and she would relive their lovemaking. And just before she fell asleep, the pillow he had used held close to her face so she could breathe in the faint scent of him that she imagined remained, she would pray that the time would pass more quickly so she could be with him again.

She had burned his letter, but she did not need to have it before her, for she remembered every word. But not once during those long, empty days did she waver in her love for him, or doubt his for her.

Now she greeted Rudge with a warm smile and handed her cloak to a footman, the ermine cloak that Owen had given her, which she now adored. When she was wrapped in it, it was almost as if she were in his arms. Now that she was back in Vienna, of course, she did not need the ermine. Soon, very soon, the two of them would be together.

She was glad when Lady Liza asked for the duke, for she was afraid her own voice would give her away when she spoke his name. Rudge told them he had gone on a riding expedition but that he would certainly see them both at dinner that evening.

Erica had to be content, although the additional waiting was very hard to bear. She spent the time choosing her gown for the evening, and bathing and having Agnes wash her hair, and then brush it until it shone. Owen had told her how much he adored her hair.

When she came down to the drawing room, she was disappointed that Lady Liza was before her. She forgot her, however, as she curtsied to the duke, trying to keep her face expressionless over the wild beating of her heart.

She was sure both of them must hear it, it was making such a dreadful din in her own ears.

Owen nodded to her carelessly. "Liza has been telling me about the remainder of your stay at Burg Kobenzl, cuz," he drawled. "It sounds as if you had a wonderful time. How sorry I am that I was called away."

"Oh, Erica was quite the petted princess of the party," Liza told him. "I have seldom seen her so gay, so animated!" She sighed. "At least *she* had a good time! As for myself, I thought I would scream if I did not get away from that gloomy Russian soon."

"But Ivan Torkashev was merely taking care of you for Prince Gorsky, dear Liza," the duke reminded her, his dark eyes bleak. So Erica had enjoyed herself, had she? Unlike the agonies he had been suffering. No doubt it was because of her heartfelt relief that he had left, and relief as well that her gaffe in taking such a man into her bed had not become known. It was all very clear to him; she could not have told him her true feelings more plainly if she had voiced them.

He searched her face as they took their seats at the table, but he could read nothing in its calm, serene contours. As she picked up her napkin, her eyes met his, and she smiled at him. The duke snapped his fingers to Rudge, and was soon deep in a discussion of the wines to be served with dinner.

Erica smiled to herself. She could see that Owen intended to go on just as he had written in that impossible note, but she had no intention of accepting such an arrangement. As soon as they were alone, she would refute all his careful arguments. She rather thought one kiss would do the trick.

But they were not to be alone that evening. After dinner the duke announced he had a previous engagement. He was everything that was polite as he excused himself, saying how sorry he was that he had not known the exact day of their return.

"But perhaps tomorrow we can attend the opera, ladies?" he asked, speaking impartially to both of them. "There is a new production that I am sure you would enjoy."

Liza shrugged, and Erica could only nod before the

duke left them. She spent the evening with a book, fully intending to wait up for him, however long it took. It was well after midnight when Rudge came into the salon to bank the fire. Lady Liza had gone yawning to bed sometime before, and the butler seemed so startled to find Erica still sitting there that she was forced to go to bed herself.

After Agnes left her, she opened her door a little, so as to be sure to hear Owen when he came home at last. She would intercept him as he went to his room, and then all the waiting, all the loneliness would be over forever.

But the Duke of Graves did not come home at all that night, and it was almost dawn before Erica gave up her vigil and fell asleep at last. As she did so, she wondered where he was, and for the first time she felt a tiny, stabbing doubt.

18

When Erica awoke later that same morning, she felt leaden and tired, and she ate very little breakfast. Agnes shook her head at the hardly touched tray, as well as the droop of her mistress's lips, her sad eyes. There was something wrong and she wondered what it could be. Of course, Miss Erica would not tell her. She would just have to wait to find out, although she knew in her bones that it had something to do with *him*.

Erica dressed at last, but even a fond note from Dorothea, asking her to call, could not lure her from the house. She was determined to have this out with Owen before another day went by.

She wrote to ask him for an interview, and told Agnes to give the note to his valet. It was almost teatime before she had his reply. He begged her pardon for keeping her waiting, but he explained he had been involved with a crush of business. But perhaps she would join him in the library now? He was, at last, completely at her disposal.

Erica barely glanced at her reflection in the glass before she ran down the stairs. She was wearing a smart new afternoon gown, chosen because its color exactly matched her eyes. Owen had told her how much he admired her in that shade of green.

As she knocked on the library door, she took a deep breath. She was confused, and a little hurt, but she would not be a coward, not now when she knew her future happiness was at stake.

The duke's harsh voice bade her enter, and she opened the door and went in to join him. He was seated behind

his desk, a pile of papers before him. When she came up
to him and curtsied, he squared them up and folded his
hands before him to give her his full attention.

As Erica hesitated at his cold, formal expression, he
waved her to a seat. "There was something you wished
to discuss, cuz?" he drawled. "Behold me, at your service."

She saw his eyes drop to the papers again, and she
stiffened. "Yes, there is something I think we must discuss, Owen," she made herself say quietly. "I was so
very disappointed to receive your note at Burg Kobenzl,
to discover you had left me."

"Indeed?" he asked her, his dark eyes empty of any
expression whatsoever. "And yet, according to Liza, you
then proceeded to have a wonderful time."

"I had to pretend to, for there was so much conjecture
about your sudden departure and that of the princes,"
Erica told him. "You may be sure you were missed—
very much missed," she added softly.

"How kind of you to say so, Erica," he replied. "But
then, I have always admired your lovely manners."

Erica rose to lean on his desk, her green eyes flashing.
"What is the matter, Owen?" she asked quickly. "Why
do you behave this way? And why did you say what you
did in that note? An enjoyable interlude, indeed! It was
no such thing, and you know it!"

The duke rose, and for a moment her heart pounded
as she waited for him to come and take her in his arms.
Instead, he went to pour a glass of wine. As he did so, he
said with his back to her, "I am sorry you did not find it
enjoyable, for I can assure you, I did. Now, however, it
is a thing of the past, and best forgotten."

He turned back then and handed her the wine. She was
forced to take it, although her eyes never left his face.

"Sit down, Erica," he said more kindly. "I was much
at fault that night, for I should have remembered that for
all the veneer of sophistication you have acquired here in
Vienna, you are still only a naive girl. As such, you place
too much importance on one night of trivial dalliance and
the emotions of the moment." He made himself smile at
her a little. "Did you think it meant we loved each
other? That now we would be wed and live happily ever
after? Poor child, that you were so misled!"

Erica sank back into her chair and put the glass down on a table beside her. This was Owen? Owen, who had loved her so tenderly, who had told her how he adored her, who had kissed her as if he never wanted to let her go? It could not be . . . could it?

"I don't believe you," she whispered through dry lips. "But even if it meant nothing to you beyond a quick gratification, I tell you it meant a great deal more to me. You see, I happen to love you."

She stopped and looked at him, her eyes begging him to relent and admit how much he cared, too. He only shrugged.

"I am sorry for it," he told her. "What I did, then, was not the act of a gentleman. But trust me. You will soon forget it, this *love* you think you have for me. I do assure you it is no such thing. It is only because you are ashamed that you gave yourself to me that now you must dress the thing up in the pink hearts and ribbons and laces of a great love affair, to excuse your behavior. Do not be so hard on yourself, Erica! It is no great matter, after all, one little fall from grace. You have seen how common these things are in Vienna. I thought you understood."

She shook her head, trying hard not to begin to cry before him. "I will never understand," she said so softly he had to lean closer to hear her.

For a minute they sat together in silence. The duke did not think he could say another word or mouth one more lie. His expression was bleak as he stared at her silvery hair as she bent over her clasped hands and bit her lip.

At last she rose. "I beg you will excuse me, your grace," she said in the deadest little voice he had ever heard her use.

He nodded, and she turned to leave.

"Erica!" he cried, her name escaping his lips before he could control himself.

She turned back eagerly, and he made himself say, "I think after the opera tonight, we will go on to Sperl's."

She put up her chin. "I must beg you to excuse me, sir," she said. "I find I am not in the mood for a gay evening out."

The duke stood up to stare at her. "I am afraid it will

not be possible to excuse you," he told her coldly. "There is someone I want you to meet in the next few days, and he may be at Sperl's tonight. You will come, and you will go on as we agreed. I trust I have made myself clear?"

Erica stared at him for a long moment before she nodded. As the door closed softly behind her, Owen buried his face in his hands. Dear God, how difficult an interview that had been! He was sure that never again would he ever have to face anything so painful as pretending he did not care, when he knew how he had come to love her.

He frowned down at his papers with unseeing eyes. She had told him she loved him too, and he remembered how his heart had quickened at her words. But now he shook his head. She was so pure in heart that of course she thought she was in love. But he knew better. And as the elder, he must keep to the course he had charted for them both. Erica would be going home soon, home to some handsome future love of her life. And even if she never forgave him, she would have a reason to thank him for saving her for that love that she would have someday, with a whole man.

Erica appeared at dinner dressed for the opera as ordered. The duke saw she was very pale, and even Liza remarked on how quiet she was. It was not that she did not respond to questions or take part in the conversation, but to the duke it was as if she had gone far away, leaving only a beautiful, empty shell, all cream and pink and gold. The same kind of shell he had seen so often on the beach, tossed up by the tides and washed gently by the waves. Lovely, and yet abandoned now by whatever creature had once called it home.

At Sperl's, after the opera, the duke introduced her to an elderly German prince, who seemed delighted at his good fortune. Later, at home, the duke told her it would be helpful to Wellington if she could discover what the Germans had in mind to do about the Jewish question. A group of German Jews was pressing for a statement of emancipation to be included in the Final Acts. Although they had had to bribe Gentz, the secretary general, to get their concern on the agenda, they had great hopes that the Germans might be pressured by the other nations to end their tyranny forever.

Erica was glad to have something to do, something that would keep her busy and out of the palace. It was such agony to be with Owen and know that the love she had for him was not returned. She knew she would always love him, but she wondered if the pain that seemed a permanent part of her now would ever lessen.

A week later, on an afternoon drive with Dorothea, their carriage was stopped in traffic near the Minoritenplatz. By now Erica had told her friend all about her stay in the country, leaving out any reference to the duke, a fact Dorothea was quick to note. At first Erica had been tempted to unburden herself to the countess, but only a moment's reflection told her that was impossible. How could she discuss yet another man who had rejected her? And even though Dorothea knew nothing of William Stone, she did know the duke.

Suddenly the countess leaned forward in her seat to peer out the carriage window. "But isn't that the Duke of Graves?" she asked Erica. "But how singular!"

Erica looked to where she was pointing. Owen was going up the steps of a house across the street from them, and he paused to exchange a few words with another gentleman who was just leaving.

"Oh, dear," Dorothea whispered. Erica turned to stare at her, she had sounded so distraught.

"What is it, Dorothea?" she asked. "Why do you look so strange?"

The countess tried to smile. "It is only that I was so surprised to see the duke at that particular house," she said.

"What do you mean? What is that house?" Erica persisted.

The countess's cheeks were rosy now. "'It is one of Vienna's most infamous brothels," she explained, and then she tried a careless laugh. "Although why I should be surprised, I do not know. Many men frequent the place, so why shouldn't the duke?" She wrinkled her nose as she said, "Men! They are all the same!"

The carriage lurched into motion again, but not until Erica had had time to see the duke actually entering the house. A little blindly, she looked away. She felt her heart must stop beating, she felt such pain. Was that where Owen had been the night she came back to Vienna? Was he yet another man who had rejected her because he preferred experienced women who knew how to give pleasure? There must be something most dreadfully wrong with her!

Dorothea stole a sidelong glance at Erica's pale profile and changed the subject. As she did so, she wondered when Erica would admit she loved the Duke of Graves, and he, her? She had known it herself ever since their day at Schönbrunn.

When Erica entered the duke's palace a little while later, she saw there was a letter from home for her on the foyer table. It was from her Aunt Anne, and she picked it up with listless fingers to take it into the salon to read. She had never found her aunt an amusing correspondent, for her letters were likely to be full of moral sermonizing. In today's letter, however, the elderly Miss Huntington was big with news.

She began her letter with an account of a carriage accident in which Erica's father had been badly injured. Quickly she told Erica that there was every hope for his full recovery, but the convalescent period was going to be long. Then her Aunt Anne begged Erica to come home. She said she was sure it would raise her father's spirits if he could see her again, and she herself could use some help nursing him back to health. Erica was sure she could. Even though she loved him, she knew General Sir Harold Huntington was an impatient, demanding man. By now he must have the entire house in an uproar!

As she sat there in the lengthening afternoon, Erica began to feel a little better. Here was a perfect excuse to leave Vienna and all the unhappiness she had known here. And surely the duke must agree to let her go, since her father needed her. After all, she had been here since October, and it was now almost March. And he did not really need her to spy anymore. The major alliance had been reached, and the nations were in agreement. The little business of international waterways, and diplomatic preference—even the Jewish and slavery problems—would soon be resolved.

Erica wandered over to the window to stare down into the street. It was snowing again, and she leaned her forehead on the cold pane to watch a sleigh go by, the bells on the team's harness gaily jingling. Across the street, in front of Kaunitz, two young boys were having a snowball fight, their cheeks as red as polished apples in the cold, crisp air. Her eye was caught then by three sturdy Viennese matrons directly below her window. They had paused to greet each other, and their breath escaped in little white puffs as they did so.

Vienna! How she had come to love it, and how her life had been changed here! She had known great sorrow in this city, and some happiness. A very little happiness, she reminded herself. But why, then, did she feel such reluctance to leave it? she wondered. She had the chance to go home at last; home, where people loved her and needed her; home, far away from the Duke of Graves.

Erica straightened up and turned with a sigh as she accepted the fact that it was Owen that made her unwilling to go. For even though it tore her heart, at least here she could be with him. And she knew that after she left Vienna she would never see him again.

She heard the first dressing bell ringing, and she made herself go upstairs. There was a ball at the Hofburg this evening that they were all to attend, and she must get ready for it.

As she climbed the stairs, she wondered when Owen would come home, and then she paused, gripping the banister hard. To think she had been regretting their separation, when now she had proof positive that he had spent the afternoon in another woman's bed! To think she had been lost in melancholy all the time he had been kissing and caressing someone else! She was worse than a little fool; she was a witless idiot!

Erica did not attempt to speak to the duke when she saw him later. She did not want to discuss her departure tonight. She had worn a white gown and the Kingsley pearls for the ball, and throughout the entire evening she had watched and listened with heightened senses. There were so many "last times" tonight. She would never sit quietly again while Agnes brushed her long hair smooth for a ball and clasped the Kingsley jewels around her throat and wrists. She would never curtsy to the Austrian emperor and empress or waltz in the Redoutensalle again, and somehow she wanted to impress it on her mind for all time.

She had no news from her elderly German admirer, for he had not attended the ball, and so there was no reason to go into the small salon with the duke when they came home in the early-morning hours. She almost wished there had been. Even though it would have been for the last time, it would have comforted her, that familiar bit of business.

Erica went to the duke's library again the following afternoon, and there she told him of her aunt's letter and asked him to release her.

The duke did not speak for a long time after she finished, and she wondered at it. At last he waved her to a chair and said quietly. "Yes, you must go home. There is very little you can do here now, after all, and it is time for you to leave."

Erica watched him as he limped over to brood down into the fire. She admired his rugged profile, those big shoulders and broad chest. As he rubbed his chin with one hand, she found herself remembering how that hand had felt caressing her, and she turned very pale.

"I shall, of course, make all the necessary arrangements," the duke told her, and she forced her mind from a luxurious bedroom in Burg Kobenzl that had been lit only by flickering firelight.

"Can you be ready in three days?" he asked her next. "It will take me that long to hire the men to accompany you and your maid, and arrange for an equerry to assist you. I rather think I shall send my groom, Albert Pray, in that role. He is fluent in French and German, and I can trust him to see you have a safe journey."

"Certainly, your grace," Erica said. When he did not turn and look at her, she rose to leave.

"You have been of inestimable value here, Erica," he told her, still staring down into the fire. "Not only to me but also to England. You may be proud always of your part in the congress, even though there can never be any public recognition of it."

Erica could only nod before she slipped way, softly closing the door behind her.

The three days passed quickly. A suddenly beaming

Agnes began packing immediately Erica told her the
news, and she nodded her head in happy agreement
when Erica told her she was not to pack any of the gowns
the duke had bought for her, nor the ermine cloak. Erica
was determined to take only the clothes she had brought
with her as Mrs. Stone. Erica Kingsley was about to
disappear.

She spent a sad afternoon taking leave of Dorothea de
Talleyrand-Périgord. She knew it was most unlikely that
she would ever see her friend again. She could not even
write to her, although she promised she would. She was
sorry that Dorothea would think her unworthy of her
friendship after she disappeared without a trace, but
when the countess asked for her address in England, she
had to tell her to give her letters to the duke, for she was
not sure where she would be living in the future. Every
lie she was forced to tell seemed worse than the last.

But it was not until the countess began to speak of
Owen that she felt the worst pain. "I am surprised that
the duke permits you to go, Erica," her friend remarked.
"Surely it is not possible that I was mistaken!"

"In what?" Erica made herself ask, although she could
not smile.

"I was so positive he was in love with you, and you
with him," Dorothea explained. "I have been waiting
this age for the two of you to admit it, fall into each
other's arms, and become as happy as Karl and I are."

Erica shook her head. "You are wrong, Dorothea,"
she said. She had spoken in an even voice, but it became
so distant suddenly that the countess was aware she had
made a grave error in voicing her suspicions.

"I am not in love with the duke, as I told you once
before. And I can assure you, he is not in love with me,"
Erica went on. "There is no reason for me to stay here
any longer, and I . . . I am homesick after all these long
months away."

She changed the subject then, and her friend was quick
to follow her lead. The two embraced when Erica left,
and tears were shed as they said their final fairwells.

As Erica went down the broad stairs and out into the
street, attended by the duke's footman, Dorothea went
over to her window to watch her.

"I am sorry, Erica," she whispered, wiping away a tear. "You, of all people, should be happy, and you are not. I wonder what happened between you and the duke that you could never bring yourself to tell me what it was? Because something did happen. I know it."

Talleyrand knocked then and entered her sitting room, and the countess made herself smile at him, and put Erica Kingsley from her mind. She could not help her friend, but she could help her uncle.

Lady Liza was delighted that Erica was leaving, for now she would be free to travel to Russia and rejoin Prince Gorsky. Vienna had not been amusing for her these past weeks. The duke and Ivan Torkashev had kept her under close surveillance, and she was bored and restless under the constraint. She made immediate arrangements to travel with a group of Russians returning home early from the congress, and her talk at dinners was all of her coming journey, the reception she would receive in St. Petersburg, and the wealth and pleasure she would have. Erica was glad she had so much to say, for the duke was brooding and reticent, and she herself had little to contribute.

She wondered, that last evening, if he would seek her out alone for a last farewell, but Owen Kingsley had himself under a rigid control. He had the rest of his life to regret Erica's departure; he would not add to that regret. He knew if he permitted himself to see her alone, all his self-imposed discipline might be to no avail.

He did, however, escort her to her carriage early the next morning. Lady Liza had not bothered to get up. She had said her careless good-byes the evening before, tossing them over her shoulder as she left for a ball. Erica was glad. She thoroughly detested the lady, and she was not the least bit sorry to be leaving her.

Now Erica came down the steps on the duke's arm. The carriage was waiting, with coachman and grooms dressed in his gold-and-gray livery, and Albert Pray already mounted, ready to lead the procession. Across the street, the Countess de Talleyrand-Périgord stood at the door of the Kaunitz, blowing her a kiss, and Erica made herself smile and wave in return.

She motioned Agnes to climb into the carriage before

her, and then she turned to the duke. She was wearing her old velvet cape, but he did not remark it or the absence of the ermine one as he took her hand in his for a moment before he bent to kiss it.

"Safe journey, Erica," he said softly, his black eyes steady on her face.

Erica searched that cold, stern face, and her eyes filled with tears. The duke must have noticed, for he held out his arm at once, to help her into the carriage. She blinked the tears away, but before she took his arm, she stood on tiptoe and reached up with both hands to bring his face down to hers so she could kiss his cheek. "Good-bye, Owen," she whispered.

Under the countess's observant eyes, the Duke of Graves did not remain to watch the carriage out of sight. Instead, he went back into the palace and up the stairs to Erica's rooms, where he closed the door behind him.

The suite was empty, of course, but he could feel her presence still lingering, a most unsatisfactory ghost. He went to her dressing room and opened the closets and drawers. As he had expected, all the beautiful gowns and accessories he had bought for her were still there, and, carefully wrapped in silver paper, the ermine cloak as well. Ripping the paper away, he buried his face in the soft fur, inhaling the scent that clung to it.

It was a long time before he left her rooms, and gave his butler orders to have all the gowns and the cloak and muff packed away in trunks and put in the attic. Owen could not bear to give a single thing away. After all, he told himself, it is all I have left of her.

The Lady Eliza Ridgely, soon to become Princess Gorsky, left Vienna two days later. Her leave-taking was not at all the wrenching emotional experience the duke had known when Erica left. As her carriage clattered away, he hoped Liza would be happy with her prince, and find some peace at last. Perhaps leaving him would be the best thing in the world for her, for he was a constant reminder of the love she could never have, that she thought she wanted so badly.

She had kissed him before she left, her eyes as full of tears as Erica's had been. As she approached him, he could see she intended to make it a searing farewell, and at the last moment he turned his head so her red lips only clung to his cheek.

She stepped back and dashed the tears from her eyes. "What a shame you are such a coward, Owen! And such a prude!" she said, her voice accusing. "I shall always regret it to the end of my days!"

"Be happy, Liza. Forget me," he told her, his deep voice even. "You and I were never a possibility."

The palace was very quiet now that he was alone. But when he was not on business for Wellington, the duke preferred to be solitary, and he rarely accepted the invitations he received.

He was sitting in his library trying to read one evening a few days later, when Rudge knocked and entered to present a note. The duke saw it was from headquarters, and so he thanked his butler and dismissed him before he opened it. He thought it unusual to receive such a direct communication, but now that the congress was almost over, perhaps Wellington did not feel the need for secrecy, as Castlereagh had.

He read the note quickly, and then he rose to his feet, cursing as he did so. The Duke of Wellington wrote to tell him that Napoleon had escaped from Elba on February 26 and was even now believed to be landing in France.

Owen crushed the note in his hand. His eyes grew distant as he remembered Robert Stewart commenting that if Napoleon ever did escape, his far-flung Grande Armée would flock to his standard once more. War would be inevitable.

But the Duke of Graves was not concerned with the possibility of future conflict. Instead, in his mind's eye he saw a carriage traveling toward France. A France that was now enemy territory again, full of soldiers hurrying to rejoin their emperor. And in that carriage was the only woman he had ever loved.

19

Erica had not allowed herself to cry more than a very few tears when she left the duke, and by the time the carriage turned the corner and left the Johannesgasse behind, she had composed herself. She could sense that Agnes was staring at her from her place beside her, but she did not explain why she had wept. Instead, she sat calmly, looking at the streets that had grown so familiar to her over the past months, and wondering if she would ever come to Vienna again. She knew it was highly unlikely.

She did not allow herself to think of Owen, for to do so would rend the tight fabric of control she had wrapped around her. She had promised herself she would think of him only when she was alone. And if her pillow were wet with tears every night for the rest of her life, at least no one would know of it. For tears, being such fragile, ephemeral things, dried quickly and left no trace.

Agnes saw how quiet she was, how pale, and wisely she held her tongue. If it had been anyone else, she would have said the girl was distraught to be leaving the man she loved. But that could not be, of course. Miss Erica and that awful duke? Never!

Still, she noticed, as the days passed, that although her mistress often pointed out something of interest in the countryside, or was perfectly willing to talk of home and her family, she would not discuss Vienna, and she never once mentioned the Duke of Graves.

Erica was glad to see that by the second day of their journey Agnes and Albert Pray had reached some sort of understanding. It was something she had worried about a little, for she knew Agnes might take a dislike to him simply because he was the duke's man. She was not to know that the two had banded together simply because they both sensed her deep hurt and wanted to make the journey as easy as possible for her.

The duke had charged Albert Pray especially with this task, and the look on his rugged face as he did so had been all the instruction his groom had needed. Miss Kingsley was obviously his master's lady, although for the life of him, Mr. Pray had no idea why the duke had sent her away. It was plain to see he loved her, and if he were not mistaken, and he really didn't think he was, she loved him too.

It was a mystery, and one he pondered often as he led the way through Bavaria and Baden. He and Owen Kingsley had planned the route together, choosing the straightest path to the Channel and a ship for home. When the carriage reached the outskirts of Strassburg, Pray knew they had only to journey across France to Le Havre, and the foreign leg of their trip would be over. Not that he was to leave the lady there, of course. He smiled his gray little smile, remembering the duke's insistence that he make arrangements for the carriage and team to be transported on the ship with them and all the servants, so Miss Erica could reach Northumberland in style and perfect comfort.

Only when he had seen her reunited with her family was he to return to Graveshead, the duke's estate in Kent, and await further orders.

Pray was a little surprised to see how rudely the French treated them whenever they stopped overnight in an inn or for a meal. They were, both men and women, not only sullen but also impertinent. He did not like it, because it was so very unusual, but he did not say anything about it to Miss Kingsley or the others. All the antennae he had developed in Vienna told him there was something wrong, something very wrong indeed. It was not just that they were overcharged for everything, although they were—he had expected that. It was something in the curl of a lip, the slow, insolent service, a barely hidden sneer.

He began to search out smaller, less populated villages to stop in at night, for the dislike, almost outright hostility, seemed more prevalent in the larger towns.

And suddenly he was very careful to check his pistols every morning before they set out again. The grooms were armed too, and he had a quiet word with them when Agnes Watts and Miss Kingsley were not around to hear.

They had almost reached St. Dizier when Mr. Pray decided to stop in a pleasant country inn rather early in the afternoon. It would give Miss Erica a rest from the jolting coach, and he knew if they went on, they would be forced to put up in the town itself.

The landlord of the inn did not appear to realize his great good fortune in gaining their patronage, and it was not until he saw the amount of gold that Mr. Pray was prepared to pay that he grudgingly agreed to house them.

Albert Pray was frowning when he helped Miss Erica from the coach to show her to the private parlor he had engaged. They were alone, for Agnes had followed the landlord up the stairs to the bedchamber to unpack for her.

As he bowed and turned to leave, Erica said, "A moment, Mr. Pray, if you would be so good."

He turned back almost reluctantly, and Erica studied his somber face. "And now I think it is time you told me what the matter is," she said. As he hesitated, she added, "It is as plain as the nose on your face that we are not wanted here, nor have we been ever since we entered France. Why is that?"

Pray twisted his hat in his hands, wondering what he should do, and Erica waved impatiently. "Come now! I am not a child or a weakling! Why are the French so unfriendly?"

"I don't know, miss," he said. "But you're right, there's something amiss. Why, it's almost as if we were their enemies still. I don't understand, but I worry. The deeper we get into France, the worse it gets. I think we'll give Paris a wide berth, head north a bit."

Erica nodded. "Very well. I trust you completely. You are armed, of course?"

At his assent, she went on, "I think it might be wise if you give me a pistol too. I am an excellent shot, and I did not like that column we passed earlier, all those men trudging along the side of the road. They were not dressed as farmers, but soldiers. Where were they going, and why, I wonder. And why did they shake their fists and curse us as we passed?"

A deep harsh voice spoke from the doorway. "Because they are marching to war with England and her allies again. Napoleon has escaped from Elba, and is even now in France."

"Owen!" Erica cried as she spun around, grasping a chair back for support. The Duke of Graves loomed in the doorway, dusty and tired-looking. She wanted to run to him, but Mr. Pray coughed, and she made herself stand still, although she never took her eyes from his face.

"Your grace!" Pray exclaimed, going toward him to bow. "I'm that glad to see you, sir!"

"And I," Erica said softly, holding out the chair. "Sit down and let me order you some wine."

Owen limped into the room. "I have already done so, and arranged for accommodations for myself and my men as well," he said.

"How very fortunate the inn is so spacious," Erica remarked, trying to hide the ecstasy she felt at being with him again. "For I must tell you, sir, if it weren't, I would not have given up a single room for you."

Owen smiled at her then, remembering, as she was, the first time they had met. He came and took both her hands in his. "You are well, Erica?"

"Very well . . . now," she replied.

Mr. Pray suddenly remembered he had to see to the team and speak to the coachman about something, and he hurried from the room, mumbling excuses that nobody heard.

The duke stared down at the lovely face he had never thought to see again. He felt he should thank Napoleon personally for his timely escape, for it had given him the perfect excuse to ride to her rescue like one of the knights of old.

He shook his head at his foolish thoughts, and Erica sighed and put her arms around him to rest her cheek on his chest. She closed her eyes and murmured a silent prayer of thanks as she felt his heart beating strongly under her head.

The duke took her into his arms just as one of her brothers would have done. They stood there quietly together until a maid knocked and brought in a bottle of wine and glasses, and then they stepped apart.

When Agnes appeared, she found the Duke of Graves and her mistress seated side by side drinking wine and studying a map. She gasped in surprise. "Why, it's *you!*" she exclaimed.

Owen stared at her, his black eyes cold. "Indeed it is, Miss Watts," he said. "Like the proverbial bad penny, I do seem to have a way of turning up, don't I?"

Agnes sniffed, and he said, "Go and find Pray for me, and then both of you come back here. We have plans to make."

He spoke so coldly and sternly that Agnes curtsied and left them at once.

When the two servants came back, the duke waved them to chairs on the other side of the table. Agnes would have demurred, but Erica gave her such a speaking glance, she took the seat indicated without a word.

The duke told them in a few terse words the story of Napoleon's escape and what he had learned before leaving Vienna. "I came after you, hoping to catch you up before you were too far into France," he concluded. "But you have made good time, and now my original plan for all of us to make a dash for the border must be forfeited.

"Here is what I think we must do," he went on, glad no one had interrupted him. He was hungry, his leg ached, and he wanted to sleep—something he had done precious little of these past few days. "Albert, you will take the coach and Miss Watts and head north toward Belgium. Erica and I, accompanied by the men I brought with me, will also head directly north from here, but in my racing curricle. We'll wait for you to catch us up in Bouillon, just over the border."

Agnes' indrawn breath was almost a hiss. "What?" she demanded. "Go off with Miss Erica alone? You'll never!"

Before Erica could reprimand her, the duke said quickly, "Oh yes I shall, Miss Watts! I want your mistress safe as quickly as possible. To travel by barouche, heavily laden with baggage, would be much too slow and much too dangerous for her." He eyed Agnes' sturdy frame and added, "There is certainly no room for you in the curricle. It is built for speed. But I do assure you the lady will be a lot safer with me and the men I brought to guard her, than stopped and perhaps ravished by a troop of French soldiers. I am sure you must agree any escort is preferable to that, even if that escort is me."

Agnes gasped and subsided, but Erica saw she still looked upset. For herself, she could think of nothing she would enjoy more than being seated close to Owen all day, even if they were tearing through enemy territory.

"I have a place in mind, some fifty miles from here, where we can find sanctuary, at least tomorrow night, as can Miss Watts and Albert when they reach it. It is the château of a Bourbon sympathizer. But, Erica, you must only bring what you absolutely need in one small portmanteau. We travel light!"

Erica stared at him. She saw the deep lines that weariness and worry had etched on his rugged face, and she asked Albert Pray to have dinner served at once. Owen was sure to feel better after he had had some hot food.

As he ate, the duke continued to talk to his man, telling him the route he meant to follow: toward Verdun, then northeast along the River Meuse. He told him the location of the château as well.

The table had been cleared, and the duke was sipping an excellent Burgundy and staring down at the bright red checkered tablecloth when Erica saw his face brighten.

"But of course!" he exclaimed. "I must have this tablecloth!"

Erica and Albert Pray exchanged glances. Agnes had gone upstairs again to pack a small bag for Erica as the duke had ordered and the three were alone.

"Sir?" Pray asked, his voice noncommittal.

"See to it, Albert!" Owen Kingsley ordered briskly.
"Say madam has taken a fancy to it, or wants a souvenir of
her journey—whatever! We'll take it with us in the
curricle. Then, if we see danger ahead, we'll leave a
piece of it by the side of the road. With the snow, it
should be easy to spot, so check the hedges, branches,
and signposts carefully as you pass."

He turned to Erica then. "I am not too concerned
about our safety. I have a letter from Talleyrand himself,
ordering our safe passage. It will be easy for me to trace
it and give a copy to Albert, to protect them as well. And
a state of confusion exists now, the army not assembled
in force, just those little bands of men trying to reach
Napoleon. You must not worry!"

He spoke to his groom again then. "Albert, go and
fetch the large parcel in my room, and bring it here."

Erica was smiling to herself. It seemed a very elaborate plan, and, perhaps, one that was unnecessary. Because if the duke had a letter from Talleyrand, why did
he bother to copy it? Why didn't he just let her continue
to travel in the comfortable coach with her maid? Why
was there any need for this mad dash by curricle, just the
two of them? Her eyes glowed as the answers to these
questions became clear to her, and she had to turn away
for a moment to compose herself.

When Albert brought the parcel, Owen dismissed him
until the next morning. He shook his hand and thanked
him for all he had done for Erica so far, and wished him
safe journey.

"Not to worry, your grace," Pray said as he left them.
"I'll bring Miss Watts and the baggage safe."

As soon as the door was safely closed behind him, the
duke rose and opened the bulky package. Erica stared as
he drew from the paper the ermine cloak she had never
thought to see again.

He held it out to her. "Wear it tomorrow, Erica," he
said. "You will need it, for the curricle is not built for
warmth or comfort."

She took it from his hands, but she was frowning now,
and he said a little impatiently, "I know I promised you
that you would have it to wear only in Vienna, but I
cannot have you getting chilled."

"It's not that," she told him. "It's just that it is such a sumptuous thing and out of place in the country. Won't any soldiers we see be suspicious of such luxury, perhaps even try and rob us?"

Now it was the duke's turn to frown, but Erica's face brightened. "But stay! I just had an idea," she said quickly. "Tell me, does Talleyrand's letter mention our names?"

Owen shook his head. "No, it only says the bearer of this letter. But why do you ask?"

"Because I have a perfect solution," Erica told him. "How would it be if I were not English at all? I could be a Swedish lady traveling home from the congress. The direction we take is right, after all, and the French do not feel the same enmity toward the Swedes that they do for the English."

"And what shall I be?" the duke asked her. "I do not speak Swedish."

"No," Erica said slowly. "There is that." She paused and then she said, "You will be a personal guard, appointed by my husband, and I can say you are a mute."

"And why are you racing along in such an uncomfortable vehicle, Erica? Are you an eccentric that you brave the cold winter weather in a racing curricle?" he asked politely.

Erica saw the amusement deep in his black eyes, and she thought quickly. "No, I am hurrying to my father's bedside," she invented. "He is very ill, and not expected to live." Silently she begged God and her father to forgive her for such a terrible, if appropriate, thought.

She waited a little breathlessly as Owen considered her carefully. Finally he nodded. "Yes, that might work," he said slowly. "Excuse me for a moment, Erica."

Bewildered, she watched him limp from the room. She was still sitting quietly at the table when he returned with a small wooden casket. As she watched, he put it down before her and unlocked it. She gasped as she saw the Kingsley jewels sparkling up at her—those emeralds, pearls, and diamonds. The duke searched through them until he found the diamond tiara, to hold it out to her.

"But not just *any* Swedish lady, Erica," he told her.

"You shall be none other than a princess, niece of great Bernadotte!"

Erica put her head back and laughed, and he admired her glowing eyes and soft skin as she did so. "Oh, Owen," she said helplessly, wiping her eyes at last. "I think you are gilding the lily, sir! Surely nobody wears a tiara in the country, at least during the daytime."

"No, but peasant soldiers won't know that," he assured her. "They will be dumbstruck; in awe. And if you can be arrogant enough, they will not dare to question you."

Erica nodded. "I have just the perfect person in mind to imitate," she told him, her eyes twinkling again. "He is proud, cold, stern, omnipotent, sarcastic, overbearing—"

Owen put his big hand over her mouth. She noted he was oddly gentle about it. "That will be quite enough from you, madam," he ordered. "Now, you must excuse me. I must copy that letter for Albert before I get some sleep. I am very weary. And, after all, we will have all day tomorrow to continue this . . . this discussion."

After he had locked the rest of the jewels away, he bowed to her. Erica waited, a little breathlessly, but although he paused then, he did not come closer or touch her. At the door, he told her he had given orders for the curricle to be ready at eight, and she nodded.

"I will be ready. Sleep well, Owen," she said softly.

Agnes was still indignant as she helped Erica dress in her warmest gown the next morning, and she muttered all the time she was doing her hair up in the familiar chignon. And when she fastened the diamond tiara on securely, and brought the ermine cloak, her homely face was set in lines of severe disapproval.

Erica grasped her arms and looked straight into her eyes. "That will be quite enough, Agnes," she said quietly. "I know what you think of all this, and of the duke, but it does not matter to me. Nothing matters except that I can be with him. I am not your little 'Miss Erica' anymore, Agnes. I am a woman, and I love him. And now, finally, I am sure he loves me. You will say no more, nor will you criticize the Duke of Graves ever again. Do . . . you . . . understand?"

Agnes stared at her, her mouth falling open a little. At last she nodded and bowed her head in submission. She knew by Erica's expression, and the tone of her voice, that this was not something she could continue to argue, or ever argue in the future.

When Erica saw her hands still twisting her apron in distress, she hugged her. "Don't worry, Agnes," she said softly. "It will be all right, you'll see."

When Erica came out into the yard of the inn, the duke was waiting for her and having a few words with the grooms who were to go with them. He came to help her to her seat in the curricle himself, bowing deeply as he did so. Before he wrapped a fur rug tightly around her feet, he reached into his pocket to get the letter they hoped would save them, and gave it to her to keep safe.

Erica could see the innkeeper and some maids and stablehands watching them, every mouth identically agape at the lady in ermines and diamonds, and she had to hide a smile.

As Owen climbed up beside her to take the reins, the curricle, being so light, rocked and quivered. It was also not very roomy, and she could feel the duke's body against hers, shoulder, hip, thigh. She settled back with a smile of complete happiness.

"Do wave to your subjects, Princess," Owen told her. "You would not care to disappoint them now, would you?"

Erica raised a regal hand, and then she giggled as the assembled maids, grooms, and ostlers bowed and curtsied in return. The curricle swept out of the yard, surrounded by the four grooms dressed in the duke's livery. As they turned the corner, Erica saw the coachman bringing the barouche forward, and she knew Agnes and Mr. Pray would soon be on their way as well. She said a prayer for their safety.

She was still smiling when the duke turned his head to look at her. They had left the village behind them now, and he had established the team in a steady mile-eating canter.

"Now, why do you look so pleased, Erica?" he asked.

"It is going to be a long, tiresome day, and there may well be danger."

Erica was sure she looked pleased. Ever since the duke had arrived and told her his plans, she had felt a bubble of happiness inside her every time she looked at his strong, rugged face. A bubble that threatened to grow larger and larger until it burst and floated her away on a cloud of pure euphoria. And even when Owen had left her last night without a kiss, she had understood his reasons and accepted them. He was tired, and he wanted to wait until they were alone—really alone. Besides, she knew he had more in mind than one good-night kiss in the parlor of a French inn. Oh, my, yes.

"Perhaps there may be danger," she replied now. "But I am happy even so. You know, when I left Vienna, I never thought to see you again. But you came after me, and now we are together. Besides, I know very well that since you have that letter from Talleyrand, there was never any need for us to race ahead of the others and participate in this elaborate charade. The only reason we are doing so is that you want to be alone with me, as I want to be alone with you. Isn't that so, sir?"

The duke stared between his leader's ears at the road ahead, frowning a little as he did so.

When he did not answer her, Erica said calmly, "Give over, Owen, do. There is nothing you can say that will convince me you do not love me—not now. Not anymore. What you told me in Vienna was a lie. I don't know why you did it, but I am so in love with you, I don't care. I don't even care that you went to a brothel there after our night at Burg Kobenzl."

The duke's hands dropped a little, and the team began to gallop. He settled them back into a canter before he said, "What are you talking about? I never went to a brothel!"

"But, Owen, I saw you going in," Erica insisted. "I was with Dorothea in her carriage near the Minoritenplatz."

She was surprised when he smiled. "Oh, *that* brothel," he said lightly. "I do assure you, Erica, my reason for visiting it had nothing whatsoever to do with the . . . business generally transacted there."

He turned a little as if to gauge her reaction. "You do believe me, don't you?" he asked a little anxiously.

"Of course I do," she told him promptly, her voice serene. "I'm sure you had a very good reason to be there, which someday, when you can, you will explain. I know that there are a great many things you cannot tell me now. I don't ask you to."

They rode along in silence for a while. The duke thought again how intelligent and quick Erica was, how comfortable to be with, no matter what the situation, and he was glad he had spirited her away from Agnes and the others, and had her completely to himself. It did not matter that she had guessed his motives for doing so, although he was delighted that she concurred with them. And although he knew that all the excellent reasons he had had for putting her away from him in Vienna had not changed, now it was as if they had been put aside, for this little time at least, until he had her safely on a ship for home. He had decided to be that selfish, because he loved her so. Of course he would have to face them again, as he had faced them once before, but not yet. Oh, no, not yet. This time was theirs.

He had not decided this in a moment; rather it had grown slowly during those frantic hours of preparation in Vienna before he could begin to chase after her, and during all the breathless, weary journey when he had found himself praying, with a fervor he had not known except when he was a boy, that he would find her and she would be safe. He had known then how strong his love for her was, what a powerful hold she had on him. He accepted it, for he could no longer deny it, especially to himself. And he could not deny it to Erica either, for she knew. Somehow, she knew, even without him putting it into words.

They stopped at a wayside inn halfway through the morning for a short rest and some refreshment. Erica was treated with an awed respect there. She made it a point to speak only Swedish to the duke, and he nodded and bowed often. She explained to the innkeeper that her driver was dumb. The Austrian grooms, of course, spoke French or German, but that was understandable and could not be remarked.

As they drove away from the inn, she felt a little better about their plan. At least they had fooled the locals there; perhaps French soldiers could be hoodwinked as well.

As the curricle bowled along, she remembered Talleyrand's letter, and she asked the duke how he had obtained it.

He smiled in memory. "It was all the Countess de Talleyrand-Périgord's doing," he told her. "And, by the way, I carry a letter for you from her. Remind me to give it to you. As soon as she heard Napoleon had escaped Elba, she came hurrying over from the Kaunitz to see me. She was very worried about your safety, Erica, for she knew that you were in danger. After we discussed what I planned to do, she begged her uncle for a letter of safe passage. Talleyrand graciously agreed. He sends his best wishes to you, by the way. But the poor man! He does not know what will happen to France, and to him, now. I suspect he hopes Napoleon will be stopped before he reaches Paris, and I am sure he has sent instructions to the government there, to that effect. But I am also sure he knows what a vain hope that is. The French have always been mad for their emperor, and fat old Louis is as nothing compared with Napoleon's magnetism and leadership.

"The countess also gave me a letter to the owner of the château I told you about. We should reach it easily by late afternoon, if there are no mishaps. I am sure this Count Duvallier will give us shelter. He is a distant cousin of the countess's husband, Edmond."

He fell silent then, remembering how the countess had begged him to admit his love for Erica when he saw her again, and told him how much she cared for him. She had asked him point-blank why he had never done so, but the duke could not share his reasons with her. He had never been able to stand pity.

"How clever you have been!" Erica said, interrupting his thoughts. "But won't this count think it very strange that we travel like this together?"

The duke turned to look down at her, so close to him in the narrow carriage. "No, he will not," he said softly as his black eyes caressed her face. "You change roles again, you see. When we reach the château, you become the Duchess of Graves."

He pretended he had to give his attention to the team then. When he looked back, he saw she was smiling at him. "But of course," she said serenely. "How lovely that will be! Oh, can we not go any faster, your grace?"

"Erica!" he breathed, delighted, before he changed the subject. It was almost as if he did not dare to continue it.

Later that morning, they came upon a small column of men marching in the direction they had come. No one challenged them, and once they were safely by, the duke sent one of the grooms circling back to the crossroads they had passed earlier, to leave a piece of red-checkered tablecloth fastened to the arm of the signpost there.

"It will take them longer, but if Albert takes the other road, he will avoid the soldiers," the duke said.

They were forced to the same maneuver twice more. Erica was relieved that the soldiers did not appear to want to do anything but gape at them, and she could see the duke had been right. There seemed to be no officers with them, and as peasants, they did not dare stop the curricle containing such a richly clothed lady who was surrounded by her own little troop of guards. Owen moved past them at a brisk pace, however, before they had time to compare the strength of their respective forces.

The duke found himself relaxing, it had been so easy. But their good fortune was not to continue. Suddenly, as they rounded a bend in the road, they saw a large troop ahead of them. Unlike the others, this one did not straggle along in disorder, but marched smartly under the watchful eye of a lieutenant on horseback.

The duke cursed under his breath, and Erica pressed his arm in reassurance.

When the French officer saw the curricle coming toward him, he turned his horse to block the roadway, raising his saber and ordering them to halt in the name of the emperor.

The duke was forced to obey. The soldiers were armed, and he knew there was no way to avoid the encounter.

Erica sat quietly beside him as the French officer approached. As he neared them, she called a long order in

Swedish to the grooms, and, prepared by the duke, they stiffened to attention in their saddles, and saluted the officer.

"Well, Lieutenant," Erica said in French as the officer reined in beside the curricle, "I trust there is some good reason you detain me? I am in a hurry, be brief about it!"

The officer stared at her as she put back her hood. The diamond tiara on her silvery hair glinted in the weak winter sunlight, and the soldiers murmured behind their hands as they edged closer.

"Your name and business, *madame*," the officer demanded, his voice cold.

"I am Princess Erica, niece of your former Marshal Bernadotte, who is now crown prince of Sweden," she said. "I am making my way home as fast as I can, for my father is on his deathbed."

"Indeed? How do I know what you say is true?" the officer asked, sneering at her in patent disbelief. Tensing, the duke saw Erica put up her chin, and he thought she looked very regal.

"Because I have just told you so!" she snapped, her green eyes flashing. Then she reached into the pocket of her cloak and drew out the letter the duke had given her. "Here, read this, for I must be on my way!" she said. "It is safe conduct from Prince de Talleyrand-Périgord himself!"

The soldiers repeated the name in awed whispers and shuffled their feet. The lieutenant read the letter slowly, holding it close to his nose.

Erica felt it an age before he folded it and handed it back to her with a deep bow over his saddle. "Your pardon, *princesse*," he said. "All is in order. Forgive me for delaying you."

Erica waved her hand. "You were only doing your duty, sir. Oh, by the way, my baggage coach comes after me. Give it safe passage too, if you should encounter it."

The lieutenant saluted, and she said more kindly, "I quite understand your concern. For now that Napoleon has returned, you must have a care for possible enemies. *Vive l'empereur!*"

She was heartily echoed by the troops, who continued to cheer even after the curricle pulled away from them.

"Whew!" the duke muttered when they were safely out of earshot. "My congratulations, ma'am! You were the complete princess. In fact, I am sorry now we did not make you a queen!"

"Thank you," Erica told him, and then, after a moment, she added, "But on the whole, if I have to playact, I think I would prefer a lower rank. Yes, a duchess will be just right. I can hardly wait to begin."

The duke stared down at her laughing face in bemusement, until she was forced to point out he was in danger of driving the team right off the road into a ditch.

20

It was dusk when at last they reached the Château Duvallier, some twenty miles from Verdun. The afternoon had been uneventful, for although they had seen other French soldiers in groups ranging from a few to well over two dozen, they had not been stopped again.

Still, Erica was tired and cold, and as the duke halted the weary team before a pair of high wrought-iron gates, she sighed a little in relief. As one of the grooms dismounted to ring for the gatekeeper, Owen smiled down at her.

"All right, Erica?" he asked her softly.

"All right, Owen," she told him, summoning a smile for the concern she saw in his eyes. "However, it will be a relief to get out of this curricle and be warm again. It may be fast, but it is very uncomfortable."

"Begging your pardon, your grace, but there's no one here," the groom called. "And no lights in the gatehouse, either."

"Try the gate," the duke told him. "It may be unlocked, since there is no keeper to see to it. It is likely he is one of the soldiers we saw this afternoon, marching off to war again."

The groom went to inspect the gate, and Erica watched him anxiously. If they had to go on—if there was no sanctuary for them here . . . But then the gates creaked open, one after the other, and she relaxed.

"Not long now, Erica," the duke told her as he slapped the reins on the team's backs to get them moving again. They trotted up a long cypress-lined drive, and Erica peered ahead, searching for a first glimpse of the château.

"There it is!" she cried a moment later, relieved that there were lights in a few windows. At least someone was at the main house.

The duke drove the team under a high arched gateway, and their hooves clattered in the cobbled yard. Erica could see very little as he circled a large fountain and halted before an impressive iron-studded door.

"Another medieval mansion," he murmured as he prepared to get down. Erica saw him open the same cane he had used at Schönbrunn. "Wait here, my dear, until I can rouse the house," he told her.

One of the grooms preceded him up the shallow stairs, and at the duke's nod, sounded the heavy lion's-head door knocker.

It seemed a long time before anyone came, but at last Erica saw an elderly butler standing there peering at them. He and the duke spoke together at length before he opened the door wider and bowed.

Owen came back to help Erica from the curricle. "Take the team and your horses around to the stables, Hans," he ordered the groom who had assisted him. "You will find food in the kitchen, and beds will be arranged."

Erica was stiff and numb from the long hours in the carriage, and she staggered a little as she got down. Owen's arm went around her quickly to pull her safe against him, and in that fashion they mounted the steps together.

The butler had lit another branch of candles, and Erica was able to inspect the hall they stood in in its light. As he bowed to her, the duke explained, "The count and his family are not in residence, but the butler assures me there will be no problem about our staying here. He has sent a footman for the housekeeper, and soon, my dear, our rooms will be prepared and you can rest."

The butler asked them if they would care to come into the salon until that time, and he showed them the way, moving at a slow, shuffling pace. Erica could see that he was a very old man, and she wondered that he was still in service.

The salon was cold, for no fire had been lit there, and she had no desire to remove her fur cloak. She noticed that Owen kept his greatcoat on as well.

"I apologize for the cold room, your grace," the butler said. "We are shorthanded here, but as soon as René comes back, I'll have him make up the fire. It's the war, you know," he added sadly.

The duke assured him they understood, and asked if they might have some wine. "It has been a long, tedious day, and the duchess could use some refreshment," he concluded.

Erica did not dare to look at him as the old butler shuffled away.

"Feeling shy, Erica?" he teased her as soon as they were alone. "And to think I was looking forward so to your performance as a duchess!"

Erica took a deep breath and smiled at him. He still had his arm around her, and she could not resist raising her face for a kiss.

"Now, your grace?" he whispered, his mouth a tantalizing inch from hers.

"At once!" she ordered, imperious again.

Wrapped in his arms, as well as her fur cloak, Erica was thoroughly and passionately kissed.

It was with great reluctance that they drew apart as the old butler coughed behind them. With him came the housekeeper, a thin little woman with black eyes that twinkled at her guests. Ah, *l'amour!* she thought to herself as she bustled forward to welcome them, a smile wreathing her thin lips.

Madame Lemieux was middle-aged and competent. In no time at all a fire was warming the salon, and Erica and the duke were seated before it enjoying a glass of wine.

The housekeeper asked when they would like dinner served, and a time an hour hence was set. As she curtsied to leave them, she was reminded of something else.

"Your grace would care for a bath?" she asked Erica. "It will take only a little while to prepare it."

"Thank you, *madame*," Erica said. "But since I have no change of clothing, I think I would prefer it after dinner. We were forced to travel light, and my baggage comes later, so I must dine as I am."

The housekeeper nodded. "These are terrible times," she said, and Erica almost giggled. *Madame* had sounded as if she regretted the war simply because it was inconveniencing the guests.

She hurried away then to see to their comfort and have their bags brought in, and Owen raised his glass to Erica in a lazy toast. "Very ducal," he complimented her. "Very ducal, indeed."

"Oh, I will never be the equal of you, your grace," she told him, feeling a little light-headed. But whether it was from the warm fire, the delicious wine, or her delight in being with the man seated across from her, she could not tell.

He smiled at her, and then he reached into his jacket pocket. "Before I forget, here is the countess's letter."

As he handed it to her, Erica's eyes asked silent permission to read it. The duke nodded, and she slit the seal. "My dear Erica," the letter began, "I write in haste, for the duke leaves soon. I must tell you, I have never seen a man so frantic with worry as he is. He loves you, I know he does. And now, Erica, *at last*, will you admit you love him too? Seize your chance for happiness, I beg you. It may never be granted to you again. I shall pray you do—as I shall pray for your safety, my friend. Dorothea."

Erica knew she had paled as she read the note, and it was a long moment before she could meet the duke's amused black eyes. As she folded the note he said, "From your bemused look, my dear, I can see I had better not ask a single thing about your letter. No doubt it was not meant to be discussed with, er, a mere man."

Erica smiled at him, noting the glint in his eyes. "No, it was meant only for my eyes," she said. "It contains some very good advice which I most certainly intend to take."

They sat together sipping their wine and talking of the day's adventures until Madame Lemieux came back to escort them to their rooms. As they climbed the stairs, she told them René would be glad to serve as the duke's valet, and she had assigned a young girl named Marie to maid the duchess. "She is very competent, your grace, she assured Erica. "Please ask her for whatever you require."

The rooms she showed them to were large, and as

comfortable as the salon had been. There were connecting bedrooms and separate dressing rooms, and a small common sitting room.

Just before she left them, *madame* reminded them that dinner would be served shortly, although, of course, she would be glad to have it put back if they wanted to rest first.

The duke thanked her, but told her they would eat at the specified time. "We are very hungry, *madame,*" he told her. "However, I foresee an early bedtime for the duchess."

The housekeeper curtsied, hiding a smile, which fortunately, Erica did not notice.

Owen did not embrace her when they were alone, although she waited rather breathlessly for him to do so. Instead, he flicked her chin with a careless finger and turned her around to give her a little push. "Go and make yourself tidy, Duchess," he ordered. "I am ravenous! And surely you know that a man must be fed?"

"To keep up his strength, sir?" she asked demurely over her shoulder.

Erica heard him laughing as he left her, and she went into the dressing room. She washed her face and hands. As she looked in a pier glass, she wondered if she should discard the diamond tiara. It looked rather ridiculous with her simple gown, now that she had removed her cloak. At last she decided to wear it to dinner, for she did not like to leave it in a strange place, unattended.

She investigated her room, noticing that her few things had been unpacked, her nightgown and robe laid across the large canopied bed.

As the dinner bell rang, she quickly smoothed her hair and hurried back to the sitting room, where Owen was waiting for her.

Dinner was a simple affair, but delicious, although Erica was hardly aware of what she ate.

"How good this is!" she said finally, smiling at the old butler, who was serving them. "I did not realize I was so hungry."

"Understandable, when you consider we have not eaten since morning," Owen said. "Do have some more veal, my dear. It is excellent."

The meal concluded with a chocolate mousse and coffee, and as the table was being cleared and the port brought in, the duke said, "Do not leave me solitary, Erica. Join me in a glass."

Erica nodded. She wondered if the anticipation she felt showed on her face, and she had forced herself not to look at Owen too often during the meal, for she was afraid she would give herself away if she did. Deep inside her, she ached with longing for him, and as the minutes passed, that feeling grew.

As the butler bowed and left them, she wondered how long it would be before they could decently retire. The thought of more desultory conversation in the salon had no appeal for her at all. And then she wondered if she were a truly wicked woman to feel this way as she moved her wineglass in a little circle, her eyes intent on the deep ruby color.

"Erica?" the duke asked, his deep voice soft.

She looked up, and was surprised and delighted to see an answering hunger in his black eyes.

"What are you thinking about, love?" he asked her.

Erica considered the question before she shook her head. "I cannot tell you that," she said shyly.

Owen laughed and reached for her hand, glad *madame* had put her next to him instead of an acre away down the long table. "You don't have to tell me, Erica," he whispered. "For we are both thinking the exact same thing.

"And now I think it would be a good idea for you to finish up your wine, excuse yourself prettily, and go and call for that bath you wanted to have," he told her. "And I will try to contain my impatience. But do not be long about it, my dear, I beg you."

Erica could not speak. Instead, she only nodded and swallowed her port obediently. As she rose, the duke rose too, to help her. She felt his lips on the nape of her neck, and she leaned back against his long, hard length, feeling shivery and weak as his arms came around her.

"Hurry," he whispered into her hair.

She made herself step away to curtsy, and as she walked from the room, she realized that she didn't care what anyone thought of such an early bedtime. It was completely unimportant.

Madame was not at all surprised when the bathwater was called for a few minutes later. It was obvious to her that this strange English couple were in love, although she doubted they were married. The so-called duchess did not wear a wedding ring. But what did it matter? she asked herself with a very Gallic shrug as she sent the maids scurrying. It was *l'amour!*

As soon as the last can of hot water had been brought, Erica dismissed the maid. "Thank you for your help, Marie," she said. "I will ring in the morning when I want you."

The maid curtsied. She was a little disappointed the duchess had not let her take down her hair to brush it. It was such a lovely color!

Erica sank down into the hot water and closed her eyes. How heavenly it felt after the cold, frightening day she had spent. She began to wash herself with the scented soap Marie had left for her, dreaming of Owen and the happiness they were soon to share.

She was seated at the dressing table to take down her hair when he knocked and came in. He had removed only his coat and neckcloth, and opened his shirt, and she wondered at it.

As she watched him in the glass, a welcoming smile on her lips, he limped up to her and calmly began to take the pins from her hair. In a moment it was streaming down her back, and he picked up her brush.

"You must allow me to maid you, ma'am," he said, his dark eyes absorbed as the brush slid through those silvery tresses. "I have always loved your hair, you know. It is the most beautiful I have ever seen."

Erica closed her eyes. Little shivers ran up and down her spine as he played with her hair.

At last he dropped the brush to bend down and bury his face in the whole glorious length of it. Erica was glad she had had Agnes wash it two nights ago. I must have had a premonition this was going to happen, she thought.

Owen stood up and held out his hand, and she rose quickly to go into his waiting arms. His kiss was deep and searing in its urgency, yet it was tender at the same time, and it made her want to cry.

His lovemaking was urgent too, and Erica was glad of

it. For some reason, she was filled with the same breathless need for haste that he was, and the slow, careful
caresses they had shared before could not satisfy them
tonight.

When he removed her robe, she was quick to unbutton
her nightgown and drop it to the floor. She heard his
sharp intake of breath and saw how his eyes kissed every
inch of her, and she stood proudly for him until he pulled
her close again.

Tonight she thought she would die with impatience
when he left her sprawled across the bed they had sought
so blindly only moments before. And then a little frown
creased her brow as he limped away to extinguish all but
one branch of candles that was set on the mantelpiece on
the other side of the room. She wished he would not. She
was greedy for him, she wanted to see all of him clearly,
watch his facial expressions as he made love to her. As
he came back and removed his clothes, she wondered
why he had done it, but her throat was so tight with
yearning, she could not ask. And then he was beside her
again, his hands and lips eager, and she forgot it.

Tonight he did not speak a single word to her, nor she
to him. Instead, he took her in silent, passionate haste.
Erica clung to him as a deluge of emotion swept through
her, threatening to carry her away to a place she had
never known. For one brief moment she tried to fight it,
for she was frightened of its power. But Owen would not
let her. His fervent body seemed to be insisting she travel
with him, and so she let herself be engulfed by the raging
torrent carrying her where it would.

She was surprised to discover she did not die from the
experience, although it had felt like death, a little, and
she had been unable to stop calling out his name with passionate fervor, over and over. It was as if the word
"Owen" had become a lifeline for her.

Now she whimpered as the flood ebbed away to little
ripples of sensation. Owen held her close, and rocked her
in his arms as if she were a child. His breathing was
ragged still, and he did not speak as one hand gently
smoothed her hair back so he could kiss each eyelid and
the tip of her nose.

Erica opened her eyes at last, and sighed. She had not

known it could be like this—so furious and fulfilling and consuming. Idly she wondered if it were the same for everyone, and then, like all lovers, decided that she and Owen were unique.

"Now what are you thinking, love?" his deep voice asked. She looked up at him with eyes full of awe for the mystery he had just revealed to her. She knew she would never be the same, that tonight she had passed through some unseen barrier and left her girlhood behind forever. She realized she was abandoning it without a qualm, and feeling only pity for all those girls who had not experienced what she had, in the arms of a man who loved them.

"I am thinking how happy I am," she told him. "How happy and awed, and somehow, finally, grown-up."

He smiled, and then he whispered to her, all the love words he had not said before. They lay close in each other's arms in the big bed, adrift from the world, but safe, because they were together.

Erica found she did not want to go to sleep, although she knew she should be tired. Instead, she wanted to talk, talk for hours. She wanted to know about Owen's childhood, his parents, his brothers and sisters. And she wanted to hear him tell her about Graveshead, the estate and countryside, and what he had done as a boy. But when she began to question him, he laughed at her.

"You are greedy, ma'am," he told her. "And if I tell you everything at once, we won't have anything left to talk about."

As she protested, he reached down and pulled up the covers. Sensitive to his every mood, Erica wondered why that fleeting expression of distaste had crossed his rugged features as he did so. Suddenly she realized she had never seen his crippled leg, that he had kept it hidden from her until she was so heedless with passion that she did not notice it.

"Owen," she said. As he looked at her, inquiring, she went on, "Why did you pull the covers up? It is warm in here."

When he did not answer at once, she asked, "Is it because you do not want me to see your leg?"

He stared at her, his face somber and dark now, and she longed to tell him it did not matter.

"Yes, that is why," he said at last. He sounded as if the words were strangling him. "I see no reason why someone as lovely as you are should have to look at a grotesque deformity. Forget it."

"Oh, my dear," she breathed. "So that is why you never undress before you come to me, why you put out so many candles! But Owen, darling, it doesn't matter to me, truly, it doesn't."

She had spoken with passionate conviction, but she saw he did not believe her. His dark eyes were bleak, and she felt he had withdrawn from her, and she could not bear it.

Quickly she climbed out of the bed and pulled the covers down to the foot before he could realize what she was doing.

"Erica!" he cried out. "No!"

She stood before him, staring at that twisted right leg. As he groaned, she saw that it was weak and thin below the knee, and strangely crooked at the ankle.

She looked back at his face, and the anguish she saw in his eyes made her put her hands on his leg and bend to kiss it.

The duke lay propped up on his elbows as her hands caressed his leg and her soft lips touched it with a score of gentle kisses. Her silvery hair hung around it. She was all cream and pink and gold in the firelight, but he could not see her clearly for the tears in his eyes. He dashed them away as she rose at last.

"It is ugly, is it not?" he demanded in harsh, strangled accents.

"Well, it is not pretty," she agreed, her voice calm. "But it is part of you, my dear, and since I love you, doesn't it follow that I love all of you? I tell you, it doesn't matter to me, it has never mattered. For as Talleyrand said, lameness does not have a thing to do with a man's worth.

"And, Owen," she went on as she climbed back into bed beside him and put her arms around him, "you are worth so much more than other men, perhaps the gods felt it only just to give you a handicap? A very little handicap?"

He took her face in his hands and stared deep into her eyes. They were as clear and honest as they had always been. He noticed she did not ask him if he believed her. But then, of course, she would not ask that for she had spoken the truth as she knew it. Erica had no duplicity. He knew it would be impossible for her to say what she had, merely out of kindness. It really did not matter to her, then, his crippled leg; she loved him still! He could not believe his good fortune, and he shook his head in wonder, his heart filled with gratitude.

"Owen?" she asked, frowning a little now. "Was it because you are crippled that you said what you did to me in Vienna? Tried to make me believe we had shared nothing more than an evening's pleasure?"

He nodded, strangely mute.

"Oh, my dear, I am so glad it was only that! You cannot know what I have been imagining," she whispered. "And to think you sent me away because of it! And I never even guessed!"

She buried her face on his chest for a moment, to breathe deeply of his warm skin. His arms came around her and crushed her against him. Suddenly she struggled a little, and he let her go at once. She pushed herself up on her arms, one on either side of his body. "But why, Owen?" she asked, as if she were still perplexed. "Why would you feel so strongly that your lameness made you some sort of monster?"

His black eyes stared up into hers, and she saw the bleakness come back into them. "Because all the time I was growing up, I was treated like a monster," he said bitterly. "My grandfather, the old duke, took it as a personal affront that his eldest son's first male child was born crippled. I knew even before I was breeched that he hated to look at me, even wished me dead. And as I grew up, he took to taunting me about it, as each successive grandchild was born normal. He called me 'Owen the Halt,' 'the Little Lame Boy,' 'Devil's Spawn'—oh, he had a dozen charming names for me!"

His harsh laugh was mocking, and she tried not to cringe.

"But your parents . . . your mother," she said quickly. "Didn't she at least try to protect you?"

"Oh yes, she tried," he agreed. "But Mama was no match for the old duke, no one was. And although she told me over and over that he was wrong, I didn't believe her. You see, I caught my father looking at me sometimes with the same kind of revulsion the old duke did. And smiling so kindly at my strong younger brother.

"Just before she died, my mother told me I would have my revenge, for the old duke couldn't prevent my becoming the Duke of Graves someday. But of course," he added more quietly as he pulled her down into his arms so he could speak against her hair, "there was no way I could escape my grandfather. He insisted we all live together at Graveshead, all three generations of us."

There was silence in the room for a moment, and he felt Erica draw a deep breath. "Well, I know it is not a good thing to speak ill of the dead, Owen," she said earnestly, "but I must tell you I think your grandfather was . . . was . . ."

"Unkind? Terrible? Awful? Vicious?" the duke suggested. Erica squirmed up until she could whisper in his ear. As she smiled in satisfaction and lay back down beside him, he howled with laughter. "Now, where did you ever hear such an expression as *that*?" he asked when he could speak again. "I shall think you have been a camp follower at some time in your misspent youth, if you're not careful, Erica."

She chuckled into his neck and nuzzled him. "No, I was never a camp follower, although I wanted to be," she admitted. "I always thought it most unfair that my brothers had all the adventures, while I had to stay at home in Northumberland. But I did hear them talking, every once in a while," she added, determined to be honest.

He chuckled again. "Oh, my love, is there no end to your delights?" he asked, wondering.

She lifted her head to kiss him lightly. "I don't know, Owen. Shall we find out?" she asked, the picture of innocence.

It was quite eleven o'clock in the morning before Ma-

rie was summoned to help the duchess dress. The hot
croissants were not as flaky as the chef would have liked,
for they had been reheated so many times, and her
grace's chocolate had to be thrown out and a new pot
made, it had thickened so, standing.

Erica could hear Owen moving around in his room,
and when she heard his deep baritone raised in song, she
smiled against her pillows. Then she had to laugh, as it
became obvious that even Owen's great delight in what
had transpired between them had not changed his inability to carry a tune.

They had decided a few minutes ago to stay at the
château another day. As Owen pointed out, there was no
sense in going unless they got an early start. Otherwise
they would not be able to reach the border and cross into
Belgium and safety, all in one day.

"You mean you don't have another cozy château waiting for us a little way from here?" Erica asked him in
feigned disbelief. "And others strung out like pearls,
only a few miles apart?" she added.

He hugged her. "No, love, I do not. I may be the
marvelous, wonderful creature you keep telling me I am,
but I am not omnipotent."

"What a shame," she mourned as he got up and col-
lected his clothes. She noticed he made no attempt to
hide his leg from her now, and she felt a great joy as she
said, "But how long do you think it will be before we can
get an early start?"

As he stared at her bemused, she added, "I mean, if
we make love all night, and then sleep to eleven, it
doesn't look too promising, does it? I wonder if the
count would care for a couple of permanent guests? For
the duration of the war, I mean."

Owen limped back to the bed. As she looked up expec-
tantly he shook his head. "No, minx, no more. I need my
breakfast," he said, trying to be severe. "And you will
rise and dress now, and try to *behave* like a duchess, at
least for the rest of the day. Do you understand me, my
girl?"

Erica sat up and saluted, and he almost forgot his good
intentions. With the morning sunlight streaming through
the window and setting her glorious hair aglow, and

those pink-tipped breasts at attention, he had to turn quickly lest he become lost in the wonder of her again.

They spent a lazy, restful day. They investigated the château from the towers to the dungeon, they browsed in the count's excellent library, and they took a turn in the cobbled courtyard for a breath of fresh air. Erica was glad of her ermine cloak, it was such a cold day. Surely it must get warmer soon, she thought, as she was forced to let go of Owen's arm to pull the fur closer around her.

The duke smiled down at her. "I am glad to see that you wear the ermine without protest now, Erica," he told her.

"I have loved it ever since our night at Burg Kobenzl," she told him. "When I have this cloak on, it is as if I am wrapped in your love."

The duke considered her, and his black eyes grew keen. She wondered what he was thinking.

"Then tonight I shall ask you to wear it again—inside out," he said at last.

"But we are not going anywhere, are we, Owen?" she asked innocently. "And why inside out?"

"You'll see, love, you'll see," he told her, and although she did not understand, the fervent light in his eyes made her lower her own, and smile.

21

They were still there in the courtyard when the barouche arrived a few minutes later. Albert Pray smiled when he saw the duke and his lady standing so close together. He saluted and dismounted before he came to speak to them, leading his horse.

"Give you good-day, your grace, Miss Kingsley," he said. "Glad to see you made it here safely, sir."

"And you and the others, Albert," the duke replied. Erica smiled at her equerry and went to greet her maid.

"I am anxious to hear all your adventures," the duke went on, although Albert noticed his eyes followed Miss Kingsley. "I shall look for you in the library as soon as you have had some refreshment," he added.

Pray saluted again, but as he turned to see to the horses and the baggage, the duke said, "A moment more, Albert. Miss Kingsley is known here as my duchess. Tell the others, will you? I do not want her to know a moment's embarrassment."

Albert nodded, although he thought the duke's warning most unnecessary. Anyone with an eye in his head could see what had happened just by their faces whenever they looked at each other. He smiled to himself. And one thing I do know, he told himself: Miss Watts, the old dragon, won't like it.

But Agnes surprised them all. She accepted the situation with more grace than Erica would have given her credit for. And when she was helping her mistress dress for dinner, and the duke came into the room after only the briefest of knocks, Agnes curtsied and left them alone together at once.

Agnes herself had been sure she would not like any situation that involved Miss Erica and the awful duke. But when she had seen the girl's face, so transparent with happiness, her awe had made her change her mind. Of course she knew it was not right, the two of them, unwed as they were, but even that irregularity seemed to lose importance in the face of their mutual joy. For she could see as well as Mr. Pray that the duke loved Miss Erica with the same fervor she appeared to have for him. As Agnes straightened the dressing room, she could hear them murmuring together, and she was reminded of the short week of Miss Erica's marriage to Colonel Stone. Not once had the girl looked as she did now. In fact, now that Agnes came to think about it, she remembered how quiet she had been then, how composed, almost stiff. She had wondered in the past if Miss Erica had been happy with the colonel and marriage; now she had proof positive that she had not been. And any man who could bring that glow, that bloom, to her mistress's lovely face could not be all bad, she told herself stoutly.

The duke and Erica ate dinner together shortly thereafter. Before the servants, they spoke only of their journey and of their plans for an early departure in the morning.

As the duke accepted a serving of the pigeon pie, he said, "It appears it will be a fine day, Duchess. I am glad of it, for I think it best that you go with me in the curricle again. We have only about thirty-five miles to go to reach Bouillon, and less than that to the border. We should complete the trip easily in one day."

Erica nodded serenely. She knew that if it had threatened to rain or snow, she would have been more than a little disappointed. For no matter how uncomfortable the curricle was, she could be close to him there. Besides, it would mean they would be alone again for one more night—completely alone. The coach was slow, and it might be forced to further diversions. She smiled to herself. Although she knew it was very wrong of her, she hoped there were a lot of them!

Owen looked at her as she sat beside him. He did not ask why she was smiling; that would have to wait until they were alone. Instead, he wondered at the strength of his love for this slip of a girl with her beautiful face and soft silvery hair. Tonight she was wearing a simple old-fashioned green gown, one she had brought with her to Vienna. He himself had not been able to carry with him the new gowns she had left behind, for in his haste to reach her, he had had to travel light. He promised himself she would have them as soon as it could be arranged. But even this simple dress could not detract from her beauty. The emeralds she wore around the slender column of her throat and at her wrists were poor things indeed to the jewels that were her eyes.

As Erica raised one brow, he realized he had been staring at her for some time. Hastily he applied himself to his dinner.

As they ate, he told her what Albert had had to say of his travels with the coach. He had spotted the pieces of red tablecloth easily, and turned off the main road whenever he saw one. Albert had also told the duke they had been forced to spend the night in a poor place, more a tavern than an inn. Erica nodded again, for Agnes had told her about it earlier.

"I was surprised, as was Albert, that Agnes was so agreeable to it," Owen remarked as the footman removed their plates.

"Oh, Agnes is a countrywoman, sir," Erica told him. "A little thing like that wouldn't bother her, or me either, if it should come to it."

"It won't," the duke assured her, his deep voice brusque.

"I know it is only important that we get to Belgium, any way we can," she went on. "I am glad I said what I did to that officer, for Agnes told me they had been unable to avoid a meeting with the same troop of soldiers that stopped us. However, he barely glanced at the forged letter before he waved them on."

"Yes, that was a stroke of genius on your part, Duchess," Owen remarked, nodding to the butler to refill his glass.

Erica smiled to herself again. How often Owen called her Duchess! She did not think it was solely for the edification of the count's servants, however, for he used the title as often when they were alone as he did in company. And his voice was a caress each time he said it.

No one could possibly remark their early bedtime that evening, for everyone was aware they were to leave the château by eight in the morning. And although the duke knew a good night's sleep was important, he could not resist showing Erica exactly what he had in mind when he told her he would ask her to wear the ermine cloak again. When he left her at last, she was glowing.

The next morning, she wore the ermines again, correctly this time, over another warm gown. She had thanked the housekeeper and the butler, and tried to give Marie some money, but the maid would not accept the coins.

"No, no, *Duchesse*," she protested. "*Le duc* has already been so generous!"

At that, Erica felt most married indeed as she took her place beside Owen in the curricle. The Austrian grooms were already mounted and ready, and she could see the duke's own servants putting the baggage on the coach. She waved to Agnes as they circled the courtyard, and then her eyes sought the windows of the room where she and Owen had loved, and slept. She would probably never see this place again, and yet she would feel warmly toward it always. As the curricle started back down the cypress-lined drive, she silently thanked the absent count for his inadvertent hospitality.

All that day, they followed the River Meuse to Sedan. They saw a few soldiers, but not many, and they were not stopped. And throughout the day, they talked—about their homes and families, and their childhoods. Erica already knew that of the two of them, hers had been the happier by far, even with her mother's early death. But she noticed that not even once did Owen speak of the future. She wondered why, and then she shrugged. Whatever his reason for avoiding the subject, she would be content. And she knew he had to have a reason, a good one. Owen Kingsley, the Duke of Graves, had spoken only the truth when he told her he was not an ordinary man.

They reached the border between France and Belgium in midafternoon, and there they had their first difficulty of the day. The officer in charge of the border guards was an important little man, and Erica could see he meant to take exception to their leaving his country. She made herself become even more imperious and Nordic than she had been earlier, for she was conscious of the silent duke beside her. She knew Owen was armed; in the close quarters of the curricle, she had been very much aware of the hard outline of the pistol he carried in his greatcoat pocket. As she drew out Talleyrand's letter, she prayed he would not make a foolish move in his desire to get her safely away.

As the officer read it, she kept up a stream of Swedish, to which Owen nodded frequently. She was glad no one could translate, for it was a relief to call the officer and his entire family complete idiots.

The pompous little Frenchman with his fierce black mustache was not proof against that magical signature, and he became obsequious, bowing low before he ordered the barrier removed. Erica sighed in relief as the French sentry post disappeared from sight around a bend in the road.

"There is no doubt about it, you missed your calling as an actress, Erica," the duke told her as he pulled up to speak to the Belgian soldiers on duty on their side of the border. "But as much as I hate to miss another performance, I shall deal with these allies of ours myself. My Swedish princess is a thing of the past."

"How sad," Erica mourned. "And just when I was getting into the spirit of things, too!"

Owen smiled as he handed her the reins and got down to speak to the Belgian officer. Erica could not hear what they said, but it was only a moment after he read the papers the duke gave him that the officer was smiling and saluting.

They arrived in Bouillon at dusk. The duke had sent the groom Hans ahead to arrange for rooms for them at the finest inn, and when they pulled up before it, everything was ready for them. The landlord bowed them to his best private parlor and hurried away to bring wine as they waited for their dinner to be served.

The inn was small, and hardly luxurious, but when Erica went to remove her cloak and wash her hands, and saw the big, comfortable postered bed that was to be theirs, any deficiencies in the rest of the room's furnishings became very unimportant indeed.

After dinner they sat on before the fire for a while. Erica was sleepy from the cold air and tension of the day, as well as the warmth of the fire, and she had to hide a yawn more often than she liked.

Owen shook his finger at her. "It is hardly complimentary to me, you know, madam, all this yawning," he growled. "Can it be that I am boring you?"

His voice was just as cold and sarcastic as it had been when they first met, but now Erica only wrinkled her nose at him. "Of course, you could not bear to think that, now, could you, you conceited man?" she asked.

As he began to get his feet, looking threatening, she laughed at him. "I doubt you shall ever bore me, Owen, but if that unlikely event occurs, be sure I shall be quick to let you know," she told him, her voice as arrogant as his had ever been.

The duke shook his head at her, and she added, carefully not looking at him, "However, I must say I find you to be rather exciting. And your inventive mind is a delight. Whenever we are together, I am amazed at how easily you manage to keep at bay any ennui I might be feeling."

At that Owen laughed with her, and Erica smiled until another yawn forced her to cover her mouth again. The duke came and pulled her to her feet and into his arms. "Go to bed, my darling duchess," he murmured into her ear. "You are tired."

Erica tried to protest, but he would not listen. "This time, as always, you will do as you are told, madam," he said before he kissed her cheek. Then he took her face between his hands and stared down into it. "There is time yet for us, Erica. Trust me."

She nodded before she raised her lips for his kiss. As she turned to go, she remembered the tiara, and she stopped and removed it. "Here, Owen, take charge of it," she said. "I shall not need it now we are safe in Belgium, and wearing it makes me nervous. If I should ever lose such precious Kingsley jewelry . . . !"

She thought he was about to say something, and she waited. But instead he took it from her hands without commenting, and bowed to her.

Erica fully intended to stay awake until he came to

her, but her eyelids were so heavy they closed in deep
sleep almost as soon as she put her head on the pillow.
Her last thought was that he was sure to wake her, but
when the duke came in a little while later, he did no such
thing. Instead, he only limped up to look at her for a
long moment, his rugged face full of tenderness. As he
got into bed beside her, he was careful not to disturb her
sleep.

But when Erica woke in the early morning, he was
there, of course, and in gray dawn they made slow,
sleepy love at last.

The coach and outriders arrived that same afternoon.
That evening, the duke was closeted alone with Albert
for quite some time, planning the route they would take
to Ostend and the Channel.

They all left together early the next morning. As the
days passed, Erica became aware that Owen was wasting
no time on this journey, although there was no blatant
evidence of haste. She wanted to ask him to go more
slowly, to stop sooner and start later, but even now that
they were so close, she did not like to. Besides, she knew
there was a reason for it, even if he did not tell her what
it was.

During the nights when they stayed in Dinant and
Uccle, she had learned a great deal about Owen, and
love, and herself. She had never imagined how many
moods there could be to making love—some so tender
they made her ache, even weep; some so passionate she
felt breathless, lost; some even bawdy and funny, with
both of them smothering their laughter in their pillows.
But no matter how their lovemaking began, it all ended
the same way, in the complete fulfillment she had come
to expect and adore.

Owen also knew how much he was learning. Since the
weather continued fair, he took Erica up beside him in
the curricle, and as they conversed, he realized again and
again how very much more there was to her besides that
beautiful face and breathtaking, yielding body. And he
learned what trust was, and acceptance, and faith. He
believed now that Erica truly loved him, and he reveled
in it. He, too, wished they might linger on the road but
he knew time was short, even though the thought of

leaving her tore his heart. But there was not only his own work to be considered, there was also the possibility that Napoleon might strike north at once and invade Belgium. He could not put Erica to that risk.

It was only a day's journey to the coast when they stopped for the night in Ghent, and then he knew he had to speak to her at last. He was more silent than usual during dinner, and when he dismissed their servants almost harshly, Erica knew he had something on his mind, something serious. She reached for his hand where it lay on the table between them, and clasped it with her own.

"You know, don't you?" he whispered, staring at their entwined hands.

"I know there is something you have to tell me, yes, my love," she said, her voice serene.

The duke sighed. "Tomorrow we reach Ostend, Erica," he said, a dark frown on his rugged face. "And it is there that I must leave you."

Erica's free hand crept to her throat. Owen was leaving her? She could not bear it! She forced herself to sit quietly, however, for she knew there was more to his story, and she did not want to interrupt him. Indeed, she did not think she could speak.

"I shall make all the arrangements, and see you safe aboard ship, but then I must go back to Vienna. Albert will go with you, and take you to Northumberland," he said. His voice was cold and even, and Erica wondered that he could be so calm, so dispassionate.

He paused then, his face still set in harsh lines, and she got up and went to him to smooth away the frown on his forehead. He did not speak, and she bent and kissed him on the cheek.

"You *must* leave me?" she asked, trying to keep the forlorn feeling she had from showing in her voice.

He nodded, and then he reached up and pulled her down into his lap to hold her close, "Yes, I must go," he said. "Even if it were not to keep a promise I made to others, there is a personal reason. But I cannot tell you of it. You must not ask me. I . . . I cannot even promise that I will come back to you. I cannot promise you anything."

He looked and sounded so distraught now that Erica

reached up and took his face between her hands—as
his hands were so wont to do with her face. "Owen," she
said quietly, "I would not ask you anything. I trust you."

She kissed him again, and his arms tightened around
her. She was breathless when he finally let her go. They
stared at each other for a long moment, and then the
duke said in a voice almost breaking with emotion, "I
will tell you something, however, Erica Huntington-Stone-
Kingsley. I do most truly love you."

She smiled at him, misty-eyed. "I know, my dear," she
said. "It is why I don't have to ask you anything, anything at all."

He buried his face against her soft breast and closed
his eyes. He knew she could not understand, and yet she
accepted his dictate without a single word of protest. He
wondered why he was so very fortunate, and yet why,
having found her at last, he was forced, as an honorable
man, to leave her so soon. For they had had such a short
time of happiness together! So little time for their love!

Yet even if that time were all there would ever be, he
knew he had been blessed by a love he had never imagined would ever be his. He would remember that, and
try to be content.

He heard her heart beneath his head. Its beat had
quickened, and as she caught her breath a little, he knew
she was trying not to cry, and he sat up straight again, to
comfort her as best he could.

"You will be careful, won't you, Owen?" she asked.

He did not know how she had guessed that he would be
in danger, but he did not ask her. Perhaps their very
closeness let her know more of him than he had realized.
"I will be very careful, my dearest," he promised. "And
if there is any way on earth, I will come to you as soon as
I can. You must believe me when I tell you this is the
hardest leave-taking of my entire life, and it will be the
hardest separation. You cannot write to me, and I will
not be able to write you, not often."

She nodded, but she remained silent. Owen did not
need her spoken reassurances any more than he needed
to be told how difficult it would be for her as well. She
knew he had come that far in learning to trust her and
her love for him.

They sat together quietly for a while, and then Erica wriggled out of his arms. "I think I will go to bed now, Owen," she said. Her eyes were glowing, and he caught his breath and came to stand beside her.

"I will be with you shortly, Duchess," he assured her, and she tried to smile. How well they were behaving! she thought. How determined they were to act normally!

Before she left him, she removed the pearls she was wearing. "You had better lock these away with the rest of the Kingsley jewels now, Owen," she told him as she held them out.

As he took them from her, he said, "You are mistaken, Erica. Oh, I shall lock them up, of course, with the others, but none of them are part of the Kingsley jewels. They are yours. I bought them for you in Vienna."

Her face was a study in astonishment. "You bought all those beautiful jewels just for me?" she whispered.

He had to smile then, she was so dumbfounded. "Of course. I could not tell you before, for you would have refused to have anything to do with them. After all, just look what I had to go through to get you to wear the ermine cloak. But I often wondered why you imagined a bachelor would be traveling around the Continent with a casket of family jewels. Did you think I brought them on the off chance I *might* find someone to wear them? My dear Erica!"

As she stared at him, still speechless, he added, "I shall give them to you before you take ship, my dear. I shall like to think of you wearing them, you know. You are what makes them beautiful."

When he came to her a few minutes later, Erica was waiting for him in bed. She had cried a little as she undressed, but all signs of those tears were gone now. She knew Owen deserved a better farewell than a weak, weeping woman, and she was determined he would have it when she saw how closely he studied her face, his concern for her plain on his own.

Her determination allowed her to smile as she held out her arms to him, her green eyes serene. As they made love, she realized that never had she felt so loved, so needed, so precious. She tried to make sure Owen felt the same way, and when at last they were lost in that wild, passionate torrent that swept them both to the culmination of their love, they cried out together.

That night it was Erica who stayed awake long after the duke's breathing deepened. Propped up on one elbow close beside him, she watched his strong-featured face relax in sleep. She wanted to memorize it, the broad forehead and strong nose, his lean cheeks and solid jaw, and his surprisingly sculptured mouth. Her eyes caressed his powerful neck and the one muscled arm and shoulder that she could see above the covers. There would be time for sleep later—all those lonely, dark nights that lay ahead of her. And it was only like this that she could study him, for she knew she must show only a calm demeanor and acceptance in the daylight. Then he could go to whatever he felt compelled to go to, without worrying about her or feeling an extra anguish because he had made her unhappy.

It was only when the candles sputtered and went out, and she could see him no longer, that she closed her eyes at last.

The final day's journey was uneventful. Owen was careful to talk about everything under the sun except their coming separation, and she followed his lead. She realized it was the only way either one of them was going to be able to get through it at all well.

As soon as they arrived at Ostend and found an inn, he left her there to go seek her passage home. Erica rested, hardly listening to Agnes' chatter as she sipped a cup of tea and stared at the waterfront spread out under her window. There were many ships in the port, and deep in her heart she prayed that not a single one of them was sailing to England in the near future.

But that was not to be. The duke came back an hour later and dismissed Agnes with a curt wave before he came to sit beside Erica and take her hands in his. "The English ship *Rosalie* from Hull leaves on the morning tide, Erica," he told her without preliminary. "They are loading the carriage and team now. You must be on board at dawn."

Erica nodded and bent her head as she fought her tears. Gently the duke raised her chin with one finger, his black eyes inquiring.

"So my prayers were not answered after all," Erica made herself say lightly. "You see, I have been sitting here hoping that not a one of those numerous vessels in port was either English or bound for England." She sighed before she added, "But perhaps it is just as well."

"Just as well?" he asked, frowning in his effort to understand.

She kissed him quickly. "Yes, my dear. For the sooner I am gone, the sooner you can see about this business you must do, and the sooner you can come back to me."

He started to speak, but she put her hand over his mouth. "Yes, yes, I know, but *shhh!* No matter what you say, I know you *will* come back to me, Owen. And I will live only for that day."

The next morning was misty and threatened rain. As they stood together on the dock waiting for the ship's boat to come and fetch her and her maid, the duke kept his arm tight around her. After loading yesterday, the *Rosalie* had moved to an anchorage in the roads for a quicker departure. By all rights, Erica should have gone aboard last evening, but Owen had made special arrangements so he could keep her with him until the last possible minute.

Agnes had gone a little apart so they might have some privacy, but strangely, they did not talk now. Erica felt it was because everything that could be said, had been, and now there was only that one sad little phrase left to exchange. Good-bye.

She turned as she felt Owen staring at her. After a moment he said, "Listen to me, Erica. If I should *not* come back, for whatever reason, I want you to write to Viscount Castlereagh. Will you promise me to do that?"

Erica had never heard him so serious, nor seen his face so stern, and she was quick to give him her promise. And then, as the sailors shipped their oars and held the boat ready, she raised her face for a kiss.

"Go safely, Erica," he told her, as he had told her once before.

"And you, Owen," she whispered. "I will be waiting for you."

As she was being rowed to the ship, a silent Agnes Watts beside her, Erica did not take her eyes from the tall figure of the Duke of Graves standing leaning on his cane at the end of the quay, alone. The gray, misty morning reminded her of the day she had come to France with so many hopes and plans all those months ago. So much had happened to her since, she could barely identify with the girl she had been then. As the duke's figure grew smaller and smaller, she was glad she had come in spite of all the sorrow she had known. If she had not, she would never have met Owen.

She saw him turn then and limp back to his curricle. After he was seated, he waved to her and drove away. It was only then that her composure slipped a little, and she had to wipe the tears from her eyes. Agnes patted her hand in sympathy.

The *Rosalie* made good time, and docked in Hull the same afternoon. Albert Pray easily persuaded Miss Kingsley, whom he now knew to be a Mrs. Stone, thanks to the duke's terse explanation, to remain in port until the following morning. There was all the business of getting the carriage and team unloaded, and he thought she would be better for the rest. The crossing had been rough, although he did not think it was that that made her so pale and quiet.

Erica did not protest the delay. She knew she should be eager to reach her father, all her family, as quickly as possible, and looking forward to seeing them again, but she could feel only apathy. Her every thought was still centered on Owen. Where was he now? Already on his roundabout way back to Vienna? He had told her he intended to avoid traveling through France, even though it added miles to the journey, and she had been relieved, For that little while she knew he would not be in any danger.

As Agnes went to fetch a pot of tea, Erica went to the window of the inn and stared back across the Channel, whispering a prayer for his safety. It was a prayer she was to repeat many times in the days and weeks that followed.

22

Albert Pray escorted Mrs. Stone to Northumberland, as he had been instructed. When Erica thanked him for his care, he smiled at her a little shyly. "I'm sure I'll see you again, ma'am," he said. Erica smiled back at him.

Her Aunt Anne cried as she kissed and hugged her, and her father beamed when she went upstairs to his bedchamber. He was, of course, still very much convalescent, but he told her the sight of her pretty face was better than any medicine. Erica noticed a suspicion of tears in his eyes too, and for the first time she was glad she had come home. Taking care of her father and trying to keep him amused as his broken hip and arm healed would give her something to do while she waited for Owen to come back to her.

Because it was a special homecoming, Miss Huntington had had a table set for dinner in the general's room, so he might join in the festivities. Erica learned then that both Geoffrey and Peter had rejoined their regiments, although her eldest brother, Mark, was there. She thought he looked much better than he had when she left, but she could tell he was fretting because he had to miss what was sure to be a marvelous battle between the allies and Napoleon. Erica hid a shudder. What was there about men that made them eager for danger? she wondered. She knew women were not like that.

Only her Aunt Anne had many questions about her stay in Vienna, and Erica was surprised until she remembered how little interest her father and brother had in society. Tonight they wanted to discuss a news item in the latest journal, about the possibility of Napoleon's invading both Austria and Belgium in tandem. As they argued the pros and cons of such strategy, Erica tried not to feel offended. She had thought she might have to answer some awkward questions about the Duke of Graves and the amount of time she had spent in his house, but the only questions they asked her concerned William Stone's death. Perversely, she wished they would ask. Didn't they care where she had been all those months, what had happened to her? Why, it seemed almost as if she had never been away from home at all, or changed in any way!

As a blustery, rainy March gave way to an equally blustery and rainy April, Erica discovered something about herself. She no longer felt at home here. When this thought first occurred to her, she tried to deny it, but she came to understand how true it was. Her aunt's dithering conversation about the household and local gossip, her father's endless reliving of old campaigns, and her brother's preoccupation with estate matters and the battle to come, seemed very boring and provincial to her now. The only time she felt at all one of them was when they studied the journals together for news of the war.

The general had her pin a map of Europe next to his bed, and every time Erica looked at it, her eyes went first to the tiny spot that was Vienna. It seemed so very far away. She wondered if Owen were still there. There appeared little left to do, unless Napoleon was victorious, and the Final Act that was to be signed was declared as null and void as he had declared the congress to be when he landed in France. How her father had snorted and ruffled up when he read that the emperor had had the audacity to declare the congress dissolved. "The arrogance of the man! The unmitigated gall!" he had bellowed. It had taken Erica quite a long time to calm him down.

But if Owen were not in Vienna, where was he? she wondered. Would he go to Brussels with the Duke of Wellington, as so many Englishmen were doing? She wished she knew where he was, for her own peace of mind.

Toward the end of April she received her first letter from him. She noticed at once that it had been sent from London, but after one heart-stopping moment of hope that the duke had returned, she realized that it had probably come in the diplomatic pouch by special courier. If Owen were in England, she knew he would not write; he would come to her as he had promised.

It was a strange letter. She had the feeling Owen did not dare to say too much, either about his love for her, or what he was doing, or even where he was. But careful rereading made her sure he was still in Vienna, although he mentioned he would be traveling as soon as he could. He told her he prayed she was well, and at the end he told her he loved her. Erica kissed his spiky black signature.

Agnes was aware her mistress had heard from the duke. Even if she had not noticed the letter on the hall table and recognized the handwriting, she would have known by her mistress's glowing face that evening as she was dressing her for dinner. Agnes had never been able to get her to confide in her since they had come home; she knew she would not do so now. But although she had expected her to become morose now that she was separated from her lover, she was surprised at how serenely and with what good nature she went about her old familiar duties as the daughter of the house. Agnes did not understand. The duke had abandoned Miss Erica, without, at least to the maid's knowledge, even an offer of marriage after all that had happened between them. How could Miss Erica be so calm?

Agnes' major concern, that her mistress might be with child, proved to be false. With great relief the maid went to evensong every night for a month, as she had promised the Lord she would, if He answered her prayers.

It was in May that several trunks containing Erica's Viennese gowns and accessories were delivered by carrier. And though there was no opportunity to wear them here in the country, even if she had not resumed wearing mourning dress again, she unpacked them herself and hung them in her wardrobe. She spent one whole afternoon and evening doing so, for she would not let Agnes help her with this chore.

Erica found another letter from Owen as she unpacked. Folded into a tiny square, it had been tucked into a beaded evening bag. Surrounded by a welter of colorful silks and laces, sandals and stoles and gloves, Erica sank back on her heels to read it.

It was much more open than his last letter had been, and full of his love and yearning for her. As she read his words, of how much he missed her, she cried a little.

Later, as she put each gown away, she remembered where she had worn it, and what had happened to her then. Here was the pale green silk she had worn to the first ball she had attended at the Hofburg; how lovely it was! And here, the silver gown that had been made especially for the Peace Ball, the night Owen had accused her being a wanton. As she unpacked the nightgown and robe she had worn the night Prince Eric and his cousin invaded her bedroom at Burg Kobenzl, and the duke had fought for her before they made love for the first time, she smiled in misty memory.

So many memories—some happy, some sad, but all of them involving one tall, dark, compelling man, the man she would always love. And yet now she was alone again, dressed in ugly black, only the young widow of Colonel William Stone. One who spent day after dreary day as the dutiful daughter on a country estate in Northumberland. It was very hard to bear.

The Duke of Graves arrived back in Vienna one rainy night toward the end of March. He had wasted no time on the road, changing teams often as he made his hasty way back through Belgium, Prussia, and Bavaria. For the last leg of his trip he commandeered one of the groom's horses and set that man to driving the curricle so he himself could cut across country and shorten his journey.

He had no idea what was happening in Vienna, for there was little news to be gleaned on his hasty stops for food and rest. But he had heard that Napoleon had not been beaten back in France, and that Marshal Ney, sent out by Louis XVIII to perform that task with the assistance of twenty thousand men, had turned himself and his troops over to his former emperor instead of bringing him to Paris in chains, as he was supposed to do.

The duke also learned that the Bourbon king, in despair at the news of Ney's defection, had fled. Paris was an open city, waiting for Napoleon to come and rule again; there was no way to stop him now. And even though he learned from one innkeeper, more informed than his fellows, that the congress had declared the emperor an outlaw early in March, Owen only grimaced. To the majority of the French, Napoleon was a hero, no matter what the rest of the world thought of him and no matter how many proclamations were passed. War was inevitable.

As he trotted down the Johannesgasse to his palace at last, he saw that the Kaunitz was brilliantly lit as usual. So Talleyrand was still there, he thought as he dismounted. Then he frowned. Where else could he go? Napoleon would not welcome him back, nor forgive him this time. As he sounded his door knocker, the duke resolved to call on the French minister to see if he could be of any assistance. They were allies now.

Rudge was delighted to see him, and assured him a late repast would be served shortly. Owen went into the library to wait for the tray he had ordered brought to him there. He was too tired to change from riding clothes, and he had no desire to sit in the large formal dining room alone.

As he ate his dinner, he decided to go to bed at once, and call on the British delegation in the morning. It was late, and he had no idea whom he would find there at this hour. And then he sat and dreamed of Erica as he sipped his port. There was the chair where she used to sit when the two of them were here alone. If he closed his eyes, he could picture her clearly, her silver hair gleaming gold in the fire and candlelight as she bent over her book while one slim hand turned the pages.

He had not known that missing someone could be such a constant ache just below your heart, but now he knew it was so. She was never far from his thoughts. It was as if they had become one person, and now, separated by circumstance and a matter of honor, he was only half a man until he had her in his arms again.

The duke arrived at headquarters very early the next morning. He did not bother to use the brothel as a shield, for it did not matter who saw him enter today. Even if Baron Hager were still spying, he would assume the visit only a courtesy call from an Englishman newly arrived back in Vienna, come to pay his respects.

The duke was ushered into Wellington's office almost at once. As he limped toward it, Owen wondered at the amount of activity he saw. For no matter how quietly everyone moved and spoke, there was an underlying sense of urgency and purpose.

Wellington dismissed the secretary who had been taking notes for him, as he rose to greet his fellow duke. "Your grace, well met at last!" he said, coming to shake his hand and lead him to a chair.

Although Owen had known Arthur Wellesley for a long time, now he studied him anew. He was a lean man, and although not as tall as he himself, he was still every inch the classical hero, from his closely cropped brown hair, still untouched by gray, to his clear blue eyes and Roman profile. Owen knew him to be unpretentious, straightforward in all his dealings, and disarmingly simple. He was even known to mock himself, once laughing loudly before he remarked to an aide as he passed through a large adoring crowd, "It's a fine thing to be great man, is it not?" Owen thought England was lucky to have someone of his caliber at the helm, especially now that war was imminent.

A great friend of Lord Castlereagh's, Wellington relayed his good wishes and messages before he said in his abrupt way, "You are just in time to bid me farewell, sir. I am for the Low Countries to take command of the army."

"Who remains in charge here, your grace?" Owen asked.

"Lord Clancarty will do the honors, and sign the Final Act," Wellington told him. "I would appreciate it if he could have your assistance and support. I have nothing specific for you to do, but still it would be helpful for us to have such a knowing ear to the ground. Just until the act is signed, you understand."

Owen agreed calmly, for he had expected this. As he rose to take his leave several minutes later, he asked if the duke knew whether the Swedish court still remained in Vienna.

The duke's blue eyes studied him shrewdly. There had been something in his cold, even voice that alerted Wellington to the fact that Graves had a special reason for asking.

"Yes, they are still here," he said

For the first time, Owen smiled, albeit grimly, as Wellington went on, "However, I am sure they are preparing to depart. Vienna seems to have lost her famous charm, for people are leaving here in droves. There is a distinct atmosphere of *déjà vu* about, I fear."

Owen became aware of it himself as he moved around Vienna that day. Of course it was Holy Week, which would account for the way the devout Viennese were making their way only to church, but there was an extra quietness, too, and the streets were almost deserted.

He spoke to both his Austrian and German grooms-spies and gave them specific orders. Only then did he call on Talleyrand and his niece. He discovered the palace in something of an upset, for Dorothea de Talleyrand-Périgord's mother, the Duchess of Courland, had recently arrived, having fled Paris. Owen had only a few minutes to speak to Erica's good friend. She seemed somewhat preoccupied, although she smiled in relief when she learned that Erica was safely in England.

"Yet you yourself returned, your grace?" she asked with an arch little smile.

"Against all my most fervent wishes, madam," he told her with an answering smile. Dorothea nodded happily.

"Would it be possible for me to see Talleyrand?" the duke went on. "I must thank him again for his letter of safe passage, for it was instrumental in my rescue of Erica from France."

The countess took him to her uncle and left them together. Owen thought Talleyrand looked worn and tired, and after pleasantries had been exchanged, and his thanks given, he asked if there were anything he could do to help.

Talleyrand bent that piercing gaze on him before he shrugged. "There is nothing anyone can do, your grace, but my thanks for your kind offer. Until Napoleon is vanquished yet again—and pray Wellington is successful this time too!—I am in exile. Although he has not communicated with me, Napoleon has cut off all funds to our mission and frozen my personal assets in France." He shrugged again.

"Perhaps some monetary assistance might be welcome then, sir," the duke persisted. "I would consider it an honor to frank you."

Talleyrand graciously allowed the duke to come to his aid, hiding his relief. These had been difficult weeks for him, and he had had to live on borrowed money and practice a stringent economy to survive, although no one would have guessed it from his usual haughty manner. It was business as usual in the Kaunitz, money or no money.

Easter weekend came and went, and the business of the congress ground on slowly but inexorably, as first one international problem, then another was solved. Owen received several reports from both the Austrian and German grooms in those days, but he did not accelerate his plans. He knew he must take every precaution before he acted. And although he had written to Lord Castlereagh asking him to tell Erica of his role at the congress if by any chance he should be killed, he wanted to prevent that happening if it were humanly possible. He had so very much to live for now.

Besides, he was sure he had the time to do so. In spite of the exodus of the general population of foreigners from Vienna, most of those in the embassies remained to jealously guard their rights while working hard to obtain their final objectives.

It was almost three weeks later when the duke sat in his library rereading the notes he had made. At last he nodded. He had set the grooms to watching Prince Eric Thorson, noting his movements and routine. Now the duke could see that although the prince went to different places at many different times, there was one constant to his days. Thursday evenings were reserved for a visit to the dancer Isabella Sabatini. He escorted her home from the theater where she was performing, and remained with her for several hours. Generally he left between three and four in the morning. Only once had he remained later. The duke nodded, his plans made.

The following Thursday, he spent the evening in his library after eating dinner at the usual time. It was very late when he summoned his butler and told him he was going out.

"You are not to wait up for me, Rudge," he ordered, and the butler inclined his head. "Send a footman to the stables. I shall require the small closed carriage and a groom to drive it in exactly one hour."

"Certainly, your grace," Rudge said, just as if the duke customarily left his palace this way, long after midnight.

As the duke rose, he said, "And if at any time in the future you or any other of the servants should be asked, I did not leave the house tonight."

"Of course not, sir." Rudge said as he bowed. "Being a gentlemen of such regular habits, which I can attest to, you ate dinner, read for a while in the library, and went to bed about midnight. I remember it clearly."

As he bowed again, Owen smiled. He had known Rudge all his life, and he knew he could trust him with his life. The butler was getting old, but time had not dimmed his understanding or his loyalty. He believed the Duke of Graves could do no wrong. Owen was aware how lucky he was to have him.

Now he limped over and clasped him on the shoulder. "Thank you, Rudge," he said. "I do not know what I would do without you."

The duke changed to black clothing and chose a matching, enveloping cloak. His valet noted he was very particular about his cane, finally choosing one with a large, heavy silver-chased handle that he rarely carried. At last the duke dismissed his man, telling him to wait for him downstairs. The valet wondered what he was doing alone in his room for such a long time before he finally came down to collect his hat and gloves.

Owen had the groom drive him to a small square near the Hofburg. The streets were quiet, for it was late, and only a very few people were abroad, hurrying homeward.

Looking around the dimly lit square, he found the building he had come to watch, and fortunately, right next to it, a vacant mansion. After telling the groom to wait for him two streets away, he limped across the square and stepped up to the dark recess of the mansion's entrance, where he took up a position, leaning

against the door to wait. He had no idea how long his
vigil would take, but he was prepared to remain until
dawn, if it should prove necessary.

Fortunately, it was not even an hour later that the
door of the adjoining house opened, and in the light that
streamed through it for a moment, he saw the handsome
face and figure of the Swedish prince he had waited so
long to confront.

He stepped forward as the prince ran lightly down the
steps, and called, "Your highness!"

Eric Thorson spun around, his hand going to his hip,
even though the duke noted he wore no sword. "A moment of your time, sir, if you would be so good," he
went on, limping down to the flagway and stopping about
twenty feet away from the prince.

"Your grace?" the prince asked, coming a little closer
before he hesitated. In the dim light from a lamppost
some distance away, he could not see the duke clearly,
but there had been that in his voice that would have
warned him this was not a social occasion, even if he did
not know already how angry the man was at his treatment of Miss Kingsley. In a way, he had been waiting for
this meeting too, especially since the wound he had received at the duke's hand had been painful and slow to
heal.

"But of course, I am at your service," he made himself
say, remembering the duke as a fool who was lame to
boot. He had little to fear; besides, it was obvious the
man carried no weapon, for both hands were in plain
sight, leaning on his cane. "I am surprised to see you in
Vienna again, your grace," he added, his voice insolent.
"I had heard you and the fair Erica had gone home to
England."

"The lady is indeed in England," the duke agreed. "I,
however, had some . . . unfinished business I had to
attend to here."

"And how is the lovely Ice Maiden, your grace?"
Prince Eric asked, leaning against the palings, completely
at his ease. Then he proceeded to catalog all of Erica's
charms in a coarse, insulting way, and to taunt the duke
by saying he had had no idea the girl was the type who
was sexually aroused by the deformed.

In spite of his fury and desire for revenge, Owen had himself well in hand, and he merely stood quietly until the prince's commentary ceased.

"Are you trying to provoke me to a duel, highness?" he asked then, almost mildly. "But I have no intention of dueling with you. No, indeed. That would be the act of a foolish man, and I am not foolish, whatever you may believe of me. Crippled, I cannot fight you with sabers, and somehow I am sure, knowing my prowess with them, you would not choose pistols.

"Besides, only gentlemen duel. And you, your title notwithstanding, are not worthy of the honor, for you are a kidnapper, a rapist, and a murderer."

Prince Eric straightened up, staring hard at that tall, broad-shouldered figure dressed all in black. He wondered why the duke suddenly seemed so ominous.

"A murderer?" he asked, trying to laugh. "Come, come, sir! You exaggerate!"

"I do not think so," the duke replied, his voice cold. "For even if you yourself did not wield a dagger on Colonel William Stone, you ordered his death. But it is not to avenge him that I am here, for in a way, you did me a singular service in disposing of him. No, I am here only to repay you for your treatment of Mrs. Stone, his widow. You knew her as Erica Kingsley."

"Erica was Stone's wife?" the prince asked, astounded. "I see. But if you refuse to duel, your grace, how is your revenge to be accomplished, and why would you even bother, when she was not a relative?" the prince asked, throwing out his hands in confusion.

"Even if she had been only a guest in my house, I would have punished you," the duke replied, his voice harsh now. "But as it happens Erica Stone is to be the next Duchess of Graves.

"And so I am going to kill you for ever daring to touch her," he went on. "I tell you this because I believe a man who is about to die should know why. You, sir, are nothing but scum, and the world will be a better place without you."

Infuriated at the insult, and sure the duke, unarmed and helpless as he was, was referring to some future meeting, the prince waited to hear no more. He drew the dagger he had concealed at his belt and rushed forward, murder in his eyes. Owen raised his cane calmly, sweeping the top of the heavy handle aside on the well-oiled hinges, to reveal a small but businesslike pistol. Just before the prince reached him, he fired.

The shot echoed throughout the square as the handsome blond officer fell dead at his feet, shot through the heart. The duke wasted no time. He limped quickly to a nearby alley and disappeared, just as the first doors were thrown open and an excited babble of voices began. When he turned into the neighboring street where his carriage waited, he heard Isabella Sabatini's scream, and he smiled grimly. She might regret Prince Eric's death, along with legions of others like her, but for all the good women there were in the world, he had done a singular service. And he had avenged Erica, as well as himself, something he had promised to do a long time ago.

The next day, Vienna buzzed with the news of yet another foul murder done in its quiet streets. Owen left his palace in midafternoon to make several calls on friends, and he heard the conjectures on every lip.

"Do you suppose it could have been the same murderer who dispatched that English colonel a few months ago?" Lady Hazelbeck asked the duke, her pale blue eyes wide.

He shrugged. "I have no idea, m'lady," he said, at his most urbane. "Was the corpse robbed?"

"No, and that's odd," her husband said with a frown. "For if it wasn't for profit, why was it done?"

His young wife sighed. She was not a pretty woman, and she knew very well she had been married for her money, but that had never prevented her from indulging in daydreams. And many a one of her daydreams had featured the handsome Swedish prince, even though he had never given her a second glance. "Such a sad waste," she murmured now, her eyes far away.

Princess Julie Zichy, who was visiting too, was quick to agree. "Especially when there are so many very ugly men in the world, are there not?" she asked, implying that it would have been much better if one of them had been slain, leaving the prince for the ladies.

Owen had no desire to smile at this feminine reasoning. Indeed, he felt humorless and heavyhearted today, in spite of his great satisfaction.

That evening, at a dinner party at the Kaunitz, he was forced to hear yet another discussion of the murder. It seemed Vienna could talk of nothing else.

"Baron Hager has no clues, no clues at all," Comte de La Besnadière informed the company importantly.

"But surely he has a plethora of suspects," Talleyrand remarked. "If what I have heard of Prince Eric is true, the baron has only to question all the husbands, fathers, brothers and cousins who had good reason to want to do away with the man." He paused, and then added suavely, "I do realize, however, that that would take much too long, since it would involve almost every male in Vienna over the age of fifteen."

His guests laughed at his sally, and the duke saw the young countess and her uncle exchange small secret smiles. His eyes went to the Duchess of Courland, and he noted the look of pain that crossed her features and was so quickly concealed. So the duchess knew her lover was lost to her, that he had fallen in love instead with her own daughter. How depressing it must be for her. Idly the duke wondered why she stayed here, when any one of her other daughters would be glad to take her in.

The duchess seemed to sense his glance, and she looked up. Immediately a charming smile lit her face, and he raised his glass to her in a little private toast. He had to admire her, she was so valiant in her defeat. A woman in her middle fifties, she still had great beauty and appeal, as well as a sparkling wit.

As the days passed, no headway was made in discovering who the unknown assailant might have been. And although Owen had thought Prince Boris might implicate him, Baron Hager did not come to question him or his servants. He was sure now that Prince Eric's file would languish along with William Stone's and others as unsolved cases.

As April became May, the duke found himself becoming ever more impatient. When would this congress ever end? When could he leave for England . . . and Erica? But the Swiss delegates labored on, trying to bring into accord the different interests of their nineteen cantons,

each one of which was represented by a separate dele-
gate. The dilemma of the German Jews had finally been
resolved, the congress voting for their freedom from
oppression, but the Germans still struggled with other
problems. Those who wanted a united Reich found themselves battling all the German princes who refused to
give up their little domains.

Of course Wellington was in Brussels now, and all
Vienna waited impatiently for news of the battle they
were sure would come. And still Napoleon and his Grande
Armée did not march. It was puzzling that he did not,
but Owen was delighted. Every day the emperor delayed
gave Wellington more time to consolidate his army and
bring into harmony all the different forces of the allies
under his supreme command.

It was late in the month before the duke learned that
the Final Act would be signed on the ninth of June. He
hurried home to the Johannesgasse at once, to order Rudge
to begin packing. "We are for home, Rudge," he told him,
his deep voice full of happiness. "Finally, we are for home!"

"For your sake, sir, I'm glad," the butler said. "I'll
start the preparations to leave, at once."

"You are to go to Graveshead, traveling through Bo-
hemia, Saxony, and Prussia to Hamburg, where I will
arrange passage for everyone," the duke said brusquely
now, ignoring the twinkle in his butler's eyes. "Any
other route would be much too dangerous at this time. I
shall, of course, go ahead, accompanied by two grooms."

The duke was ready to leave Vienna the moment the
document was signed. He had bidden his friends and
Talleyrand and his niece farewell, visited Mimi Lebrun
with a last generous payment for her help, and dismissed
the two grooms. Taking his leave of Lord Clancarty as
well, he had been thanked fervently again for his service
to England's cause. Now he paced his library impatiently
until the footman sent to wait at the first—and only actual—
convening of the Congress of Vienna came home with
the good news that released him from duty.

When Rudge learned the duke meant to leave that
same day, he tried hard to convince him it would be
better to make an early start the next morning. After all,
as he told his master, it was almost three in the afternoon.

Owen smiled at him. "But I can put three hours of traveling behind me before I have to stop, Rudge," he said. "No, no more. I am for England!"

He shook his butler's hand and wished him Godspeed before he limped quickly down the steps to his racing curricle. Rudge shook his head and smiled a little. He knew well it was not so much England the duke yearned for as it was Erica Kingsley. He had known it this age.

The first person the Duke of Graves saw when he arrived at General Sir Harold Huntington's estate in Northumberland some weeks later was not the lady he had been traveling toward for such a very long time, but her maid, Agnes Watts. The butler had been called away to deal with some crisis in the kitchen, and when Owen knocked she had been passing through the hall, and so she opened the door for him.

Agnes' hands went to her heart in astonishment as she saw him. "Why, it's *you!*" she exclaimed.

As he stepped into the hall, he sighed. "Really, Agnes," he complained as he handed her his hat and gloves, "surely you can find another way to greet me? This constant repetition grows tiresome."

Agnes curtsied. "Oh, your grace," she said, ignoring his sarcastic remark completely, "I'm that glad to see you, I can't tell you!"

For a moment the duke's famous aplomb deserted him. He appeared as astonished as she had been when she opened the door, but then a look of consternation crossed his rugged face. Quickly he grasped her arms in a hard grip, and Agnes gasped. "Tell me at once! Is Erica sick . . . or with child?" he demanded in a cold harsh voice.

Agnes tossed her head and sniffed in quite her old way. "No, she's not," she said, and he released her. As she straightened her crushed sleeves, she added tartly, "Although I'm sure *I* wouldn't be a bit surprised if she were!"

"Nor I, Agnes, nor I," he murmured, blasé again, although a reminiscent smile lit his dark eyes. "But why were you so glad to see me, then, if it was not to make an honest woman of your mistress?" he asked. "Surely such a welcome is most unlike you!"

Agnes looked away from those keen black eyes to study the Turkey carpet beneath her feet. "It's just that Miss Erica has missed you so," she told him, swallowing hard in her honesty. "And even though she is the same kind lady, I can tell she has been unhappy."

"Where is she, Agnes?" Owen asked quietly.

"She went out to pick some roses for the drawing room," the maid told him. "This way, your grace."

She led him through the hall into a small, old-fashioned salon that had long doors opening to a terrace. Owen looked past her eagerly, but Erica was nowhere in sight, although the rose garden lay directly before them.

"She's probably down by the stream, your grace," the maid told him as she unfastened the door for him. "There's a favorite spot of hers there she's always loved."

The duke nodded as he brushed past her. She watched him limp through the garden, realizing for the first time that he was not his usual sartorial self. It was obvious he had been so eager, he had come in his traveling clothes, the moment he arrived. Agnes smiled to herself.

Erica was seated on a large flat rock next to the stream, her back against an oak. It was a warm day for late June, almost sultry, and after she had picked the roses and laid them in the flat rush basket she carried, she had wandered down here to think in the shade. She was very confused. It was such a long time since she had seen Owen, even heard from him. She knew the Congress of Vienna had signed the Final Act at last, and only a week ago news had come of Wellington's victory over Napoleon at Waterloo. That evening had been a most festive one for the Huntington family, one that Erica had tried to participate in with a good grace, even as sad as she was.

But now she sighed, feeling lonely and depressed. Where *was* he? She was so worried about him! Last night, unable to sleep, she had wandered over to her window seat late at night, trying to decide for the first time whether she should write to Lord Castlereagh now, as she had promised the duke she would do. Yet she could not believe that Owen was dead, although she knew that only death could keep him from her side. Now she closed

her eyes and sighed again. She *would* not believe it!
Surely she would sense it if he were hurt, or in trouble,
or forever gone.

It was peaceful there under the tree, and the sounds of
the stream had always soothed her before, for this was
where she had brought her troubles always, to ponder
them alone. Today she could not be comforted.

Some premonition, something, made her open her eyes
and turn her head. The tall, familiar figure of the Duke
of Graves stood a little distance away, watching her.
Erica closed her eyes quickly. Was she going out of her
mind? Did she yearn for him so much she was beginning
to see things?

"I must admit I had looked forward to a less . . . tepid
welcome," she heard his deep voice remark, and her
eyes flew open. "However, no doubt it is just the lesson
in humility I deserve," he added.

Erica rose quickly to her feet, tumbling the basket and
scattering the roses it carried as she did so. Not even
noticing, she ran to meet him as he limped closer. In only
a moment his strong arms enfolded her to hold her close
to his heart.

"Oh, Owen, my dear," she cried, her voice breaking
as her hands came up to cup his face, "it is really you! It
is!"

"So I have always been told, madam," he said in a
shaky voice.

Erica did not reply, for she was pulling his face down
to hers so she might kiss him.

It was a very long time before they could do anything
but hold each other, murmuring again and again of their
love, and their joy in this reunion.

At last the duke led her to the flat rock and sat down
beside her. He brushed the bruised roses aside as he did
so. Their sweet scent was all around them, and Erica
picked one up with a rueful smile.

"Now look what you have made me do, Owen," she
scolded him. "I shall have to pick more, for these are sad
specimens for a bouquet."

Ignoring the roses, the duke smiled down at her. She
was in black, of course, and her hair was braided in the
old tight coil at the nape of her neck she had worn as a

girl. Surrounded by the rich pinks and yellows and deep
reds of the roses, she looked liked a prim Puritan at
some Bacchanalian feast. He realized he could do nothing about her gown, but he began to undo her braids. "I
never want to see you with your hair this way again," he
ordered. "It is a sacrilege to wear it so tightly braided
when it is so beautiful."

As he loosened those braids to run impatient fingers
through her hair Erica smiled. Owen buried his hands in
it as he kissed her. "Now you are my Erica again," he
told her, reluctantly lifting his mouth an inch from hers
in order to do so. "At least you will be when you change
from that ugly gown," he added.

"But you know I must wear black for a full year,
Owen," she said.

The duke shook his head firmly. "You and I know that
Colonel Stone did not deserve such homage, my dear,"
he told her. "But even if he did, I do not intend to wait
for my duchess another day. I have a special license in
my pocket. As soon as I have explained the matter to
your father, we will be wed. Quietly, and here, in deference to your situation, but wed. Then we will travel to
my estate in Scotland, where we will remain, most happily I am sure, until fall. And when we return to
Graveshead, and London, you will be Erica Kingsley in
truth. And since everyone knows you by that name already, there is no need to tell them you were married
before, now is there? Not that I care if society knows,
Erica, believe me."

She smiled at him. "You cannot know how delighted I
am to agree to all your plans, your grace," she said
demurely. Then she abandoned her conventional pose to
throw her arms around his neck. "Oh, Owen, I have
been so lonely, and I have missed you so much!" she
cried.

"I know," he said. "For I have missed you the same
way." He kissed her cheek before he put his own hard
cheek against it. "Tell me, love, what were you thinking
about when I first saw you today?" he asked. "You
looked so quiet, so sad."

"I was thinking I must write to Lord Castlereagh soon,
as I promised you. I was beginning to think I would

never see you again," she whispered. "But why did you want me to write to him, Owen?"

The duke settled back more comfortably against the oak, keeping his arm around her as he explained. "I wanted Robert to tell you what I have been doing," he said. "You see, I always wanted to help my country, if I could, even if I am lame. You were not the only English spy, Erica. I was the master spy. And besides you, I had an Austrian and a German groom in the Hofburg working for me, and that brothel you saw me entering near the Minoritenplatz housed a young French prostitute named Mimi Lebrun who was of great help to me. It was also the safest way for me to make my reports, for I could leave Mimi's by the alley and enter headquarters through the back door."

"I am so glad to have *that* explained," Erica teased him, and he hugged her closer.

"I did not mean to be mysterious when I left you in Ostend," the duke went on. "But I had promised Castlereagh to remain in Vienna until the Final Act was signed. I had to go back, but I could not tell you why, for I did not want you to worry. If it had ever become known that I was a spy, I might have been killed. That was why I was so careful to appear a fatuous man, who was only interested in horses, and who was bored by international affairs. But if anything had happened to me, Robert would have told you the truth, and why I died. You see, it was important to me that you at least knew the kind of man I was, if I never came back to you."

Erica buried her face on his chest as she said a silent prayer of thanks for his safe return. The duke stared down at her as he gently smoothed her silvery hair with one big hand.

"There was another reason I had to go back," he went on, his voice constrained now. "I had to avenge you. Prince Eric Thorson is dead. I killed him."

Erica sat up and drew away a little, her green eyes searching his somber face. "You killed him?" she whispered. "How?"

"I shot him one night as he was leaving Isabella Sabatini's house," he told her. He seemed to see the

doubt in her eyes, and he added, "In the eyes of the
world, it was a fair fight, Erica. I told him all about you
and William Stone, and I waited until he came at me
with a dagger before I fired. Even so, I know my retribu-
tion was murder. I intended it to be murder, for I could
not have him alive in any world that held you, my love,
not and live with myself."

Erica was frowning, and he waited a little anxiously,
afraid she might draw away from him in disgust. "But if
he only had a dagger, why did he attack you?" she
asked. "Surely he could see a dagger was no match for a
pistol!"

"But he did not see it," Owen told her, relieved at her
reaction. "He was attacking what he thought was an
unarmed cripple. I shot him with the gun that is built into
the handle of one of my canes. You do remember I told
you I have an interesting collection of canes?"

He waited until she smiled at him. It was a tremulous
effort, but it was still a smile, and he was not at all
surprised at the relief he felt.

"So that is why you said you might not come back to
me, why you said you could not promise me anything, or
tell me anything either. I understand now," she said.
"But oh, my dear Owen, how clever you have been! But
I always knew you—"

But the future Duchess of Graves was not allowed to
finish her sentence. Owen Kingsley pulled her close to
him again, and bent his head to kiss her. Soon the
intensity of that kiss made her forget spies, Prince Eric,
Vienna—everything and everyone but the two of them
lost in their own private world under an English oak
beside a murmuring English stream.

About the Author

Although Barbara Hazard is a New England Yankee by birth, upbringing, and education, she is of English descent on both sides of her family and has many relatives in that country. The Regency period has always been a favorite, and when she began to write nine years ago, she gravitated to it naturally, feeling perfectly at home there. Barbara Hazard now lives in New York. She has been a musician and an artist, and although writing is her first love, she also enjoys classical music, reading, and quilting.